THE
PRICE
OF
REDEMPTION

THE
PRICE
— OF —
REDEMPTION

The Tides of Magic:
Book I

SHAWN
CARPENTER

SAGA PRESS

LONDON SYDNEY **NEW YORK** TORONTO NEW DELHI

SAGA **PRESS**

AN IMPRINT OF SIMON & SCHUSTER, LLC

1230 AVENUE OF THE AMERICAS, NEW YORK, NEW YORK 10020

An Imprint of Simon & Schuster, LLC
1230 Avenue of the Americas
New York, NY 10020

First Saga Press trade paperback edition July 2024

SAGA PRESS and colophon are trademarks of Simon & Schuster, LLC

Simon & Schuster: Celebrating 100 Years of Publishing in 2024

For information about special discounts for bulk purchases, please contact Simon & Schuster Special Sales at 1-866-506-1949 or business@simonandschuster.com.

The Simon & Schuster Speakers Bureau can bring authors to your live event. For more information or to book an event, contact the Simon & Schuster Speakers Bureau at1-866-248-3049 or visit our website at www.simonspeakers.com.

Interior design by Lewelin Polanco

Drawing on page 352 by Shawn Carpenter

Manufactured in the United States of America

1 3 5 7 9 10 8 6 4 2

Library of Congress Cataloging-in-Publication Data

Names: Carpenter, Shawn, author.
Title: The price of redemption / Shawn Carpenter.
Description: First Saga Press trade paperback edition. | London; New York: Saga Press, 2024. | Series: Tides of magic ; 1
Identifiers: LCCN 2024011280 | ISBN 9781668033739 (paperback) | ISBN 9781668033746 (ebook)
Subjects: BISAC: FICTION / Fantasy / Action & Adventure | FICTION / Fantasy / Historical | LCGFT: Fantasy fiction. | Novels.
Classification: LCC PS3603.A7713 P75 2024 | DDC 813/.6—dc23/eng/20240315
LC record available at https://lccn.loc.gov/2024011280

ISBN 978-1-6680-3373-9
ISBN 978-1-6680-3374-6 (ebook)

This book is dedicated to my daughters Becca, Caitlin, and Christian who finally read it, and to my son and daughter Armyn and Veronica who haven't. The five of you are the best things I have had any part in creating.

Shawn Carpenter
The Pup House
2 February 2024

Note from the Board of Domestic Peace: All names in the dedication above are listed in alphabetical order as they are presented. No order of precedence is intended or implied.

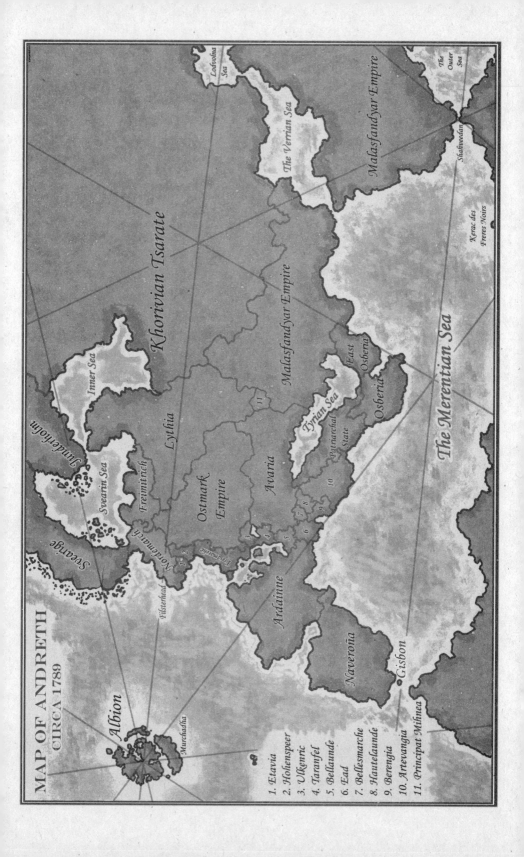

MAP OF ANDRETH
CIRCA 1789

1. Etavia
2. Hohenspeer
3. Ulkenric
4. Taranfel
5. Bellaunde
6. Ead
7. Bellesmarche
8. Hautelaunde
9. Berengia
10. Artevangia
11. Principat Mihnea

Albion

Murchadha

Svearige

Svearin Sea

Jundérholm

Inner Sea

Khorivian Tsarate

Freimtrich

Nordemnich

Filsterhead

Lythia

Ostmark Empire

Ardainne

Naveroña

Avaria

Framarche

Malasfandyar Empire

Tyrian Sea

Vhatmarchal State

East Osberia

Osberia

Gisbon

The Merentian Sea

Malasfandyar Empire

The Verrian Sea

Lodvolnia Sea

Shafrvedan

Kerac des Freres Noirs

The Outer Sea

THE
PRICE
OF
REDEMPTION

chapter 1

At any other time in her twenty-five years, Enid would have found her circumstances invigorating. Blue water crowned with snowy foam sang past the hull as the sails and rigging snapped and hummed in accompaniment overhead. A fine spray peppered her angular face and left a brisk trace of its salt perfume as it passed. A part of her recognized the perfection of the day as it unfolded beneath a rare clear sky over the Straits of Albion, but the rest of her was conscious of only one thing: the hostile frigate closing in on her ship from the starboard side.

Without the impromptu tutelage of the vessel's master, a rotund fellow named Arnaud Efarge, Enid wouldn't be able to put a name to the type of ship pursuing them, nor the quarter from which it approached. She was a student of True Art, not of ships and the sea. As far as she could discern, there was no real difference between the merchantman carrying her toward a destiny she prayed was rich in vengeance and the predatory warship that snapped at its watery heels. Certainly, this "frigate" carried more cannon. That was obvious to even her untrained eye. Still, reason seemed to decree that their smaller ship, with its rakish lines and gallant spread of sail, could bear her past the reach of those guns.

Unfortunately, reason held little sway over the affairs of wind and wave. The frigate grew visibly larger with each passing moment, despite the frantic activity of the sailors in the merchant's rigging and the master's grim concentration as he paced the rail of the quarter-deck. As he passed, she put out a hand to stay him and asked how so large a vessel could close on a smaller, fleeter ship, something as incongruous to her as an ox running a hare to ground.

"She has the gauge of us," Master Arnaud snapped, even as he gently scratched between the ears of the long, six-legged otterkin draped over his shoulders like a living stole. Seeing the blankness in Enid's eyes, he said in a softer tone, "The weather gauge. It means she has the favor of the wind. She can match our every move and still close on us."

"But surely its sheer bulk will slow it! We are smaller, lighter, and faster, are we not?"

The master's fatalistic chuckle did not please Enid or the otterkin, which chittered nervously. Arnaud soothed it absently as he explained.

"Milady, we are smaller and lighter, of that there can be no doubt. But faster than a frigate under a full press of sail?" He chuckled grimly and shook his head at her naivete. "Size has its advantages in many things, milady, and sailing is one of them. All those yards and yards of canvas she spreads would tear the masts from our poor *Marie*, but they push the frigate there along at a pace we can never outstrip without abandoning all our cargo, water, and passengers to the sea."

Enid's brow furrowed slightly at the mention of abandoning passengers to the sea and her hand strayed toward the hilt of the small sword dangling from her hip.

Master Arnaud raised a hand in apology and was about to speak when a fluttering noise floated down from above. The broad-faced commoner cursed under his breath as he squinted up at the sails.

"We're losing our wind, milady."

A glance at the frigate revealed it was more fortunate in finding loyal zephyrs. Her sheets still bellied with wind and a great spume of spray greeted her blunt prow each time it rose above one wave to fall upon the crest of another.

The sailors high in the little merchantman's rigging whistled tunelessly like a flock of artless birds.

"What is the meaning of that racket?" Enid asked absently as she allowed her will a looser rein. She grew lightheaded as her being encompassed both more and less than her physical shell. The coppery taste of magic welled up in her throat and she felt the other sorcerer in the depths of the frigate, in some dark place below the waterline. Dying sylphs surrounded him, slowly suffocating in that dark place. He was literally killing their wind.

"To call up a wind, milady," the master answered. "Whistling for a fair wind is a common practice at sea."

"I do not think the winds can hear them. I will see what I can do to help."

The master took a cautious step backward and muttered his thanks as she closed her eyes and reached out toward the foam-wreathed frigate with her hand and will.

There he was: a small man in more than physical stature, the sort who reveled in such small cruelties as extinguishing the spark of minor spirits. Still, he was strong in his own element, and she doubted she could counter his workings without time to properly prepare. So be it. If she could not stop him, she would lend her strength to him. She felt his terror as the surrounding sylphs began to expire more rapidly than he could control. Each sylph took some of itself with it as it perished in a dying inhalation, each leaving the small room more airless with its passing.

Enid's outstretched arm tensed, and her hand curled into a fine-boned claw. The master backed into the quarterdeck's rail and his thick-fingered hand clutched the prayer beads around his thick neck as she drew in a seemingly endless, whistling breath. She barely noticed him. She was somewhere else, across a narrowing expanse of tumbling waves, and while she saw a face sinking into a mask of fear, it was no common sailor's.

Here was a petty sorcerer. A mage of the fifth or sixth rank, she reckoned, highly capable at the casting of a few rote processes, but no true practitioner. It was disheartening to see how low the Theocracy had brought the greatest nation in the world, a nation once famed and feared for the prowess of even its lowest-ranking mages. Still, she had no pity for this traitorous wretch and worked against him with a will. There was a moment when, if he had known more, he could have made their encounter a true duel, but, in the face of an *Institut*-trained mage he was all but unarmed. Still, she grinned in wolfish delight at sending one more Theocrat to hell.

As she came back to herself, she was aware of the cheers of the surrounding sailors. The wind had slipped from the *Artagny*'s sails, which now hung limp like so much laundry on a charwoman's lines. The little merchantman's topsails scratched up a breeze and filled with a satisfying snap of canvas. Even in such light airs, she was pulling away from the becalmed frigate. The *Marie*'s crew and passengers voiced their joy as the distance between the two ships widened.

The celebration was short-lived. The *Marie* did not make more than a mile before the frigate's topsails filled and she began to make way again.

Enid raised an inquisitive brow at the master, but he shook his head.

"She will still run us down, milady. Even without a mage, her natural advantage over us is too great. We have gained some time, but not much. I expect we'll be under her guns before dark. Then the killing will begin."

"It has already begun," Enid said, the little mage's blue face in her mind's eye, his hands clawing at his throat as he struggled fruitlessly to draw one breath past his last in an airless chamber beneath the waves.

It seemed the ardent pursuit of revenge was as poor a shield against Fortune's indignities as hope. The frigate closed steadily despite the loss of its ship's mage. The *Marie*'s crew struggled gamely, fighting with the sails to urge every inch of headway from her. So far, no baggage or cargo had gone over the side to coax another quarter knot out of the merchantman. Master Arnaud said that he doubted it would make any difference and if, by some miracle, the *Marie* was able to escape, the refugees aboard would be left destitute. As the frigate closed with them, though, he looked grim enough to reconsider his position on the matter.

He had good reason: the fluttering black pennant at the frigate's masthead meant she carried a Confessor aboard.

Were the *Marie* to fall into the hands of a Confessor with highborn émigrés aboard—such as the Marquise Enid d'Tancreville— the ship would be taken up by the state. The *Marie*'s master would be hanged on the spot for treason. His men would be sentenced to a life in service to the Theocratic Navy. For most of the fat little brig's passengers, falling into the hands of a Confessor was a fate that rivaled capture by the inhuman Darghaur that haunted the dark fairy tales of their youth.

The frigate loomed near enough that Enid could discern the small details of her construction and spot the scarlet-robed figure of a Confessor upon her quarterdeck. The black maws of her cannons, which seemed large enough to swallow the merchant ship, drew Enid's eyes with a morbid gravity.

Following her gaze to the guns, the *Marie*'s master said quietly, "They'll keep closing and eventually fire a gun across our bows, unless the dogs sailing for the Theocrats have abandoned tradition altogether."

"And what shall we do, then?"

The master took a deep breath, which stretched his brown coat tight across his barrel chest. He shook his head and cast his eyes toward the deck.

"You'll call it cowardly, milady, but we'll heave to. The *Marie* wouldn't survive a single volley, and if she did, my men would be slaughtered. I cannot let that happen, milady. They rely upon me, and their families upon them."

"Considering the welcome the Confessor will give you for harboring aristocrats, I would not call surrendering to save your crew cowardice. You are a brave man, Master Arnaud, and an honorable one."

Master Arnaud frowned and colored slightly. "I hope you will feel the same an hour or two hence, when I surrender my pretty little *Marie* to that bastard of a Confessor, Redeemer rot him!"

Enid d'Tancreville offered a chilly sniff at the unwonted familiarity embodied in the commoner's profanity, but she could not help but share his assessment of the scarlet-clad figure pacing the command deck of the approaching frigate.

The sun hovered just above the horizon, its bottom half grossly deformed, giving it the shape of a baleful orange pear. To Enid, it seemed to cast a heavy, reluctant light that illuminated in broad strokes but refused to add more detail than the occasional flash of a polished surface or glitter from a breaking wave. Perhaps its desultory performance was due to the rapidly approaching night. Why bother to reveal what darkness would soon devour? If this were the sun's excuse, she felt a strong empathy for its case. After all, she showed no more energy as dusk approached, its blackness eloquently presaged by the dark mass of the frigate growing visibly larger to starboard.

She stood at the rail, still in body and mind. When a second sail was spotted an hour ago, a rush of desperate hope had seized her and the rest of the ill-fated *Marie*'s passengers and crew. That hope was soon crushed. After a few moments of reckless cheer, a keen-eyed young sailor in the tops discerned that the vessel upon which they had hung their hopes of rescue flew the same hated black pennant as the frigate.

Master Arnaud identified the vessel as another frigate, though smaller and more lightly armed than the one that had dogged their heels during the course of the long afternoon. In the patient tones of a doomed schoolmaster, he informed her it was a "28" and the larger ship was a "40." The numbers, he said, referred to the number of cannons borne on each. The twenty-eight, he opined, had witnessed the chase, and piled on sail to assist, or, failing that, claim a right to a portion of the prize money for being in plain sight of the capture. Enid raised an eyebrow curiously at the mention of prize money and the master's round frame shook for a moment in what passed for humor under such dire circumstances.

"Prize money, milady! Why do you think any sailors volunteer for service in the navies of Albion and Ardainne when they can command twice the wages aboard a trading vessel like the *Marie* than aboard a first-rate ship of the line?"

"For the honor of serving their king and country?"

The master brought his laughter under control as Enid's features darkened. He held up an apologetic hand.

"I do not make light of you, milady, and indeed there must be some who do just that. Most of 'em, though, are gamblers. They are wagering their lives the man-of-war they are aboard will take enough prize and head money to more than make up for the difference in basic wages."

Master Arnaud explained that ships and cargoes captured at sea became the property of the capturing ship's sovereign. By long tradition, those sovereigns showed their gratitude for such windfalls by awarding most of their value to the crew who had hazarded their lives to secure it. A captured merchantman would be valued according to its cargo and the condition and type of its hull, while a captured warship was usually valued at the cost of construction less the cost to bring her up to the capturing navy's standards of seaworthiness.

"The *Marie* is a fine ship and is low in the water with a hold full of wine bound for the Spice Colonies. If they can prove we have so much as one escaping aristocrat aboard, we're in forfeit of our bond and those ships"—Master Arnaud gave a spite-filled wave in the direction of the closing vessels—"may claim us as a rightful prize. The two captains will no doubt make enough from us to refurnish their fine manors or perhaps buy a few more horses for their stables. Their sailors will make as much in prize money for this one day's work as they would have in a month or more of regular wages. So, you can see why they crack on so. Ah, it appears the little frigate intends to play an active role in our capture rather than taking her money just for watching. See how she is coming on? She means to cut across the forty's bow and head us off. Now they're racing to see who closes us first."

And so Enid spent her last hour as a free woman, and most likely as a live one, watching the slow dance performed by the three ships, each occasionally altering course or making some arcane adjustment in sails intended to urge a little more speed across the rising sea. Master Arnaud stood beside her, feeding his greedy otterkin biscuits. Between calming words for the nervous animal and the occasional shouted commands, he kept her informed of the purpose behind each movement of the cumbersome minuet. At one point, he snorted derisively and threw his hands up in disgust.

"Look how sloppily the twenty-eight is handled! See how her sails have gone slack? She's lost the better part of her headway and the race as well! See how her crew struggles to bring her around? A pity. She was so close to her mark. Now she'll pass aft of her larger sister for certain. She'll be in position to rake us there, but we'll strike our colors long before I let him turn my *Marie* into a slaughterhouse."

"Rake? What does this mean, to be positioned to rake us?"

Arnaud maneuvered his thick-fingered hands to show the positions of two ships and raised his right hand slightly. "This is our *Marie*. My left is the small frigate. When the light frigate passes behind us, she'll have her broadside facing toward our aft, like so." The master's hands made a T. He frowned a moment before continuing. "Were she to fire a broadside into us from such a position, her shot would sweep down the length of our ship, slaughtering man after man as it passed. The carnage would be dreadful."

A few moments later the small frigate was all but invisible on the far side of the much larger 40-gun frigate, which now stood so close Enid could see the gunners peering around their cannons through its gaping gun ports. She noted the hateful smile upon the scarlet-cloaked Confessor as he leaned indolently upon the rail of the quarterdeck. One of the frigate's guns boomed and belched smoke and actinic fire. Enid was startled despite herself. An alarmingly large plume of water erupted just past the *Marie*'s bow, bathing the front half of her deck in acrid-smelling water. Master Arnaud turned to her, his expression halfway between apology and resignation, and shouted for his men to strike the colors and bring the *Marie* around to be boarded.

The big frigate erupted in boisterous cheers as the Ardain flag was lowered aboard the *Marie*, her crew and officers apparently untouched by the irony inherent in the little merchant striking the same flag that flew from the frigate's mizzenmast. Enid leaned heavily on the rail, her face set in an expression of sour resignation. The frigate lowered a boat to ferry across the boarding party. Arnaud came to join her and when she turned to glance at him, he seemed smaller somehow, as if the last orders he'd shouted as the *Marie*'s commander had taken all his energy and vitality with them. She shrugged to herself and doubted if she looked much better to him.

"Will the Confessor come with them?" She gestured with her chin toward the boat bobbing at the frigate's side. Sailors and a few marines swarmed down ladders on the ship's side to take their places in the boat. It was difficult for her to imagine the scarlet eminence of a Confessor duplicating the feat.

"No, milady. A lieutenant will be sent across with the compliments of the frigate's captain and demand I present myself and my ship's papers to him at once. They'll take me across while the lieutenant and his men make a quick survey of the *Marie* and search the passengers and crew for hard coin. Any money aboard is forfeit to them at once, you see."

Enid made a disparaging remark about piracy as the smaller frigate slowly emerged from behind the bulk of her sister ship, passing her astern, just as Master Arnaud predicted. Her second remark, regarding vultures arriving late behind the wolf, was drowned out by the deafening roar of a cannonade and the aft third of the *Artagny* vanished in a thick cloud of gray-white smoke and splinters.

chapter 2

"Strike that black rag and run up the king's colors," shouted Commander Rue Nath, captain of His Majesty the King of Albion's ship the *Alarum*. His voice was powerful enough to be heard over the bloodthirsty cheers of the *Alarum*'s gunners, despite originating from a slight, unimpressive frame. "Reload with a will and let's give the Rats another before they can recover!"

Magister Dunaughy, next to him on the quarterdeck, smiled. He'd seen robust officers a head taller and far broader of chest forced to resort to charms to ensure that their orders carried to the topmast. Nath, minikin though he was, required no enchantments to make himself heard.

"There's no mage aboard the frigate now, but there was. I can smell his workings from here," Dunaughy said in his lilting Murchadhan accent.

"Hiding from you, perhaps," Nath said, producing a dented, tarnished pocket watch to time the gun crews as they reloaded, as if this were just another drill rather than a desperate fight with a superior vessel. "Some sort of magic concealment?"

"No," Dunaughy said firmly. "He's dead. I'm sure of it. I'll wager there's a mage of estimable talent on that fat little brig. Should I—"

"Don't waste your attention on it now," Nath replied, giving his magister a fond pat on the shoulder. "The merchant is showing her heels. We'll catch her up later. Let us focus on the fight at hand."

The *Alarum*'s broadside roared again, pouring hot iron through the Rat frigate's shattered stern gallery and chewing great furrows down the length of her tumble home. This time Nath's voice joined the gunners' joyous howl, and he clapped the taller Dunaughy more forcefully on the shoulder. "Only a bit over two and a half minutes between broadsides! Redeemer bless them. I could not be prouder of our people! You recall how slow and cack-handed the crews were before—"

At that moment, Master Harde called up from the waist. "Her rudder's loose!"

Nath rushed to the rail to see for himself and grinned like a wolf at what he saw. A lucky shot had damaged the Rat's rudder, and the ship was clearly not responding to her wheel.

"Oh ho," he exulted. "There's an end to any fighting from her! Hail 'em, Magister, and tell 'em to drop sail and prepare to be boarded, else we blast her down to the waterline!"

Effortlessly summoning a friendly zephyr to carry his words directly to the Rat's quarterdeck, Dunaughy passed on his little captain's words. Nath, watching through his come-hither glass, was surprised to see an obvious argument break out among the officers there. A lieutenant and a man Nath took to be the enemy frigate's master were obviously pleading with a tall man in red. Even through the shaking image the collapsible telescope presented to his curious eye, the man's expression was clearly flushed with maniacal rage.

"That's a Rat Confessor," Dunaughy drawled. "It appears he'd rather see the frigate and her crew reduced to dust and splinters than surrender. Ah! But look—the young lieutenant there has made a compelling argument!"

The lieutenant in question leveled a pistol at the Confessor's face. Nath snapped his glass closed and handed it to Lieutenant Bascombe, who stood at his left.

"Ardain discipline has descended lower than the farcical standards of the old regime," Nath drawled.

"The Rat lieutenant might be excused for his reluctance to see his frigate and all her people sacrificed to the bloody-minded whim of a supernumerary, for that accurately describes Confessors, who have no legitimate military rank." Dunaughy's voice dripped with hatred and disdain.

A moment later, both the Ardain flag and the black Confessor's pennant were struck. Nath grinned at the glorious sight.

"Regardless, this has been as neat an evening's work as I've ever seen," Nath said. "A grand prize snatched up and not a drop of Albion blood spilled in the process!"

Dunaughy frowned and tapped the wood railing, a gesture common among sailor-folk to offset the risk of any hubris in their thoughts or deeds. The sea hated the arrogant as much as she hated the meek. Nath chuckled at the gesture.

"You're as superstitious as the meanest foremast jack," he said. "Which is strange for such a learned fellow!"

"Learned enough to know not to tempt Providence," Dunaughy said, smiling despite himself.

"As am I. That is why I'd admire it if you'd join me in the boarding party. I don't want to rely on my own pitiful magic if their magister does make a surprise appearance."

"As you wish, sir. But he won't, I assure you." The mage cast a quick glance over the opposite rail, where the little merchant ship's topgallants were sinking below the horizon.

The sun dipped closer to the horizon as the boats bearing the boarding party approached the Rat frigate. A party of red-coated marines
scrambled aboard, covered by the *Alarum*'s great guns. Once the marines had the Rat sailors and officers under their muskets, Nath and
Dunaughy came aboard, followed by Lieutenant Bascombe and her
prize crew. Alston, Nath's steward, brought up the rear, his captain's
portable writing desk clutched under one arm and an endless stream
of grumbling curses on his lips.

Nath took a moment to survey the Rat vessel's state. She was a bit of
a shambles, but nothing a work crew couldn't set aright in an hour or so.
The damage the *Alarum*'s two broadsides wreaked was on full display.
Guns were dismounted and wide sections of railing had been reduced
to splinters, some of which were embedded in the deck and, presum-
ably, in the bodies of the wretches whose faint screams he heard rising
from the orlop below. Fortunately, the masts seemed undamaged and
the standing rigging, though cut up, still appeared serviceable. Nath
nodded his approval at the sight. The *Alarum*'s gunners had done as
they were trained and aimed their guns "twixt wind and wave" to cause
maximum damage to the Rat frigate's hull and crew. She was a seaworthy prize despite the mauling she'd received and would certainly be accepted as a fine addition to Albion's frigate-hungry fleet—and provide
further evidence to the Admiralty that he was an active officer, not the
malingering layabout the *Alarum*'s sad state might lead the credulous
to describe him.

Against the far rail, stacked like cordwood, were the bodies of Ardain sailors and officers who were slain outright under the *Alarum*'s
guns. The tangle of their limbs made their number difficult to estimate,
but Nath reckoned over a dozen corpses lined the rail. The broken
body of the Ardain captain lay a respectful distance away, her mauve
uniform coat darkened to a deep purple red around the oak splinter

protruding from her chest. Nath paused for a moment, his alert eyes locking for a moment with the unseeing orbs of his opposite number. Despite the cloudy murk that spread across them, they radiated resignation and remorse. He leaned over to close her staring eyes and, gazing upon her face in repose, was certain that she would have been an insightful and supportive comrade to any who held her respect and returned it in kind.

"A sobering butcher's bill," Nath said softly.

"You are a good man to feel thus at the sight of the enemy's dead," Dunaughy said. "Bless you for it."

"Pardon, Captain," said a young Ardain woman with a crimson-stained bandage on her right cheek. Nath took her to be a mid based on her uniform. "His eminence, Confessor Faucher, awaits your company on the quarterdeck. He has taken command of the *Artagny* with the death of our captain."

Nath noted the quaver of fear in her voice and gave her a reassuring smile. Should the fortunes of war turn on him someday, he hoped the officer that laid him low would treat as gently with his young mids. "Then let's not keep him waiting. Please lead the way."

As they neared the quarterdeck, Dunaughy leaned close to Nath and whispered, "I've placed a warding on you, sir. I fear this Rat might bite."

Nath nodded as he took in the Confessor's deeply lined face. His vicious scowl revealed no courtesy or complaisance. He regarded the approaching Albion officers and the marines flanking them with such visible malignance that it was nearly palpable. Still, he stood quietly, his arms at his sides under a cassock of finely woven scarlet cloth. The lieutenant who Nath had seen threaten the Confessor with her pistol stood to his right, the weapon now snug under her belt.

Nath schooled his features into an expressionless mask and held out his hand to the Confessor. "I am Captain Rue Nath, of His Majesty's Ship the *Alar*—"

The Confessor lunged forward with a bestial snarl. His hands appeared from beneath the cassock, each filled with a spell-lock pistol. Nath was momentarily blinded by a bright violet flash mere inches from his nose. He felt a hammer blow to his forehead and his vision contracted to a tiny dot of light before the darkness consumed it completely.

When his vision cleared, he was seated on the deck, ringed by the worried faces of Lieutenant Bascombe, Alston, and the lieutenant of marines. Chief among them was the young Rat lieutenant, who grasped his hand and kissed it.

"Upon my word, sir," he said, "I had no part in this treachery! Faucher is a rabid dog! Were you to cast him overboard, not a single *Artagny* would raise a hand to stop you!"

Nath smiled weakly and regained his feet with Alston's assistance, who hissed in his ear, "March the lot over the taffrail and leave the world a better place, sor. It's a miracle yer head ain't a hollow melon!"

"No miracle, just solid spellwork by Magister Dunaughy," Nath said, rubbing the bruise between his eyes. "You were right, Spells. This Rat did bite."

There was no answer from Dunaughy, and Nath's officers all avoided his eyes. Alston placed a hand on Nath's arm and pointed to starboard with his chin. There, a few feet away, Dunaughy lay sprawled full-length on the deck. There was a charred spot over his heart and a pool of blood spread sluggishly beneath him. Nath's heart froze.

The Confessor lay at Nath's feet; the bridge of his nose laid open by a recent blow and his left eye closed by clotted blood. His remaining eye, bright as a viper's, locked with Nath's. He bared his teeth aggressively through blood-spattered lips. Nath answered the glare with silence and an expression of cool contempt.

"After emptying a brace of pistols at you and poor Spells, he drug out his sticker and made for Lieutenant Bascombe," Alston said. "But

Lieutenant Harcourt would have none of that and disarmed the das-tard after cutting 'im up a bit."

It took every fiber of Nath's resolve, but he refrained from running his hanger through the throat of the snarling dog at his feet. The eyes of the *Alarums* around him stayed his hand. If their captain took out his grief on an unarmed prisoner, how could he expect them to do better? Instead, he willed his wrath to transform from a raging fire to a blood-freezing chill.

He looked down at Confessor Faucher and sniffed in contempt. "What sort of gentleborn strikes a blow after their colors are struck? You, sir, are a craven dog and a murderer."

"Better a dog than one of your *gentleborn*," Faucher spat and rose unsteadily to his feet. "Or the sort of coward that dispatches demons over the horizon to murder a good man!"

"Murder is a strange word to hear on the lips of a bloody-handed killer," Nath drawled.

"I feel no shame in ignoring your effete rules of war to avenge my brother's death. I only wish he'd had time to enchant another ball to pierce magical defenses, so that your heart's blood mixed with his on the deck. You are as much a murderer as the diabolist I struck down. It was at your behest that he sent his fiends to slay my poor brother!"

Nath and his officers exchanged bewildered looks. This confessor was mad, he thought.

"Magister Dunaughy was no diabolist," Nath scoffed. "You're a fool to believe in such children's tales. He sent no demons after your brother. If he could do such a thing, why would he strike your brother down rather than you?"

"Poor Olnierre was more of a threat to him! He was a magician of growing power."

"Magister Dunaughy had nothing to do with your brother's death.

He must have been slain by some émigré mage on your chase." Somehow, the tragedy he shared with Faucher heightened Nath's cold fury.

"You lie," Faucher raged. "You lie! Curse you all for aristocrats' dogs who stand in the way of progress and enlightenment. May you all live long enough for your severed heads to gaze upon your broken bodies! And you, Captain Nath, I will be avenged for the crimes you and your brigands committed against me and my command!"

The man literally frothed as he raved, his spittle spraying the lapels of Nath's coat. Despite himself, Nath took a step back from the Confessor, whose visage had transformed from arrogance to outright lunacy.

Faucher turned his head to spit toward Dunaughy's broken body.

"And he, the instrument of the worst of your crimes, this Magister Dunaughy! I curse him, body and soul! May his spirit know no rest and wander the seas eternally, a bodiless revenant, a—"

Alston silenced the Confessor with the brass pommel of his cutlass, knocking him to his knees. "That'll be enough cursin' from you, ye devil."

Nath stared at the dazed Confessor for a long moment, fighting back images of the bastard's body sinking beneath the waves, unshriven and unmourned. Or perhaps clear a circle on the deck, put the insect's sword back in his hand, and kill him one humiliating cut at a time, leaving his left hand, that truly sinister hand that slew poor Dunaughy, for the penultimate stroke. The final affront against the villain's person would be a slash that opened his windpipe and left him gasping out his last mortal breaths like some loathsome, bottom-feeding fish thrown on the shore by a contemptuous fate. He broke this reverie with an effort and turned his icy gaze on the Ardain officer.

"How are you called, Lieutenant?"

"Themideaux, sir," the woman answered and made a nervous knee. "Third Lieutenant, *Artagny*."

Nath nodded and pointed at an ornately engraved, gold-hilted small-sword lying on the deck. "Is that Confessor Faucher's sword?"

"It is, sir."

"Bring it to me, please."

He accepted the sword and turned it over in his hands appreciatively. After his study was complete, he plunged the point of the sword into the deck and placed his boot in the middle of the blade. He bore down until the slender length of steel snapped loudly under his boot.

"Throw this trash over the side." Nath handed the ruined weapon to his steward. "There is no more honor in it than there is in the creature for whom it was forged."

Alston accepted the sword as if it were coated with filth while Faucher watched from his knees, his face frozen in a paroxysm of rage. Nath ignored him and turned his attention back to Lieutenant Themideaux.

"You are the highest-ranking *naval* officer remaining, are you not?"

"I am, sir."

"Then I will accept your sword in surrender, sir."

Lieutenant Themideaux bowed and presented Nath with a plain, brass-hilted hanger. It was the cheap but serviceable weapon of an impoverished junior officer.

"It is a mean weapon," Themideaux apologized.

"It is a good weapon that has been used in action," Nath replied, running a thumb along its faintly notched edge. "And it belongs to an honorable woman, so it is far superior to that gilded piece of trash, which was nothing more than an accoutrement to a costume donned by a parasitical louse to pass among us as a man."

Confessor Faucher attempted to surge to his feet but was brought up short by Alston's boot in his face. "Yer betters is speakin', ye wee sow. Keep yer peace!"

Nath ignored Faucher's display and returned Themideaux's weapon to her, hilt first.

"You have acquitted yourself with honor, Lieutenant Themideaux. I suspect you will be an officer of some distinction. I am not comfortable depriving you of the instrument of your trade, sir."

Themideaux's mouth gaped for a moment before she accepted her sword and quickly sheathed it. "I will carry your words fondly for the rest of my days, sir. I hope someday we might meet when our nations are at peace."

Nath nodded and glanced about the ship. He was gratified to see that Lieutenant Bascombe's prize crew, thin as it was, had already secured the Ardain crew belowdecks and was in the process of putting the ship to rights. Dr. Rondelle had finished ensuring that the Rat wounded were cared for properly by their own ship's doctor and now knelt by the fallen Dunaughy, his instrument bag at his side. He had covered the dead man's face with a handkerchief.

He was surprised to see tears in the doctor's eyes as the wizened fellow looked up at his approach. Nath knew there was no love lost between Rondelle and Dunaughy, but it was clear now that Rondelle held his former nemesis in some respect, if not friendship.

"There was nothing to be done, sir," Rondelle said, the brassy edge of his voice giving his words a strange mix of aggression and defensiveness. "Had I been here the moment his head struck the deck, there was nothing I could have done. I regret that dearly, but that is the physical reality which no amount of grief will alter."

"I understand, Dr. Rondelle," Nath said, staring down at the body of his ship's mage. It had taken no small effort on Nath's part to earn the man's estimable respect and, as time passed, his genuine friendship. Perhaps something beyond friendship, approaching the paternal. Over the last month, Nath felt as if Dunaughy had adopted him and was grooming him for higher command with his instructional tales of life aboard an admiral's flagship.

"The ball destroyed his heart," Rondelle carried on. "Quite destroyed it. There was naught within my power I could have done, even were I here."

"I understand," Nath repeated patiently. "Now if you will, sir, please see that Magister Dunaughy is borne back to *Alarum* in all dignity. We will see to his service at nightfall."

"I fear he was a heathen, sir," Rondelle said with a disapproving sniff. "A practitioner of the old ways. One of those dancers in bogs one hears about. The sort that marks the seasons with nonsensical rituals from the primitive past. He said as much once when we conversed after dinner—"

"Thank you, Dr. Rondelle. You have your orders."

Nath joined Lieutenant Bascombe, who was locked in conversation with the carpenter's mate and his assistants. Bascombe cast a glance over Nath's shoulder to where Dunaughy's mortal remains were being carefully rolled into one of the hammocks that littered the deck.

She touched the brim of her bicorn hat and said, "A sad loss, sir. May Providence carry Spells to his glory."

"Amen, Lieutenant Bascombe," Nath replied, and pushed on to business. Mourning now was not in the best interest of the king or his naval service. He'd confront Dunaughy's loss later. "Chips, what is the state of the rudder?"

"The cordage was cut clean, sor. An easy splice to fix, if'n ye ain't dodging splinter and shot. No damage to the rudder post or rudder herself. She'll be right as rain within the hour."

Nath nodded and gave the *Alarum*'s carpenter a subdued pat on the shoulder. "Have you surveyed the stores, Lieutenant Bascombe?"

"Yes, sir. There are ample rations to run her in to Middlesea and just enough powder and shot if we are cagey in our course. I won't have enough hands to fire a full broadside, at any gate."

"Keep that in mind, Lieutenant," Nath cautioned her. "Avoid all enemy contact. Run fast and true for Middlesea. Those are my orders."

"I understand, sir."

"Good. I will leave half a dozen marines with you, though it will leave the *Alarum* short. Use them wisely."

"Thank you, sir. I'll keep the Rats confined below and set guns loaded with grape at the hatches."

"Keep an eye on Faucher, the Confessor. Trust nothing the worm says, nor any gesture he makes. You know your duty and you are as skilled an officer as any that has worn the king's coat. There is nothing left for me to do than to wish that fair seas and fine winds bear you safely to Middlesea."

"Thank you, sir," Bascombe replied with a grin. "You needn't worry! We'll be safe as houses on the voyage. Good sailing to you as well!"

They shook hands and Nath took his leave, eager to finish the chase that the *Artagny* began.

chapter 3

I n the morning, Enid was awakened by a sailor informing her that Master Arnaud sent his compliments and requested her attention on deck.

"I'm certain that Master Arnaud can survive without my attention until a more reasonable hour," Enid said. "I am not accustomed to leaving even as poor a bed as this until after the cock crows."

Truth to tell, yesterday's efforts had left her exhausted. Snuffing out the *Artagny*'s little mage had required more effort than it should have, due to the ambiguities of working such a sending in a realm of wind and water. The interplay of elementals in this strange environment left her all at sea, as it were. Later, her labored efforts to fill the little brig's sails to overflowing with beneficial breezes and loosen the grasp of the sullen waves that resented the passage of land-born intruders through their watery empire had depleted the last of her reserves so thoroughly that she had no memory of collapsing in her box cot.

"Begging your pardon, milady, but Master Arnaud sends his compliments and *requires* your attention in his cabin. And it's only an hour before the noon bell, milady, so the cock has done crowed."

"Damn the bird, then, and damn you for waking me!" Enid snapped. "Tell your master that I'm a passenger and he can keep his *require-ments* for those under his petty power!" She rolled over in her hanging cot and pulled her blanket higher over her shoulders, dismissing the sailor with her back.

"Begging your pardon, milady, but it's not truly Master Arnaud's requirements, milady. It's more the Albion commander's orders. The one what has made a prize of our poor *Marie*."

Enid groaned. All last night's efforts were obviously fruitless.

"Make yourself useful then and help me out of this infernal box!"

She dressed quickly but carefully and made her way across the *Marie*'s strangely silent deck toward the master's cabin. Heavily armed Albion sailors and marines held most of the little merchantman's crew at bay in the forecastle, while another group gathered the passengers against the lee rail. Behind them, Enid could plainly see the ship that had rescued them the evening before, her guns run out and an Albion pennant streaming from her tallest mast.

An Albion marine snapped to attention by the master's cabin door and opened it for her. She ducked her head as she entered, frowning slightly as her eyes struggled to adjust to the dim interior after the brightness of the deck. Soon she could make out the vague form of Master Arnaud standing beside his desk, behind which was seated a smallish man in the uniform of an Albion navy officer.

To Enid, he looked more like a merchant's clerk than a military of-ficer. The same avaricious glint so characteristic of the hardened usu-rer gleamed in his eyes as his finger ran down the column of figures on a ledger page. She noted that those eyes were the blue-gray color of the forget-me-nots that grew in a riot around the ruins of her family's old keep in Tancre. At first glance, he seemed about as imposing as one of those minute blooms. She estimated that he stood no higher than her shoulder and nothing about the hang of his rather worn and drab uniform indicated anything impressive about his musculature.

Still, there was a definite grace and sureness to his movements. She imagined he was quite the thing on the dance floor or, perhaps, the salle. She appreciated the fact that he did not powder his hair as so many Albions did and found its unapologetic auburn hue quite pleasing. She decided it would take little more than a squint to ignore the deficiencies of his frame and declare him a handsome man.

Master Arnaud cleared his throat and said, "Captain Nath, may I present the Marquise Enid d'Tancreville."

The Albion officer glanced up from his hurried survey of the *Marie*'s papers at the master's voice. He stood and bowed slightly at the waist in consideration of her rank and introduced himself.

"Captain Rue Nath, His Majesty's Royal Navy, HMS *Alarum*. An honor to meet you, I'm sure."

Enid acknowledged his courtesy with a vague nod. "A captain, you say? And yet you only wear a single epaulette?"

Nath eased his narrow frame back into the master's chair. "I am a commander in rank, but a captain in authority."

Enid shrugged, her expression indicating she didn't care one way or the other about the foolishness indulged in by her inferiors. She turned to Master Arnaud and said archly, "There. I have presented my compliments as you requested. Now, if you will excuse me, I wish to return to my berth and safeguard my belongings from this horde of Albion locusts."

The husky master dabbed perspiration from his broad brow with a plain handkerchief and waved it at Nath. "Captain Nath wished to make your acquaintance, milady. I beg your pardon for disturbing you, but under the circumstances—"

The Ardain noblewoman turned back to Nath with a smile that did not quite reach her frosty eyes. "Well, then, it has been a pleasure, Captain Nath. Now, if you will excuse me?"

Nath arched a brow and was about to speak when Master Arnaud interrupted, "Milady, the captain has made a generous offer that would seem to benefit you both. I humbly implore you to give him your attention for a moment or two."

Enid shrugged and settled into a low canvas chair in front of the desk. After adjusting her costume to her liking, she gestured for the Albion officer to speak.

"Marquise d'Tancreville, Master Arnaud told me of your part in counteracting the *Artagny*'s magister. He also indicated that you are bound for the Spice Colonies, where you intend to arrange a passage to Albion. Is this an accurate representation of your intent?"

Enid pursed her lips and nodded.

"What do you intend to do in Albion, Marquise? Do you have family there?"

"No, I do not. If it is any of your business, my intent is to offer my skills to assist the Crown of Albion in bringing down the so-called Theocratic Republic of Ardainne, perhaps through service in one of your king's cavalry regiments."

Nath nodded somberly. "You wish to offer the king your skills as a sorceress, milady?"

"I understood that Albion already had enough seamstresses, so sorcery seemed my next most valuable skill to offer."

Master Arnaud visibly winced, but Nath ignored the barb and said, "Why the cavalry, of all things? Were you in a regiment before the uprising?"

"No." Enid's tone was sharp, and she shifted uneasily in her chair. "I was not. I have never served in the military in any capacity. As to the cavalry, well, it seems the logical choice."

"What aspect of cavalry service provided the framework for your logic?"

"The cavalry has been the traditional arm in which the highborn have served since time immemorial. I flatter myself to believe that while my blood may not allow me to aspire to a queen's throne, it is of sufficient quality to permit a seat atop a king's horse. And as for seats, well, I have been told mine is a good one. It has certainly never failed me on a hunt, no matter how rough the ground."

"I have no doubt as to the quality of your seat," Nath answered wryly and glanced at the seat in question, which was presented in semi-profile as she sat angled on the edge of her chair. Her lips compressed with annoyance as his eyes snapped back to her face. "Nor do I argue the nobility of service astride. But have you any interest with the Horse Lord? An influential friend on his staff, perhaps? A relationship to one of his generals? Colonels? Majors?"

She shook her head at each point, and, in the end, Nath threw up his hands with a perplexed frown.

"You must truly love the idea of fighting on horseback, then, if the idea of playing step-and-fetch for someone more fortunate in influence or wealth than yourself—"

"I will do no such thing!" Enid snapped. "I would not be made a mere servant! I am a skilled sorceress! There would surely be a place for me on some general's staff!"

"Oh, certainly there would be. You could work the cantrips to keep his tent warm and snug and perhaps he'd allocate you a corner of it to keep you out of the rain. I'm sure he'd also value you for chilling his wine, keeping the mildew from his hose, and, when dire military need arose, he might turn to you to charge his spell-locks for him."

"You dare imply my skills are no more worthy than that?" She stood, her fists clenched at her sides, and glared down at the little Albion officer.

Nath raised a conciliatory hand and smiled easily. "Nothing of the sort, I assure you. I'm mortal certain that your skills are anything but inconsequential, else we would not be engaged in this conversation. My only intent is to warn you of the sort of treatment you can count on if you present yourself to the Horse Lord with no one to speak for you and no treasure with which to purchase a suitable commission. Placement in the regiments has nothing to do with skill and everything to do with patronage and purse. I would hazard you are familiar with such practices even in Ardainne?"

Enid bristled at the little officer's words. "I believe my title as a marquise should stand in good stead for petty social connections. I believe it carries as much weight in Albion as in Ardainne, does it not?"

Nath's sad, compassionate expression seemed genuine as he said, "It would, if an actual marquisate was associated with it. I fear that is not the case for you as things currently stand in your homeland. Your title is sadly empty."

"Be that as it may," Enid snarled. "I am no pauper!"

"Enjoy that state while you may, then," Nath said. "As the price of commissions doubles or triples for Ardain refugees."

Her anger subsided under the calm scrutiny of Nath's water-blue eyes and was replaced by a dejected certainty that he spoke the truth. She resumed her seat with a disconsolate sigh.

"Well, I cannot see any alternative. My pride would suffer less participating, however menially, in the defeat of the Theocracy than it would idling away my time peacefully while others fought my war for me."

"Ah!" Nath said and leaned eagerly across the desk. "But there *is* an alternative! I can save you the humiliation of service beneath your abilities as well as a long voyage fraught with risk of capture by Ardain privateers all in one stroke!"

"How so?" Enid treated the Albion officer to the same sort of skeptical expression she might have worn had he attempted to sell her a handful of magic beans.

"It was our misfortune to lose our own ship's magister in the action against the *Artagny*. I have enough sorcery to plot a course or charge a match, but not enough to scry or work magic against an enemy vessel." Nath paused and gave an almost apologetic shrug. "After hearing Master Arnaud's description of your part in countering the *Artagny*'s magister and your desire to repair to Albion, I asked to speak to you to offer you a temporary warrant aboard my ship, the *Alarum*. It is a solution that will relieve me of some difficulty and gain you the opportunity to arrive in Albion as much as a year earlier, and, as a bonus, to take up arms against the Theocrats immediately and in a capacity more suitable to your obvious rank and talent."

Her eyes thoughtful, Enid reached into one of the voluminous pockets of the blue jacket she wore and produced a pair of cigarillos. She offered one to Nath, who waved it away with a polite word and regretful smile. He watched silently as she nipped off the end of a cigarillo between white, even teeth and, without applying any flame to its tip, puffed somberly. An instant later, the tip of the cigarillo began to glow and the cramped cabin was filled with the smell of aromatic tobacco. Just as the weight of silence was about to squeeze a word out of Nath or the *Marie*'s unusually nervous master, the marquise spoke.

"I had thought to offer my services to one of the cavalry regiments accepting expatriate Ardain nobility into their ranks." Her warning glance stilled a heartfelt entreaty from Master Arnaud, who obviously felt the better this interview went for Nath, the more generous he would be in his reckoning the *Marie*'s fate. "However, there is much to be said about your offer, especially in light of what you have said regarding the sort of duties I could expect were I even accepted into a regiment. But I must own I have no more influence with the lords of your navy than I do with the Horse Lord. How different could service aboard your ship be than on some general's staff?"

"Why, as different as night and day!" Nath assured her. "A ship's magister is entrusted with tremendous responsibility and respect in equal proportion. You'd be no lackey aboard the *Alarum*. You'd be a key figure in making her a fearsome weapon against the Theocracy."

"She certainly seemed fearsome enough against the *Artagny*," Enid said, then puffed on her cigarillo. "Still, I'd hoped to put my magic to work in support of an entire regiment, to play a role in turning the tide of battles that might decide the war . . ."

"Do not discount the importance of one frigate, Marquise," Nath said. "It is my firm belief that one frigate in the right place, at the right time, with the right people aboard her, is worth a dozen plodding regiments. We move freely and we strike fiercely."

"Hmm." While it was clear that the Albion captain believed his own words, Enid was not entirely convinced. She doubted that even the grandest ship of the line represented anything like the fighting power of a cavalry regiment. Certainly, even a smallish frigate such as the one under this "Captain" Nath's command was possessed of a respectable number of cannons and was able to move them hither and yon with great speed—but did that match the focused power and glory of a heavy cavalry charge? Surely not.

Still, everything the man had said regarding her likely treatment at the hands of the Horse Lord rang true. She had little desire to be relegated to the role of ensign until she was able to earn the interest of some Albion lord through deeds of valor or sycophantry. She rolled her cigarillo between her thumb and fingertips and contemplated her options. The voyage to St. Iphrygia in the Spice Colonies was a long one and, as this lieutenant pointed out, it exposed her to capture at the hands of Ardain warships and privateers—not to mention the risk of encountering an Albion commander with more interest in her value as a prisoner than as a mage. Then there was the matter of finding passage from Iphrygia to Albion, probably aboard another merchant engaged in semilegal trade and smuggling. An expensive and risky proposition.

Captain Nath took her silence for an eminent refusal. He leaned back in his chair and said, "I might be reluctant to accept such an offer myself, were I in your position. After all, you've never even considered service at sea and you've only my word that you'll be treated with any more respect than you'd receive in a cavalry company."

Enid nodded silently, leaving the onus of persuasion on this young officer.

"Let us look at it in this light," Nath continued evenly, ticking his points off on his fingers as he named them. "You wish to reach Albion but your current plan places you at extreme risk. Once there, you wish to take up arms against the rascals who have overthrown your king."

He paused for her nod of agreement before continuing. "I am in great need of your skills, if only until the Naval Board can appoint a permanent replacement for poor old Dunaughy. Here is where our disparate desires might happily converge: If you act as the *Alarum*'s interim magister, I will release you from the post upon the *Alarum*'s return to Albion. If we do not find ourselves there within three months and you do not desire to continue our association, I will release you at Gisbon at the first opportunity. From there, you can easily find a berth on a warship or legitimate merchantman bound for Albion. Regardless, you will find my offer far safer and significantly less expensive than sailing all the way to the Colonies and back to Albion. Who knows? You might even find the Sea Service to your liking."

"I seem destined to further sailing regardless of my decision and doing it aboard a formidably armed vessel is more appealing than aboard one which is unarmed."

Nath's face split into a cheery grin, but before he could enthuse, she pressed on firmly. "There is the matter of training, however."

Enid paused to flick ashes from the tip of her cigarillo, eliciting a frown from both sailors until they noticed that the gray flecks faded out of existence before touching the deck.

"I have had formal training at the Université de Vermandoix and I am a member of the Institut, but I fear I have had little in the way of military, let alone naval, instruction."

"Magister Dunaughy left behind a fine collection of books on the subject of maritime sorcery, milady. I don't doubt that you will find all you need to know in them. Besides, considering what the Theocracy has left Ardainne for ship's mages, a first-year neophyte could make a credible showing against them. I'm sure you'd serve us quite well!"

Enid sniffed irritably and flicked ashes toward the deck. "At least as well as a first-year neophyte."

She took another long draw on her cigarillo as Nath watched. In the background, Master Arnaud assured her that the honorable Albion captain meant her no offense, but his words were lost on her as she studied Nath's sparkling eyes, taking a measure of their depth. She liked what she saw and silenced Master Arnaud with a vague wave in his direction.

"It is better to serve as a neophyte against the Theocrats than to be captured by one of their seagoing Confessors—or serve as an overblown valet for some Albion cavalry captain. So, how does one go about *temporarily* enlisting in the Albion Royal Navy?"

"It's the simplest thing in the world!" Nath smiled broadly and pushed a piece of paper across the desk toward her. "The serious circumstance of being without a ship's magister gives me wide latitude in rectifying the lack. That, coupled with Master Arnaud's account of your sorcerous efforts on behalf of the *Marie* and the evidence of those efforts aboard the *Artagny*, provides me with ample grounds to extend you a temporary commission as ship's magister aboard the *Alarum*."

Enid picked up the commission and skimmed over the terse, almost brutal composition. Her eyes lingered for a second on the words "fail at their peril." A powerful oath, this temporary commission. "This calls for proof of 'ability and education.' You have proof of my ability, but what of my education?"

Nath raised a brow as he placed a wide-bottomed inkwell and quill next to the commission. "Evidence? You said you received an enviable education just a moment ago. The word of a lady of noble birth is evidence enough for me, I assure you."

Enid made a noncommittal noise and put her name to the paper, adding an intricate flourish beneath it. She lifted the page to her lips and whispered a cantrip to dry the ink. When she offered the paper to

Nath, he snatched it with an alacrity that troubled her. She hoped she had not just made a fool's deal based on the clarity of a man's eyes.

"Mr. Bell!" Nath bawled in a voice that vastly exceeded his frame. When a lean, balding sailor thrust his head through the cabin door and tugged at a nonexistent forelock, Nath told him, "See to Magister d'Tancreville's dunnage! Stow it in Magister Dunaughy's cabin."

He then turned to the merchant commander and spoke in a tone only slightly less peremptory. "Master Arnaud! Be so kind as to send some hands to fetch her belongings stored in the hold. When you return, we will discuss what we shall do with your vessel."

Once the burly little shipmaster was gone, Nath said, "We'll speak more of your duties and privileges aboard the *Alarum*, Magister. For now, I must negotiate this vessel's ransom and have time for little else. Let it suffice that from this moment on you must address me as 'Captain' or 'sir' and obey my commands briskly."

Seeing a flicker of doubt cross her face, he continued a little less brusquely: "Never fear, though. I won't ask anything of you that you are not capable of, or which is beneath your status as ship's mage."

"Which status you will explain to me more fully later?"

chapter 4

Enid departed the cabin in a quiet rage, leaving the minikin Nath behind, his shoulders hunched as he pored over one of the *Marie*'s ledgers.

Within ten minutes Master Arnaud appeared, his face flush from activity. "Milady, your baggage has been whipped over, as Captain Nath ordered. If you'll permit it, I'll share this rail with you while he determines whether my poor *Marie* will be taken as a prize or—"

Nath appeared like a devil summoned by his name. Enid was not sure if he was wearing a closemouthed grin or just squinting against the sun after the darkness of the master's cabin.

"Or. Master Arnaud. I have settled upon 'or,' unless you find the terms disagreeable." Nath ignored the Ardain master's ardent exaltation of his generosity and took several sheets of paper from the dispatch case hanging from his shoulder. He pressed them into Master Arnaud's hands. "Read this before you praise too much, Master Arnaud. I trust you are familiar with Notes of Ransom?"

"I am," Arnaud said.

"Good. I'm sure you'll find my reckoning fair and accurate."

Arnaud glanced down at the paper, and his face transmuted from pleased acceptance to fury. Enid smiled openly as he shook the Notes of Ransom under the Albion captain's nose. It was good to see more of the fellow's stubborn pugnacity so in evidence during yesterday's chase.

"Five thousand livre? You mistake my poor *Marie* for a treasure galleon, Captain! I assure you she is not!"

The red-faced master ranted and stormed about the iniquitous greed of young naval officers and the importunities heaped upon honest merchants at every turn. As he raved, Nath glanced over the rail and studied the sails and rigging of his own vessel. At last, he flung out a silencing hand.

"Do not mistake my generosity for weakness, Master Arnaud! I would rather not put a prize crew aboard you, but if you will not accept my terms, God as my witness, I shall!" The last words of the declaration were uttered with a force that would have borne them clearly over screaming gales or roaring guns. It left silence hanging heavily in the air for a long moment.

Nath cleared his throat and smoothed his threadbare coat before continuing in a more conversational tone. "The ransom is reasonable, and it is not negotiable. It will leave you with a comfortable profit at the end of your voyage. I do not expect you to pay it in hard specie, but rather in the transference of goods from your hold to the *Alarum*'s. Do not forget, either, that if you refuse the ransom, I am within my rights to seize your cargo and, should I choose not to part with a prize crew, sink the *Marie* to deny her services to the enemies of Albion. I don't think either of us wishes to see such a fine vessel reduced to flinders for my gunners' practice, do we?"

Master Arnaud sighed in resignation, defeated. "No, sir, we do not. Five thousand is a fair demand, but it was my duty to attempt to reduce it, just as it is yours to fire at least one broadside before striking your colors to a superior opponent."

Nath stood with his hands behind his back and ignored Enid's glare while Master Arnaud stamped into the darkness of his cabin. When he stepped back on deck, he had a countersigned copy of the document in hand and a wan smile on his face.

He handed the paper to Nath and said, "There. It is done, and may it bring you joy, Captain Nath! I don't doubt I owe you my life for rescuing us from the *Artagny* and her thrice-damned Confessor!"

Nath's expression darkened at the mention of the Confessor. He tucked the signed document into his cartel and said, "It was a costly favor. There are very few rascals I would wish to see entombed in one of His Majesty's prison hulks, but such a berth is more than that worm deserves."

Enid was momentarily taken aback by the sheer hatred in the little officer's voice, but she could not resist a barb at his expense.

"I give you joy at your victory over the *Artagny*, Captain Nath," she said. "Did you ransom her as well or did you 'reduce her to flinders' for your gunners' amusement?"

"No, it is not proper to ransom a warship. They must be taken as a prize or sunk. She was quite the shambles before our little dance was complete, with dozens dead and wounded and many of her guns dismounted. Still, she was seaworthy, so I placed a prize crew aboard her, which was good news for the owners of the *Marie* here." Nath paused and offered an amiable wink to Master Arnaud.

"If I had more men available, I doubt I would have ransomed such a sweet vessel as this." The Albion officer caressed the *Marie*'s rail with an appreciation that bordered on the amorous. "Such are the fortunes of war! Now, Master Arnaud, there are a few minor issues we must resolve before parting company . . . Oh, Magister d'Tancreville. Mr. Bell will see you across to the *Alarum* and settled in your cabin. You will do me the honor of dining in my cabin this evening? We shall discuss the duties of your warrant and get to know one another better. We will be working closely in the future."

Enid gave her answer to the back of Nath's head as he became lost in the important business of transferring stores and gathering information from Master Arnaud.

———

Bell was obviously surprised when Enid negotiated the spray-slick ladder down the side of the ship with casual grace and leaped nimbly into the boat bobbing beside the *Marie*. She registered that surprise with some annoyance. The fact that she was not a sailor born did not mean she was some sort of clumsy dullard. She wondered how sure-footed the bald-pated commoner would be on the narrow, rocky trails that crisscrossed the uplands of her beloved Tancre. Judging by his rather ungainly stride and bowed legs, she was less likely to come to mischance at sea than he would be in the mountains of her homeland. She noticed the coxswain staring at the smooth white flesh exposed by her open collar and pulled her coat tightly closed in a gesture more evocative of contempt than concern. Bell merely shrugged and barked a hoarse command. The sailors aboard the boat bent to their oars and in a moment, it was slicing a credible path through the choppy blue-gray waves of the strait.

Seated in the stern sheets, Enid watched the *Alarum* grow steadily larger with each sweep of the oars. She was bigger than the *Marie*, being both longer and taller above the water than the merchantman. Her masts seemed higher and thicker as well. While many of the crew were actively involved on the frigate's deck, hauling aboard stores taken from the merchant vessel and going about other arcane tasks which were beyond Enid's meager maritime understanding, there were not as many crewmen visible as she expected. She remembered the great mass of sailors that crowded the *Artagny*'s rails just before the first lethal broadside swept them into bloody oblivion. The *Alarum* seemed all but deserted in comparison. Still, undermanned or not, the *Alarum* had proven more than a match for the much larger Ardain frigate, and that sure knowledge produced in her a confidence the more pragmatic part of her being prayed was well-founded. A moment later the boat bumped against the *Alarum*'s side, and she sprang as easily up its battens as she had descended from the *Marie*.

Once on deck, Bell quickly reported to a tall, dark-skinned woman in the same sort of single-epauletted coat Enid had seen Captain Nath wearing. She wondered if asymmetry was the current fashion in Albion's military circles. The officer was engaged in a rather heated discussion with a man Enid took to be either a person of some authority or an extremely impudent sailor. She waited patiently with Bell while a short but sharp argument unfolded before them.

"I tell you that lot *must* be stored for'ard!" The man gestured wildly at a net full of provisions confiscated from the *Marie* that hung suspended over the deck. A group of sailors loitered nearby, watching the debate with interest.

"And I tell *you*, Master Harde, that the *captain* has declared otherwise." The lady officer answered Harde's heated exclamation with cool certitude, instantly winning her points in Enid's estimation. "He believes we are heavy in the bow and that it is affecting the *Alarum*'s sailing properties. I've noted your opinion on the matter, but Captain Nath has the final say. I will obey his orders and I expect you will as well."

"Heavy in the bow, by the Redeemer, and we with barely enough weight in the hold to settle us proper in the water!" Harde seemed about to spit on the deck but thought better of it. "You have more time at sea than this jumped-up minikin, Lieutenant. Surely you see the madness of it! A solid officer like yourself would leave the master to do his duty as he saw fit instead'a poking your nose in just to see if it would fit!"

"A solid officer like myself would also report any further remarks of this sort to her captain, so he could take the actions merited by such insolent and undisciplined talk. Now see to your duties *as ordered*."

As the man stalked off, cursing under his breath, Bell rushed forward and begged the lieutenant's pardon. After a few moments of hushed conversation, Bell knuckled his brow in salute and hurried over the side to lend a hand in transferring fresh food and wine from the *Marie*. The lieutenant turned to Enid, her hand outstretched and a smile upon her angular features.

"Lieutenant Augusta Merryweather, ma'am. Acting first lieutenant, the *Alarum*." Her handshake was firm, but not the bone-crushing clench many military officers she'd met in the past attempted when she took their hands palm to palm rather than fingertips to palm. Enid had difficulty gauging the lieutenant's age due to the deep lines around her eyes, but her clear blue eyes and frank smile gave the impression of youth, whatever her actual age might be.

"Bell tells me you've taken up old Dunaughy's warrant?"

"Yes, *temporarily*. Captain Nath was kind enough to offer me a trial at it before requiring any more permanent commitment." She found herself uncomfortable under the lieutenant's amused and speculative gaze and said, rather lamely to her own ear, "He said he would explain the duties associated with the post over dinner tonight."

"I dare say he will." Merryweather cleared her throat and called a couple of sailors by name, ordering them to take up Enid's baggage. "If you'll accompany me below, Magister, I'll show you to your cabin."

Enid followed Merryweather through a hatch and down a narrow set of stairs into a cramped room with a rough table running down the center. The air was a little stale, but no worse than she'd experienced aboard the *Marie*. They ducked through a short door at the room's end and stopped at a door on the left side of the hall. Merryweather held the door open for her to enter and then stood in the doorway.

"This is Dunaughy's cabin. He kept a small workroom below on the orlop. That'll be yours, too. I had it locked tight when he packed it in. I mean, passed away, may the Redeemer take him."

The cabin was no more than six feet deep and perhaps five wide. She had to stoop not to bump her head on the ceiling. A single chair and a wooden-sided cot suspended from ropes, similar to the one in her cabin aboard the *Marie*, consumed most of the room's space. After the sailors carefully piled her baggage in the room, there was barely room for her feet on the floor. Merryweather cleared her throat again. Enid suspected it was affectation meant to cover her amusement.

"We'll have some of that struck below, Magister, after you determine what you need handy. While you're at it, you might go through the seabags on your cot there. Those are Dunaughy's belongings. We were going to auction them at the masthead this evening, but as his successor, you have first choice of his gear. Just pick what you want and set it aside. The rest will go on the block after the evening meal."

Enid did not deign to hide the disgust in her voice. "You *auction* off the possessions of your fallen comrades?"

Merryweather chuckled. "Not an old salt, are we, Spells? The auction isn't as hard-hearted as it sounds. Everyone pays at least purser's price for whatever they buy, and the proceeds will go to Dunaughy's family or toward a memorial for him if he don't have any. Any truly personal items are kept by the captain and sent home to his kin with whatever money the auction raises."

"Oh. Well. That is different," Enid admitted reluctantly.

Merryweather informed her with a wry smile that dinner was taken early aboard the *Alarum* and it was as formal an affair as possible, out of respect for the captain. She assured Enid she'd send someone to guide her to the captain's cabin and suggested she stay in her quarters until then.

"Wouldn't want to see you clobbered by a block or some such tragedy, ma'am." She sketched an amiable salute and left Enid to the claustrophobic solitude of her new home.

With little else to occupy her, Enid sorted through her baggage and found a few items of clothing and toiletry she felt were both essential and suitable for shipboard service. She transferred these items to her smallest sea chest. A few moments more saw the most useful of her sorcerous tools and books consolidated into a second small chest. After repacking her goods into her remaining chests, Enid restored the dweomers that protected them from rodents and mildew. She stacked the items to be "struck below" next to the cabin door and then turned her attention to the bags on her suspended cot.

Both bags were made of canvas, reinforced with leather. She emptied one bag on the cot and found it filled with clothes, mostly uniforms. The dead man had been shorter and leaner than her, which left her oddly relieved. The thought of wearing a dead man's clothes, or worse yet, feeding any parasites residing in them, disgusted her. The second bag contained a few personal items, a journal, and a few books on maritime magic. She set the books aside, and after a moment's consideration, the journal as well. Everything else went back into the bags, which she set outside the cabin door.

Overhead, she heard an alarming rumble of feet rushing back and forth across the decks, followed by a horrible, screeching whistle. Her first thought was that the ship might be under attack, but after several minutes passed without the roar of cannons, she settled into the writing desk's rickety chair and blew on an ancient-looking orb lamp to coax forth a faint blue glow. Flipping through the maritime spell books, she saw nothing which seemed beyond her abilities, although some processes used terminology which was foreign to her. She found one book, *Herbstrom's Naval Arts*, included a glossary that should be sufficient to overcome the unfamiliar jargon. She set the books aside and took up Dunaughy's journal.

The journal's leather cover had once been dyed a deep red, but was now worn to a dull rust brown, the only traces of its original glory visible in a few deep recesses and folds. The cover was plain and unembossed, but the first page bore an impressive print of the Seal of the Albion Royal Navy, below which were written the words "Presented to

Magister Ian Fitch Dunaughy. Filsterhead Remembered, 1773." She flipped past the ostentatious seal and memoriam, skipped from place to place in the journal, and read snippets at random.

Dunaughy's journal was encrypted, but it was a standard variation of the so-called Naveroñian Exchange Code. She was able to mentally translate much of it and simply skipped sections that were beyond her. She would revisit those later. From what she could gather, the journal picked up in the middle of Dunaughy's long service as a ship's magister after a certain naval action that had in some way proven pivotal to his career. This was no doubt the "Filsterhead Remembered" on the journal's opening page, and she made a note to look into what had happened there. The journal only gave her glimpses of the battle's aftermath. Dunaughy's crabbed script spoke of lost friends, perhaps a lost brother, and of men so mutilated by flying splinters and shot that they were ruined for sea duty and forced to seek whatever livelihood they could find ashore. The mage was quite affected by the plight of these invalids and left all his worldly wealth to their succor through the auspices of the Naval Relief Fund.

Nor had he come out of the battle untouched himself: He lost his left eye to a shard of oak from the shot-torn scantlings of the man-of-war on which he served, the *Reaver*. The wound was serious, and he spent months recuperating. When he was at last well enough to resume shipboard duty, he found he had difficulty focusing, not only with his remaining physical eye but also with that extension of self that made truly effective sorcerous processes possible. As the extent to which his arts had suffered from his injury became clear, his career suffered commensurately. His journal bitterly recounted his fall from duty aboard first rates like the 110-gun *Reaver* to exile aboard sixth rates like the *Alarum*.

Dunaughy had obviously been a proud man, and Enid admired his refusal to abandon his beloved navy despite the lack of esteem it seemed to extend him. He was also a brave man. Bedeviled by his inability to focus properly on his sendings, he experimented with different methods of increasing his clarity. He finally settled upon the simplest expedient of all and abandoned the sheltered workroom on the orlop for a spot on the deck where he could physically observe the enemy through the one good eye left to him. This stratagem left him exposed to shot, shell, and more personal perils, such as the one that eventually took his life. It also made him useful to his commanders to the very end of his days.

As Enid read her predecessor's terse but evocative account of life and death at sea, she was struck by his obvious love for service in the navy. His accounts and the events they described were undoubtedly stirring. Here were accounts of bravery in the face of the enemy, whether that enemy was the fleets of Albion's rivals or the primal forces of nature itself, but also of the simple loyalty and bone-deep camaraderie of a group who were, quite literally, all in the same boat.

It was clear Dunaughy had found more than fleeting glory in the navy. He discovered his higher purpose, a goal whose pursuit was a reward in and of itself. Enid read on, barely noticing the deepening gloom that settled over the cabin as Dunaughy recounted triumphs as trivial as the successful repair of a damaged spar to Captain Nath's remarkable chain of victories over the past three weeks. Regardless of the relative scope of the accomplishment, Dunaughy's voice never sank to the dismissive nor rose to hyperbole. The tale he told was one in which no success was either inconsequential or so far out of reach as to seem remarkable when finally attained.

She read his account of the last two months in search of clues about the character of her new commander, Captain Nath. The half-blind mage had thought little of Nath at first and wrote openly of his contempt for the young officer's "childish" figure and "flash" mannerisms. Enid could all but taste the sarcasm dripping from Dunaughy's pen as he consistently referred to Nath not as "captain" but as "commander." She found the dismissive nature of the word confusing, as Nath's role was obviously to command the ship. What could be more natural than to be called its commander? She assumed "captain" was an elevated form of address that Dunaughy chose to withhold from Nath from distaste for his character and doubt in his ability.

After the first week at sea under Nath's command, however, Dunaughy referred to him only as "the young Captain." The small, "flash" officer had obviously won the old magister's respect even before leading the *Alarum* against the enemy for the first time. After his blooding as the ship's commander in a victory against a competently commanded and efficiently manned Ardain privateer, Dunaughy dropped the "young" from Nath's title and spoke of him in tones of quiet admiration which, for him, must have been akin to exaltation.

She was drowsy by the time she reached the end of the journal, and as she read Dunaughy's unexcited prose describing the sighting of the *Artagny*'s topsails over the horizon and the opening maneuvers that would eventually bear him to his end at the hands of the treacherous Confessor, her eyelids drooped. The script swam before her eyes and a part of her mind argued that surrendering to sleep would not be such a bad thing. She tended to agree and allowed her chin to fall to her chest. She felt herself slipping fully into sleep's embrace just as she became aware that someone was standing by the desk, staring at her appraisingly.

She jerked upright with self-righteous approbations poised upon her lips, only to find no one at whom to let fly. The cabin was empty save for a strangely powerful smell of licorice. Before she could reprove herself for such nervousness, there was a sharp rap on her cabin door, sufficiently unexpected under the circumstances to elicit a curse-worthy start, and a young man's voice braying, "Begging your pardon, ma'am, and the captain desires your attention prior to dinner!"

chapter 5

A pock-faced young man who introduced himself as Mid Yeardly while gazing in frank interest at her bosom led Enid to the captain's cabin. It was at the rear of the ship on the main deck, forcing her to follow Yeardly up the short, narrow flight of stairs and offering him the opportunity to stand at their top and enjoy an overhead view of her decolletage. By the time they crossed the narrow end of the weather deck to the captain's door, she was more than a little annoyed by the young man's roguish grins over his shoulder. He opened a door and led her through a dining room barely large enough to accommodate the table, chairs, and cannon that vied among themselves for space.

Yeardly knocked on a door set in the middle of the stateroom's rear wall to announce her arrival and then, impervious to her cold glare, used a stumbling attempt at a courtly bow to bring his face near her person and, to her utter amazement, sniff loudly. Her stunned silence at his effrontery was interrupted by a loud bellow from within the cabin: "Enter, then! Enter!"

Enid pushed the door open and burst into Nath's cabin, nearly braining herself on the low ceiling. She found the place well-lit by orbs in reflectors and the waning orange light of dusk flowing through the broad, low windows that dominated the cabin's back wall. Captain Nath was seated on one of three padded chests, apparently engaged in a struggle with his shirt's high collar. He smiled up at her and was obviously about to voice some sort of pleasantry when she blurted out, "Captain Nath, I demand you have that young dog flogged!"

Nath's face lost all signs of joviality and took on such a grave aspect that Enid was momentarily taken aback. "Yeardly? What has he done? He can be a bitter-tongued brute! Did his speech offend you?"

"No, Captain Nath. He said nothing untoward but he . . . If my word was proof enough for my qualifications for a warrant, shouldn't it be enough to have that rogue flogged?"

Nath regarded her somberly for a moment. "Only a ship's captain may order a man flogged. Your word is enough to ensure my serious consideration of your recommendation, however. Now, if he did not speak rudely to you, did he lay hands upon you?"

Enid stiffened with disdain, again nearly braining herself on the ceiling. "He did not. Had he touched me, I would have dealt with him directly."

"I don't doubt that you would have, Magister d'Tancreville." A little of the gravity was washed out of Nath's narrow, delicately chiseled features by the glimmer of a smile in his eyes. "Although we must talk about how directly you or anyone other than myself may deal with the crew. That can wait, however. What exactly did Yeardly do to deserve a flogging if he did not speak offensively or lay hands upon you?"

"He looked upon me in an unwonted and licentious manner," Enid replied coolly.

Nath nodded thoughtfully. "Such openly coarse behavior deserves censure. You'll have no argument from me on those grounds. You are now an officer of this ship, and your fellow officers must respect your dignity if the crew is to be expected to follow suit. Flogging seems a little too severe. Flogging officers is never good for discipline."

"That . . . that *creature* is one of your officers?" The idea of it left Enid aghast. Yeardly struck her as utter gallows. She would hardly consider trusting him with the feeding of hounds, let alone a share in the command of a ship.

Nath answered her patiently. "Yeardly is a mid, Magister d'Tancreville. He finds himself lost in a nebulous realm somewhere betwixt the ranks of village idiot and king's officer. Now, did he exhibit any other unseemly behavior that might warrant a flogging?"

Enid colored slightly, something she had not done in many years and which she found quite annoying under the circumstances. She cleared her throat and said in as cold a tone as she could muster, "He smelled me."

Nath raised a brow. "He smelled you?"

A deep frown creased her forehead. "Yes. He contrived to bring his nose quite close to my bodice and then sniffed about like a hound on the scent!"

She was about to launch into further commentary comparing Yeardly to various beasts of the field, but the look of frank astonishment on Nath's face struck her as quite humorous. In her experiences with him to this point, he had kept his mien dressed in the currently fashionable cloak of languorous disinterest, but now his eyes were wide with disbelief and his mouth agape. Despite herself, she laughed.

Nath sputtered for a moment and then barked out, "That will be enough levity, Magister!"

As Nath surged to his feet, Enid noted he was in little danger of striking his head on the ceiling, an observation that did not make controlling her amusement any easier. The little captain's stony-faced stare demanded decorum, though, and her mirth evaporated like cooling mist under a harsh sun.

"That's better." Nath cleared his throat. "Now. Smelling is certainly more than staring. You'd have been within your rights to box his ears." He raised a hand to stay her as she exhibited an eagerness to redress the omission of her rights. "No, no! It is too late for that now. I won't have my officers chasing each other from stem to stern to commit mayhem upon one another! Now, this pup Yeardly is well loved by his division and has been cutting it a bit rough lately. This latest atrocity leaves me with no doubt that he must be reminded of the fact that he is a gentleman and the consequences of forgetting it."

Nath paused and turned to gaze thoughtfully out the stern gallery, his hands clasped behind his back. After a long moment of silent consideration, he turned back to Enid, a sly smile on his face. He winked at her before turning to the door to shout for his steward. Enid heard the shout repeated down the length of the light frigate and a moment later Alston popped his head through the door and pressed a bony knuckle to his forehead. He was a tall man with a habitual stoop born of the low deckheads of men-of-war. The sailor was more than twice his captain's age, with leathery brown skin that spoke of decades of exposure to sun, wind, and salt. His long braided hair was the color of polished steel.

"Mr. Alston," Nath said in a brisk tone. "My compliments to Mr. Yeardly, and would he do me the honor of dining with me tonight. That is all."

Alston knuckled his brow and departed without comment.

Nath seated himself at a small chart table and gestured for Enid to take the chair opposite. Once she sat, he began explaining her duties and outlining the ship's organization as if the earlier portion of their conversation had never occurred. Much of what he told her she had already read in the section entitled "Orders and Instructions for a Ship's Mage" in *Herbstrom's Naval Arts*. Although the sorcerous processes her duties would require of her were highly specialized, none of them seemed so far removed from certain basic practices to be too difficult to master in a short time, although she was a bit concerned by the prospect of studying under the prevailing conditions. A tossing ship filled to the brim with noisy and noisome sailors was not the best environment for her for scholarly pursuits.

She dreaded "Instructing the Young Gentlefolk in the Higher Arts as Befits both their Station and Duty," however, especially now that she knew Yeardly would be among those "gentlefolk." Even that was only mildly daunting, though. She'd instructed students in the Foundational Arts before, she just hadn't relished it. The ship's organization, though, was all unfamiliar territory, and she listened to Nath describe it with genuine interest.

The common sailors were at her command as long as those commands did not interfere with their regular duties or unduly compromise their hours of rest. Since Enid had no idea what might interfere with a sailor's regular duties, she determined to rely on the services of the ship's "young gentles" as much as possible.

Nath made it clear that part of a mid's training was learning to cope with the rigorous schedule of command, so she needn't worry about interfering with their time off-watch. She was made to understand that any mid not actively involved in the supervision of their watch division was at her immediate disposal. Despite his recommendation to turn to a mid for the most subservient of tasks, Nath made a point of reminding her they were officers. While the thought of beardless young rogues like Yeardly being used for anything more responsible than stepping and fetching was alarming, Captain Nath assured her that mids were a vital part of the *Alarum*'s command crew.

Next, he described the roles of officers above the rank of mid, explaining that all officers were divided into two classes, "commission officers" and "warrant officers." The only commission officers aboard the *Alarum* are Captain Nath and Lieutenants Merryweather and Oxley, who each held their commissions from Albion's Admiralty. There had been another lieutenant, Bascombe, but she was absent commanding the prize crew aboard the *Artagny*. All other officers, other than the young gentles who are classified as "volunteers," held warrants from the Navy Board or Admiralty.

"Now you must understand that there are warrants and then there are warrants," Nath explained carefully, something in his tone and manner reminding Enid of an old pedagogue patiently holding forth for a slow student. She kept her irritation at his insolence from her face, though, and listened patiently. "Some warrants are of the wardroom, and some are not."

"I'm sure that is so," Enid agreed flatly. "But what is the difference?"

Nath smiled tolerantly. "Well, all the difference in the world, I assure you. Officers of the wardroom keep their quarters near the wardroom and take their meals there together in a genteel fashion. All the other officers have cabins forward and take their meals among the common divisions."

"And in which strata do I find myself?"

"Oh, never fear! Yours is a wardroom warrant." He smiled reassuringly. "I would never put a person of your social standing among the common sailors."

"So, I am to dine in this wardroom?"

Nath chuckled mildly. "Our little *Alarum* is too small a vessel for a wardroom. We have a gunroom that serves the same purpose."

"Then it would seem more appropriate to refer to 'officers of the gunroom' than to 'officers of the wardroom,' wouldn't it?"

"Certainly not." Nath smiled. "It would fly in the very face of tradition, and you'll soon learn tradition is more durable than oak in the king's navy. Now, the officers of the wardroom are the master, the purser, the surgeon, and, of course, the magister. By courtesy, the captain of the marines and his lieutenant are also part of the wardroom. We have only a small contingent of marines aboard, though, commanded by a lieutenant."

"Is he referred to as 'captain,' too, out of deference to authority?"

"He is indeed referred to as captain, due to some mysterious tradition among the lobsters of giving their shipboard officers a brevet rank one higher than their actual commission."

"So the marine lieutenant is a captain while aboard ship. Doesn't this cause confusion among the sailors as to whose commands take precedent?"

"Not in the least," Nath chuckled. "The marine captain holds no authority over the ship's people."

"I believe I begin to understand. You are each in command of your own people."

Nath nodded his approval. "Exactly!"

"Still, there must be occasions when the captain of marines' views differ on how their marines are used in battle. How are such matters resolved?"

"There is no conflict at all. The captain of marines is under my command. He does with his men as I direct."

"But if he were an actual captain, raised to major by virtue of serving at sea, then he would outrank a naval captain, correct?"

"No one outranks a captain aboard his own ship, except he is a flag captain, who is in the singular position of having an admiral aboard—"

"Perhaps we should leave the intricacies for later and restrict our discussion to conditions aboard this ship alone?" Enid tried to keep her tone light but wasn't entirely pleased with the result. Nath, on the other hand, seemed oblivious to her exasperation. He agreed to "lay closer to the wind," though, and limit his remarks to the empirical, leaving the hypothetical for some future date. The following hour went by more smoothly as Nath described the duties, and, to a lesser degree, the personalities of his various warrants and petty officers.

The master, he informed her, would not be in attendance at dinner, as he would be standing a watch at that time. Based on her initial impression of him as an impertinent and foul-mouthed boor, she doubted he would be much missed. Nath explained that the master was second only to the captain in authority, which seemed to conflict with Nath's description of Lieutenant Merryweather as his second-in-command. She found it best for her nerves to ignore such inconsistencies, however, and was more intrigued by the coolly polite manner in which Nath spoke of the *Alarum*'s master, Isembarde Harde.

Despite the unrelenting propriety of Nath's complimentary description of Master Harde's "officer-like" behavior, it was clear to Enid there was friction between the two men. She wondered what lay behind it but was not so curious that she felt the need to make a rude inquiry. She would also be meeting the surgeon, and the captain of marines, though, and the discussion of those worthies took them to dinner, which was announced by Alston's loud knock on the door and stentorian cry of "Vittles is up!"

Enid followed Captain Nath into the cramped dining room and fought down a momentary surge of claustrophobia. The room seemed minuscule enough empty. Crowded as it was now with three officers besides Captain Nath, a waxy-faced, nervous mid, and herself, it had all the homely appeal of a coffin. The strong odor emanating from the covered pewter platters on the table did nothing to make the close quarters any more bearable. Still, she smiled politely as she was introduced to each of the captain's dinner guests in turn.

She noted that Merryweather was clad in a fair uniform that, despite its slightly frayed cuffs and one mismatched button, was of a far higher quality than the one she had greeted Enid in upon her arrival aboard the *Alarum*. The other guests were equally well turned out, all in their finest coats and shirts. Even the pale-faced Mr. Yeardly looked fairly presentable, although it was apparent, despite his efforts to conceal it through a stratagem involving hunched shoulders and elbows kept bent at all times, that the sleeves of his jacket had long since been outstripped by the length of his arms.

After the formalities were complete, Nath took his seat at the head of the table. Enid took the open place beside Lieutenant Merryweather, who sat at his right. Once everyone was in their places, the captain gestured for the "servants," consisting of Alston and a marine sergeant, to fill his guests' wineglasses.

Alston, whom Enid had heard in passing was Captain Nath's steward, was dressed in his best: a truncated blue waistcoat over a more or less clean white shirt. His dungarees nearly matched the shade of his jacket, and he wore well-polished, stack-heeled shoes adorned with gleaming silver buckles. He stood as tall as the low ceiling would permit and schooled his face to a blank expression that in no way concealed his disapprobation for the profligate waste of his captain's stores this gathering of officers represented.

"You are in for a treat," Nath said, raising his glass to his guests. "The blackstrap has been banished and replaced by this pleasant vintage, courtesy of Master Arnaud!"

The officers laughed and made a show of wishing Master Arnaud safe sailing wherever he might be. Enid's expression remained noncommittal and complaisant. She thought it was poor form to crow over extorting wine and other goods from an unfortunate merchant ship employed in delivering expatriates to safety. If Nath noticed her reticence, he showed no sign of it. Instead, he cleared his throat and called out in a strong, clear voice, "Ladies and gentlemen, I give you the king!"

Amid cries of "The king! The king!" Enid began to stand, as was the custom when toasting a sovereign, but Lieutenant Merryweather lay a surprisingly powerful, slim-fingered hand on her shoulder and saved her the embarrassment of banging her head on the low ceiling as a reward for her enthusiastic courtesy. Her cheeks colored a bit at the barely avoided blunder, but nobody other than Merryweather seemed to notice. Relieved, she drained her glass with the rest of them. As she held up her glass to be refilled by Alston, she contrived to lean close to Merryweather to mutter her thanks, which were answered with a quick smile and a wink.

After the glasses were refilled, Nath continued, "Now, all of you have met our new magister. I'm sure that you will all make her feel welcome and give her whatever assistance you can in learning the ropes. She is a masterful sorceress, but if you'll forgive me, Magister D'Tancreville, a thorough landsman. I expect you'll all be patient tutors in our plain art of seamanship, considering her mastery of the High Arts themselves."

A hearty round of assent circled the table and Enid was bombarded with pledges of assistance and assurances that "even the admiral of the fleet was once a lubber."

Enid was amazed at the clamor such a small group could raise, even in so tight a space as the captain's dining room. Each of them, even the otherwise painstakingly obsequious Mr. Yeardly, spoke far louder than was called for at such a narrow table. Otherwise, their manners, though a bit plain in some cases, seemed courteous enough. She assumed the volume of their speech was not a product of vulgarity, but rather a natural condition among those used to shouting orders above the wind, waves, and banging of guns.

Once the general assertions of goodwill died down, the servants began dishing out food at a gesture from Nath, who apologized to Enid for the meanness of his larder.

"We put out rather hurriedly, you see," he said, looking around at his officers, who all nodded their glum affirmation. "We had very little time to put any decent stores together. All was done on very short notice, and you must accept my apology for not providing you a finer meal for your first evening aboard the *Alarum*, for such shortcomings are inevitably the captain's responsibility."

Here Enid noticed a significant glance exchanged between Lieutenants Merryweather and Harcourt, a glance she interpreted as their shared belief that in this matter, at least, Captain Nath was taking on more responsibility than they deemed proper. Oblivious to the exchange, Nath forged on.

"So, while I cannot offer you a particularly fine meal, Magister D'Tancreville, I can at least offer you one that I'm sure you'll find unique in your experience thus far. The main course here is what we sailors call a sea pie. I'm afraid that this one is a fourth rate that was nearly razeed when Cookie Wycke couldn't find the potted hare."

Nath smiled a bit smugly at his own wit, and his self-congratulation was supported by the appreciative chuckles of his audience. Enid smiled, too, but it was only a polite gesture, unfounded on any understanding of the joke itself.

"Fortunately, he was able to rouse it up at last, so here we have the last of the pressed goose and potted hare all in as fine a pie as you're likely to see till we reach the Fist. I pray you will enjoy it."

The "sea pie," as Nath called it, was a thick, two-layer pie, one layer containing hare, the other pressed goose. All of this was mixed with a dense, savory filling and flavored with onion and sage. She took a bite and found that though the crust tasted a bit stale, the pie itself was more than passable. After assuring Captain Nath that it was quite good and that she had a taste for such simple foods, she settled back to pick at her plate and idly observe the others while they were distracted as Alston and the marine sergeant filled their plates.

The surgeon, Heston Rondelle, sat across the narrow table from her. Elderly, tall, and desiccated in form, the surgeon's narrow face was dominated by so large and hooked a nose that one barely noticed his other features, which by penury of contrast seemed mean and cramped. When he spoke, his voice was too hard and brassy to leave any warmth in even the kindest words, making his every comment seem a challenge or insult. To Enid, he seemed a prickly fellow, too rapid and birdlike in his movements, his small, round eyes too porcine to be trusted.

Seated next to the surgeon, as if in conscious comparison, was the *Alarum*'s captain of marines, a man whose deportment seemed aptly matched to his name: Amiable Harcourt. Enid paused a moment in her survey of the captain's dinner guests to reflect on the question of the marine lieutenant's apparent character. Was he so named because his mother and father detected in his infantile person some sign that predicted his adult affability and named him accordingly, or had he, influenced by the power of a given name, grown into the sort of man his parents' choice portended? For the moment, she put the question aside for future examination, content to note the lieutenant's handsome face, fine hair the color of cornsilk, and open, *amiable* expression.

She allowed her eyes to drift past Mr. Yeardly, who, despite being obviously cowed by his sudden summons, seemed unable to remove his eyes from her bosom for more than a moment.

At her right sat Lieutenant Oxley, an unremarkable fellow whose uniform was nearly as worn as the expression on his haggard face. Like Merryweather, the poor fellow was forced to stand watch after watch to make up for the absence of Lieutenant Bascombe, who was in command of the prize crew aboard the *Artagny*, and the senior mids aboard the lesser prizes. Philby and Osteen, according to Dunaughy's journal, had been given command of a pair of captured merchant ships that did not merit the attention of a lieutenant.

Even discounting the fact that his manner was deeply affected by his current discomfiture, it was apparent that he would make a relatively glum and lumpen companion under the best of circumstances. He was obviously older than Merryweather, who was nonetheless his senior in rank, indicating that Oxley had either not earned his superiors' acclaim in as timely a manner as the younger officer or had failed his lieutenant's exam repeatedly. Neither prospect inspired Enid's confidence.

To her left, of course, sat Lieutenant Merryweather. Her sparkling blue eyes glittered as she noticed Enid's gaze skim over her on its way to the head of the table and Captain Nath, who was in the process of dispatching his pie in an efficient and prolonged assault. As the practice seemed to be to eat in virtual silence, Enid followed his example and

dug into the plain but tasty viands, her first untroubled meal since the
Marie's sighting of the *Artagny*.

After the arrival and swift destruction of a rather anemic pudding,
the *Alarum*'s officers pushed their plates away and launched into a series of convivial exchanges made all the merrier by Alston and the marine sergeant, both of whom were quick with the bottle and apparently
loathed the sight of a glass less than half-full. For a while conversation
dwelled upon Enid's history, birthplace, and sorcerous experiences,
most of which involved more assumptions on the part of her interro-
gators than admissions from her. Finally, she turned the conversation
away from herself by asking how the *Alarum* succeeded in taking the
much larger *Artagny*.

"You saw the way we raked her, did you not?" Nath plunged on without awaiting an answer. "That was the key to our victory, and it was
firmly clinched in the plain, good hands of the *Alarum*'s crew, whether
they were manning the sails or feeding the guns. Heel-taps to them,
gentles. And Alston! Order an extra tot of wine for the crew with their
captain's compliments!"

Alston knuckled his brow and rushed off with an expression of
such avidity that Enid had little doubt who would receive the first of
the captain's tots. Nath adroitly drained his own glass and continued
with his tale.

"Those raking volleys took most of the fight out of the Rat frigate—
if you'll excuse the term, Magister?" Enid waved a hand dismissively.
She'd called the Theocrats much worse herself. Reassured, the captain continued. "The blast through the stern gallery served us best, as
we learned later, as it slaughtered most of the Rat's officers."

"Served their first lieutenant up like a goose in a mid's berth: nothing left of them but a bit of gristle and the odd gizzard," Merryweather
interjected, grinning at her own imagery. If she expected Enid to
blanch, she was disappointed. "All it lacked from being a perfect volley
was that the thrice-damned Confessor was not bathed in shot as well!"

"He lived then?" Enid inquired.

A tinge of melancholy tainted the formerly high spirits at the table as Nath nodded. "He did, and more's the pity. It was he that slew poor old Dunaughy after we boarded her. Shot him with ball enchanted to pierce magical wards. He'd have taken my life as well, had he two such accursed balls. Still might have if Lieutenant Harcourt here hadn't intervened. You weren't so amiable aboard the *Artagny*, were you, Lieutenant?"

Harcourt smiled patiently at the ancient jape on his name and raised his glass in a gesture that Enid, despite her best efforts to the contrary, could only think of as amiable. Sighing inwardly, she asked if the Confessor was sorely hurt in his capture.

"Not sorely enough," Nath answered. "Although not for want of the good lieutenant's efforts. A shallow cut to his nose and a gash across his left eye."

"That is correct, sir, and I have no doubt but that he'll lose the use of that eye," the surgeon bleated harshly. "There was certainly damage to the sclera, whether he would admit it or not, and the pupil was already beginning to occlude."

"It fell out?" Yeardly gasped, breaking his long silence at table. Rondelle rewarded him with a charry eye and a disapproving downturn of the lips that seemed to pull the tip of his nose down with it.

"No, Mr. Yeardly," the surgeon corrected in a voice dripping with self-righteous contempt. "It certainly did not *fall out*. The pupil is integral to the structure of the eye. How could it conceivably *fall out*?" Satisfied with the mid's hangdog expression, Rondelle continued in a tone that contrived to sound both smug and strident, "The pupil did not *extrude*, it had begun to *occlude*, to become milky at its perimeter. I would hazard that the pupil is fully obscured by now."

The surgeon paused to take a sip of wine and then cast a baleful eye up and down the length of the table. "And I could have saved the eye with a salve and cantrip or two but that he had pretended to conceal the severity of his injuries to me. Let that stand as a lesson to any on the importance of honesty with one's physician."

Silence fell over the table for a moment as every person seated around it cut their eyes from one to the other except for Rondelle, who, satisfied that he had made his point, helped himself to the last of the pudding. Eventually Nath reclaimed the thread of his narrative and proceeded to describe the evolutions by which the *Alarum* brought the *Artagny* to bay after raking her with double-shotted broadsides.

"Her captain and most of her senior officers were dead by that time," Nath explained. "Much of the credit for the fortunate outcome of the encounter must rest with their corpses, in all honesty. If a naval officer had been in command, things might have gone very differently. Instead, the Confessor took command and his ignorance allowed us to close with minimal damage to ourselves and board."

Lieutenant Merryweather and Mid Yeardly raised their voices in protest of the captain's modesty, insisting that it was his skill and not the Confessor's lack that undid the *Artagny*, but Nath raised a silencing hand and plowed implacably forward with his account.

"In any case, we battered her around far longer than should have been required, but the Confessor refused to strike her colors until the last living lieutenant persuaded him with a cogent argument from the mouth of his pistol. Once *Artagny*'s colors were struck, we were able to board."

Nath described the fatal events that occurred on the *Artagny*'s quarterdeck as he attempted to accept the Confessor's surrender and their aftermath.

"A shame for such a learned man and skilled practitioner of the True Art to be lost to a pistol shot." Enid shook her head, remembering her uncle's last breaths in a stinking Ardain alley.

"You know of Dunaughy from some past acquaintance, m'lady, to speak so reverently of his accomplishments?"

"No, I fear I knew nothing of the name Dunaughy before setting foot aboard this vessel. Still, I have heard both the officers and crew speak of him with some reverence, so I assume that he was a man of shining parts."

Nath gave a slow nod. "He was indeed. A bit obsessive in some interests, but a very learned and officerly mage." The captain sighed and called for a drink to the fallen man's memory. The subdued joviality that characterized the conversation since Rondelle's outburst suddenly dissolved. Even the aptly named Amiable Harcourt's congeniality evaporated, leaving him looking as grim as the affable set of his features allowed. Obviously, Dunaughy's death had profoundly affected these men.

"The tragedy is that the Confessor's murderous wrath was founded on a fallacy: he believed Dunaughy killed the *Artagny*'s magister."

"Who was his brother," Harcourt added.

Enid said, "How is this villain named?"

"I can only tell you what he told us," Nath answered, "and it is likely the name he gave was a nom de guerre. He called himself Guillaume Faucher."

"His surname translates to 'scythe' in Albion," Enid said. "He declares himself a mower of the Theocracy's foes. As you say, almost assuredly a self-assumed and self-aggrandizing epithet."

"He lived up to his new name," Lieutenant Harcourt said. The other officers nodded sadly, and a doleful silence fell over the table.

"And that was that for the *Artagny*," Nath said at last. "Her last living lieutenant surrendered her, and I gave her to Lieutenant Bascombe to take back to Middlesea. She was battered around pretty badly, but still seaworthy. Over half her guns were dismounted, but I was only able to spare Bascombe enough people to serve an eighth of 'em, at any rate. She had a favorable wind for Albion, though, and with any luck, she'll be rounding the Serpent before week's end."

Nath gave a resigned shrug and reflexively rapped a knuckle against the table's bare wood. Enid shook her head slightly as the gesture was repeated around the table. A superstitious lot, these Albion naval officers.

Conversation drifted into thin pleasantries as an equally thin brandy was served, along with a worn pewter plate sparsely laden with slices of hard cheese and harder biscuits. Nath apologized again for the meanness of the fare.

"By now you're all too aware of the coarseness of the *Alarum*'s captain's larder. Have you had a chance to form an opinion of the rest of the ship and her people?"

"I have not yet had the opportunity to acquaint myself with your vessel, sir," Enid replied demurely. "Although what I have seen of it has been very tidy. As to her people, I have only had the pleasure of the company at this table, which I have found unfailingly charming."

A fresh round of bonhomie circled the table, culminating in Nath's declaration that Enid was a fine judge of character.

"They are a charming lot, indeed," he agreed. "And talented as well. The good Lieutenant Merryweather here is as fine a navigator and as taut an officer as any captain could wish for. Lieutenant Harcourt is a bold and gallant swordsman, tried and proven in combat. Dr. Rondelle is a surgeon of great skill and perception." Nath paused to take a sip of brandy and then waved casually at Yeardly with a biscuit in his left hand. "Even Mr. Yeardly here has a special talent, don't you, young sir?"

Yeardly nearly choked on a mouthful of hard cheese, quantities of which he had consumed since its arrival on the table.

"Me, sir? I . . . I am sure that I do have, but . . ." The young man's face colored deeply under his captain's apparently congenial scrutiny, striking a sudden pang of sympathy through Enid. ". . . but, well, sir, I fear I cannot quite put a name to it!"

"Oh, come now, Mr. Yeardly," Nath chided amiably. "We are all friends here. If you are too modest to name your special talent, pray allow me to name it for our new ship's magister."

Without waiting for any further comment from the young man, the captain turned to Enid and spoke in the tones of a proud father describing his child's accomplishments.

"Mr. Yeardly is blessed with an amazing sense of smell which, I am told, he uses tirelessly in the execution of his duties. I have even heard it said that his powers are wasted with too much sleep and that his remarkable nose would be put to far better use sniffing out the enemy than buried in his pillow."

Enid raised her glass to her mouth to cover an unseemly smile as the captain carried on earnestly.

"I find myself quite persuaded by this argument. As thinly manned as we are with so many prize crews away, we would be foolish not to take full advantage of every intelligence available to us, would we not?"

Enid expected chuckling to accompany the captain's droll remarks, but the other officers seated at the table limited their amusement to glittering eyes and barely detectable smiles. She maintained her hauteur with some effort. Yeardly himself seemed to visibly shrink in on himself as his captain spoke of his "gift," and visibly blanched as Nath fixed him with a cold gaze and said sharply, "With this in mind, I have ordered a special watch position established for Mr. Yeardly just forward of the roundhouse. From there he should be able to utilize his talent to the advantage of us all. Until I am confident that his services in this regard are no longer needed, Mr. Yeardly will stand watch and watch in order to man this new post and fulfill his established duties. Is that understood, Mr. Yeardly?"

"Aye, sir. It is."

"And in understanding, you take my full meaning, Mr. Yeardly?"

Yeardly shot a nervous glance in Enid's direction and nodded. "Aye aye, sir! I take your full meaning, sir!"

"I am most gratified to hear it." Nath produced a battered silver pocket watch and read the time. "Well, gentles, as enjoyable as this evening has been, I fear it must draw to a close at last. Mr. Yeardly here has a watch to stand and I'm sure the rest of us have duties to attend to as well." Nath smiled graciously as each of his officers, including the thoroughly abashed mid, offered their compliments on the meal. He exchanged a significant glance with Enid and requested her attendance during the afternoon watch.

"Rest yourself tonight. I'm sure you've had a trying day. Tomorrow we'll delve more deeply into your duties and further acquaint you with the ship and her other officers."

Enid stepped out of the captain's quarters and found Lieutenant Merryweather awaiting her. The lieutenant smiled cordially and offered to escort her to her quarters.

"It is gloomy belowdecks, and you are new to the vessel, after all."

"Thank you, Lieutenant Merryweather. I'm happy for the company. It gives me the opportunity to ask a question that occurred to me as Captain Nath spoke to Mr. Yeardly."

"Oh, a right scalding that young scamp received, and may he profit by it! I wonder what the rascal has got his nose in now." Merryweather chuckled. "But what was your question?"

"What is the significance of the roundhouse?"

Merryweather grinned wryly. "Well, it can be quite significant when it is needed, which it often is. Ashore, you might say the room is *necessary*. Yeardly is bound to smell *something* there, d'ye see?"

Enid saw but was not particularly amused by the low humor involved. Still, it was a just punishment, and she had no doubt it would make a lasting impression on the young gentleman in question. She thanked the lieutenant for her kindness in escorting her to her quarters and watched after Merryweather for a moment as she headed farther aft on some errand or duty of her own.

The thin lath door of her berth opened with a slight squeal and closed with a juddering shudder that reminded her of the painted canvas doors used on theater stages. She smiled inwardly at the impression and the passing feeling it engendered: for an instant she felt as if she were an actress on the stage, portraying, perhaps, the imperiled damsel in some nautical farce.

She'd seen just such a production a year or so before the horrors of the Harrowing descended upon Ardainne. She found her recollections of that fiction far preferable than the reality she faced now. The sets, after all, had been tall enough for the actors to stand, had been well lit, and, unless she missed her guess, had not been redolent with the odorous legacy left behind by decades of unwashed bodies, smoke, and other, fouler sources. She did not know how the gentle officers of the *Alarum* lived amid such a reek. She'd detected no traces of the sort of cantrip she was using to deaden her own sense of smell among the officers gathered at Captain Nath's table. In fact, she'd sensed very little in the way of dweomers among any of the ship's officers, other than the spells that kept their ubiquitous pocket watches calibrated. She'd heard that sailors were a superstitious lot, so it was possible that Nath and his fellow officers eschewed magical accoutrements out of superstition.

Enid sank tiredly into her small desk chair and self-consciously removed the combs from her hair before sending her shoes off under her suspended bunk with a practiced kick. Smiling demurely, she turned in her chair to face the empty corner of her berth, just behind her swinging cot.

"Do not expect me to undress further, sir. I am not in the habit of disrobing in front of strangers, be they living or dead. Now, what is your business with me?"

⋘ ▶

As her rounds took her back topside, Merryweather noticed light streaming from beneath Magister d'Tancreville's door and decided to pause long enough to wish her good night. She was about to knock when she heard a lowered female voice within. The new mage was apparently in the habit of talking to herself. Grinning wryly, Merryweather dropped her hand, reluctant to embarrass the magister by interrupting her discourse with herself. She turned to walk away, a small smile on her lips, and then came to a sudden halt, the back of her neck and arms puckering with gooseflesh. Apparently, she thought, looking over her shoulder one last time before scurrying up on deck, the new magister was also in the habit of answering herself . . . in a man's voice.

chapter 6

Enid found Nath on the quarterdeck the next day, instructing Yeardly and another, older mid in the art of fixing the ship's position relative to the nearest ley lines. Yeardly looked down at his feet as she approached, mutely tugging at his forelock as Nath introduced her to the other lad, a young man she guessed to be approaching his twentieth year. "Magister d'Tancreville, allow me to present Mr. Eanis Cullen, currently the senior mid aboard. We are lucky to have him, although he doesn't deem himself lucky, do you, Mr. Cullen?"

The young man shook his head, his rather unremarkable features rendered momentarily and breathtakingly handsome by the sudden flash of his smile. Enid was so pleasantly taken aback by the transformation that she missed the first few words of his reply: ". . . sir, but it is not too late to take another prize. My turn will come."

"Perhaps you are assuming too much when you place yourself so high in my esteem that you imagine yourself in command of a prize, Mr. Cullen," Nath answered dryly. The young man stiffened under the rebuke and made to excuse himself until he noticed the glint of humor in his captain's eyes.

"One can only hope, sir, and diligently do one's duties."

"Well said, sir." Nath chuckled and held out a hand for the slates upon which the two mids had plotted the ship's position. He looked at Cullen's first and gave a brisk nod of satisfaction.

"Diligent indeed, Mr. Cullen. Should Master Harde come to harm, the *Alarum* would be safe as houses under your able navigation. As would any prize you might command." After handing the slate back to the beaming Cullen, Nath turned his attention to Yeardly's slate. "Very good, Mr. Yeardly. Excellent, in fact. Just the quality of work I expect from you when you've applied yourself."

Enid was astonished to see the lad's cheeks color at the compliment and, despite herself, felt her repugnance for him lessening. Nath returned Yeardly's slate and clasped his hands behind his back.

"Dismissed, gentles. I enjoin you to share your wisdom with the youngsters. Their slates were deplorable." Nath paused thoughtfully and then pointed a finger at Yeardly. "Perhaps they can share your special watch for a few nights, Mr. Yeardly? The combination of your sagacity and the bracing atmosphere should do wonders for their perspicacity."

"Aye, sir." Yeardly touched his fingers to the brim of his hat and strode off, manfully ignoring Cullen's playful elbow in his side as they left the quarterdeck. Nath offered Enid a conspiratorial smile as he watched them go. "Mr. Yeardly is taking his extra watches with good grace. According to Lieutenant Merryweather, he is using his time at the roundhouse to study. I'm sorry he made such a poor impression on your first meeting. He has great potential if he does not do himself harm."

Enid bowed her head and made a courtier's gesture with her hand. "I'm sure you would know more of what makes a good sea officer than I, so I'll accept your judgment without reservation."

Nath cleared his throat. "There's no need for all that. I'm a captain in His Majesty's Navy, not the Malasfandyari emperor. Our manners aboard ship are simpler than what you are used to, I'm sure."

"Different, perhaps, but surely not simpler!" Enid replied with a smile. "I've been reading Magister Dunaughy's service manuals, you see, and find it all somewhat bewildering. Practice must be the only way to keep all your naval courtesies straight, so until I have had some of it, I beg you to excuse me if I fail to bow or knuckle my brow at the right moment. I assure you any failing is out of ignorance and never from insolence."

"It is not as difficult as all that," Nath assured her. "But do not worry. I understand it takes time to adjust to our ways. I'll help you learn the ropes just as I was taught them, and I'm sure your fellow officers will too. Don't turn your nose up at the advice of the common sailors, either, as many of them are wiser than a handful of admirals."

Enid shifted her gaze forward, taking in the sight of dozens of sailors scurrying about deck, each involved in tasks arcane to her. Some occupied themselves with hauling on the myriad ropes that adorned the *Alarum* while others scrambled up into the dizzying heights of her rigging. Everyone seemed to have a purpose and to be about it with a will. She saw none of the brutality for which all navies of the civilized world were notorious. It was commonly held ashore that all of a sailor's labors were accompanied by beatings with rope ends and canes, but the crew of the *Alarum* went about their business with a certain amount of good cheer, their arduous labor often accompanied by laughter and song. None of the silent, sullen looks she'd grown accustomed to from the common folk of her father's holdings were anywhere in evidence, a fact that Enid found at once comforting and troubling.

Here, at least, was a sign that no leveling poison had been at work in Albion, convincing her common folk that the aristocracy should have no special privileges associated with their enormous responsibilities, so she need not fear death in a sudden, revolutionary uprising among the crew. She was forced to wonder how the general mood of a mass of commoners could differ so greatly aboard a ship at sea, where hard daily labor and great physical peril were the norm, and a prosperous fief overseen by a lord as kind and generous as her father. Was there something so inherently flawed in Ardainne's social order that even the most comfortable serf in the most congenial of fiefs would always be more sullen and resentful than the meanest sailor aboard one of Albion's smallest vessels?

She shook herself from her revery and nodded.

"The dullest sailor aboard knows more of the sea and shipboard duty than I, so I'll treat each of them as I would a potential savant, sir. I may, with your permission of course, even attempt to develop an acquaintance with one or more of them, assuming such fraternization is allowed by your custom."

"Oh, I'm sure you'd make the acquaintance of more than a few of them, whether I will or no, Magister. They're a curious lot and would seek you out even if you locked yourself away in your cabin. They're all dying to find out what the new Spells is like."

Nath paused a moment to shout an order that was repeated down the length of the ship and then turned his attention back to Enid, a speculative look in his eye.

"As for fraternization: Well, there is fraternization and there is fraternization. I expect you will find some of our people, both gentle and common, whose company you find pleasurable and diverting. I do not expect my officers and warrants to lock themselves away like monks in their cells, but I also expect them to always behave in a seemly manner that is not prejudicial to discipline or their own good name. Do you follow me, Magister d'Tancreville?"

"I believe I do, sir."

Nath nodded thoughtfully and continued in the offhand tone of a person reiterating a well-known and mutually agreed fact.

"Familiarity that does not pass the bounds of discipline and good order is acceptable. Discretion must be applied to ensure that such familiarity does not engender feelings of either superiority in its recipients or resentment in others. For this reason, no guests should ever be allowed in one's cabin, especially guests from before the mast. Only the captain may receive visitors in his cabin on any other pretense than duty. All others must use the common areas of the ship." He paused and gave Enid a searching look. When she offered no comment, he raised a brow and continued. "I suppose I should have warned you of that sanction before now. You are certainly blameless on that account, being but lately put to sea."

"I am blameless indeed, sir," Enid responded stiffly, but chose her words carefully. "And in the hard specie of fact, not on account, as you put it. No living soul has entered my cabin since Lieutenant Merryweather and one of the ship's people brought my luggage . . . my 'dunnage' . . . aboard."

"Hmm. I beg your pardon, then. I was given to believe that you had a guest in your cabin last night after dinner. I assumed you had taken up such an engrossing conversation with one of my other officers and they forgot themselves and the rules of behavior that governs them." Nath continued to regard her calmly, awaiting some sort of reply.

"I cannot answer for what you were given to believe, sir. I can say that the only person to enter my cabin last night was myself." Enid returned the captain's gaze evenly, but she could not keep the offended and somewhat challenging chill out of her voice.

"Well," Nath said, nonplussed, "Apparently a mistake has been made. Still, it is good for you to be aware of my policy toward wardroom dalliances. It is not one that is held universally throughout the fleet, after all."

Enid stiffened further, her face becoming an icy, emotionless mask. "I assure you, sir, that I have no interest in dalliances of any nature aboard this ship. Now, if you require nothing more of me, I beg to be dismissed. I have further studies to pursue if I am to perform my official duties in a more satisfactory manner than I have apparently discharged my social duties."

Nath returned her icy gaze for a moment, like a cold gray sea reflecting a glacier, and then gave a single, brisk nod. "Very well. You are dismissed."

Nath watched the woman stride off as purposefully as her landsman's gait would allow on the ship's rocking deck and cursed silently. *Well,* he thought, *there's a fine start.* He was already at odds with the *Alarum's* master, the one of two warrants aboard that a successful captain was always sure to cultivate an amicable relationship with, and now he had obviously offended the second. *Damn me for my talent for choosing exactly the wrong word at the right moment.*

*Wardroom dalliances, indeed! I would have been offended myself. Not dalliances, damn it, but—what? Certainly not trysts! Lord Redeemer, no, that would have been even worse. Audiences, perhaps, or visitations—*He shook his head and frowned, drawing a startled glance from one of the hands at the wheel. After calming her with a smile and a nod, Nath turned and strolled farther aft, deeper into the publicly private domain traditionally carved for captains out of their quarterdecks.

If it were anyone but Merryweather, he would simply write the matter off as a mistake, but he knew the lieutenant was a solid, trustworthy officer. She was hardly the sort to pester her commander with imaginary voices. No, he'd stake his career on Merryweather's report: the lieutenant definitely heard the new magister conversing with a man in her cabin. She could not hear any of the actual conversation—blast. There was the word he should have used. Who could find offense at "wardroom conversations"?—nor had she been so indiscreet as to actually eavesdrop.

Still, Enid had been quite adamant that none save herself had entered her cabin last night. She did not seem the sort to lie over a simple mistake in judgment or to resent gentle correction. Indeed, she had requested correction if her manner varied from that dictated by naval regulation or tradition. There was also the matter of her magic skills to be considered. Her bona fides left him with no doubt that she was the most learned mage he had ever met, let alone sailed with, so she may have told the truth when she said no one had entered her cabin. After all, she had not denied the conversation itself, only the presence of another person within her berth. But if she was in magical communication with someone, who was it?

He doubted it would be anyone among the Rats. Her distaste for the Theocrats was obvious and, he believed, unfeigned. Perhaps she spoke to some lover with sorcerous powers as highly developed as her own and was embarrassed to admit squandering energy and talent in such a mundane conversation? He frowned at the idea. *Damn me*, he thought, *I have no business being unsettled by the thought of a woman I have barely met having a lover. I am the captain of a warship, not some simpering clerk from one of Marbury's plays!*

Nath leaned on the rail with a sigh and stared out over the sea. A freshening breeze was lifting white spray from the peaks of the waves and the uncharacteristically blue sky over the strait seemed to lose its color to the leaching effect of a wall of gray clouds that darkened the northern horizon. He allowed himself to be distracted by an analysis of the wind, waves, and clouds and their portents.

Rain before sundown, he was certain, and a stronger breeze that would serve the *Alarum* as a soldier's wind for her destination, Gisbon. No truly foul weather in the offing, though. He touched the wood of the rail at the thought of such good fortune. One could never be too careful, after all.

The same held true for Enid d'Tancreville, he thought. One cannot be too careful with her, either. Perhaps she was telling the truth within the very limited confines of her answer, but perhaps she was not. The only way to be as certain of her was to come to know her in the same way he had his other trusted officers: Observation of her at her duties and enough time spent in her company to gain a feel for her character. The observation of duty would begin on the morrow, he decided, but the time spent in her company would begin tonight. He shouted out for Mid Cullen to pass on his regards to Magister d'Tancreville and would she join him in his cabin for dinner and a reading?

chapter 7

Careful of her, Cullen," Yeardly warned the older boy in a low voice as they made their way below toward the magister's cramped workroom on the orlop. "She is a termagant, no matter how fine she looks. Look at me, if you need proof: watch and watch standing guard by the roundhouse, all for noticing she wore a sweet scent!"

Cullen laughed and gave Yeardly a playful cuff to the head.

"I look to you as proof that Fortune favors fools! Any captain but ours would have put you before the mast for carrying on so in front of an officer! Why, if we behave like rutting hounds, how can we expect the ship's people to act any better?"

Yeardly reflexively counter-cuffed his friend and groused, "I only noticed that she wore a sweet scent! That is hardly rutting like a hound!"

Cullen stopped for a moment, pressed his back up against a bulkhead to allow a hand laden with a replacement block to pass, and laughed out loud at the younger mid.

"If I know you, and I do, it was *exactly* like a rutting hound. I remember how you sniffed my arm on watch after I came back from liberty at Merent. If you'd ply your nose with such zeal for secondhand perfume, I can imagine what a frenzy the genuine article put you in! That nose of yours will get you in trouble if you allow it and that other protrusion below your decks to lead you around!"

Yeardly tried to sulk, but his friend's laughter was too infectious. "All right, all right! Perhaps I was a little too forward! Even so, you must be careful of her, Cullen! She's Ardain and a full mage, which makes her doubly unpredictable and perilous!"

"You forget she is a woman, too, Yeardly, and so triple-shotted rather than merely doubled. Now, you'd best get about your duties. Just because she didn't blow you to flinders with some death magic or another the last time she saw you don't mean she won't this time! Besides, your 'special' watch awaits!"

Cullen chuckled under his breath and shoved Yeardly toward the hatch. Yeardly stumped off, casting the occasional sour glance over his shoulder before disappearing up the companionway to the deck above.

Once he was sure his friend was safely removed, Cullen rapped lightly three times on the door to the magister's workroom, half hoping she would not answer. Despite all his cheerful bonhomie with Yeardly, he was truly apprehensive about delivering the captain's invitation to the new Spells. He'd seen them quarrel on deck earlier and anyone who had the nerve to speak so sharply to a captain, let alone *this* captain, was no doubt half-mad. He had no desire to put himself in the way of a lunatic mage that many of the older men in his division had already assured him had the power to kill or maim with a glance.

The door opened to reveal Enid d'Tancreville and, behind her, a small cabin crowded with carefully secured shelves of sorcerous materials and implements. The room was lit by a globe of softly glowing light that hovered just over the mage's left shoulder, casting her features in sharp relief. For a moment Cullen felt he was face-to-face with a painting by one of Nordmarche's "Old Masters" sprung to life. The globe's gentle glow illuminated the portion of Enid's face toward it, accentuating her exceedingly fair, blemish-free complexion and casting the rest of her face in vague, beguiling mystery that intensified the strong but delicate character of her features. Although the Ardain lady was modestly dressed in a plain blouse and what appeared to be a pair of worn hunting breeches, clothing perfectly suitable to work in her laboratory, the globe's light shaded the graceful arch of her neck and the soft pools of shadow beneath her collarbones with such a suggestive brush that he found his breath catching in his throat for a moment. At last, his cheeks coloring despite himself, he blurted out, "Captain Nath's compliments, Magister, and will you be so kind as to join him for dinner and a reading afterward?"

"A *reading*?" Enid spat.

Cullen took a step back as the mage's expression transformed from one of vague annoyance at an interruption to obvious ire at some sort of slight.

"Does your captain think I am some sort of hedge witch? Some sort of common *soothsayer*? You may inform him, with *my* compliments, that if he wishes to have his palm read or the lumps of his head deciphered, I wish him joy with any charlatan ashore. For myself, I am a Mage of the First Circle, and I prefer to pay for my meals with silver rather than chicanery!"

Cullen's blush darkened another shade or two as he attempted to stammer an answer, finally finding his voice just before Enid slammed the door in his face.

"No, no, Magister, you mistake my meaning! I do not mean that sort of reading at all, lady! I'm sure Captain Nath would never insult you with such a request!"

Enid opened the door a little wider and snapped, "Do not presume to speculate upon how Captain Nath might contrive to insult me. Instead, explain exactly what sort of 'reading' I am invited to attend!"

"Why, a reading of lines, Magister! Simply a reading of lines." The words rushed out of Cullen in a torrent of relief at being allowed to explain himself to the magister rather than being forced to tell his captain how he transformed a courteous invitation into a grievous insult.

"Captain Nath is a devoted follower of the theater, whose themes and examples he believes have an ennobling effect on the young volunteers—the proper sort of theater, of course—and to provide ample opportunity for them—us—to polish our reading skills, history, and knowledge of classical allusions."

"Line reading? Even so?" Most of the wrath drained from Enid's face, leaving behind a surprised, wary expression. "What work will you and the other young gentles be reading from tonight, then?"

"Marbury's *Cierengarth*, Magister." Cullen puffed up with pride and announced, "I am to read Murchadha!"

"I see." She did not seem particularly impressed with either the drama or Cullen's part in it. "An Albion work. I suppose that is natural, but if these readings are a regular part of the ship's routine, I must introduce the captain to the works of Maubin and Ribera."

"Oh, Captain Nath speaks very highly of Maubin. We're to read a translation of his *Bridge of Three Duels* when we're finished with *Cierengarth*." Cullen didn't comment on Ribera, a name that sounded Naveroñian to him. He doubted that the scribbling of some simpering don had anything to offer him, but he was too polite and overawed to share that opinion with the new magister.

"Very well. I beg your pardon for snapping at you. Something was said earlier that offended me and colored my initial reaction to the captain's invitation." Enid sounded genuinely apologetic, and Cullen assured her that the misunderstanding was of no consequence to him.

Before he could get out more than a blurted "milady," however, she pressed on, trampling his sentiment with her acceptance of the captain's invitation. "Pray inform the captain that I would be honored to share his table again and attend this reading. I may even bring a folio or two that I have in my luggage. I'm an avid follower of the theater myself, you know."

Cullen did not know, of course, and wasn't particularly pleased to be so enlightened as to the magister's enthusiasms. He touched the brim of his hat and assured her he would bear her acceptance and compliments to the captain immediately. As he scrambled up the ladder to the upper decks, he muttered, "Wonderful. Now there will be two critics with the power of life and death at each reading!"

Dinner that night was a smaller version of the previous evening's affair, the captain only attended on this occasion by Enid, Yeardly, Cullen, and a pair of younger mids: Dinwitty and Harlech.

Harlech was a girl of no more than eleven or twelve, Enid estimated, and she looked just as ridiculous in a waistcoat, breeches, and hose a size too large as Dinwitty, a golden-haired lad with the face of a cherub, if cherubs ever had their faces scrubbed nearly raw to remove smudges of dirt and tar. He appeared to be a year or so older than the girl. All four mids dug into the food Alston served them as heartily as decorum permitted. Alston refilled their plates with a parsimonious frown on his face. Enid was sure the steward would have voiced his displeasure at their greedy destruction of the captain's meager pantry if it had not been for a meaningful glance from Nath at the onset of the meal.

From beneath her raven lashes, Harlech's luminous blue eyes seemed to follow Enid's every move and, she noticed, the girl imitated what she saw. It occurred to her at that moment that she might well be the only gentle-born lady Harlech had seen since parting with her mother for service at sea. Her duty to "aid in the education of the youngsters" took on a whole new dimension, and she made a mental note to set aside some private time for a conversation with Harlech to determine if she knew the things a noble girl of her age should.

When the mids's appetite moderated—Enid was certain the ravening beasts that must dwell within their bellies could never be sated by any amount of food—the table was cleared away. Alston filled each of their glasses with wine and left a flat-bottomed decanter on the table. His part in the evening's entertainment apparently at an end, he withdrew.

"Well, now to the real meat of the occasion!" Nath announced with a grin.

The mids dug out their hand-copied scripts and jostled cheerfully with each other as they took up their prearranged positions. Enid was impressed by Nath's obvious enthusiasm. After Cullen left, a niggling worry that the evening's exercise would be exactly that, an exercise that Nath enforced out of a sense of duty to educate the youngsters and which they participated in out of duty to him. That was obviously not the case, however, and Enid settled back in her chair, determined to savor the spectacle if not the thin, watery wine in her glass.

"Now," Nath said, speaking more to Enid than his troupe of "actors," "this is act nine, scene three." He gave a brief description of the action, which ended with a warning to the youngsters. "There is no room in here for any mock combat, so we'll make do with simply reading the lines. There will be no brawling, real or simulated. I trust you will not forget this injunction in your enthusiasm?"

The three boys' heads waggled in a confusion of nods and shakes as they tried to convey both their understanding and avow they would not forget themselves in their excitement. The result was less than convincing to Enid's eye, but Nath nodded, satisfied by the display.

"Good enough. Dinwitty . . . here, Dinwitty! That is no place for your finger to go! Dinwitty will read Eomaine, Cieran's trusted advisor." Redeemer save Cieran, Enid thought with an internal chuckle. "And Harlech is Owain's boon companion, the valorous Eochaid of Maeredd."

Nath allowed his ersatz troupe a moment or two to review their lines and then clapped his hands. "I do not believe Magister d'Tancreville requires us to set the scene for her." He glanced at Enid, who smiled in agreement. "So, let us begin with Cieran's line, the one that begins, 'If we are to number our foes, let us get among them and number those that have fallen to our swords and spears . . .' "

Although Cullen obviously mistook volume for emotion, he delivered his lines with spirit and a clear understanding of their meaning. Dinwitty, on the other hand, stumbled through his lines as if they were written in a foreign tongue and might, if spoken too clearly, summon some malefic entity into their midst. Harlech spoke her part in the singsong style of the profoundly amateur, the last word of each sentence rising as if her dialogue were an endless train of questions. All these failings were to be expected among youngsters who were likely reading the words of a master aloud for the first time. What truly surprised Enid, however, was Yeardly's performance: he seemed to grow several inches taller and decades older as he read his part and contrived to portray his character's deep umbrage at being maneuvered into a death duel with his childhood friend, a friend who was willing to forget the joys of their shared youth in pursuit of his regal ambition.

When the scene was finished, Enid applauded politely and congratulated them each on the excellence of their performances, and shook their hands in turn. She held on to Yeardly's hand, refusing to relinquish it until he looked up and met her eyes, which glittered with amusement.

"It seems, sir, that you have as keen a nose for subtext as you do for Lithain water. I hope your nautical talents are as finely honed as Captain Nath says, otherwise your thespian talents are criminally wasted at sea."

Yeardly blushed furiously and mumbled his thanks.

Nath added his compliments to Enid's, assigned the mids a scene to read the following week, and dismissed them for the evening. When Enid made to follow them, Nath, to Harlech's obvious disappointment, motioned for her to stay. Once the young people were gone, Nath invited her to join him at the table. He replaced her glass with one filled with a better vintage, no doubt some of the wine liberated from the *Marie*, and asked her frank opinion of the night's entertainment.

"I found it quite diverting, sir," Enid answered coolly, willing to allow her lingering displeasure with Nath's insulting remarks earlier in the day to surface now that the mids were no longer present to witness it. "I'm sure the practice is edifying to your mids and makes your evenings pass the swifter."

Nath cleared his throat. "It is not the habit of post captains to apologize, Magister d'Tancreville." A retort formed on Enid's lips, but Nath silenced it with a raised hand. He locked his gaze with hers and spoke earnestly, saying, "But I am not a post captain. I am but the commander of a vessel whose captain's ambitions took precedent over his duty to the Service. Apologies offer no shame to me, so please accept my regrets for a deplorable clumsiness with words. I did not mean to impugn your character earlier, I assure you, or to accuse you of involving yourself in any dalliances. I only meant to make clear my policy against using cabins for private conversations that do not revolve around specific duties."

The captain's tone and expression were so sincere that Enid could not help but be convinced. She nodded her head and replied, "Anyone with a love of theater knows that one poorly chosen word can change the entire tone of a scene and that even master playwrights may err in their choices. If they can fail, how more likely are we to do the same? Do not trouble yourself over this matter any further, sir, and accept my apologies for being so thin skinned. I will endeavor to think the best in the future, rather than assuming the worst."

Nath smiled and looked relieved. "I am gratified to hear it. I hoped not to get off on the wrong foot with you. The relationship between a ship's captain and her magister is as important as that between captain and master, and I'm afraid things are less than convivial between the sailing master and myself. It is my hope that you and I can avoid misunderstandings and unnecessary hard feelings."

"I noticed he resisted your orders which Lieutenant Merryweather passed on to him when I came aboard."

Nath's face darkened. "It's a sad state of affairs when troubles between a ship's officers are so obvious that even a landsman can perceive them. No offense meant, lady."

"None taken, sir. What is the root of these troubles, if I'm permitted to ask?"

"I think it is permitted in this case. I only fear you might find the details tedious." Enid assured him her interest was sincere and Nath seemed pleased, saying, "It is a relief to have someone to discuss it with, Enid."

The prickly part of Enid's nature rose at his free use of her given name, but she forced it down. Nath meant no disrespect. His forwardness was clearly an invitation to a more open and friendly relationship. Such an advance beyond mere comity could only benefit them both. "Some problems are diminished by shared confidence."

Nath nodded. "True. But I cannot speak freely about the matter to Merryweather or any of my other officers. To do so would be to encourage factions among the officers and crew, and that is one thing I will not countenance aboard a ship under my command. I saw the tragic effects of it at far too close a range aboard the old *Robust* frigate when I was but a mid."

"And yet you can speak to me?" Enid bristled. Was she such an outsider or so minor a power aboard ship that she could be confided in without fear of consequence, like a handmaid or lapdog?

"The relationship between a captain and his ship's mage is often one of special confidence," Nath said. "Dunaughy and I became quite close before his passing. I hope that sort of confidence might develop between us, Magister."

Enid felt a twinge of guilt at Nath's words and offered him an apologetic smile. "I hope so as well, Captain Nath. I can assure you that anything you discuss with me will enter my ears but never pass my lips. The necessities of discipline aside, such discretion is the least requirement of both honor and the gratitude I owe you for entrusting me with such an important post in your command."

Nath chuckled and waved a hand dismissively. "If anyone should be grateful for your posting to the *Alarum*, it is me. The *Alarum* hardly rates a mage of your accomplishments, milady, and your agreement to serve aboard her even temporarily is a great boon to us. We were fortunate to have Dunaughy, God rest him, and wouldn't have if certain blockheads in the Naval Department had not confused infirmity of limb with decrepitude of faculties. A keener mind or talent than old Dunaughy's you're unlikely to find in the navy or out. It is a shame you did not have the opportunity to meet him."

"Yes. It is a shame he died before I came aboard," Enid answered carefully. "Now, this friction with Master Harde—if it does not stem from your relative youth, then what is the rub?"

"He's another man's creature, and that man means me ill," Nath said with a resigned shrug. "Roughly a third of my crew is under his sway to some extent."

"How did this come to pass?"

"Harde sailed thrice with the Honorable Captain Carlysle Ambrose, Lord Aixely, first in the *Dauntless*, one hundred, where Ambrose was third lieutenant, and again when he was commander of the poor old *Vigilant*. Both of them were quite accustomed to each other's ways from their time together." Nath frowned at his own tone. "And that is as it should be, truly, between a captain and his sailing master. It was quite fortunate that they were so eminently compatible."

"Speak to me of this relationship, if you would," Enid interjected. "I fear I'm still uncertain of what Mr. Harde's role is aboard the *Alarum*, though I perceive it is important."

"Indeed it is. A ship's master is responsible for navigating her, keeping her in proper trim, and oversees the carrying out of sailing orders received from the officers. His authority is on a level with a lieutenant, but he is not a commissioned officer, so he is subordinate to them. Harde and his mates are invaluable in the ship's handling, particularly in battle, when the commissioned officers' attention must be focused on fighting her."

Enid frowned. "So, your right hand cannot be trusted?"

"Not completely, alas," Nath said. After chewing his lip thought-fully for a moment, he continued his tale. "When he made post, he was shifted from the *Vigilant* sloop to the command of *Brazen,* 32, for her last cruise. When she paid off, the Admiralty gave Ambrose command of the *Alarum*, a mere twenty-eight. He was vociferous about his belief that his service merited a forty-gun frigate at the very least. Then he delayed reading himself onto the *Alarum* at the advice of his uncle, Gareth Ambrose, Duke of Ardeth."

"Why did the duke advise Lord Ambrose to delay?"

"This was before Captain Pertwit delivered the infamous Ourest Shot to the House of Lords, so while war seemed imminent, it wasn't declared yet. This was also a short time before our long-serving sea lord, Aryl Dunbow, Earl of Dunbow, took leave due to his declining health. He was too bloody-minded to retire, but few expected him to live through the winter. His withdrawal necessitated the appointment of an acting sea lord—Theon Morrin, the Duke of Morrin, of the Old Charter Party. He immediately took to passing out plums like Father Winter at Winter's End. One of those plums was the *Trenchant*, a new forty-gun frigate he promised Lord Aixely once she was accepted into service."

"Ambrose had no orders relieving him of the *Alarum*'s command and assigning him to a new one, mind you, but he felt the sea lord's word was good enough. He retired to his father's estate to await new orders, leaving the *Alarum* to languish in port."

"Ahh. He scorned the bird in hand for the fatter fowl in flight?"

"Indeed, and he nearly lost them both, just as the parable warns.

Old Devil Aryl was so worked up by Morrin's ineptitude and favoritism that his health rebounded from spite. He resumed his position and sent Morrin packing."

"So all of Duke Morrin's plums turned sour?"

"Worse than sour—poison! They don't call Dunbow 'Devil Aryl' for nothing. He's got a black streak of temper that has ended many a career, and he was not pleased to see two fine frigates anchored in a home port due to one officer's ambition. I was given the *Alarum* as her commander and Ambrose was beached."

"Why is Harde not stranded with him?"

"Poor luck for both of us," Nath said. "Ambrose sent him and a skeleton crew aboard the *Alarum* on pretense of preparing her before he read himself in. When Ambrose was stripped of command of the *Alarum*, Harde and his picked men from the *Brazen* were left on the *Alarum*'s roster pending Ambrose's assumption of the *Trenchant*. Then he'd use his captain's prerogative to move them all aboard his new command. Alas, there are many a slip between cup and lip and I inherited his crew."

"Well, it seems Providence favored you," Enid said.

"Immediately, yes. But trouble will come of it, have no doubt. Ambrose is enraged and feels the Young Briar Party is behind all his misfortunes—and he has decided I'm their very embodiment. He will do all he can to destroy me and Harde is his enthusiastic lackey. They believe I used my interest to steal Aixely's crew and command."

"That seems foolish," Enid said. "Why would you try to hold on to men with no loyalty to you?"

"Experienced sailors are so scarce that most captains would happily take damned souls from hell's deepest pit to fill out their roster."

"Most captains, but not you?"

"My family has always been fortunate in recruiting hands," Nath said with a modest smile. "I was able to come close to a full complement for the *Alarum* despite the short time I had to prepare for sea—Devil Aryl demanded she be out as scheduled, and Pertwit and her little brig-sloop the *Alacrity* had been fired upon by the batteries at Ourest by then, so there was an urgent need for frigates. The price of Ambrose's dithering fell to me to pay."

"I see. So, Ambrose lost his sailing master and chosen men to you, and Harde is intent on making you pay for that, too. How does he go about collecting?"

"Initially, he attempted to discredit me with the crew—decrying my youth and experience." Nath leaned back in his seat, clearly tamping down his anger. "By his attitude, he made it clear that he believes I am little more than a jumped-up landsman in a captain's costume."

"Do such creatures actually exist, or are his misgivings completely arbitrary?"

"Oh, they exist," Nath sighed. "Interest often takes a man further than talent, after all, and I own to an abundance of interest. I would not have begrudged him his doubts if they had subsided after I proved I was a true tar-handed officer. He has retained them, though, even after I demonstrated my skill, even after I proved him wrong as to the best rake of the masts for the old *Alarum*! He insisted they should lean aft when they clearly would serve better raked for'ard.

"You may not credit it," Nath said as he stood and poured them both another glass of wine, "but I went aboard my aunt Dolorous's *Alianor*, seventy-four guns, at the age of nine, and not just on paper, but actually *aboard* in the flesh, or at least as much of it as I had at the time. There is no better sailing school than the sea, and I have been enrolled longer than most officers my age. Six years longer than Ambrose, at least."

Enid sipped her wine thoughtfully and allowed Nath to fume in silence. She lit a cigarillo for each of them. Nath accepted his gratefully and when he spoke again, his tone was more dispassionate.

"His rot was spreading steadily until we took our first prize. A ship's master is a persuasive creature, but nothing gains a common sailor's loyalty more surely than prize money. Even the old *Brazen*s began to see the advantage of having an 'active' commander that put silver in their pockets. Harde pretended his approval as well. To do otherwise would risk alienating himself entirely."

Enid raised a brow. Nath's remark narrowly skirted an accusation of cowardice. "Ambrose and Harde were not active in their duties?"

"I would never call another gentle shy unless I had seen it with my own eyes. I can only say that neither of them took so much as a smuggler as a prize in two independent cruises during the Winterlands Crisis." Nath pushed a small pewter salver between them on the table and tapped the ashes from his cigarillo into it. "Most captains would not receive a second independent cruise if they returned so empty handed."

"Is Harde resigned to his defeat?" Enid tapped her own ashes into the salver before accepting a fresh tot of wine from Nath's own hand.

"No, he resists any decision I make that falls, however arguably, under his purview."

"Does he attempt to stir the crew against you?"

Nath took a long, thoughtful draw on his cigarillo before answering. "Not overtly. He's not foolish enough for that. I don't believe his intent is to incite a mutiny—I believe he simply takes pleasure in compromising the efficiency of my command. He hopes to find or contrive some failing with which he can blemish my record. Masters turn in their logs along with a ship's captain and lieutenants—and his scribblings might get more attention than most, thanks to his friends."

Enid felt genuine sympathy for Nath. She was only too aware of what it was like to labor under constant, hostile scrutiny. She still occasionally woke at night drenched with terror's sweat from dreams in which some ill-thought remark at table during a dinner party brought the wrath of the Theocracy upon her head. Those final months before her escape aboard the *Marie* had been torturous, and she had only to govern her own tongue and tone to avoid her enemies' snares. Nath was forced to command a ship, knowing that any of the hundreds of decisions he made each day might be called into doubt. He rose a few more notches in her esteem for the sanguine way in which he bore the pressure under which he labored.

"Are you worried he will succeed, Captain Nath?"

"Not especially . . . and pray, call me Rue when we speak in private." He grinned and waved his cigarillo at her. "Especially if you intend to continue sharing such wonderful smoke with me!"

Enid flashed a smile of her own. "My humidor is yours, sir, so long as you keep it safely from the bottom of the sea! But come, are you so certain of your abilities that Harde and his lackeys' desire to catch you up in a mistake causes you no particular concern?"

"Such tale-telling can ruin an officer's reputation and put him in foul odor with the Admiralty, but carrying such tales can have much the same result. I'm no clergyman's son forced into sea service, though. I'm a career officer from an ancient naval family—I'll put my patrons against Harde's or Ambrose's any day."

"Even so?"

Nath nodded confidently. "The Naths have been in the Sea Service since time immemorial, as they say. We're one of the oldest of the Westlands navy families. I've kin serving at every level from mid to admiral, which translates into an embarrassing wealth of interest, at least as long as the Westlands families are paramount in the Service."

"Ah." Enid contemplated this as she produced a pair of cigarillos from the pocket of her coat. She offered one to Nath, who accepted it gratefully. They avoided eye contact as they leaned forward to light their smokes from a small ball of conjured flame that hovered over the upturned palm of Enid's left hand.

"Still, this friction between you must be a great distraction."

"It's worse than that," Nath said. "Harde and the worst of the

*Brazen*s are an illness on this ship—a fever that has subsided but may return more virulent than before. The man is insolent—he is only as civil as is required by my status as the *Alarum*'s captain and I, despite my best efforts to the contrary, can only bring myself to be as civil to him as is required to maintain the discipline of the ship. Ashore, the demands of the service set aside, I'd surely call the fellow out."

A chill traversed Enid's spine at the last remark, which was uttered as a simple statement of fact, devoid of any trace of bluster or hyperbole. Here, she thought, is someone who is utterly confident in his dueling skills or utterly contemptuous of personal hurt. Perhaps both.

"You are in the habit of going out, then? I've heard it is nearly as popular a pastime in parts of Albion as it once was in Ardainne."

Nath shook his head. "No, I don't duel for sport. I only call for satisfaction when someone has honestly and severely injured me. Harde has done so repeatedly with his damnably patronizing tone and veiled comments before the crew. He is a canny 'un, though, and always keeps his sauce just on the safe side of sedition. On a less fortunate ship, his insolence would pose the peril of mutiny."

"But mutiny is not his goal?"

Nath shook his head. "No. An uprising would destroy him as surely as it would me. Still, he'll do whatever he can to make life difficult for me and those loyal to me. Do not let him draw you into any compromising situations. He may try to antagonize you—he is a master of that art."

Enid stiffened in her seat and then realized that her reaction was exactly what Nath was warning against. She'd been in a position to allow her temper to run free in the past—but that past was long gone. She relaxed and nodded. "I'll be on my guard around him."

"Good," Nath said. "And keep your ears open. Some of the crew will be more open around you than the other officers. The common sailor looks upon the ship's magister as a protective spirit. Dunaughy's death was a severe blow to morale—your arrival has cheered them up immensely."

"I'm happy to be of service, Rue. I assure you, you will have my full support in the eyes of the crew and other officers. If I have any concerns, I will bring them to you personally and discreetly." Enid smiled and tapped ash into the salver. "And I will strive to avoid showing my temper publicly as well."

Nath smiled warmly at the pronouncement. "Good! Very handsome of you, indeed! I hope I have not burdened you too much with my own concerns, but as I said . . ."

"No, not at all. It is good to have someone to share confidences with and I had already gleaned that was the custom between captains and their mages before this. Later, when I have problems of my own to discuss, whether personal or duty-related, you can rest assured that I will even the exchange."

She looked down at her cigarillo for a long moment. Without looking up, she said, "I would prefer not to discuss my past, however. There are too many painful wounds there and none of them healed sufficiently to bear the pain of examination. I pray you will not take that reticence as a sign of distrust, because it is none of that. It is only a sad weakness on my part, coupled with a dread of bringing to the front of my mind that which I have only recently and with great effort banished to the back."

Nath reached across the table to give her a companionable pat on the shoulder that she received with only a faint stiffening of posture.

"Do not trouble yourself on that account. I can certainly understand your wish to put your hardships behind you for a while. Some things are best seen from a distance."

Nath leaned over and opened the nearby transom window and flicked his cigarillo through it. Enid's eyes followed its path for a moment: a tiny comet tracing an arc against the *Alarum*'s phosphorescent wake. She fancied she could hear a faint hiss over the chuckle-gurgle-slap of the ship's running as the waves took it. The sky was dark and, just as Nath predicted, she felt a cool shock as a wayward drop of rain found its way through the transom and spattered against the back of her hand.

As she followed his example with the butt of her own smoke, Nath refilled their wineglasses. When Enid made to object, he raised his hand and said, "One last, in recognition of an evening well spent, milady. I have enjoyed your company greatly this evening. You have been both a charming audience and an agreeable confidant."

Enid smiled and removed her hand from over her glass and allowed him to refill it. One more would not undo her, after all. She'd consumed less wine tonight than in a casual evening at a salon in Arden.

"I hope to prove useful as well. I have made as close a study of the regulations and manuals at my disposal as time has permitted, but I am afraid I am still 'all at sea' when it comes to the finer details of my employment."

Nath chuckled and nodded. "We will remedy that on the morrow. From tomorrow morning on I will have you on the quarterdeck at my side. There I can make use of your talents and indicate to you where you can use them of your own initiative to serve the ship most usefully."

"That will be a great relief. I detest feeling useless. We will sail about some more in search of more boats to capture?"

Nath smiled wanly. "No, we will not be actively seeking prizes. I have an appointment to keep with Earl Weymouth, admiral of the Merentian fleet, at Gisbon and cannot afford to be late or, worse yet, so undermanned that I lose the *Alarum* in some sudden blow. We're shaping a fairly direct course for Gisbon now and should arrive there in a week's time. With luck, we'll find Admiral Weymouth on station and receive new orders."

The marine posted at the captain's door snapped to attention as the new magister emerged through it. From the side of his eye, he observed that she was as handsome a woman as the fellows were saying, although a bit severe of feature for his taste. As she passed, his nose also confirmed that she smelled as sweet as poor Yeardly claimed before taking up his "special watches." *Lithain water,* he thought as he settled back to a rest position. *Very expensive and not applied too liberally as some were wont.* His nostrils expanded as he took a second sounding. *Oh!* he thought. *Damned fine tobacco, too!*

⸻ ◄ ► ⸻

Nath nodded with satisfaction as his cabin door shut behind Enid. That had gone far better than he'd dared hope. The lady had a true love of theater and a nature generous enough to forgive at least one faux pas. He'd known others of Enid's stature who would have never forgiven even the most innocently offered slight, no matter how trivial— for them, the ice once frozen would never thaw. He was grateful his new magister was not cut from that cloth.

He'd carefully avoided broaching the "conversation" Merryweather overheard in hopes that she might volunteer more information without goading. She apparently preferred to believe that the only significance to the accusation lay in Nath offending her with it—or perhaps she placed it in the same parcel as her past: wrapped up tightly and not to be opened till some time in a more comfortable future. Either way, he was sure the truth would eventually come out, whether through confidence or chance, and was content to let the matter lie for now.

As he undressed for bed he was amazed by his admirable state of relaxation. Voicing his concerns to Enid had been a tonic, no doubt of that. He felt sure tonight's sleep would be the best since coming aboard, if only he could drive the image of his new magister's exquisite neck from his mind long enough to sink into oblivion. And the surprising little dimples that appeared when she smiled.

"It went well, I hope?"

Dunaughy was making a conscious effort to moderate his accent or Enid was becoming more adept at deciphering it.

"Yes," she answered sharply. "Now lower your voice. I don't relish being accused of having a man in my cabin again, thank you! I really do not understand why you do not just allow me to explain the situation to Captain Nath. He seems a very reasonable and tolerably well-educated man!"

"Aye, he is both of those," Dunaughy's disembodied voice whispered at her ear. She found the invisible apparition less disconcerting than the sight of the horrible chest wound that had made a wraith of him. "He is also a sailor. For all his manner and schooling, he was raised by a gunner who had a greater hand in his education than his father, uncle, or any tutors he may have had aboard. At heart he is as superstitious as any tar-handed rascal before the mast and if there is one thing those lads fear worse than a ghost, it is a *ghost-talker.*"

Enid didn't agree with Dunaughy's assessment, but since the dead man had known Nath far longer, she felt she must take his word on the matter. Still, it troubled her to treat a fellow gentle for whom she had a growing respect as if he were some backwards commoner. After their recent frank discussion, she felt more than a little guilty for withholding her confidence from him. The deception, even by omission, seemed counter to the "special relationship" Nath hoped to cultivate with her, a relationship he described as formerly existing between himself and Dunaughy. She wondered if the shade was truly counseling her to silence based on Nath's sailorly superstition or from resentment at losing his place as the captain's confidant. The dead, she had found, were a uniformly jealous lot.

"I will not tell him now, but I warn you if I am confronted with the matter directly again, I will tell him the full truth of the matter. I will not have Rue believing me a liar, nor will I sully my own integrity by resorting to half-truths and sophistry! If my only choices are maintaining my honor or being ostracized from superstitious dread, I must choose my honor. It is the only wealth left to my family's name."

"You must do what you think is best, of course." Dunaughy's lyrically accented whisper came from beside her other ear, causing her to start slightly. "I only hope you have the opportunity to earn the captain's full trust before revealing to him your particular talent. But that may not be so difficult, if you are already referring to him by his given name, eh, lass?"

Enid colored slightly, a reaction that instantly angered her. "He has given his consent," she snapped sharply. "And I act on it based only on the cordiality of a growing friendship and a desire to become the sort of confidant he seeks—and that you have so eloquently convinced me he requires if he is to survive this cruise with his career intact!"

"Tsk, tsk! I meant no rebuke. There is no reason to lash out so!"

She could clearly hear the low chuckle behind his words, which now came from the vicinity of her cabin's minuscule writing desk. She noticed the neck of a decanter of brandy from her dunnage frost slightly and knew it was from the ghost's touch. The dead longed for the pleasures of the living, especially the recently dead. She was pleased to see that Dunaughy refrained from the sort of wailing and gnashing of insubstantial teeth that most spirits resorted to when they found those longings beyond their reach. Instead, he merely sighed and continued in a low tone, "It is good that he has brought you into his confidence so soon. It proves he is both an excellent judge of character, as I always thought, and that he has learned the importance of confidants and allies. When he first came aboard the *Alarum*, he was quite standoffish. I know he has had a command or two aboard prizes and the like, but I do not believe he has ever been able to fully trust the officers or men beneath him till now. A crew at sea resent a distrustful captain and soon become worthy of distrust."

Enid again wondered at Dunaughy's veracity and motivations. "Since meeting him I have not noticed that he was the least bit aloof. Is it possible that his character could have changed so much?"

"Oh, he has definitely changed, but not so much as all that." Enid could tell by the location of the ghost's voice that it was now "seated" in the writing desk's chair. *How long would he hold on to the fiction of his physical form?* she wondered.

"He can be as chilly and remote as the best of them, I assure you. You just haven't been there to see the weather change yet. Never underestimate him. He is cleverer than even he believes and once his mind is set on some ambition, his pursuit of it is as inexorable as a glacier's progress. He may move fast, or he may move slow, but those who oppose him will eventually be ground to dust.

"Unfortunately," Dunaughy continued, "he is also somewhat precipitous and does not always see the subtle nuances of a situation. As his new magister, it is your duty to temper his proclivity for instant action and help him recognize subtleties that, left unheeded, might prove his undoing."

"At least till we part company," Enid said with a sniff. "I have no intention of making a career of playing social governess to a grown man. Or do you mean I should temper his foolhardiness in naval matters?"

"For the Redeemer's sake, no!" The shade sounded scandalized at the suggestion. "Leave the handling of the ship to him! He has an understanding of wind, wave, and tactics involving them that far outstrips his experience. If that buffoon Harde weren't such a bootlicking sycophant of Unbearable Ambrose he'd have recognized that by now, too. Help shield him from the stratagems of his foes and, perhaps more worrisome, the foolishness of his friends, but leave the naval matters to his own discretion."

Enid nodded irascibly, thoroughly put out with annoyance at this enforced and unseemly discretion Dunaughy forced upon her.

"As you will, for he seems a decent, capable man. Only till we part company, though, and that will be as soon as I set foot aground within range of either an Ardain royalist company or an Albion regiment that will have me. This sailing about and disrupting merchant traffic is all fine and well, but it is still my intent to do the Theocrats as much direct hurt as possible, the sort of hurt best done with a regiment of cavalry."

"How very *noble* of you, Marquise," Dunaughy drawled, his lilting accent somehow magnifying the contempt of his words. "It is a shame that Destiny is not in accord with your will, lass. You will see far more of foreign seas than you shall ever see of your native land and when you pass, you will pass beneath the waves."

Enid was seized with a sudden chill of premonition. For an instant it seemed to her as if the room were transformed into the gloomy green depths and the glowing orb lighting it became the faint gleam of the sun seen from far below the wrong side of the waves. She shook her head to clear it but was left for several moments with the afterimage of a string of glittering silver bubbles drifting slowly upward toward a land of air and light that, in the flash of the vision, she knew she would never see again.

"Damn you!" she gasped at Dunaughy's shade. "Trifle with me again, ghost, and I will confine you to a bead that I will toss into the foulest depths of this vessel's midden! Doubt that I can do so at your peril!"

A sad, disembodied chuckle filled the room. "It is called a bilge aboard ship, milady, not a midden. I do not doubt that you have the ability to do just as you've said, and no fear of you wasting the effort to do so. Your vengeance is reserved for more than mere trifles."

"Do not be so certain that I have none to spare!" She could barely control the quaver that threatened to enter her voice as she spoke. Other spirits had tried to bend her will to theirs with dire presentiments in the past, but what she had just seen was different: she was certain she had just witnessed her own weird.

"I do not mean to offend you, milady, and would not do so purposefully." Dunaughy's voice became theatrically mournful. "Some things are beyond my control. You of all people should know that the dead can never bring anything but sorrow to the living . . ."

"Unless it is deep annoyance," Enid groused, still slightly shaken by the vision of her mortality, but willing for the moment to allow bygones to be just that. "Now, you said last night you would elucidate further on the techniques used for detecting another vessel by its sympathy with the ley line it steers by . . ."

She sat down at her writing desk and watched as the appropriate manual opened of its own accord and pages began flipping to the chapter containing the necessary formulae.

Outside, Dr. Rondelle, always Dunaughy's particular rival, paused in his passage through the wardroom, a chill running up his spine and the faint odor of licorice in his prodigious nostrils.

chapter 8

Determined to make a credible showing as the *Alarum*'s interim magister, Enid arranged to meet with the mids after Master Harde finished checking their calculations of the ship's current position. Based on Lieutenant Merryweather's sardonically humorous account of the suffering Harde inflicted on the mids in the name of instruction, she calculated the young folk would come to her in a mental state so cowed and downtrodden that their youthful enthusiasm would not prove too much for her admittedly limited patience to endure. Her stratagem proved eminently effective. The youngsters Lieutenant Merryweather ushered into the cramped space of Enid's workroom could not have looked more crestfallen and doom-laden if they were being led to the gallows.

"Here are your pupils, Magister," Merryweather said sternly, but the shadow of a smile and a quick wink gave her gravity the lie. "If they prove intractable, do not hesitate to dispatch them to the gunner with your compliments. I understand Gunner Gannis has worn out his old cane and is afire to break in its replacement."

Harlech's eyes could not have gone wider if the lieutenant had announced a Darghaur had taken over the mids' berth. Enid had to steel herself to follow Merryweather's lead. Still, she thought, fear of a caning might prevent the pain of one.

"He will certainly find the opportunity to do just that if any of these young officers try my patience."

As Merryweather ducked out of the workroom with a wry smile on her face, Enid held her pupils' eyes for a long moment before taking a seat behind her narrow worktable. She pointed at the makeshift bench a pair of sailors had set before it at her direction. Cullen and Yeardly sat at either end of the bench to stabilize it, Yeardly's eyes fixed on his hands, which were clasped nervously in his lap. Harlech and Dinwitty sat between the older boys and immediately began kicking their feet in unison. Enid's lowered brow reduced the pair to wide-eyed, slack-jawed statues.

"Now, I have here Master Dunaughy's notes on your progress in the study of the High Art." Enid tapped her finger on a cloth-covered log on the table before her. "And I must say that his observations do not please me. They do not please me at all."

Her words elicited varied responses from the obviously nervous mids. Cullen sat at attention, his face a mask of military discipline, while Yeardly continued to stare uncomfortably into his lap. Tears welled up in Harlech's large blue eyes and her cheeks colored with shame. Dinwitty chewed his lip and picked at a scab visible through a tear in his hose.

She allowed the grave silence to stretch uncomfortably. When the cord of the youngsters' anxiety seemed taut enough, she slapped the ledger on the table and allowed the trace of a smile to enter her voice.

"It is my practice, however, to prefer my own observation over that of others, no matter how illustrious they might be. Unless you have some objection, I believe we will start with a fresh slate."

A subdued chorus of polite, youthful voices assured her that there were no objections to her plan.

"Very well, then."

The attentive, trepidatious faces of the mids sent Enid's stomach into a slow churn. These young people did not have the advantage or opportunity to attend a proper sorcerous academy—they must learn what they could aboard this rolling classroom. For them, the High Art was only one of many arcane sciences to be mastered even as they worked watch after watch, their duties sometimes calling on them to put lessons only just learned into practical use, often under dire circumstances. They relied on instruction quickly parceled out between rigorous hours of hard labor and scant hours of sleep to guide them. They were often required to extrapolate from previous lessons the solutions to emergent problems their instructors had not yet had the opportunity to address. She wondered, briefly, if the gunner, sailing master, and lieutenants found the task of educating these young officers as daunting a responsibility as she. And what of Captain Nath?

She struggled to imagine what it must be like to be responsible for every mortal aboard this complex instrument of war, especially for a man as young as Nath. It could not have been so long ago, she thought, that he sat in some dark space between decks and struggled to make his fatigued, adolescent mind wrap itself around the intricacies of sorcerous formulations. Had he shown the military decorum of Cullen here? Had his stomach growled as audibly as Dinwitty's?

She gave her head a mental shake to clear it of both unwonted apprehension and self-indulgent introspection.

She pointed at Dinwitty and asked, "We've long known that similar items are connected by an intangible but powerful bond, a bond that skilled sorcerers use to reduce the effort required by a formulation. What is this fundamental principle of sorcery called?"

Dinwitty swallowed forcefully and redoubled his assault on the scab on his leg. After glancing left and right, no doubt in hope of some telepathic message from one of his peers, he clenched his eyes closed for a second or two and then, just when Enid was about to point to Harlech for an answer, he blurted out, "Pathetic magic!"

Enid sat back in her chair, her eyes wide with surprise at the boy's outburst. The combination of Enid's expression and Dinwitty's mala-propism proved too formidably comical for the mids's military bearing to withstand. Cullen restricted himself to a single sneeze-like exclamation, which, while shocking, paled in comparison to Yeardly's brief but ear-jarring guffaw. Harlech laughed merrily and hid her face behind tar-smudged hands. In a pause between giggles, she gasped, "Silly *Dim*witty!"

"Enough!" Enid barked, bringing her open palm down on the tabletop. The gunshot-like report straightened all four of the mids in their seats and put an effective end to any further jocosity. "You will refrain from subjecting your classmates to ridicule and malicious frivolity unless you wish to suffer the same at my hands—and name-calling! Really, Miss Harlech!"

Harlech wilted under Enid's disapproving glare, her lower lip trembling with the effort required to restrain her tears. Cullen's and Yeardly's heads drooped with shame, but poor Dinwitty seemed more discomfited by the incident than any of the offenders. Enid resisted the urge to treat the other mids to a blazing diatribe against such promiscuous incivility, but something in Dinwitty's morose expression told her that such an effort would cut him deeper than Cullen, Yeardly, or Harlech. She took a deep breath and continued in as near a dispassionate tone as she could manage.

"Now, Mr. Dinwitty, I assume that by 'pathetic' you meant 'sympathetic.' Is that not so?"

"Yes'm," Dinwitty answered glumly. "Magister Dunaughy talked to us about it the day before—before the *Artagny*. He ex-explained about how ley lines and a rock or handful of soil from a port can fine-tune a day's working."

"A day's working?" Enid asked.

"He means fixing the ship's position on the charts at the end of the day, Magister," Cullen answered in a humbled tone. "We call it the day's working."

"Very good. And did Mr. Dunaughy explain why these pebbles and dirt can help you more closely define the ship's position?"

Dinwitty nodded nervously. "Yes'm. He taught us how they would resonate with the place they was took from. The Hejnmeiher Device can measure that and give you an angle you can mark across the ley line on the chart. The 'X' it makes is where the barky is."

"Very good, Mr. Dinwitty." Enid treated the lad to a brief, reassuring smile. "Your grasp of the practical application of sympathetic magic more than makes up for your earlier slip of the tongue."

Dinwitty sat up a little straighter and screwed up his face at Harlech while Enid consulted Dunaughy's ledger. His face was the perfect image of smudged decorum when she glanced up, however, so Enid turned her attention elsewhere. "Mr. Cullen. Pray describe the concept of affinity."

"Affinity," Cullen answered briskly, "describes the bond that makes sympathetic magic possible. It is the link that connects two like objects."

Enid nodded slowly. "That is correct as far as it goes. Affinity also extends to potentiality, and it is primarily the affinity that some entities have for certain potentialities that makes most of a magister's formulations possible."

"I thought it was mostly elemental formulations?" Yeardly asked boldly. His eyes widened as if his own words had escaped his grasp and slipped behind him to catch him off guard. Enid swallowed the urge to respond sharply. He would not profit from spite, but an example of objective professionalism might serve.

"Elemental magic plays a large part in naval formulations," Enid agreed, acknowledging the validity of Yeardly's observation with a nod. "In part due to the obvious applicability of the elemental entities' powers within their dominion. Sylphs influence the winds, undines affect the nature of the water in which they reside, salamanders hold sway over the fires that draw them—but none of this would be of any practical use for us if it were not for the fact that there are some among their kind who have an affinity for potentials that are useful to us. The skilled sorcerer can recognize, attract, and successfully entreat entities with a propensity for the outcome they desire to effect."

"By shouting the right spell! I seen Magister Dunaughy shout up an undine to loosen our fouled anchor in Middlesea." Harlech's eyes were round as saucers at the memory of the spectacle. In a breathy stage whisper of an awed child, Harlech said, "He was prodigious loud and cursed uglier than old Caxton! That was the first time I ever heard the word____."

Enid blanched as Harlech uttered the infamous word and assured her between dark glances at the smirking Yeardly and the sniggering Dinwitty that neither volume nor profanity were necessary to the magister's art.

"To the contrary, a composed silence and a placid mind will achieve far more than any howled imprecation, no matter how loud or foul it might be."

"A composed silence? Then you do not speak an incantation as a part of your castings?"

Enid made a mental note to castigate Dunaughy for the shocking ignorance of even his oldest students but kept any note of her disgust from her answer to Cullen. "When dealing with elementals? No. Words are both the instruments and architects of reason. The creatures we are speaking of are as great a stranger to that virtue as we are to the bottom of the sea. Words are valueless in our dealings with elementals."

Cullen looked skeptical. "If they don't understand words or possess understanding at all, how does a sorcerer make their will known to them?"

"Affinity," Yeardly stated authoritatively before Enid could voice her answer. "The sorcerer must have an affinity for just the sort of elementals that likewise possess an affinity for the action required of them."

As he finished speaking, Yeardly seemed to become aware of himself and his audience—and most particularly of the perilous Magister
d'Tancreville, who now studied him closely, a speculative expression
on her face. He begged her pardon in a voice as halting as Dinwitty's
when his stutter was on him.

"Nonsense." Enid cut him short. "There is no reason to apologize
for answering correctly. But come, tell me, you studied the Art before
going to sea?"

"No, ma'am. I've had only what there's been time to learn in the
Service."

"Well, a remarkably intuitive answer then."

"Perhaps he has an affinity for the subject." Cullen smiled hand-
somely and tipped his friend a wink.

"Perhaps he does," Enid agreed softly. "Perhaps he does at that."

<hr>

Nath was forced to withdraw his invitation to spend the day at his side
owing to some difficulty in the hold, so Enid spent what remained of
the day making herself better acquainted with the ship, its people,
and her duties as magister. Lieutenant Merryweather, whom Captain
Nath had assigned to assist in her nautical education, proved most
charming and helpful in this endeavor. There was an almost girlish
eagerness in the lieutenant's otherwise earnest desire to share her
knowledge of the ship and its arcane workings, which Enid recognized as a true love of the subject. She would evidence the same barely
subdued enthusiasm were she called upon to demonstrate a complex
formulation for Merryweather. The ship's people, when called upon to
describe their duties and the importance thereof, did so with the same
zeal. The weather was fine as they meandered about the ship, careful
to avoid interfering in its running, and Enid found herself enjoying
Merryweather's company as much as the glimpse she provided into
the *Alarum*'s mysteries.

The time, though pleasant, proved most instructive. She learned the sails could be taken up in sections to reduce the amount of force the winds exert against them, thus slowing the ship or easing the stress on her masts. This was accomplished by folding the sail along horizontal bands and securing those bands with stout canvas ties provided for that purpose. The work was accomplished by a team of sailors known as "topmen" who leaned over a spar to gather up the sail, all the while standing on a rope which was all that prevented them from plummeting to the deck or into the sea, either of which would generally prove fatal. The operation was known as "taking in a reef." Untying a section of sail to increase its surface area was called "letting out a reef." This binding and unbinding of reefs was apparently quite an important undertaking at sea, as Merryweather gravely informed her that one must be able to both hand and reef before being rated as an able seaman. She didn't explain what it meant to "hand," but Enid assumed it was quite an important task by the reverence with which she spoke of it.

While observing the topmen at their work, Enid noticed what appeared to be a feathered serpent undulating lazily between the masts and occasionally wrapping itself around a spar as if to rest. While wingless, it flew through the air with same sinuous ease as a water snake wriggling effortlessly after its unsuspecting prey. Its iridescent feathers shifted from a brilliant green to a vibrant purple as it passed from sunshine to shadow. She estimated the thing to be the length of both her outspread arms, and that she could easily wrap both hands around it with fingers touching at its thickest point. The sailors in the rigging seemed unaffected by its presence, other than to laugh when it raced them up or down the ratlines.

"What is that flying feathered snake? A pet of some sort, I assume? I've never seen its like."

Merryweather smiled and Enid was momentarily distracted by its brightness and the sparkling clarity of her eyes. "Why, that's *Alarum*'s other foreign lady! She's an umoki from the southern Shards. The hands named her Lady Chum-Chum."

"Chum-Chum?"

"For the sound she makes while eating. She's a comely lass but a rough feeder!" Merryweather laughed.

Enid eyed the soaring antics of Lady Chum-Chum and felt the vague prickle of innate magic emanate from the serpent. "Does it serve any purpose in the ship's running?"

Merryweather stood beside her, shielding her eyes with her hand as she watched the umoki's aerobatics. "Purpose? Well, umoki are said to be good luck, so there's that. She brings a chuckle to the ship's folk, too. All but the meanest wretch afore the mast are cheered by her and the games she'll play for extra bits of biscuit or beef. Distraction and amusement are of great value to those whose days are defined by hard, repetitive labor."

"I would think it would be a distraction. I'm surprised pets are allowed aboard a warship."

"Well, your most tyrannical captains don't permit pets or mascots, but that can make for a sullen crew. Sailors love to keep little pets as reminders of good times in strange lands and to console them when they're in the blue doldrums. A wise captain will allow a few, but not so many as to convert a barky into a menagerie with cannons."

"So, you find Captain Nath to be a wise commander?"

"Indeed. Wise and active, which is a welcome change from—" Merryweather stopped and smiled silently for a moment before saying, "I'm tasked with acquainting you with the ship and her parts. It's best we leave aside any commentary on the merits or lack thereof of her officers, past and present."

Enid nodded. "Agreed. I did not mean to pry."

Next, Merryweather showed her to a great circular spool on the deck and said, "Here you have the ship's capstan, Magister. Note the holes bored about its circumference? Those are meant to accommodate the great bars which the landsmen aboard seize up and pace a circle about the capstan."

"And the purpose of all this winding and unwinding is?"

"To haul up the *Alarum*'s great anchors, for the most part, though the capstan can be pressed into other services when need be."

This led to a foray to the catheads, from which the *Alarum*'s great anchors depended. Enid marveled at their size and that of their hawsers.

"You'd find their stench a marvel, too, were you required to venture down to the cable tiers," Merryweather said, chuckling lightly. "I was once banished down there for a double watch, albeit on a much larger ship, the sixty-four-gun *Tigress*."

"For what cause?" Enid asked, her nose wrinkling at the odor of the cables in the open.

"Crimes against humanity." Merryweather grinned. "Another mid made disparaging remarks about my hair, which had a large streak burned off by a defective spell-lock, so I gave him my rum ration and shaved his head while he was in a stupor."

Enid's cheeks dimpled in amusement. "So, they banished you to this cable terrace to consider your sins and repent of them?"

"They did. And it was lenient of the captain, too. The shorn sheep was a lord whose mother was a creature of some influence."

Enid's smile vanished. "So, you made a powerful enemy that day."

"Not so," Merryweather said. "When she heard the whole tale from me, she laughed and said it served her son right for his ill manners. It doesn't hurt that the young lord and I became fast friends before we left the *Tigress* for other, separate posts. We still correspond to this day."

During the next few hours, Merryweather peeled back the top layers of the *Alarum*'s mysteries. When they parted ways with a smile and mutual salute, Enid's knowledge of the ship's layout and working was much improved, and her opinion of Lieutenant Merryweather was cemented. She was literally raised at sea, and like Nath, her conversation did occasionally lurch into coarseness, but her mind was keen. A natural instructor, she introduced Enid to the ship and its parts without baffling her with extraneous jargon. Nor was she as prone to digressions as Nath when discussing maritime inconsistencies. She felt she'd made a good impression on her as well.

In the following days, Enid set herself to performing the various daily tasks described in *Herbstrom's Naval Arts*. She found her duties took her to nearly every corner of the ship, from stem to stern and from orlop to weather deck. Her daily rounds would greatly accelerate her understanding of the *Alarum*'s geography. They would also allow her to mix more freely with the crew, half of whom were deferential or even friendly, while the other half were distant and suspicious. She hoped that familiarity would ease their distrust. She wasn't overly concerned either way. What did a lady of her standing care about the common folk's opinion of her?

She inspected the spell-locks on each of the great guns to verify that they were fully charged and functional and learned the fanciful names given to them by their crews, such as Billy Raker, Spliniferous, and Olde Bunnecrusher. She found each lock immaculately maintained by the gun crews and freshly charged by the gunner.

In the hold, she found the dweomers that discouraged vermin and slowed the putrefaction of the ship's common stores were weak but effective. *Herbstrom's* indicated that this was acceptable, as all shipboard dweomers were kept to a minimum to avoid detection by enemy mages. It rankled Enid that the ship's people must endure weevil-tainted biscuits and increasingly rancid salt beef but suffer they must until she was more confident in her ability to mask her work.

While the morning sightings were taken, Enid double-checked the enchantment of the navigational instruments and found them active and accurate. When she was finished, Nath joined her and asked, "How did the ship fare under your scrutiny, Magister? I trust we haven't run too far afield from old Mr. Herbstrom?"

"Very well, in the main," Enid replied. "Your people did their duty, despite the lack of a ship's mage to oversee them. Magister Dunaughy instructed them very well indeed."

Nath nodded and led Enid to the windward rail. After a moment of introspective silence, he said in a low voice, "You know, the old fellow didn't like the cut of my jib at first. In fact, I initially assumed he was a partisan of Mr. Harde."

Enid overcame her reluctance to share Dunaughy's thoughts, as recorded in his journal, and said, "He thought very highly of you, sir. I have read it in his own hand."

"Thank you, Enid," Nath said. "It was clear his opinion had changed before he lost his number. He was a good man, loyal to a fault to the Service. I'm glad you think highly of him. I'm sure he would have returned the sentiment."

"That is most kind of you," Enid said, her nostrils filling with the faint odor of licorice. She ignored the spectral odor and pointed at a group of hands hauling on a cable connected to one of the myriad blocks adorning the *Alarum*'s rigging. "While watching the people the more experienced crew refer to as landsmen, it occurred to me that much of the unskilled labor on a ship could be accomplished by automata, which would greatly reduce the perishable stores needed for a cruise. Has the Navy considered their use?"

Nath's head snapped up, his eyes narrow and cold. "Do you contrive to jest with me, Magister d'Tancreville? For if you do, I counsel you to reconsider, as I find more insult than humor in your foray."

Enid felt her temper rise and tamped it down. She'd obviously trod on a sore toe of which she was unaware. She bowed apologetically and said, "I meant no jest or insult, Captain Nath. My question was born of ignorant curiosity, not malignant intent. I apologize without reservation for offending you. It was not my intent."

She saw Nath's face visibly relax as his passion cooled. The last of his ire escaped in a long sigh through his pursed lips.

"It is I who owes you an apology, Enid," Nath said. "My father has squandered a fortune on unsuccessful experiments revolving around automata, and I have been the butt of some of the ridicule attached to his obsession."

Enid was deeply intrigued by the infamous automata experiments but swallowed her curiosity in the interest of Nath's bruised feelings. "Think nothing of it. I will step lightly around the subject in the future."

After an uncomfortable silence, Nath said, "We do not use automata aboard ships because no clockwork mechanism can act with the alacrity and instinct of a flesh-and-blood human. This is compounded by the fact that multiple mages would be required to pass orders to the various divisions at work during a blow, say, or a battle. The seconds lost could cost the lives of everyone aboard."

"Ah, I had not considered that."

"You would have arrived at the same conclusion eventually, I have no doubt," Nath said. "But there is a second reason: a hostile mage might wrest control of the automata from a lesser practitioner. Remember, too, that the majority of the Royal Navy's mages do not approach your level of power or erudition."

"Phah," Enid said with a self-deprecating smile. "Not so erudite that such an obvious flaw would occur to me."

"Ah, well, we are all caught blind by some inspiration from time to time," Nath said. "And, on the topic of inspiration, I'm sure the younkers would find your presence most inspiring at tonight's reading, if you wish to join us?"

"I can think of nothing more gratifying," Enid said with a genuine smile.

At week's end, the *Alarum* relaxed from its usual taut discipline. Enid was a little awed and ill at ease by Nath's recitation of the Articles of War to the assembled crew but found the dour spectacle with its heart-chilling litany of "shall be punished by death" ushered in a day of rest and pleasant diversion. Sailors laundered their clothes, shared gossip, napped in the sun, and assisted each other in unplaiting and re-plaiting their hair into long tails. A fiddle and hand drum played merrily amidships, providing the meter for a wild hornpipe.

She spent a portion of the morning in quiet conversation with Nath, sharing fine cigarillos, the *Marie*'s wine, and easy conversation. She told him of Yeardly's remarkable aptitude for sorcery and suggested a separate, more intense set of lessons for the lad. Nath, or Rue, as he insisted she call him in private, applauded the idea and gave it his immediate approval.

As evening fell, she wandered above deck, at last making her way to the ship's forward-most region, where she could watch the waves break against the little frigate's bluff bows and feel the refreshing sea breeze riffle through her hair, worn loose today to the obvious gratification of several sailors who admired her respectfully as she passed. Once it was clear she intended to remain forward, the few sailors gathered there withdrew to leave her to her privacy.

She stood alone for a long while, admiring the way the vessel stalwartly braved the waves and wondering at the import of a long line of darkness on the seaward horizon. Just as she was about to seek Nath and ask if the clouds portended foul weather, there was a footstep behind her. She turned, half expecting to find him there behind her, his serious features broken by that amiable smile she found suited him so well, but found instead the sadly pockmarked face of Mr. Yeardly.

"Ah. Mr. Yeardly. Pray, do not let me interfere with your duties. I will be on my way and leave this place." She made a lost gesture with her left hand and sighed. "Whatever you call it."

"It is the fo'c'sle, milady," Yeardly answered in a subdued tone, his hands clasped firmly behind his back and his eyes on the carefully polished buckles of his shoes. "But there is no call for you to leave, Magister. It ain't—isn't duty that brings me here. I hoped you might allow me a private word?"

"Well, I suppose this is as private as one can hope for in a wooden keg packed so tight with humanity. What would you have of me?"

"Your pardon, ma'am. I acted most abominably at our first meeting and worse—"

Enid carefully resisted the urge to smile. Although he could not bring himself to meet her eyes, it was clear his sentiments were sincere.

"And worse?"

The young man seemed to shrink in on himself under the weight of his embarrassment. "Yes, milady, and worse—worse, that I blamed you for being offended by it rather than accepting the blame myself. It was unfair of me; I see that now in the example of your fairness."

"My fairness?"

"I've just come from Captain Nath. He says you've spoken kindly of me on many occasions and have taken a special interest in my education—and all this while I was resenting you for a harridan."

"I see."

"Your speaking so kind and taking such an interest when you had a genuine reason to resent me, hate me, even. It has shamed me, m'lady, and I beg your pardon most sincerely."

"Look up, Yeardly," Enid said sternly. "When you offer an apology, you do it with your eyes as well as your lips. Now, there are two things I'd have you know: First, it is unseemly to think of a woman as a harridan and doubly so to admit it in her hearing. There are some sentiments which are best kept to oneself, whether recanted later or not. Second, it is always easier to find fault in someone we've offended than to find it in ourselves for offending them. You are not alone in that, but you are in rarified company for admitting it. I accept your apology and assure you the matter is closed between us."

She offered him her hand, which he held, obviously torn between shaking it and kissing it. Enid allowed herself a tiny smile and said softly, "As you are offering your apology privately, as a gentleman to a lady, a kiss on the hand would not be inappropriate."

Yeardly hurriedly pressed her knuckles to his lips and then backed away, blushing furiously. "M'lady?"

"You are excused, Mr. Yeardly."

Enid waited till the young man had scampered belowdecks before allowing herself a rare unguarded smile.

The next few days saw the *Alarum* steadily run down the distance twixt her and Gisbon despite increasingly heavy weather. Enid's stomach, which had found life at sea perfectly agreeable thus far, railed against the ship's lurching ascents and violent descents of each towering wave that confronted her. Her only comforts were the shelter of her cot and a concoction that Dunaughy coached her through preparing. Though bitter to her tongue, it was soothing to her belly.

She was nestled deep in that cot when a forceful rap on the door roused her from a state of partial slumber to fuzzy awareness. Merryweather's raised voice followed the rap.

"Spells!"

Merryweather's voice keened above the roar of the storm and the loud grinds, booms, and squeals of the ship struggling against the height of the violent storm. Enid prayed it was the storm's height, at least, as she couldn't imagine any escalation that wouldn't involve the Merentian Sea being torn from its bed.

Enid dressed herself with difficulty and staggered to the door. Every movement tasked her will, agility, and strength, but she reached the door and flung it open.

"The ship is in danger and the captain requires you on deck to assist with your magic in—" Merryweather's eyes widened in concern at the sight of Enid's ghostly complexion and hollowed eyes. "Gods! Magister, you look half in the grave! Are you well enough to stir from bed?"

"I'm well enough," Enid snapped weakly and tried to force her way past Merryweather.

"I can see that," the lieutenant said drolly. "You'll need this rain gear, though."

Enid accepted Merryweather's assistance in shrugging into the raincoat and let her tie the large rain hat in place.

"Come, Enid," Merryweather said, her arm around the taller woman's waist. "The ship's movements are unpredictable. There is no shame in leaning on me until we are above deck."

Enid appreciated Merryweather's kindness and leaned heavily upon her until they gained the open gun deck, where Nath and Harde stood staring up at the tops of the mainmast. She stood upright and walked unsteadily to Nath's side, who grasped her by the arm and pointed skyward.

"Enid, we are about to lose the main topmast under this blow," Nath shouted near her ear. "It was damaged during the *Artagny* set-to but seemed sound enough to stand. Now it seems about to give way under these winds. Can you—"

"Of course," Enid said in the strongest voice she could muster. "Consider it done!"

She heard Nath say something, but the wind carried his words away as she allowed her mind to open to the storm. She could do nothing about the storm itself, but she could manipulate the mighty sylphs in the *Alarum*'s immediate environs. It would take a great deal of effort, particularly with no preparation, but she was confident she could relieve the amount of stress on the masts until the winds blew themselves out. She gathered her power and augmented it with that of the stray energy created by the storm. As she began her formulation, she heard Dunaughy's faint voice in her ear, demanding to know what she was about. As Enid focused more tightly on her intent, his ghostly voice faded from her awareness, along with the bucking deck and the howling wind in the rigging.

In her mind's eye, she saw the storm for what it was: a mad, elemental dance composed of preternatural forces ranging from tremendous undines to sylphs, aetheric beings, and galvanic forces. The storm was mindless and absolutely devoid of malice. Its only purpose, which it pursued with implacable dedication, was to rage until its rage was spent. The forces that comprised the storm were of various sizes and strength and Enid used this to her advantage.

She reached out and redirected the more powerful sylphs, directing them away from the *Alarum*, replacing them with more moderate winds drawn from the storm's periphery. The formulations required were not complex, but the sheer energy involved was immense. Her frame shook and her ears buzzed with the effort. She faintly heard the raised voices of both Nath and Dunaughy through the noise, but she pushed the distractions away and bent her will to cementing the weaker sylphs to their tasks and creating an aversion in the stronger ones nearby.

She felt the *Alarum* slow under her feet and had the vague impression of people shouting all around her. Cheering her success, she surmised, and smiled as she returned fully to herself.

"Enid! Enid!"

Her eyes opened to find Nath shaking her by the shoulders, his face contorted with concern. They were clearly not out of danger.

"Do I need to relieve the stress on the mast further? I can reduce the wind more."

"For the love of the Redeemer, no!" Nath barked. "Restore the wind immediately! We may lose the main topmast, but we will certainly be pooped if you don't!"

"Pooped?" Enid wasn't sure if they were practicing on her.

"One of the great, bloody waves astern of us will crash down on our stern and drive it under the sea!" Master Harde shouted, pointing aft. "Else dismast and throw us on our beam ends!"

"I—" Enid said, but Nath cut her off.

"Now, Enid, let the winds in and we'll take our chances. We are doomed as things are now!"

Enid nodded and closed her eyes. She understood she was working against time, so she wasn't able to unknot her formulation as cautiously as she'd like. Exhaustion and illness forced her to take whatever shortcuts that came to hand. She left the smaller sylphs in place but exhorted them to greater effort. The great sylphs were harder to deal with. Once set on their path in nature, only mountains or the great wind rivers of the sky could turn them aside. Driving them from the *Alarum* had been difficult but required little precision: she needed only to coax them a hundred feet to either side and forget them. To lure one of them into a specific space and bind it to a course was far more difficult indeed.

She cajoled, threatened, and begged the breath of a gale to roar against the *Alarum*'s bare masts, opening her reservoirs of power to pour forth with her will and determination. As she sank to her knees, completely spent of magical, moral, and physical energy, she felt the conscious-less monster of wind she'd summoned seize her body and roll it down the slope of the deck toward the grasping waves.

───◄ ►───

Blood gushed through the smoking hole in her uncle's coat, just to the left of the third button below his collar. The spell-lock ball that pierced his breast was fired by a person of noble blood, many of whom were as bloodthirsty in their desperation to prove their loyalty to the Theocracy as the common rabble with whom they associated, like ticks on a rabid beast. Enid was infinitely more concerned with the severity of the wound than its political significance, however, and pressed her hand against it to staunch the flow of blood, which came in pulses so strong she would have deemed them farcical in a scene playing out onstage rather than in this grimy alley.

A cantrip to ease pain came to her lips without a pause for thought as her fingers struggled to coax her uncle's aging flesh to reknit itself. She was not a healer by trade, but she had gathered enough knowledge of the gentle art at the Institut to stabilize any but the most grievously wounded. Still, she felt her uncle's skin cool perceptibly under her fingers and the large black pool spreading beneath him served as an eloquent criticism of her competence. Enid watched his kind, intelligent eyes cloud from crystalline blue to foggy gray. He didn't blink when one of her tears fell heavily on his cheek and pooled in the corner of his left eye. Her magic could not contest with mortality.

Comte Emile d'Erbonne, her mother's eldest brother and one of the greatest living authorities on sorcerous theory, was dead. Enid lowered his head gently to the blood-slick cobbles, hands shaking as she struggled to tamp down her overpowering rage. This man had been her earliest mentor in the sorcerous arts, her guide through the treacherous and duplicity-laden tracks of the Golden City's high society. He had placed his own life at extreme risk to deliver her from Revolutionary Arden's devouring maw, remaining behind with her as his peers at the Institut fled to Albion because she stubbornly refused to accept the ending of her world. Through his devices, much of her disposable wealth had been clandestinely transferred to the banks of Albion, the colonies, and Ostmark. When he realized there was no stopping the revolutionary forces consuming Ardain, he arranged for their escape aboard a respectable merchant ship bound for the colonies. They were making their way to that very vessel when they ran afoul of a Theocratic mob.

Now he lay here, in a rat's warren near the Dolorous Gate, slain by a coward, a worm in the corpse of Ardainne whose treachery left her with no companion but grief to accompany her into her new life. Grief and a lust for revenge. Revenge for her uncle, for her father, her brothers, the whole of her line. Revenge for the loss of a golden idyll and damn the foundation upon which it was built. Enid wiped her bloody hands on Uncle Emile's brocade travel coat and vowed to see the Theocrats pay for laying waste to his great heart and incomparable mind and the culture that birthed them.

His last words had directed her to find the postern gate if they became separated. "Find the city wall and then follow the slope down toward the sea. Always toward the sea!"

Flickering orange torchlight and the sudden gabble of excited voices from the far end of the alley drew her attention back to the present. The vanguard of the revolutionary mob came into view around one of the crazed alley's corners. When they spotted her on her knees on the filthy ground next to her fallen mentor, the mob voiced a blood-thirsty halloo of discovery, which would have made any pack of wolves proud. Enid brushed a strand of salt-and-pepper hair from her uncle's face, closed his eyes, and pressed his mouth closed. When he was arranged with as much dignity as the environs permitted, she stood and turned to face the mob milling in the alley's mouth behind her.

The front rank of the mob, perhaps a dozen ragged-looking commoners, straggled to a halt. Enid suspected they would keep their distance until the rest of the horde trailing behind them arrived. Then, bolstered by the encouraging presence of another two or three dozen of their kind, they would screw their courage to the sticking point and descend upon her. Although the mob was, for the most part, armed with the most rudimentary of improvised weaponry, she was confident their sheer numbers would overcome the hastily prepared dweomers of protection woven into her plain brown traveling cloak. Besides, there was still the matter of the turncoat nobleman. Her coat might blunt a sword stroke or cushion a cudgel's blow, but it would not stand against a spell-lock ball. So—where was this traitor and his spell-lock now?

She opened her mind and sought for him. It *had* been a man's face she'd seen momentarily limned in the cyan flash of a pistol. She remembered him, his eyes in particular, more than well enough to form a connection with him. It took only a moment's concentration to find him. Alone in the crowd of commoners, he stood out to her like a beacon in the night.

Her uncle's murderer lacked any protective dweomers at all, she noticed. Perhaps that indicated his arrogant confidence in the mob's power or, more likely, he was all but ignorant of combative sorcery.

Whatever its cause, his defenselessness gratified her. She gave her perception its head and sensed the spell-lock pistol in his hand, recharged and ready to fire. She felt the ripple of potential as his finger tightened on the weapon's trigger and bent her will toward the ball in its barrel. Cold, concentrated rage seemed to amplify her ability. Only a minute amount of effort drastically increased the sympathetic bond between the spell-lock and ball. This accomplished, she extended her will in all directions, calling for sylphs, salamanders, and shadowy umbrae amenable to her purpose.

The mob's angry cries drew her back to the physical moment. Their jeers and savage, incoherent challenges redoubled in volume as the nobleman stepped to the front. He towered over the commoners for whom he'd betrayed his own kind. His face twisted into a spiteful grin of triumph as he took in the sight of her standing by her fallen uncle, her eyes stained with tears. He obviously mistook her vacant expression and lack of flight as proof that shock and tragedy had robbed her of the will to flee—to live. He raised the pistol to shoulder level and aimed down the length of its elegantly tapered barrel. A wolfish grin split his face as the rabble shouted, "Kill her! Kill her!" His eyes filled with triumph as he jerked the trigger.

His form was so poor that she doubted that the ball would have struck true even if it had exited the barrel. The point was moot, as the ball remained stubbornly lodged in place, bound by a sympathetic attachment encouraged and greatly magnified by Enid's sorcerous art. Pressure built behind the blockage and the spell-lock exploded with a tremendous noise and a blinding cyan flash that consumed the nobleman's hand and a good portion of his forearm.

The deafening report stunned the crowd into a short-lived silence that soon turned into frantic screams as Enid turned her sorcery on them. The flames of the crowd's torches leaped high into the pitch-black reaches of the alley's upper shadows. The fire danced there with a disturbing and malevolent life of its own. It squirmed and darted down the torch shafts and found purchase in the filthy sleeves and dirt-caked flesh of the wretches who held them.

The alley was instantly choked with flaming, panic-stricken victims of her magic. Some fled down the alley, away from Enid, their horror-racked brains frozen in the hope they might escape their agony if they put enough distance between themselves and its author. Others turned to their companions for deliverance, grasping them in a desperate embrace which offered no salvation, but visited the same fiery fate on their fellows. Some rushed toward Enid herself, either to beg her mercy or to strike her down before the flames consumed them. The same silent winds that circled her and lifted her raven locks in soft waves hurled them back.

All but a few of Enid's persecutors writhed out their last moments amid the alley's piles of offal and debris within a few heartbeats. Some wretches at the back of the mob threw away their torches and turned to flee from the sudden hell that consumed their comrades. The fiery salamanders pursued them relentlessly. Tendrils of flame slithered through the stinking darkness to caress them with the feathery, skin-scorching touch of all-consuming flame. The stricken stumbled into mounds of urban detritus that bordered the alley, igniting new bonfires and expanding the salamanders' reach.

As the last of her persecutors succumbed to fire and shadow, Enid walked purposefully down the alley. The sylphs that swirled protectively about her stirred up ashes and the foul smell of burning flesh—none of which they allowed to come within proximity of the ward they mindlessly adored. When she reached the fallen noble, collapsed around the ruin of his right arm and sobbing softly to himself, she allowed her mind to move through formulations that would have disgusted and appalled her only an hour ago. Now they seemed insufficient by half.

She heard the hue and cry raised a block or two away. Another pack of Theocratic murderers would soon descend upon her, drawn by the noise of the confrontation and the flickering firelight of the opportunistic salamanders still idly chewing away at the buildings bordering the alley.

In her heightened state, Enid felt the brooding hatred of the massed commoners who made these tangled, claustrophobic slums their home. A part of her empathized with the wretched urban poor and their lives of near starvation, subjugation, and abject poverty. She understood the callous attitudes of her own kind were responsible for their suffering and the hatred that arose from it. The knowledge shamed her. But the kinder, more sympathetic part of her character was not ascendant now.

If the salamanders hunger yet, she thought, *then let them feed*.

She raised her arms and loosed her will, sending most of her coterie of sylphs radiating outward in a stiff breeze, each carrying fiery seeds in the form of dozens of hungry salamanders. New cries of panic and alarm replaced the Theocratic hunting calls as fires spread quickly in all directions. The ravenous motes of fire found purchase in the ancient, smoke-dried timbers of ramshackle rows of tenements. Fire bells rang out, followed shortly by the tolling of chapel bells as a false dawn spread over Arden.

Enid became more sharply aware of her immediate surroundings as she released the elementals from her dominion and allowed them to run free. Her skin prickled from the heat emanating from the salamanders that fed greedily on the corpses that littered the alley and the buildings on either side. Acrid smoke burned her eyes and throat despite the deference in which the fire elementals held her. A great, greasy black cloud rose into the heavens around her, underlit by leaping flames.

Tears ran down her cheeks, but they were born of the smoke. She felt no regret for the mayhem she'd wrought or its potential consequences for her beloved city. Arden could burn to the ground for all she cared. The golden age of Ardainne was at an end, and she doubted its lost glory could ever be restored. Better for it to burn than continue to rot under the cancerous regime of the Theocratic Republic.

That would not happen, though, not tonight. Without the impetus of her wrath to guide them, the elementals would quickly lose interest in the destructive tasks to which she'd set them. Soon other mages, loyal to the Theocracy or simply motivated by humanity, would descend upon the quarter to banish the few remaining salamanders or put them to work, reversing the spread of their handiwork.

Arden would not burn to the ground tonight, but a sizable portion of it would serve as her uncle's pyre.

"Merciful Redeemer, do not leave me here to burn!"

Enid looked down at her uncle's murderer lying maimed at her feet. He was clad in the sort of earth-colored, adornment-free clothing favored by the Theocracy's supporters and those who wished to avoid casual denouncement to the feared Confessors. Gone were the days of hair colored by dweomer to match the shifting colors of a fine coat or gown and held in fantastical arrangements by minor magics. Embroidered images no longer capered and flowed around cuffs or hems. Jewelry, if worn at all, hung flat and lifeless on a chain against the breast rather than orbiting like a glittering satellite around their owner. If the Theocracy had given her no other reason, she would have despised them for robbing her world of so much of its color, grace, and visual drama.

"Please," her would-be killer groaned again, raising his ravaged right arm in supplication. "Please do not leave me to *burn*."

"There is nothing further from my mind, sir. I would not dream of leaving you to the flames." Enid smiled and extended her will to push the flames back in all directions. She and her uncle's murderer were left in a pool of flickering shadow ringed by a palisade of flames. He began to thank her for her mercy, but the words strangled in his throat as the shadows descended on him with all their dark savagery.

The umbrae insinuated themselves between their victim and the faintest glimmer of light, wrapping him in a primeval darkness that smothered rational thought and robbed his benighted soul of all hope. Loathsome fears emerged from the dark corners of his mind, banished since childhood and left to fester. Free to roam unhindered, they rent his sanity with claws as cold and black as wrought iron.

The screams of his passing rose shrill and broken above the roar of flames as she made her way through the twisting, smoke-choked maze of streets, following the slope down toward the sea, always toward the sea.

When she found her uncle's retainer awaiting her at one of the postern gates near the dockside, she rushed toward her in relief. The woman turned and the hood of her cloak fell away; she saw the blue face, yellowing eyes, and black, bulging tongue of the *Artagny*'s inept mage. His smile was all dry gums and dull gray teeth as he said, "Welcome, lady. We have a place prepared for you!"

She was bustled into a coffin-like box in which she'd be smuggled to Ourest hidden under the cargo of a slow-moving hay wain. It was dark, warm, and redolent with the comforting smell of fresh-cut hay. Racked with fatigue and sorrow, she began to sink into slumber. As her eyes began to droop, her nostrils were assailed by the odor of sweat and vomit. She felt something cold splash against her lips and licked them in reflex. Seawater.

Enid awoke in her berth with a start, her mind churning with the memory of her actual last hours in Ardainne, albeit haunted by the taint of guilt and self-loathing. As her thoughts cleared, she found herself racked with seasickness and utterly fatigued. Lying there with no one for company, Enid nearly sank into despair for a time. Her dreams were troubled by images of men and women dying horribly, engulfed in flames and shadows that charred and flayed the flesh from their bones. She wanted to hate them as her enemies, but she could only sob in horror at their suffering. The bloodshot, accusatory eyes of the *Artagny*'s pathetic mage glared at her from the flames rising in the Dolorous Quarter, whose black clouds of smoke hid unknown numbers of other victims who had no hand in her uncle's death.

Even her waking hours were burdened with ghosts: Dunaughy sat at her writing desk and regarded her morosely.

"What happened after I lost consciousness? I perceive that the weather has cleared, and I still live, but beyond that . . ."

"You spent an inordinate amount of power and reduced yourself to such a weakened state that you nearly expired from *seasickness*." Dunaughy practically spat the last word.

"I see."

"Do you? Your rash action and ignorance were nearly the death of every mortal aboard. What in the gods' names were you thinking?"

Enid breathed a fluttering sigh. "Rue said we were about to lose a mast due to the strength of the gale, so it seemed logical to reduce the pressure against it by reducing the wind."

Dunaughy put a weary hand to his forehead. "Your plan would have been effective if the main topmast were standing ashore. But it is not. It is secured to a moving ship, a ship that *must* move away from the following sea or else be swallowed by it."

"I understand that now, but I had no hint of it in the moment of crisis."

"I tried to warn you, but you would not hear me!"

"Could not," Enid snapped. She collected herself and continued the dialogue in a low voice. "Could not hear you. Your voice was too weak to hear."

Dunaughy leaned back in the chair. He was increasingly less conscientious about replicating his mortal shell, as illustrated by his current lack of legs below the knees. Even his torso was little more than a cloudy suggestion. His worried expression was crystal clear, however, his concern evident in every well-defined crease and wrinkle.

"I am tethered to this room," he sighed. "It is my axis mundi. The farther I move from it, the more effort it takes to make myself noticed among the living."

"And without your counsel, I am prone to fatal error. Should I choose to make my position here permanent, we must take steps to improve our situation."

"What do you suggest, milady?"

"That you leave me be for a time, as the room is swimming before my eyes."

Enid's brow was dotted with perspiration and her voice faded to a whisper as she spoke.

Dunaughy stood beside Enid until her breathing became regular. When he was certain she was resting peacefully, he withdrew into the twilight land the separates the dead from the living.

———

For the next three days Enid suffered from a second bout of illness that Rondelle blamed on her use of a self-concocted cure rather than coming to him for a sound medicinal treatment. She was shaken by fevers, chills, and fits of delirium. Nath checked on her daily and ensured that Rondelle was attentive to her every need.

At one point, she was so tortured by the effort of emptying an already ravaged stomach that Dr. Rondelle insisted she must not be left alone lest she find herself too weak to rouse herself and come to mischief in her own cot. It was during this time that she awoke from a heart-rending dream of mothers and infants dying as their burning homes collapsed around them. She looked up through tear-streaming eyes to see none other than Yeardly staring down at her, his face contorted in the most genuine expression of sympathetic woe that she had yet witnessed on any face other than her mother's. The young man dabbed the perspiration from her forehead with a damp cloth and gently murmured "there, there" as if her afflictions would flee before the heartfelt repetition of that incantation. For a brief, shining moment, his belief was well founded. She slipped into an untroubled sleep for the first time in days, her hand clasped over Yeardly's where it grasped the frame of her hanging cot.

chapter 9

W e're all happy to see you materially improved, Magister."
Nath smiled at her as she crossed to the windward side
of the quarterdeck, where he stood in company with Lieutenant Merryweather and Master Harde.

Harde was a stout-looking fellow who towered over Nath and was
only a bit shorter than Enid. His head was as smooth and hairless as a
round shot. His features were pleasingly regular. As he knuckled his
brow and greeted her courteously, she noted his eyes were a brittle
shade of yellow brown she always associated with a loyal hound.

All in all, there was little of the villain evident about Isembarde
Harde. This was no surprise to her. She'd learned long ago that evil
often found its home in the hearts of otherwise decent men who suffered under the delusion that they must act counter to their nature in
order to prosper.

"Thank you all for your concern," Enid said, smiling weakly. Her
stomach and throat still ached from the last few days of exertion, but
she had been able to hold down Dr. Rondelle's despicably thin portable soup without any effort that morning. The weather had much

improved, and she found the air that raced across the *Alarum*'s bow as she dashed along under a bright sun and wind-tattered clouds extremely bracing. Lieutenant Merryweather stepped aside to allow her to take a position at the rail between herself and Captain Nath. Glancing around, Enid immediately noticed two things: first, a dozen or more ships and boats of various sizes dotted the waters around the *Alarum* and, second, that a large, red, cliff-faced mountain rose out of the sea before them and that no great distance beyond it, a vast expanse of mountainous land was visible.

Nath noted the direction of her gaze and smiled, obviously pleased with himself. "That prodigious large rock is Gisbon, Magister d'Tancreville. We laid the *Alarum*'s course just so despite our wandering in the Straits of Albion and that touch of rough seas that laid you up."

He glanced sidewise at Harde, obviously assuring himself that his fling at the sailing master's doubts of his navigational abilities had registered and then cheerfully continued, "Master Harde and Lieutenant Merryweather and I were just discussing the aptness of the name Albion's sailors give the island: the Fist. I have suggested that it resembles an enormous head more than a fist, but my reasoning flies in the face of tradition. It stands two to one against me at the moment, but perhaps your opinion will bring the matter to a draw. Would you care to hear the two positions offered?"

Enid assumed the officers' joviality resulted from the intoxicating nearness of land and shrugged her shoulders in assent.

"I will weigh your arguments if you wish, as long as they are not too nautical in nature. If there were any doubt that I am still a landsman at heart, my recent illness must banish it entirely."

"There is nothing nautical in it, my dear magister," Nath reassured her. "It is more a question of poetic license."

"More like poetry given too much license," Harde drawled with a wink to underline his humor. Whether either the humor or its herald was genuine, Enid could not say. Both the captain and Merryweather chuckled amiably, though, so she smiled as well.

"Allow me to present my argument, then. If I cannot persuade you to my position, Master Harde and Lieutenant Merryweather will present their arguments against it." Nath grinned boyishly before putting his hands behind his back and holding forth with a somber earnestness that was only belied by the sparkle in his eye and the chuckles and sniffs of the opposition party.

"I remarked to Mr. Harde that far from a fist, Gisbon resembled nothing more closely than a giant's head. Observe the island as it now lies: See that it is tall and rounded at the top, where a patchwork of trees and shrubs resemble the closely shorn bristles beneath an oldster's wig. Note, too, that the island's face is as deeply lined and as dark a red as that of any tar-handed sailor. Finally, see how the waves break upon the island's chin to form just the sort of white fringe that many of our older hands grow and are shameless enough to refer to as beards. There before us is the head of a giant who stands with his feet planted wide apart on the sandy seafloor and bathes himself to the chin in the warm waters of the Merentian Sea. That is obvious to anyone with eyes. Calling it a fist just won't answer. What sort of fist has hair atop it or has such a patriarchal look thanks to wrinkles and a white beard?"

"As to hairy fists, sir, they are a-plentiful 'tween decks," Harde answered slyly, prompting both Nath and Merryweather to laugh and glance at Enid as if they expected her to fly out in offense. She had no idea where offense was in the relative hirsuteness of sailors' hands, so she shrugged noncommittally.

"And them wrinkles is found just as much on a sailor's sunbaked hands as on their phyzes and made all the more obvious by the tar that is as hard to wash away as cats is to kill. An' that fringe of white looks more to me like the lace that hands is given to sewing on the cuffs of their shore-goin' rig for the astonishment of the folks found there. It looks like a fist, I say, as generations past has as well, and that fist is a-shaking right under the nose of them damned Naveroñians, which I beg the lady to forgive my language in this instance."

Enid waved the curse away, impressed with the sailing master's reasoning. He may be old-fashioned and tradition-bound as Nath held, but he had a sharp wit for a man of simple origin.

"I may be forced to recuse myself," she said with a slight smile. "I find both arguments equally convincing."

"Them's only the poetical arguments, Magister," Harde said. "There's practical arguments as well."

"Then, by all means, let us hear them!"

"Well," Harde said, casting a sly glance at Merryweather, whose eyes shone with amusement as she gave the master an encouraging nod. "Well, it ain't delicate to refer to someone's home as a head. It ain't calc'lated to put 'em on good terms, is it? There's nothing offensive about a fist, though, even if it is a bit hairy at the knuckles."

Enid raised a brow. "A compelling argument, indeed. Your rebuttal, Captain Nath?"

Laughing, Nath raised his hands in surrender. "To argue past such a well-reasoned argument would be boorish. I concede both the point and the argument, Master Harde; your pragmatism has vanquished my poeticism! I rely on the same deft hand and keen wits to bring us in. I desire to present my log and journals to Admiral Weymouth before dinner."

"Aye, sir." There was a trace of wryness to Harde's smile as he touched the brim of his hat and strode away, briskly shouting orders as he went.

The *Alarum*, whose atmosphere had been relaxed and complacent a moment before, was transformed into a whirlwind of activity. Enid watched as sailors swarmed across the deck with obvious energy and zeal. She could put no purpose to their toil yet, but it was clear from the confident manner with which they went about their business and the briskness with which they responded to Harde's commands that they knew what they were about. She found the scene oddly exhilarating, a surprising turn of events since she had never been one of those smug nobles who gained satisfaction from the indolent observation of others laboring on their behalf.

This was different from watching her father's serfs trudging behind a plow, though. Very different, indeed. She found herself desirous to understand the duties at which these sailors were employed, what that gang of men intended to accomplish by tugging on that rope, or why those men and women in the rigging were furling one set of sails while another snapped open at the wind's urgent insistence. She felt the deck's angle change under her feet and heard the gurgling song of the waves change pitch as they rushed past the ship's hull. She felt the last vestiges of seasickness evaporate in the moment's joy and, despite herself, her grin reached a broadness unseen since her father presented her first pony to her as a mere girl. Nath noticed and returned her grin, tooth for tooth.

"This is one of our Service's best-kept secrets, Magister." Nath made a broad gesture that took in all the brisk activity aboard the ship and then leaned closer to say in a stage whisper, "It can be quite pleasant!"

"Yes," Enid agreed, her embarrassing grin banished and replaced with a more decorous but still radiantly genuine smile. "This almost makes up for the last few days. But tell me, aren't we headed into that harbor at a rash pace? As pleasant as the day is, I have no desire for a swim."

"We are standing sharply in, but not rashly, I assure you. Admiral Weymouth, the lord and master of all Albion's warships afloat in the Merentian Sea, may watch from up there." Nath pointed to a white-faced building high on the side of the mountain that formed most of Gisbon's landmass. "Master Harde will want to bring her in smartly, but not precipitously. The eyes of a higher power are a fine inspiration and for those of us in the Service there are few powers higher than an admiral of a sea."

Enid gazed skeptically at the white face of the Admiralty building, a structure that appeared monolithically forbidding from a distance.

"I wonder if you jest with a landsman, sir. What sort of 'higher power' has the leisure to stand by his window and observe every ship that chances to sail in?"

"You'd be surprised," Nath drawled amiably. "And recall that higher powers are not limited to their own eyes for observation. Every ship in the harbor will attend our approach quite closely, as will the admiral's creatures ashore. If we miss stays or otherwise present a lubberly spectacle, you can bet your last ha'penny that Admiral Weymouth will hear about it before I'm halfway up the hill."

"Then I would think you would wish to take personal command of the evolutions that bring the ship into harbor." She was painfully aware of Dunaughy's injunction against interfering with Nath where naval matters were concerned, but trusting an avowed enemy to perform a duty that might bring disgrace to his command seemed to be just the sort of thing the wraith had enjoined her to endeavor to prevent. "Is it wise to trust your reputation to—"

Nath silenced her with a wave of his hand and the sort of affectionate smile the wise offer to imbeciles. In a voice quiet enough to stay between them, he reassured her that Harde was too proud of his own sailing ability to make a fool of himself bringing the *Alarum* in.

"That pride, while in no small way contributing to our disagreeable relation, is also my best assurance that he will perform this maneuver to my highest expectation."

"I'm sure you know best." She had her doubts, but his reasoning seemed sound. "So will the admiral send for you once his 'creatures' have informed him of our arrival?"

"Oh, no. There's no need for him to. It is my duty to report to him immediately, bearing with me my journal and any other pertinent documents or charts."

Nath snapped his cuffs nonchalantly, but he was clearly a little nervous at the prospect.

"This will be the first time I have presented myself to an admiral. I'm told it can be quite an ordeal. They are quite interested in uncovering the smallest piece of valuable intelligence their officers may have observed and can be relentless in their interviews to uncover it. They are also very busy men and have no patience for fools that waste their time."

"I'm sure that will not be an issue in your case. You are certainly no fool." Enid recalled his manner in conducting business with Master Arnaud of the *Marie* and had no doubt he could be quite businesslike when circumstance decreed.

"Thank you for your confidence." Nath offered her a slight bow and a strained smile. "And may it be well-founded, please the gods. Annoying an admiral, especially one with as deep an interest and long a reach as the admiral of the Merentian Sea, may put a permanent halt to an officer's ambitions. It is never a light undertaking to go before beings of such power, especially when they have a reputation such as Weymouth's!"

"He is known for his ferocity, then?"

"He is a fire-eater, as we say in the Service. 'Ferocious' applies wondrous well to him, both in action against the enemy and in his dealings with ineffectual underlings. It is widely held that Weymouth's enmity keeps Lord Grove, one of His Majesty's favored nephews, languishing in the worst vessels in the fleet. Something about him being reluctant to bring his ship too close in among the perilously shifting shallows off Filsterhead."

"Filsterhead? Weymouth was there? It was a battle of some note, I take it?" In her mind she could see the commemorative "Filsterhead Remembered" in Dunaughy's journal.

Nath's face revealed as much pure astonishment as if she had denied any knowledge of the sun.

"You surprise me, Magister! I thought the fame of Filsterhead was universal, and Weymouth's with it. You may recall, perhaps, that Albion and Nordmarche were at war for a short time over the Great Scarp fisheries and the possession of some islands in the Western Ocean, specifically the islands known as the Three Sisters?"

Enid nodded noncommittally. She vaguely recalled some such unpleasantness, but the details were inconsequential to her at the time and so nonexistent to her now.

"Well, that war owes its brevity to Weymouth's action off Filsterhead: He was there with thirteen of the line when Admiral Gunerwald came out of Exen with his fifteen of the line and attempted to force a passage to the Great Scarp, there to drive our fishers from the area and destroy any other Albion shipping he chanced upon. They played cat-and-mouse among Nordmarche's perilous shallows for several days until Weymouth could finally close sufficiently to force an action."

"Despite the shallows? He was not daunted by the prospect of running his fleet aground?"

"Not in the least, Redeemer bless him!" Nath exclaimed with genuine admiration. "He had a Nord master's mate aboard who knew the shallows like the back of his hand. All that nonsense about frigates going in and sounding before the action is quite exploded, I assure you!"

"And the admiral trusted this master's mate? He was a man of gentle birth, I take it?"

Nath chuckled and shook his head. "No, not in the least. As common as sand on the beach."

Enid's expression of incredulity elicited a second, deeper chuckle.

"No, my dear lady, it is not such an enormity as all that. The Sea Service makes the most of its people. Common folk are not dismissed as mere muscle and grist for the great guns. A good officer will make full use of their experience and wisdom, which often exceeds that of their supposed betters."

"In much the same way that my father relied on the advice of his hunt master, I suppose."

Enid drew a pair of cigarillos from her coat pocket and offered one to Nath, who accepted it gratefully. As she and Nath lit their smokes from a small ball of flame hovering above her palm, she reflected again on the differences between common folk she knew from her father's holdings and those she'd observed aboard the *Alarum*.

"Actually," she continued in a ruminative tone, "it is probably very little like the relationship between my father and his hunt master, whose name I'm ashamed to say I cannot recall despite an association that began in my early childhood and continued well into my adult years. My father respected his hunt master for a single facet of expertise and then only when that expertise was of use to him. Outside of the hunt and its various preparations and evolutions, I can safely assume that the hunt master never entered my father's thoughts. No matter how warmly he regarded him during the limited times that his skills and lore were of value, the hunt master occupied no more of my father's mind at other times than, say, an itch experienced sometime in the distant past. He was used and then forgotten—and I can say that without fear of subjective bias: I was there when the hunt master's son took over his father's duty, the older man having fallen to a flux of the lungs at winter's height, and my father took no notice of it. He behaved as if it were the same man, or, more accurately, the same animal. He took less heed of it than if one hired mount had been replaced with another."

Her diatribe gathered heat and volume as she plunged ahead, and Nath felt obliged to place a hand on her shoulder and mutter some placating words. The unexpected, and yes, unwonted, display of passion made him quite uncomfortable and for a moment he wondered if he had inadvertently introduced some sort of radical into the ship's carefully conservative society. Her words sounded very much like the sort of "leveling" cant that most people blamed for the bloody horrors unfolding in Ardainne, not to mention the growing unrest in Middlesea's own crowded streets. Enid seemed to grasp the loose reins of her decorum at his touch, though, and treated him to an even less expected flush. She colored prettily, he thought, and lost for a moment in the depths of that observation, missed the first few words of her apology.

". . . but that is neither here nor there. I simply must apologize for flying out so. I really have no excuse that seems adequate."

"Well," Nath said in a low, humane voice, "I'm sure that if there were anything to apologize for, and I must assure you to my mind there is not, the strain of your recent illness coupled with the stress of your recent travails could crack the most courteous of demeanors."

"You are kind, sir."

Enid turned her eyes back toward the rapidly approaching Fist. The truth, however, was that even a short time aboard the *Alarum* had brought home for her the true cause of the horrors consuming her homeland. Little as she wished to admit it, she knew that the atrocities suffered by her class were not solely the result of the ambitions of a few radical clerics or the animalistic urges of commoners who wished to reduce the glories of Ardainne to a sad, dingy shambles. Ardainne's aristocracy and their stubborn devotion to traditional privileges had helped fuel the flames that consumed them. It was a bitter thought to harbor and, for the moment at least, she eagerly sought some other subject to occupy her mind.

"Will the crew spend the night ashore? Is that the custom when coming to land after such a long cruise?"

"No, it is not," Nath answered with an amiable chuckle. "In fact, it is never customary for the entire crew to spend the night on shore."

"Never? Not even when their vessel is being repaired?"

"If she were careened, perhaps. But in most other circumstances, absolutely not. A ship is not something to be left unattended, after all. They are too prone to go to rack and ruin at the first hint of inattention. Rot and fire are always waiting in the wings to swoop down on a ship and have their way with her." He rubbed the smooth rail under his hand affectionately. "No, she must always be chaperoned, our *Alarum*."

Nath stood there for a moment with the live deck beneath his feet and the fair breeze on his face. He wore the most contented smile Enid had seen on a man's face outside a boudoir, and she could not help but smile a little with him.

"There is also the matter of the crew's behavior ashore, of course," he continued absently, still caught in the moment. "They must be chaperoned, too, you see, and their own ship is the best matron of all to look after them."

Enid glanced around at the sailors working on the deck. They seemed excited, she decided, noting that they moved with an extra spring to their steps and called out their arcane communications to one another in a heartier tone than seemed the norm. One or two of the rascals even dared to smile and wink at her as they caught her glance. She turned coolly back to Nath and observed that the thought of shore had an evidently invigorating effect on his crew. The captain visibly snapped out of his reverie and turned to her with a somewhat rueful grin.

"Oh, they're full of vinegar and . . ." He coughed into his hand. "Quite full of vinegar. They'll each be issued a bit of the prize money owed them before going ashore and some of them are likely to cut it up to a sorrowful degree. It is not uncommon for entire watches to be brought back from leave too drunk to walk, carried aboard by the Harbor Watch. Put extra money in their pockets and they will raise dissolution to a harrowing level of perfection."

Enid frowned at the sailors laboring on the deck as if they were already drunken and self-befouled lunatics.

"I'm surprised you let them ashore at all if they make a habit of such debauchery," she said, sniffing.

"Often we do not," Nath answered lightly. "Although not on account of debauchery, of course. People who risk their lives for king and country have every right to the occasional tear. No, no, it is the running that keeps us from being more liberal with their leave. Not much of a worry here at Gisbon, though. No place to run, you see."

"Does this reluctance to grant leave extend to a ship's officers and . . ." She fumbled for the word *warrants*, but it would not answer her call, so she continued, "And other persons of responsibility?"

"Certainly not," Nath assured her. "Although as many must stay aboard as is required by good discipline, of course, and the responsible lady or gentleman is usually loath to take liberty when those around them are constrained to remain aboard."

Enid nodded. "So, it would not be precipitate of me to pack a few things for the night? A bed planted firmly on unmoving earth seems a vision of heaven to me at the moment."

"Well, I should wait if I were you. Unless you have decided to resign your warrant and take passage to Albion from the Fist? If so, I can—"

"No, no, no," Enid interrupted, touched by the sudden, raw emotion in Nath's voice. "I have decided to extend my warrant for the duration of the *Alarum*'s—tour? Campaign? What is the word you use?"

"Cruise," Nath answered with a broad smile.

"For the duration of the *Alarum*'s cruise, then, if that is acceptable."

Nath took her hand and gave it an affectionate squeeze. Her impulse was to extricate it from his grasp immediately, for she had no love for such displays of intimacy, but she resisted the urge. His smile was so warm and genuine that she dreaded dampening it with her prickly eccentricities.

"I could not be happier to hear it, milady! If I may ask, what led you to this portentous decision?"

"It is hard to say. The truth is, I made the decision just now, as the words left my mouth. I suppose the scale was tipped by a number of considerations, not the least of which is my own stubborn refusal to abandon any pursuit until I have excelled at it."

"This is not a choice to be entered into precipitously, Enid," Nath said, his tone transforming from celebration to concern.

"I am precipitous by nature," Enid assured him. "But there are other factors, I assure you. Your arguments on the satisfaction of naval service weighed against service ashore were persuasive, and, despite its rigors, I find life at sea agrees with me. I find that I function better in a smaller community—there are fewer social forces intent on raising my ire."

She left unspoken the growing obligation she felt to Dunaughy's revenant. Despite how his presence grated on her patience at times, he was generous with his aid and his genuine regard for Nath was contagious. She found, like him, that she truly enjoyed Nath's company and found his devotion to his ship's people refreshing and worthy of respect.

She gently freed her hand and steered the conversation to less personal terrain.

"So there will be no furlough ashore for any of us?"

"Not immediately," Nath said. "No one will be given liberty to go ashore until I have delivered my compliments to Admiral Weymouth and received his leave to stay awhile. No, no—there is no cause to look so concerned, Magister! With the state of our stores, I don't doubt we will spend enough time here for you to turn your vision of heaven into a reality! Now, I must beg your pardon and see to the salutes and dress appropriately to be received by Admiral Weymouth."

Harde brought the *Alarum* in as sharply as Nath could have wished, and the gun crew fired off the salute with equal smartness. These were small but clear indications to the other ships anchored in Gisbon Reach that the *Alarum* was a taut ship with taut officers. Small as she may be, as old and under-gunned for her class, she was handled as briskly as any ship in His Majesty's fleet. No mean feat considering the condition she and her crew came to him in. These thoughts filled him with pride and confidence as he set in the stern sheets of his gig, swiftly propelled toward Admiralty Steps by the strong strokes of his immaculately turned-out boat crew. Still, a kernel of icy dread lay heavily in his stomach and made occasional hot forays up into his throat.

He had no reason to expect rough treatment at Admiral Weymouth's hands, but he had no cause to expect a warm greeting, either. Weymouth was from a Westlands family and had thrown his support behind the Earl of Dunbow's appointment as sea lord, but he was notorious for his stubborn independence. Nath sighed and shrugged to himself. Weymouth was like a strange sail on the horizon—he'd only discover his true nature by standing on to face it.

＊　＊

He smoothed the front of his best coat with one hand. At least he had no worries about his appearance. His uniform was impeccably tailored, but not ostentatious. He didn't look the pauper, as many commanders did, but there was nothing flash about his appearance, either. He was the very image of a solid, well-set sea officer.

The logbook and manifest clutched beside his left elbow told a different story. His men were already on reduced rations after the short cruise from Albion to Gisbon. Most of his shot and powder were spent. Spars and sails needed replacement. His stomach knotted tighter as he thought of the list of deficiencies that must be resolved before the *Alarum* would ever be granted new orders, let alone allowed out of anchorage. How could he ever hope to accomplish so much within the meager limits of the Admiralty's beneficence and his own credit? The Nath family name would only go so far for an as yet unproven scion.

With such concerns crushing his spirits, he was only tangentially aware of Mid Cullen's anxious, inquisitive expression as he stepped onto the worn, sea-slick stone steps of the landing.

"Yes, Cullen?" His voice sounded harsh and inhuman to his own ears.

"Will you be staying ashore tonight, sir, or shall I return to take you up later?"

"Keep a watch on the Steps. I'll wave my hat when I am ready for a boat."

With that, he straightened his hat on his head, snapped his cuffs into place, and stalked darkly up the stairs toward a volley of shouted invitations to part with his silver for some service or another.

Cullen lingered for a moment, watching him go. He'd never seen his captain's face so dark and grim, not even during the action aboard the *Artagny*. What could vex him so after such a marvelously successful cruise? As if reading his mind, Hornesty, an old salt with a fiercely scarred face and gentle manner, said softly, "Now don't stand frettin' o'er matters past yer ken, young sor. Fierce as a cap'n seems t'you today, that much more fierce seems admirals t'cap'ns. An' for good cause, too. If an admiral takes a wrong turn against you, it's rough seas and rotten bottoms till the sea takes you."

Cullen shot a worry-filled glance at Hornesty. "You think . . . ?"

"I think no more than the king requires of me, lad." The scar on her face wriggled to accommodate a gap-toothed grin. "Nor should you. Our cap'n is a smart'n and levelheaded in storm an' fire. Ain't likely he'll go on his own beam ends no matter what kind of gale the admiral sets on him. Now, shouldn't we be back to the barky afore the smell o'all them fine spirits ashore gets too strong for even our stouthearted *Alarum*s here?"

Nath stepped gingerly out of the donkey trap and carefully folded a pair of coins into its driver's outstretched palm. He manfully ignored a pair of post captains who chuckled at the ignobility of the conveyance that had borne him to Admiralty House. Better to make a ridiculous impression on them by taking such cheap transportation, the best that his currently depleted purse could afford, than to appear before the admiral covered in sweat and grime from the long, hot walk up the Fist. He touched the brim of his hat in salute to the two officers as he passed into the cool shadows under Admiralty House's arched stone portico. A trick of acoustics brought one of the captain's low words to Nath as plainly as if he whispered in his ear.

"Poor fellow."

Poor fellow indeed, thought Nath. *Poor in pocket until the prize court condemned his prizes, perhaps, but not in prospects—and certainly not so poor in character to require some scrub's pity!* He took a moment to adjust his uniform and allow the spark of anger lit by the casual remark to cool. No point in entering battle with the rigging aflame, after all. Satisfied that he was cleared for action, he adjusted the lay of his sword at his hip and entered Admiralty House's main hall.

chapter 10

The baleful gaze of a cadaverous old clerk with rheumy eyes greeted him. They held a generalized enmity that set Nath's temper a-smolder at their first shared glance. Nath waited in vain for the ill-looking cur to speak. A sour expression and the faint elevation of one age-frayed eyebrow proved to constitute the extent of the clerk's courtesy, however, so Nath introduced himself.

"Commander Nath, is it?" The clerk's tone was short, shrill, and altogether of a kind with his odious and arrogant appearance.

Nath smothered an urge to violently remind the wight of his manners and replied coolly, "*Captain* Nath, the *Alarum*, with compliments to the admiral."

The clerk grunted. "Airs, is it, sir? Newly appointed and mortal sure that the news of it is of great importance to everyone in the Service. Well, you must behave as you see best, but Admiral Weymouth does not take any pleasure from the sight of his officers puffed up by their own good opinions of themselves!"

Nath's only response was a cold stare of his own, which lasted until the clerk let out a long-suffering sigh and scratched something in the enormous ledger that took up most of the surface of his desk.

After sanding and blotting the entry, the old man levered himself out of his chair and crepitated over to a heavy oaken door. He knocked sharply three times before opening it and announced Nath in a creaking crow's call.

Nath swept past him and into the admiral's office. He heard the door slam sharply behind him as he made a leg before a figure out of legend.

Physically, Admiral Cormaend Heort Weymouth, Earl of Filsterhead, was everything the stories said: a powerfully built man whose unusual height was obvious even as he sat folded up uncomfortably behind a massive desk. His bluff, strong features were still handsome despite his advancing years and his eyes, when they glanced up from the papers arrayed on the desk before him, were the palest gray he'd ever seen. Nath would have found their ghostly hue and intensity disconcerting even if they had not reposed within an admiral's august phyz. The fact was, however, that they did, and as they lingered on him for a long moment, Nath felt the heat of his ire raised by that horrendous relic of a clerk replaced by a cold dread of his master.

"Captain Nath, the *Alarum*, reporting, sir," he said, praying his voice did not sound as strange and unnatural to the admiral as it did to his own ears.

Without speaking, Admiral Weymouth extended a powerful hand for Nath's log and other ship's documents. The hand, Nath noted, was the color of walnut, and the palm had roughly the same texture as that wood's bark. The admiral silently scanned the log pages, his face as immobile as Nath, who remained at attention before his desk. After an interminable amount of page flipping and unreadable glances, Admiral Weymouth finally pushed the documents away and gestured for Nath to take a seat, an offer he accepted with no small amount of trepidation. He was always more comfortable standing before his superiors, feet braced firmly, chin up, hands clasped behind his back. A place for everything and everything in its place. Seated, though, he was all at sea. His hands were never comfortable wherever they rested and had the ill-natured habit of mutilating any hat or papers held in his lap. With this damnable habit in mind, and aware that this bicorn was the last dress hat in his possession, he crossed his legs one over the other and thrust his hands between them. Weymouth seemed to wait for him to settle before plucking the abbreviated report from Nath's logbook. His expression was indecipherable as he read, but he looked up occasionally to regard Nath over the top edge of the report. At last, he set it aside and spoke.

"You may not be aware of it, but your late ship's magister was my particular friend. His death is a blow to me personally and to the Sea Service as well."

Weymouth's voice was a rich baritone, exactly the sort of voice Nath would expect of a national hero. His own sounded dreadfully dull and nasal when he replied, "I was honored to serve with Magister Dunaughy, and felt his loss keenly as well, professionally and personally."

"I am to understand that you have filled his position with an ex-patriate Ardain gentlewoman of some skill?" Weymouth's tone was coolly noncommittal, betraying neither approval nor censure. Nath suspected he was leaving it to him to fashion his own noose.

"Yes, sir. I have extended a warrant to Marquise Enid d'Tancreville, a graduate of the University of Vermandoix and a member of the Institut de l'Arcane. Her entire family has fallen to the Theocratic mob, so her zeal to oppose them is as great as ours. She had already served our cause before I clapped eyes on her by eliminating the *Artagny*'s magister."

"I commend you for your initiative and ingenuity," Weymouth said. "And give you joy of your prizes taken en route, Captain Nath. You will do me the service of writing a more detailed account of your action against the *Artagny*. I wish to include it in my next dispatch to the Admiralty."

"I am honored by your kindness, sir."

"Kindness has little to do with it, Captain. I admire a young officer who shows such skill and bold initiative."

Nath cleared his throat nervously. Perhaps this might not go so badly after all. "Thank you, sir. It is my intent to serve my king and the Service with all the energy allotted me."

The admiral grunted and drummed his fingers on the cover of the *Alarum*'s stores ledger. "There can be no doubt of your energies at sea, sir. But perhaps there is some indication that they are much dissipated ashore. Do you follow my course, sir?"

Nath shifted uncomfortably in his chair. Here it was, the moment of dread that had haunted his idle moments since taking the *Alarum* out of Middlesea.

"I do, sir. You refer to the ship's stores. I can only assure you that all my energy was bent toward setting the *Alarum* up as well as possible. Any failings in that regard must be laid at the meagerness of my means, not my fervor in expending them."

The admiral raised a bushy red brow.

"You take responsibility for the deplorable state of your ship's stores, then? No flings against the peculation of the Naval Board or the Admiralty's unreasonable demands?" Weymouth's voice rose steadily as he spoke until his last words were nearly bellowed. He leaned across the desk, a blunt cannon of a finger jabbing toward Nath's chest in time with his words.

"No, sir." Nath looked ahead, his gaze fixed on a spot some six inches above Weymouth's stormy gray eyes. "I received my orders to command the *Alarum* and read letters of command to the crew. Any deficiencies in her fitting out are my responsibility."

The admiral grunted again and settled back in his chair. He eyed Nath from beneath his thick brows as he stuffed a large-bowled pipe with tobacco. After the pipe was lit and a few puffs filled the room with a sweet odor, Weymouth said in a more normal tone, "Good on you, sir. That is exactly the sort of answer a proper sea officer should give. Exactly the sort that these letters from Vice Admiral Emuel Barrington"—Weymouth slapped a heavy hand down on a small twine-tied stack of envelopes on his desk—"would lead me to expect from you. I believe you are familiar with the gentleman, as he speaks most highly of you."

Nath nodded warily. "Yes, sir. He was my commander aboard the *Redoubtable*. I'm gratified that he found my service worthy of comment."

"Well you should be," Weymouth said, taking a long draw on his pipe. "I've also received recommendations on your character from several others, including your aunt Dolorous, with whom I sailed as a young post captain under Old Harry himself. You have a prodigious amount of interest marshaled in your favor, sir."

Nath detected a note of disapproval in the remark, so he restricted his response to a nod and a quiet "Thankee, sir."

Weymouth tossed the packet of letters to one side.

"Too much interest, frankly. Enough to make me suspect that such a torrent of praise must be intended to hide some serious flaws. Your performance on the cruise from Middlesea and acceptance of responsibility for every aspect of your command have given me cause to reconsider my stance, though."

The admiral paused to shout for his clerk, demanding a pitcher of shrub for himself and Captain Nath. The old clerk's rheumy eyes shied away from Nath's face as he filled two glasses with cool rum shrub. As refreshed by the old devil's discomfiture as the chilled drink's restorative virtue, Nath relaxed enough to lean back slightly in his chair. Still, he kept the hand not holding his drink clamped firmly between his knees.

Once the clerk departed, Weymouth continued in a low, serious tone. "Now, it is not my habit to speak poorly of my officers without they have some recourse to answer me, especially in front of those officers' inferiors, so I trust you will take this comment in the manner

in which it is offered: Not all sea officers are as ready to take responsibility as you are. There are many who would rather shift any duties
that do not add a shine to their name to anyone they can land them
on, particularly their subordinates. Steer a careful course around such
officers, sir, for you will find them as merciless as any lee shore and
possessed of a malignancy not found in the natural world."

His stomach knotting, Nath nodded. He'd made the same assessment of Captain Ambrose, who'd obviously taken pleasure in leaving
the *Alarum* all but forgotten in the Middlesea basin until Nath was assigned as her commander. Ambrose thought himself rid of a command
that was beneath his stature, a treat sweetened by thrusting it upon
the scion of a Westlands naval dynasty. The surly and beaten-down
state of the *Alarum*'s people did not reflect well upon his character as
an officer or human being.

"I will steer carefully then, as you say, sir."

"It would be wise. If you have not encountered them yet due to
your youth, be forewarned that they will view any success you achieve
as a blemish on their glory and will seize on any of your failings as
means to advance their own reputation. Do you take my meaning, sir?"

"I do."

Weymouth nodded briskly and pointed at the stores ledger with
the stem of his pipe. "Now. What shall we do about this, sir? You don't
have enough biscuit for the weevils, let alone your crew, nor enough
powder to blow your own nose. Not to mention the article of men, of
which you are blessed short. What do you propose to do about it?"

"I hoped to find a prize agent willing to provide me with some credit
based on my captures so far. If I spend carefully, I should have enough
to lay in whatever the Navy Board will not allow me by way of reissue."

Weymouth rubbed his chin thoughtfully. "Well, you'll find everything in scandalously short supply. A blockade of Ardainne's Merentian ports is in the offing and the whole Red Fleet has been here before
you, preparing for long stations. Everything of value and anything that

walks like a man and smells of tar will have been snaffled up by now. Government sources will yield precious little, but private speculators may still have something to offer."

Nath sighed and mentally bade his entire share of the prizes taken thus far goodbye.

"I'll make shift as best I can, then."

Chewing his lip, Weymouth pulled a blank sheet from a stack of papers and scribbled something on it before passing it across the desk to Nath.

"That is the address of my personal prize agent. Call upon him in the morning. He will be expecting you. I think you'll find that he will be most generous."

Nath accepted the sheet of paper with the same pious respect he would have given a relic of the faith. An *admiral's* prize agent expecting *him*? It beggared belief!

"Thank you, sir! Your generosity is . . . is . . ." Words failed him, and he found himself waving the paper like a signal flag.

"Is not entirely without self-interest," Weymouth broke in, saving Nath further embarrassment. "Although I flatter myself that I would have extended the same courtesy based solely on your services so far, it also serves to allow you to do me a further, more personal service."

"It would be an honor to serve you in any way, sir," Nath assured him earnestly.

"Hmm." The admiral steepled his fingers and leaned back in his chair, which creaked ominously under the strain. "Well, it is an opportunity for you as well as a service to me. And also to the memory of a good man and a taut officer who has been much maligned by history. Do you recall Captain Wilhem Ourey?"

Nath nodded slowly. Who would not recall the name of a man commonly believed to have been the cruelest, most arbitrarily savage captain ever to command one of His Majesty's ships? Ourey's name was synonymous with sadism and bloody mutiny, but Weymouth's words and tone warned Nath away from making any comment beyond, "Last Albion captain of the *Redemption* frigate, sir."

"Precisely. And as fine an officer as ever came under my command." Weymouth caught Nath's doubtful expression before he could hide it beneath a reserved mask.

He frowned and continued with quiet force. "I know that is contrary to everything you have heard, Captain Nath, and yet it is true. Ourey was no tyrant or martinet. He dealt with his crew fairly and kept the cat in its bag for all save the most serious offenses. 'Fair' and 'firm,' those were his bywords. 'Fair' and 'firm.' He was also a thoroughgoing sailor who could reef and splice with the best of the foremast jacks and they loved him dearly for it. He knew each of their names and was free with his praise. This man was no monster, Captain Nath."

Moved by the force of Weymouth's obvious affection for Ourey, Nath asked, "As you say, sir. But as that was the case, what happened?"

Weymouth seemed to collapse around his center, as if the question undermined some support essential to his certainty.

"I cannot say. I truly cannot say. I only know that the Ourey those murdering dogs described to the court-martial was not the Ourey I set in command of 'em. You know as well as I that it only takes one or two bad seeds to poison the entire crop. Perhaps Ourey missed the signs before he could take action. I doubt we'll ever know. I can only say that Ourey was not a man to take any pleasure in songs sung at the grate. Any man who would call Wilhem a flogging captain is a liar, and you have my warrant on that, sir!"

Nath nodded. Weymouth was right. What really happened that bloody night aboard the *Redemption* would probably never be known. There were so many things that could go wrong between officers and crew, things that might not directly involve the captain at all, at least not until he was up to his neck in bloodthirsty mutineers. Nath served on unhappy vessels himself and was aware infection could spread belowdecks without the notice of any but the most perspicacious captain.

Under the right circumstances, it was but a short step from grumbling to mutiny.

As to the reports of Ourey's cruelty, well, those may be true or not, but one thing was certain: such accusations were a mutineer's best hope for leniency, especially if no witnesses to the contrary were left among the living.

"A greater tragedy than I had thought, then, sir. I'm heartsick at the thought of losing an officer of such caliber to men who would so freely defame his honor to save their own worthless necks."

"Not that it has saved any of them so far. Six have been recovered and six have filled gibbets." Weymouth's smile left Nath with no doubt that it would be a sad day indeed when one found himself the object of this man's enmity. "But now, the business at hand: If you know who Captain Ourey was, you're no doubt aware of what became of the *Redemption* after the mutineers seized her?"

"Sold to the Naveroñians for pocket silver and asylum, if I recall correctly, sir."

Nath's lip curled in uncontrollable contempt. To mutiny against officers sworn to the king was hellish bad in and of itself, but to sell a king's ship to his enemies after it was wrested by force of arms from one's fellows in the Sea Service was a sin for which no pit of damnation was deep enough.

"Even so. It has long been my fondest dream to see the *Redemption* retaken, to undo the infamy against both the crown and my friend. Unfortunately, the Naveroñians take as much pride in possession of her as we are shamed by it. They have gone to great pains to keep her location a secret and to keep her out of our sight."

"Why are they so cautious? We are not at war with them."

"Because no civilized nation on earth condones the sale of national ships by mutineers. They would prefer to let the world forget about their base behavior, even if it costs them the service of a well-founded frigate. And were we to retake her? They would be doubly embarrassed." Weymouth warmed to his subject and leaned forward, again using jabs of the stem of his pipe to punctuate his points. "They were careful to keep her in well-guarded harbors and under as many guns as possible. Places that would require us to send a squadron in to cut her out, and thereby precipitate an open war. And so things have stood until recently."

Nath sat bolt upright in his chair.

"She's been moved! They decided her mooring was too exposed! Probably somewhere up toward Purparde, too close to Ardainne? Now they're trying to creep her down the coast to a more secure harbor!"

Weymouth smiled broadly and laid a finger beside his nose. "Barrington is right about you. You are a canny one. She's been creeping down the coast, just as you say, probably planning to lay into Santo Caterina and wait for a good wind into Cahors that blows foul for Gisbon. If she ever gains Cahors, we'll never lay hands on her again short of open war. We must bring her in before that."

"A frigate or two placed between her and Cahors would put things to right in no time."

"Yes, if I had any to spare, Nath. But I need anything remotely resembling a frigate covering the Gap and the approaches to Arleonne. If Ardainne's Merentian fleet breaks free to join their Ocean Sea fleet, we'll be fortunate if our blockades are not reversed . . . or worse."

"An oversea invasion," Nath muttered grimly.

"Indeed. So, I cannot spare enough frigates to post a picket for the *Redemption*." Weymouth took a slow draw on his pipe while regarding Nath with a speculative gleam in his washed-out eyes. "But I do believe I can spare one for a few weeks to reconnoiter the coastal approaches to Cahors. What say you?"

"With all my heart, sir!" Nath barked, his mind afire with the opportunity. The ship that recovered the *Redemption* would become famous everlasting and her commander, well, her commander could not fail to see advancement. Weymouth was notoriously miserly with his interest, but that wouldn't matter a whit in comparison to the glory of redeeming the *Redemption*! "This is a singular honor, sir!"

Weymouth nodded absently and took a rolled chart from the edge of the desk. He spread the map out, anchoring its corners with a lamp and Nath's logs and ledgers. He circled an area of the Naveroñian coast with a thick, tanned finger.

"Last verifiable report we had of her was here, under the guns of Hertamosa. I think we can safely assume she has moved since then: probably to Puerto Galeno, but perhaps as far as Alcada—here."

Nath nodded, closely studying the areas the admiral mentioned.

"You shall have a packet of orders by noon tomorrow giving specific details, but suffice it to say that I desire you to take the *Alarum* to this area and attempt to locate the *Redemption*. If you can determine which harbor she has slunk to, I desire you to stand off and on to cover its approaches, there to endeavor to take the *Redemption* in the offing."

"Or cut her out if the opportunity arises?"

The admiral frowned and shook his head. "I do not think that would be wise. Both Alcada and Puerto Galeno are well covered by shore guns. With frigates so dear, I must forbid your risking the *Alarum* against shore batteries of such strength. While I trust you will not need the reminder, that proscription will be clearly worded in your orders."

Weymouth held Nath's gaze for a moment to add a moral underscore to his statement.

"Aye, sir," Nath said. "I'll see to the *Alarum*'s preparations immediately."

"If you find yourself short of any necessity, contact my clerk and I will remedy the situation."

Nath's face must have revealed his astonishment at those words.

"Did I not say this was a *personal* service, sir? Ourey was my protégé, and Earl Eoward Aixely and his toadies have made much of his loss of the *Redemption*. They were unable to use it to lever his stern into the sea lord's chair, but it worked admirably to pry mine from it.

Earl Aixely's feud with me made Viscount Morrin sea lord and made it very unlikely I'd ever hold the title myself."

Nath nodded gravely and wondered if the appointment of each sea lord resulted in a cyclone of political disaster.

"It was one of my protégés that lost the *Redemption*, whatever the circumstances, but she'll be recovered by a young officer whose interest is my own."

"It will be as you say, sir," Nath answered, amazed at the steadiness of his voice, considering the pounding of his heart and the chaotic reel of his senses. The Hero of Filsterhead had just announced an interest in his career! Familial connections and the kind support of former commanders was one thing, but the friendship of a bona fide hero of the realm was quite another. The rest of the interview, which consisted for the most part of an overview of the cruise and the most likely places to catch the *Redemption*'s trail, was overlaid with an odd buzzing behind his ears and his waistcoat suddenly seemed too constrictive to allow easy breathing. The condition was immediately exacerbated by the admiral's invitation to sit at his table during a dinner and ball to be held the following night.

"You may find the affair with the *Artagny* mentioned," Weymouth rumbled around his pipe, a faint gleam of amusement in his killer's eyes. "It seems unfair to make you wait to be feted until your dispatch is published in the *Naval Journal*, as I assure you it shall be. It will also provide an excellent opportunity for me to gently suggest that the worthies gathered at my table lend you whatever hands they can spare to replace those you've lost to prize crews. I also intend to reinforce your marine contingent. It would be a sad turn to track the *Redemption* down and have too few men to board her."

When he was finally dismissed, Nath was in such high spirits that he barely noticed the speculative gaze of the admiral's ill-aspected wretch of a clerk and made no more than an offhand and rather amiable fling at silently damning the old fool to hell as he swept past him and out of Admiralty House. He strode to the edge of the colonnade, mindless of the oppressive heat that settled around him like a mantle. Baring a fierce, unrestrained grin at the stars twinkling to life in the deepening royal blue of the Merentian night, Nath laughed.

A pair of local servants gave him a wide berth as they passed, released from their duties for the evening and on their way to their little apartments at the base of Admiralty Hill. Nath laughed again and took a step toward one of the coaches loitering outside the house to carry officers with late business back to the Admiralty Steps. His hand was half-raised to hail one of them when he recalled the state of his purse. Whatever its notional value tomorrow, it was still empty tonight. Even that sad realization coupled with the long, wearisomely hot and humid walk ahead of him could not dim the twin beacons of a heroic admiral's interest and an independent cruise that promised fame and glory at its end. He set off down the hill with a smile on his face and as much spring as his sailor's rolling gait would permit.

chapter 11

I s there something amiss with your new shoes?" Enid asked as Nath paused in the shade of the cobbler shop's awning to fuss with the shoe on his left foot. He cut a far more respectable figure now that he'd spent a little of the coin Weymouth's prize agent had allowed him on a new uniform, complete with new hose, shoes, and hat. The rest of his funds went to making up for what the yard lacked in supplies by purchasing them from commercial sources.

"No, there's nothing wrong with them," Nath assured her after straightening and stamping his feet in place a few times. He would have looked comical if not for his dour expression. "I'm just not used to shoes with any heel left to 'em. I'll have the set of their rake in time for the party, I'm sure."

Enid nodded but suspected his frowning discomfort had more to do with the pinch to his purse from buying powder, shot, and rations than his shoes pinching his toes. Altogether, despite the alleged generosity of the admiral's prize agent, he'd had very little to spend.

"The merchants of this place are rapacious. You could have bought three pairs of shoes in Ardainne for what you paid for them here."

Nath nodded and wiped his brow. The heat was horrendous. "It is the way of any port city. Few work harder for their pay than a sailor, and none are as mercilessly bilked of it at every turn."

"I'm no expert in such matters, of course, but it seems that the bilking began with your new prize agent. It is scandalous that a great warship like the *Artagny* should have brought you so little reward."

"Oh, old Japhot was wondrous fair in his assessment," Nath assured her. "The money he paid out was for several merchant vessels I sent into Gisbon. The *Artagny* hasn't been presented to the Prize Court yet."

"Your other prizes have arrived and undergone your piracy court's scrutiny. Why is she so tardy?"

"*Prize* Court," Nath corrected her. "I placed Bascombe under orders to take the *Artagny* back to Middlesea. It's a longer voyage, but she's less likely to run into Ardain patrols the nearer she approaches Albion."

"That seems a reasonable course."

"And a profitable one as well. The *Prize* Court at Middlesea will condemn the *Artagny* for far more than the bloodsuckers here in Gisbon."

Enid frowned. "This prize system of yours seems to encourage an avariciousness that might drive an officer to take unnecessary risks to enrich themselves."

"It might seem so to a landsman," Nath said, shrugging. "But the lords of Albion's navy—and Ardainne's as well—know that a lucrative prize is more likely to goad a reluctant officer to greater zeal than it is to turn a diligent officer foolhardy."

Enid's frown deepened, but she allowed the subject to rest. Nath's day had been trying enough without burdening him with an argument over an institution that would continue to prosper, no matter their opinion of it. Although the day began pleasantly enough with the easy and enriching interview with Ephram Japhot of Japhot and Hayes, the admiral's prize agent, it soon turned into a frustrating ordeal in the face of the monolithic intransigence of Gisbon's naval yard. It amazed Enid

that the most powerful navy in the world was supported by such an obviously corrupt and self-interested institution. Even with the admiral
of the Merentian Sea's writs under their noses, the lords of spar, tar,
paint, and powder refused to stir so much as a finger to rouse up any
of the much-needed supplies on Nath's list without first seeing their
palms crossed with hard currency. Even then, their efforts were half-
hearted and, for the most part, futile. In the end, Nath had been forced
to turn to private suppliers for fresh sails and decent powder for the
Alarum's starving guns and Enid had seen his respectably bulging
purse reduced to sad flaccidity. After purchasing a new uniform to
wear to the admiral's soiree, he was left with barely enough for his
steward, the pugnacious Mr. Alston, to convert into meager viands to
fill the captain's cupboard.

Enid was tempted to offer him a loan. After all, the estimable Mr.
Japhot had been perfectly sanguine about extending the admiral's
faith in Captain Nath to his ship's magister, the whole of which barely
signified against the carefully warded letters of credit in her sea chest
or the least of the rings she currently wore. She feared he might take
offense at such an offer from so recent an acquaintance, though, and
held her peace for the moment.

When Nath finally seemed satisfied with the fit of his shoe, she
asked if he knew of a reputable jeweler in Gisbon.

"A jeweler? I thought you said you were adequately prepared for
tonight's entertainment?"

"I am. This purchase has nothing to do with tonight's event."

"Hmm. Well, I seem to recall there is a jeweler somewhere on
Avery Street that some officers trade with. I cannot vouch for her
quality myself, however." He took her elbow and turned her down the
street. "I must warn you, though, that I doubt anything you commission will be finished before we leave."

She dismissed his concern with a slight shrug. "I'm sure I'll have no trouble finding what I need before we set sail again. If not here, then elsewhere."

Enid was correct. At first, the jeweler, used to dealing with officers in search of exquisite baubles to aid in the seduction of their seniors' husbands or wives, balked at such a simple commission. Enid offered her a price worthy of gold and emeralds and banished her reservations. The ring, she was enthusiastically assured, would be ready for her on the morrow.

"So," she announced as they stepped out of the jewelry shop and into the sweltering heat of the sun-swept Gisbon street, "that is the last of my errands ashore. The sorcerous tools I purchased will be delivered to the *Alarum* tonight. Alston can be trusted to see to their stowage in my workspace on the orlop should they arrive after our departure for Admiralty House?"

"He can, or else explain himself to me." Nath glanced from Enid to the jewelry shop door. "And speaking of explanations, if my curiosity does not offend your sense of privacy . . . That ring?"

"It is a necessary component to a sorcerous operation I intend to attempt before we set to sea again."

Enid paused to examine a sample of cloth displayed in one of Gisbon's quaintly anachronistic window displays. She folded it back into the sill tray and waved away the merchant attracted by her interest. Turning back to Nath, she waved the same hand airily. "You needn't worry, however. It is nothing that concerns the *Alarum* directly. It is more of a ritual to placate the dead than anything else."

"Oh, Lord!" Nath came to a sudden halt and addressed her urgently. "Redeemer save us! Do not loose some specter or ghost upon the barky, or the crew will never be the same! You would not credit the depth of their fearful superstition where spirits outside their grog ration are concerned!"

Enid smiled and put a reassuring hand on Nath's arm. "Upon my honor, I have no intent of inflicting any ghosts upon the *Alarum*, sir. Now, perhaps we should find you a new stock? Yours seems more a shade of faded blue than black."

As the coach trundled up the final switchback to Admiralty House, Nath tugged crankily at his stiff new stock and stole another glance at Enid, opposite him. He'd served with female officers before, some of them regular beauties, but never with one of such casual grace and apparently instinctive taste. He assumed the qualities must be innate to Ardain ladies, but he admired them nonetheless. Envied them a bit, too, he was forced to admit as he compared his rather drab appearance to her sartorial excellence. He could not fairly blame the disparity on the fact that he was constrained to a uniform. Enid had obviously selected her apparel with an eye toward marking herself as a serving sea officer, rather than a mere civilian attendee. The gown she wore was simple without being austere, and its deep blue hue instantly brought the Sea Service to mind. He could not help but notice that its décolletage, although perfectly respectable, suggested other types of service. He turned his face toward the heat-purpled glass of the coach window to banish the imprudent thoughts.

"Well, it seems we have arrived," Enid remarked matter-of-factly as the coach rumbled to a stop and the footmen struggled with the latches on its door. "I do not know the proper military precedence, I'm afraid. Who should disembark first?"

Nath smiled and clutched his hat to his breast. "This is a civil function, milady. It would be my honor to hand you down."

Nath stepped down from the coach and into the stifling heat of a Gisbon summer night and replaced his hat. Its band had a rough spot not yet smoothed by wear, a reminder of its newness that Nath found comforting. He assisted Enid and a somewhat-baffled Merryweather out of the carriage. Together they joined the immaculately turned-out throng of Gisbon's best wending their way through the colonnade and up the wide marble stairs leading to Admiralty House's official ballroom. He felt relatively plain compared to the opulence exhibited by some senior officers in attendance, but at least his uniform was clean, new, and respectable. He would not be shown up as a scrub in this crowd, nor would the officers he'd chosen to attend him. Enid's understated elegance had already attracted some admiring glances and Merryweather had used the promise of her prize money to secure credit toward the purchase of a new dress uniform.

Admiral Weymouth hailed Nath with a smile and a voluble greeting from the ballroom's broad, ribbon-festooned entrance. The old warhorse was posted there in full naval panoply to greet guests as they entered. His wife, a tall, aristocratic lady whose handsome face contrived to turn the lines of age to her advantage, stood beside him.

"Captain Nath! Pray, allow me to present you and your officers to Lady Hypatia Weymouth."

Nath made his most elegant leg before the lady as her husband continued loudly enough to be overheard by anyone on the stairs.

"Captain Nath is the young officer of whom I spoke earlier. He led the gallant little *Alarum* against the much larger Ardain *Artagny* frigate, a notable-enough act on its own, but even more so when laid alongside the string of captures before it."

Nath accepted her hand in his and bowed his head rather than indulge in the increasingly popular and, to his mind at least, vulgar practice of pressing his lips to a strange lady's hand without her leave. Lady Hypatia raised an appreciative brow and gave his hand an amiable if decorous squeeze.

"I see that some young officers still adhere to the old practices of courtesy rather than embrace any fly"—she pronounced the word with infinite disdain—"affectation. It is a pleasure to meet you, Captain Nath, and I give you joy for your accomplishments."

Nath bowed, murmured his thanks, and stepped aside as Merry-weather and then Enid were presented to the lady.

"*Marquise* d'Tancreville?" Lady Weymouth repeated wonderingly, her eyes narrowing slightly as she gave Enid a second appraisal. "I rarely have the pleasure of greeting so exalted a grand seigneur in our remote little posting. I beg your pardon, milady! My husband and I should have made our courtesy to you, as your title has precedent over ours!"

Enid waved the apology away and said lightly, "My title is worth no more than the breath required to utter it. For all the tangible foun-dation upon which it rests I may as well name myself Impératrice de la Lune as Marquise d'Tancreville."

"You are as graceful as you are kind, milady, but what else should one expect from the scion of such a politically powerful and influential line?"

"We were not so powerful or influential to avoid contributing our heads to fertilize the weed of revolution. To my knowledge, I'm the last of my line and I only escaped Ardainne by dumb luck."

Lady Weymouth laid a consoling hand on Enid's arm and said, "And yet you are far from alone, my dear. I imagine you will find many of your family's old connections remain unbroken among the many emigres in Albion and, of course, your part in Captain Nath's gallant victory over the *Artagny* will earn you many admirers among native Albions as well. You may soon find yourself as influential in your new homeland as in your own."

Enid's smile was polite, but there was a faint chill in her voice as she answered. She was discomfited by the undivided attention Lady Weymouth heaped on her, given the impatient queue of guests await-ing their turn to present themselves and begin the serious business of eating, drinking, and dancing. Worse yet, there was a probing edge to the woman's questions and observations, which were rendered more worrisome by the prickling sensation within Enid's nose that warned her that more than cosmetic magic was nearby. She reflexively raised a minor ward and the sensation in her nostrils faded slightly.

"I won't detain you any longer, Lady d'Tancreville," Lady Weymouth said, her eyes glittering with amusement. "Perhaps we can speak together more privately at some point? My nose tells me we might become fast friends."

"It would be my pleasure." Enid stepped away from the greeting line and joined Nath inside the ballroom door. Merryweather had already absented herself to take full advantage of the fine buffet laid out at the opposite end of the room.

"What was that all about?" Nath asked in a tense whisper. "Is there something I should be aware of?"

"Many things, but my private conversations are not among them," she said in a bantering tone. "We should make way for others to pass before Merryweather has emptied every platter in the place!"

Nath nodded but felt a cold seed of doubt taking root despite his best intentions. First that odd ring that she'd been so evasive about, now this. He firmly believed officers had a right to the privacy of their own affairs, but secrets were another matter entirely. He would have to discuss this with Enid later, he decided. There must be absolute trust between a captain and his mage, after all. If he had not known that before, the way the *Alarum* had suffered until he won Dunaughy's full and genuine support had provided inarguable proof.

That he'd accepted an Ardain national as his ship's mage should be proof enough to Enid of the trust he'd extended to her on faith. He felt it was only reasonable to expect the same courtesy in return. He fought down resentment at the necessity of considering such matters at his first entertainment ashore since his cruise with Barrington. Nath vowed not to let the matter destroy his enjoyment of the evening.

That vow, it turned out, was the easiest to keep he ever made. He had taken no more than three steps toward the table laden with food and wine before a prosperous-looking, narrow-faced post captain with amazingly bushy muttonchops confronted him.

"Captain Nath, isn't it? I thought I overheard the admiral introduce you as such!" The captain grabbed his hand and pumped it energetically. "Wish you joy, sir! Wish you joy! Jarvies of the *Badger* frigate, sir!"

He gestured at a group of officers by the punch bowl, who observed the conversation with keen interest. "My fellows and I would be most honored if you'd share a glass with us and relate the particulars of your engagement with the *Artagny*!"

Nath flushed with pleasure at such open praise from a man who'd made post. "It would be *my* honor, sir, my particular honor! But perhaps you'd like to meet Lieutenant Merryweather as well, as she was key in the boarding action's success?" He called across the room for Merryweather, who hurried over with one hand holding a plate heaped with anything but cold pease pudding or hard biscuit and the other clutching a glass of powerful punch.

"What has become of Magister d'Tancreville?" Nath asked her. "She should describe her row with the *Artagny*'s magister. Impressive bit of spellwork. I believe you'll agree upon hearing of it, sirs . . ."

"If you mean that lovely creature yonder," one of the gathering ring of post captains said, pointing to where Enid stood, attracting a crowd of officers herself, many of whom wore the plain uniform of a magister. Others were obviously interested in admiring more than her sorcerous skills, however. Nath felt an odd tugging that exacerbated his resentment toward her secretive behavior and sensibly dimmed his enjoyment of the moment. But only for a moment. The eager faces of his audience as he recounted the taking of the *Artagny* coupled with his joy in telling of it produced an inner glow that no shadow of melancholy could stand against.

"It is a pleasure to meet one of Ardainne's best, whom Fortune has allowed to raise arms against her oppressors." The cavalry major's white, even teeth flashed in a smile that was bright against his soldier's tan. "There are quite a number of your countrymen in my regiment, as a matter of fact. Fine horse riders all. Your people truly have a natural gift for the noble virtues."

Enid smiled icily. "If that were true, as flattering as it is, I somehow doubt my countrymen and I would be so beholden to Fortune for allowing us to raise arms against the Theocratic Republic. Unless you count that wretched body among the fine and worthy things my country has produced?"

The major coughed, brought to a stand. "Well, um, no, certainly not . . ." He fumbled with the tassel of his sword for a moment, searching for another route of advance and was promptly ridden over by one of his own colonels.

"I believe what the major meant to say is, the best of Ardainne are among the best in the world." He took Enid's hand and pressed it to his lips and cast a mocking, sideways glance at his discomfited junior officer. The expression froze on his face as Enid delicately extricated her hand from his grasp with a haughty sniff.

"What nonsense. It is self-evident that the best of any group would be found among the best in general. Even the best dung would qualify for such a comparison. Do you think to flatter me by comparing my people to dung?"

"I made no such comparison," the colonel blustered. "I . . ."

"Pray excuse the interruption," Merryweather said, appearing at her side like a delivering angel and holding out her hand in invitation. "But this piece was written with the Ardain échange de bonheur in mind, and I would admire a lesson in the dance's evolutions from someone who knows them far better than I."

"I would be delighted, Lieutenant Merryweather," Enid said, and parted company with the crestfallen officers without a word of apology.

"You have my gratitude for the rescue," Enid said, settling into the meter with Merryweather. "My patience for tiresome attention is in short supply and I must husband it carefully if I'm to last the night without inciting an incident."

"I am happy to be of service." Merryweather's eyes sparkled with humor. "But I must admit to having a personal investment in cutting you out from that crowd of lubbers."

"Oh, and what might that be?"

"Your graceful comportment is visible to any with eyes," Merryweather said. "When I first saw you cross the deck on the *Alarum*, I thought, there is a woman I must dance with. Dancing is one of many passions I cannot indulge in aboard ship, sadly, but now I find myself with the opportunity to fulfill my ambition and learn new movements all at one go."

Enid surveyed the dancers around her and saw they moved with a sedate complacency that did not suit the dance at all. The precisely rotating dancers carefully avoided crossing the orbits of other couples and replicated the base movements of the dance with the clockwork precision of a minuet. Enid was appalled by the sight.

"The échange de bonheur may not be suitable for the more proper deportment of Albion's gentlefolk," Enid said. "It is meant to provide dancers with an opportunity to showcase their passion above their precision. The basic movements are only a structure—the dance's geometry is not rooted in the mind, but rather in the heart. Or, more accurately, the loins."

"Then let us show them how the dance is meant to be performed," Merryweather said as the échange's movements brought her lips near Enid's ear. She was at once surprised and elated at the whisper's husky timbre.

The pair followed the dance's path through its first movement, meant to represent the nascent attraction and preliminary advances of two new lovers. Merryweather was, indeed, a competent dancer, and Enid found her partner eager to elaborate beyond the rote steps. By the opening bars of the second movement, which portrayed the recognition and acceptance of an eventual tryst, their steps were sure and forthright as the mutual pursuit evolved into a melding of passionate rather than romantic intent. They were both flushed by their efforts, although Enid assumed the misting of sweat on Merryweather's brow was, like her own, the product of more than athleticism and Gisbon's balmy evening air.

By the third and final movement, all but a few couples whose imitations had locked them into the same hot gravity as Enid and Merryweather abandoned the floor to join a hushed ring of spectators. The tempo increased incrementally as the échange drew them closer together and the steady thrum of the cello and viola seemed to synchronize with their pulses and rumble in their chests. They found themselves with their hands lifted high over their heads, fingers tightly interlocked, and their lips mere inches apart as the final chord faded. Enid stared into Merryweather's eyes and saw the same determined, predatory heat that burned in her own.

"We must dance again," Merryweather said. "Soon."

Enid nodded wordlessly as they separated, bowed to each other and to the applause of the onlookers whose faces were one part admiration and another part shame. Inwardly, Enid scoffed at them. There was no place for shame in the échange de bonheur.

———

Nath had no great ear for music, but the quartet was lively enough to set his toe tapping. He'd been passed from one conversational group to another and told his story a dozen times now. All the wine and punch that had eased its telling coursed through his veins, suffusing him with an inner, affable glow of such self-satisfied warmth. After the shameless Ardain dance, Nath found himself the recipient of a fresh round of partygoers begging for "a drink with you, sir!" Each conversation turned inevitably to questions regarding his relationship with his magister and whether she was available for the approach of respectful suitors. He countenanced the intrusion into his private life and Enid's virtue for a short time and then migrated to verge of the merrymakers and drank the admiral's fine wine for an hour or two.

He stood on the edge of the dance floor, his hands clasped officerly behind his back, and watched couples turn and whirl in rhythmic tides from one end to the other. One pair of gentlemen were particularly graceful, and he watched their movements with admiration. *Devils on the dueling salle*, he thought. Watch out for the ones that can dance, his old dueling master had instructed him, they are likely killers.

His ears perked up at a conversation between two captains who stood a short distance behind him, but he didn't turn to join. His appearance would instantly switch the topic to the defeat of the *Artagny* and he was interested in a story other than his own.

"I tell you, Genilden, it is no exaggeration," one of them said, and Nath recognized him as a post captain a few years his senior by the name of Shae. "The Darghaur are venturing forth from their fastness and poking their noses into the Shards."

"And I tell you, sir," the gentleman named Genilden replied, "that every time one of the eyeless devils' galleys is seen east of Cape Despair, the Shards' great merchant barons begin screaming 'Darghaur invasion' and demand the protection of ships put to better use against the damned Rats."

Nath took another long sip of deliciously citrus tinged-shrub and thought, *Well said, Genilden, well said!* Shae, on the other hand, was unconvinced and continued with news from the Far West.

"I'll grant you that the wealthy dophirs are an excitable lot," he agreed. "But Commodore Bishop is a month late returning to Far Port, and it is feared he was lost with his command."

Gods, Nath thought, *that can't be true!* He followed Captain Bishop's career with interest because he was a distant relative. He remembered reading in the *Naval Times* that Bishop had been dispatched to the Shards to deliver Far Port's new governor and undertake an extended patrol to discourage any cooperation between the Rats and the pirates that prowled the Shards. He was in command of the *Tireless*, 74, the *Venture*, 40, and the *Firebrand*, 40, three new ships, all well provisioned and crewed. Any one of them would have been more than a match for several Rat corsairs or light frigates that currently cruised the Shards. Together and under Bishop's capable command, they were practically invincible. Unless they were overtaken by a Darghaur war barge.

Distracted by the conundrum, he barely noticed Enid's approach and greeted her touch on his arm with a pleased but simple-minded expression.

"Captain Nath," she said, leaning forward to speak quietly near his ear, filling his nostrils with the delightful and arousing scent of Lithain water, "perhaps we should take our leave? The hour has grown late. Did you not say every moment must count on the morrow?"

"Ah. Yes, even so." He glanced around, still smiling in a pleasant muddle. "We should gather up Merryweather, though. Wouldn't do to maroon her, would it?"

She guided him toward the door with a firm hand on his elbow. "She awaits us in the coach, sir."

They gave their regards to the admiral on the way out, their passage well lubricated by his intoxication, which matched or exceeded Nath's. They stepped into the muggy warmth of the early morning. No sooner had she bundled Nath into the interior of the coach than he was asleep, his head resting on the shoulder of the equally somnolent Merryweather. Enid sighed and cooled the interior of the coach slightly with a half-hearted cantrip and leaned back to let the wine fumes dissipate from her head. Fortunately, she had not been as free with the spirits as her fellow *Alarum*s. She'd needed a clear head to deal with Hypatia Weymouth.

That woman, Enid thought, would have been quite at home in the court of Achard XIV. She had a keen nose for evasion and a subtle conversational technique that left one wondering just how much they'd revealed each time they opened their mouth. In retrospect, her brief exchange with the woman felt more like an interrogation than a conversation. Or perhaps an interview? If so, she felt she'd comported herself well. While she had no particular secrets to keep, she took some satisfaction in preventing the Earl's perspicacious lady from prying anything from her she didn't wish to share. She didn't believe she'd necessarily found an ally, but she was certain she had not gained a foe.

Nath and Merryweather recovered enough on the winding trip down to the steps to rouse themselves out of the coach and signal the *Alarum* for a boat. They could also make their way up the side and into their cabins under their own power. Enid had no desire to test her agility in a gown against the mute treachery of the battens, so she troubled Yeardley, the officer on watch, for the use of a bosun's chair. He helped her to the deck with an unnoticed deference that bordered on worship.

⊰ ⊱

"So you spoke to her?"

The admiral felt some regret as the philter his wife had prepared for him washed away the lugubrious warmth of a fine and genteel drunk. He wouldn't miss the pounding head and stormy gut in the morning, though.

"But of course, dearest," Hypatia answered in a low, comforting tone. She chilled a cloth with a pass of her hand and used it to dab at the lingering perspiration on his forehead. They'd seen the last of the guests able to steer under their own wind on their way, an arduous task for a man as easily punished by Gisbon's heat as her poor Cormaend. She escorted him upstairs to their bedchamber and assisted him into his bedclothes. His limbs were still a bit heavy from the remnants of his earlier near-stupefaction and the gathering effects of fatigue. He was no dotard, she thought as she helped him into bed, but he wasn't as young as he once was. "You don't have to worry about her. She has more reason to hate the Theocrats than anyone in Albion. She's not one of their agents."

"How can you be so certain?" Weymouth gave his wife an appreciative squeeze that proved he was neither too old nor insensitive to her beauty. "Because she's noble? The Rats have other nobles among their ranks."

"None that have so much to lose if the Theocrats consolidate their hold on Ardainne, or so much to gain if they are overthrown."

Weymouth's ears pricked up at the sound of that. "So highly placed as that, then? Perhaps she'd be better off in a more protected location than a sixth-rate frigate? Particularly one employed as perilously as the *Alarum*?"

"No, no. Leave her where she is to finish what she's started." Lady Hypatia's breath was warm and sweet in his ear as she settled next to him in the bed. "And let us leave the question altogether for now and finish what *you* have started."

Enid gathered up her ring from the jeweler on Avery Street in the morning. The rest of the ship's stores were loaded by the afternoon, their stowage manfully supervised by a bleary-eyed, sour-faced Lieutenant Merryweather. The crew, she observed, was nearly as out of sorts over their lack of debauchery ashore as Merryweather and Nath were from too much of it. To be so close to one of the Royal Navy's most famous liberty ports and not be allowed so much as an evening of roistering struck them as prodigiously grievous. Oddly, though, Nath's appearance on the quarterdeck with a face drawn and pain-pinched from last night's overindulgence produced a more cheering effect. The crew seemed to take heart from his misery, which was obvious no matter how heroic his efforts at stoicism.

"It is good the ol' man got to cut a dido or two ashore," she over-heard Hornesty say to a grumbling landsman in her division. "You owe all th'prize money ye been countin' inside that thick head o'yourn t'him. Give 'im joy of it and think of the carouse ye'll be able t'afford after *this* cruise!"

The landsman frowned, unconvinced, and snarled, "Cruise t'where, I ask ye? T'where, in such a tearin' great rush?"

She shared the landsman's question and hoped Hornesty would have an answer, or at least a theory, to satisfy them both. All she heard was the older woman's assurance that wherever the *Alarum* was bound, wealth and glory awaited. Perhaps that was so, Enid mused philosophically as she went belowdecks to her workspace in the orlop and began preparing the ring. Still, it would be comforting to know the route taken to all that treasure and fame.

She suspected there was more behind Nath's grim expression than last night's wine and rum. Those suspicions deepened when, shortly before setting sail the next morning, a contingent of fresh marines marched aboard to augment Lieutenant Harcourt's command.

chapter 12

The *Alarum* plunged and rolled in the aftermath of a sudden summer squall that erupted with brief and impotent violence two days out of Gisbon. The small knot of crew members gathered in the cover of the fo'c'sle were no more bothered by the ship's motion than they were by the occasional misting of warm sea spray produced as the ship's bluff bows cut the waves. The presence of the ship's new mage a short distance away was another matter, however, and one that elicited frequent wary glances and constrained conversation to a low murmur.

"You can't be sure what ye heard," Landon Averill, one of the *Alarum*'s respected part-of-ship captains, muttered against the subdued clash of wave against bow. "We have no ken a'what a sorceress a'her powers may get up to in her workroom. She may well a'been palaverin' with some ol' Spells back in Gisbon for all we know!"

"A foreign sorceress at that," Clotty, one of the topmen, added with a sour glance over his shoulder at the elegant noblewoman standing at the rail, her raven hair loose and trailing out like tendrils of black smoke caught in the squall's last gasp of wind. He found the mage's beauty added to his fearful suspicion of her. "Mayhap she was passin' word on our course back t'some Rat Confessor."

"No, damn you all," Master's Mate Kendal growled, glaring them all into silence. "It was Dunaughy, dammit! I'd rec'nize that canny ol' bastard's brogue in a gale with an ear full o' Markham's pease slop! She were talkin' t'the *dead*. All o'you know what that means."

Those present exchanged dread-filled looks and made whichever sign with which their faith or superstition greeted such fell news. There was no worse luck than having a ghost-talker aboard. They were dreadful enough ashore where they drew the spirits of the dead not yet passed to their reward like lodestones gathered iron shavings, but at sea the matter was even more perilous. Every sailor knew that the bottom of the sea was a tangled boneyard of drowned sailors, most of whom died as they fought to keep their battered vessels afloat. Died, in other words, unshriven, their souls forever entombed within the green depths. It was obvious to the meanest of wits among them that for every spirit a ghost-talker on land might summon, they would attract a score or more at sea . . . and each of those ghosts brought with it a burden of bad luck and implacable enmity for the living. Bad luck for a landsman meant a poor harvest, sour milk, or some such triviality. Bad luck for a seaman meant gales, shattered timbers and spars, and a last look at a storm-racked sky before the waves closed over their face and cold water filled their lungs.

"Mayhap someone should speak t'the captain about it . . . ," one of the other larbowlines suggested reluctantly, her voice cracking slightly as she cast a fearful glance in Enid's direction.

Averill shook his head. "No. Wouldn't be proper like. Might carry a smell o'conspiracy with it an' none of us wants t'sing at the grate or dance at the yard for that, do we?"

"None of us want t'be dragged down by ghosts t'feed the worms, either," Kendal barked, causing a half dozen eyes to dart aft. The mage was gone, though, so Kendal continued with the same venom. "I'll not see us all damned out o'fear o' offendin' some pup of a jumped-up luff!"

"You'll see yer worthless hide flogged 'round the fleet and hung like the dog ye are if ye keep actin' the mutinous fool!" Averill took a handful of Kendal's slop tunic and jerked him close, putting his superior height to good use as he glowered down into the shorter man's upturned, hostile face. "An' ye'll hang alone, damn ye, fer there ain't a one of us who'd risk the rope for your sorry neck! The captain ain't done nothing but good by us an' if he trusts this foreign Spells, so'll we till we have better cause than yer yammerin' t'change the set o'our sails!"

He pushed Kendal away with a savage thrust and gave each of the others such a fierce look they ducked their heads and nodded in mute, reluctant agreement before slowly dispersing.

Kendal watched them leave, an expression of utter contempt twisting his face into a mask of hatred.

"We'll see about you, Mr. Averill, and about yer boot-lickin' curs as well. We'll see what Master Harde has to say about trustin' your puffed-up lumpkin of a luff with *his* barky!"

Enid looked up at the soft rap on her door. She recognized it as Yeardly's and gave a satisfied nod. He had arrived exactly at the specified time, just as he had for the last two lessons. She cleared the notes from her desk and placed them carefully in a leather portfolio. Dunaughy's exasperated sigh susurrated silently in her mind.

"I agree the lad has some talent," Dunaughy's whiskey-and-cigar-voice tenor purred between her ears, "but we were reaching the culmination of a challenging formulation that might well save your ship at some point. Surely your own education should take precedence over— never mind then."

Even as Dunaughy protested in her ear, Enid called out, "Enter."

She rose to greet Mr. Yeardly, who was still bashful after his second visit to her berth. He stood in the doorway, holding a straight-backed chair he'd borrowed from Dr. Rondelle. Enid smiled and stepped out of his way.

"Please, Mr. Yeardly, take your place!"

He shuffled carefully past her and set the chair on the other side of the writing table and sat down once she'd taken a seat herself. She waited patiently as he produced a journal and pencil from his coat pockets, arranged them precisely on the desk, and then looked up expectantly. She smiled inwardly, pleased with the display. Whatever else Mr. Yeardly might be, he was eager to learn.

"Our last couple of lessons were a review of the basic foundations of the Art," Enid began. "And I'm happy to say that your attentiveness to Magister Dunaughy's lessons have set your feet on solid ground. I notice, however, that while you are very proficient at prepared for-mulations—spells, if you will—you are less confident with impromptu ones. We will begin addressing that today and it will be our focus for the next several lessons."

Yeardly frowned but nodded.

"You disagree with my assessment? Please, speak freely. I believe a mentor and their student must be in honest accord with each other for either to prosper at their task."

"I don't disagree at all, Magister," Yeardly said cautiously. "But I wonder if a sea officer requires much more than a few spells. After all, the ship's mage is there if any sophisticated workings are required."

Enid resisted the urge to scoff, and said evenly, "Where was the *Alarum*'s mage before I assumed his post?"

Yeardly's frown deepened. "Dead, but . . ."

"But what?"

"It flies in the face of tradition for a lieutenant to be too deeply schooled in the Art!"

"Fortunately, you are not a lieutenant, Mr. Yeardly," Enid drawled. "Now, shall we continue?"

Yeardly opened his mouth, closed it, and then mumbled, "Yes, Magister."

Enid eased the young man into magic's deeper waters, explaining that "formulations" were intellectual constructs upon which a mage might hang one's intent while casting about for the appropriate elemental. It could then anchor the elemental in place while the mage pitted their will against it to secure the desired service.

"This framework is not required," Enid said. "It is a crutch for the neophyte or ungifted. In fact, for a person of my ability or yours, though I daresay you'll doubt me, it is an impediment. The time and, more critically, *energy* required to recall or construct a formula is wasted."

Yeardly nodded his understanding. After scribbling a few notes, he looked up and asked, "But how does one work magic without a formula?"

Enid patted a small pile of books on her desk. "These books and a thousand more strive to explain that, often in terms mathematical or poetic. The truth is that each caster must approach unfettered power in their own way. They must become the formula."

"So, you lean toward the poetical explanation," Yeardly stated with a covert twinkle of amusement in his eye. "I'm still not certain how I can become a formula."

"You already are the formula. When you cast a preformulated spell, you *are* the formula. The paper from which you memorized the formula cannot activate the formulation. Nor can simply reading from a page. The formula can only actualize after you have internalized it, powered it with your essence, and directed it with your will."

"I think I understand in theory, but I fear the practice is beyond me."

"It is not," Enid assured him. "Here. See this unlit candle on my desk? Light it."

"How?"

"Are there salamanders in the room?" Enid asked.

"Of course," Yeardly answered confidently. "They can be found anywhere there is the potential for fire."

"So, there is no reason to summon one."

"I understand, but how will I bind it to my will without a formula?"

"Why must you bind it to your will? There is potential for fire in the candle, is there not?"

"There is."

"So, there must be—"

"A salamander with an affinity for the candle!"

Enid smiled encouragingly. "Even so!"

"If I bend my will to the candle's potential for flame, the salamander with an affinity for burning the candle should light it for me."

"Not should. Will. Clear your mind and try it now."

Yeardly took a deep breath and before it was fully drawn, the candle flickered alight.

"I did it!" He stood up so quickly that the chair toppled over behind him, to rest against the curve of the ship's hull. "Did you see that? I did it!"

"I saw," Enid said with a laugh. "And half the ship must have heard as well."

Yeardly set the chair upright and returned to his place at the desk. He grinned excitedly, happily glancing from the lit glim to Enid. "There was a moment of resistance—it seemed to last forever, and I was about to give up. Then I saw clearly!"

"It took you no more than the space of a heartbeat. The tricks casting plays on one's mind is something we'll study later. What did you see?"

"It's impossible to describe," Yeardly said, his grin fading. "Not shapes, but . . . patterns? They shifted like a kaleidoscope until the candle lit."

Enid leaned across the desk and placed her hand over the young man's, which still shook with excitement.

"Most practitioners do not see what you saw," Enid said. "They describe a more symbolic vision. Salamanders as sparks or tiny flames, sylphs as clouds, undines as fat drops or streams of water, and so on. This indicates that they are still bound by intellectual structures that can be distracting and, worse, deceptive."

"What did you see the first time, Magister?"

Enid stiffened and withdrew her hand. "I saw . . . fundamentally what you saw."

In her head, Dunaughy said, "This is the first time I've heard you lie, Lady d'Tancreville. I saw what you saw as he asked the question. What . . ."

She willed Dunaughy to silence and smiled apologetically at Yeardly, who looked concerned.

"All is well," she said. "I was drawn back by memory for a moment, but you have my full attention now."

Yeardly nodded slowly and latched on to the tail of the topic with the alacrity of a foxhound. "Fundamentally the same, but different?"

"Yes, we all see something different. You describe it as shifting patterns. I likened it to undulating threads."

"What is it?"

"A perspicacious question," Enid said. "And one that is rarely heard from one of your youth. It is the Wall of Creation, according to d'Alismere, the father of arcane formulism. It is formed of the building blocks of creation, the materials, though immaterial, of which the world is made and manipulated."

"What is on the other side? The void?"

"Far from it. If the Wall of Creation comprises the building blocks of reality, beyond it are the tools to bend those blocks entirely to one's will. It is there that the very greatest of magic is performed unbound by the rules or reality of creation. Only mages that are the most gifted of practitioners can access that level of power without being driven mad, slain, or consumed by it."

"Mages such as yourself, then."

Enid chuckled. "I've had glimpses of that power, but I've never commanded it. My uncle was able to do so with some effort but refused—even at the cost of his own life."

Yeardly's brows raised inquisitively. "Why?"

"He believed—and taught his students—that it is impossible to know the consequences of pretending to godhood. Even the gods themselves couldn't foresee that their act of creation would spawn the Darghaur. What horrors might we unleash?"

"Copper-bottomed reasoning," Yeardly said with a slow nod.

"Indeed," Enid said. "Now, let us see if you can snuff the candle in the same way you lit it."

Since the evening of Admiral Weymouth's ball, Enid made it her habit to take some air on deck during Lieutenant Merryweather's evening watch, a practice that Nath endorsed, believing that Merryweather used her spare time to further Enid's knowledge of the mysteries of the ship and life aboard her. He was correct in so far that most of their conversations turned on nautical matters. However, these evening classes also allowed for less formal communication that deepened their friendship through familiarity. Tonight Enid stood at Augusta's side gazing studiously down at a chart of the region. They'd finished discussing the meaning of the various markings and scribbles on the map some time ago, but it still provided an admirable excuse for quiet conversation with their heads together.

"He is a natural mage," Enid muttered, while tracing a random line on the chart. "I've rarely seen the like, especially in one as young as Yeardly, who has had only the most basic magical education. It is a shame to see his potential wasted as a mere mid!"

"I doubt he'd agree with your assessment," Augusta said with a grin. "And I beg you never to characterize his service as a waste within his earshot. He would disagree and hotly, I'm sure."

Enid nodded. "You would know best. It simply irks me that he is not in a decent school receiving instruction from—"

"From whom?" Augusta interrupted. "I'm not a sorcerous adept, but I know superior talent when I see it. You pretend someone at some boring school ashore would be a better mentor than you for a young hotspur like Yeardley?"

Enid frowned. "There is some sense in what you say. I demanded obscenely high wages for classes in Ardainne before the Theocracy. It is not as if I have no experience in such tutelage, but . . ."

"And consider this," Augusta said. "When you first devoted yourself to the study of the great arts, how would you have reacted if someone you respected, even admired, suddenly announced that you were wasting your time and should become a sculptor instead?"

"I would say that they never saw my attempts at sculpture," Enid said. "But I take your point and will hold my tongue on the subject unless Yeardly broaches it."

"Perhaps even then," Augusta said. "Now, I've put some thought into places we must see together once we reach Albion. The Old Royal Theatre, of course, though I imagine Captain Nath will see to that. There is a bookstore near it that I'm told is packed with volumes devoted to dramas and the dramatic arts. We'll want to dine at Ordell's, which is frequented by actors, fabulists, and playwrights. And we simply must spend a night at the Green Queen's Rest, which, in addition to fine food and wine, boasts obscenely large, soft beds."

"Obscenely large and soft," Enid repeated.

"Even so," Augusta said.

"Perhaps we should start there."

chapter 13

The next afternoon found Master Harde and Captain Nath at the quarterdeck railing, carefully studying the rock-strewn Naveroñian coast through their glasses. Enid stood near at hand, admiring the wild clash between mountainous shoreline and the foam-crested waves crashing against it. Even from such a distance as their current position, the thunderous boom of the waves ending their long charge across the Merentian Sea against the rugged walls of impervious red stone was easily audible.

"Puerto Galeno lies beyond yon promontory, sir, which the Naveroñians call Monte Ybarre." Harde pointed toward a craggy thrust of land. "Mark ye the road what follows the shoulder of the mountains and winds round the coast? Most common in these parts as the interior is so up and down like as t'make it easier t'lay yer roads along the coast than t'try to run 'em straight from town t'town as we do at home."

"Most of their coastal towns are built at the mouths of rivers," Enid remarked absently. "They find a bit of flat space there and enough delta lands to support crops sufficient to feed them most years. The interior, once one has risen high enough, is more hospitable."

Nath nodded distractedly. Harde shot her a glance that made it clear he felt she was impinging upon his territory. And something more, she thought: a speculative distaste that she'd never seen from him before. She could think of nothing she'd done to offend the man, but then the mysteries of seagoing society were still relatively opaque to her. Perhaps she'd used some word that should not be uttered on the quarterdeck or had left her foot for too long on some sacred seam in the steadily rocking deck. She gave a resigned shrug and returned her attention to the lovely, if forbidding, shoreline.

Nath closed his glass against his thigh with a snap. "We will stand off and on here, twixt Puerto Galeno and Santo Caterina. We can plan with more exactitude later, Master Harde, if you will attend on me before dinner and bring your charts. Plan to dine with me as well. I have a matter to discuss with you and the other officers this evening."

"Aye, sir. There's a matter I need t'aquaint ye with meself," Harde said, glancing quickly in Enid's direction. Nath failed to notice the glance as he reopened his glass and resumed his study of the coastline.

"Yes, yes. We'll discuss it this evening," he muttered. "Set a good pair of eyes on watch. I want to be told the instant any southing sail is spotted. Carry on, Master Harde."

"Aye, sir."

Enid found something cold and impersonally inimical in the master's smile as he passed her. She frowned after him, absently fingering the plain silver ring on her right hand.

The captain's table boasted a considerably finer fare than she'd found on her first night aboard the *Alarum*. The company was largely the same, save that Yeardly and Rondelle were replaced by Master Harde. Harde had arrived early to discuss a private matter with the captain, and it was apparent that the audience had done no good for either of their moods. The two men exchanged dark glances throughout the meal and some of Harde's remarks verged on actionable insolence. Oxley, in stark comparison, contrived to arrive late and sat in stony, embarrassed silence throughout the entire affair.

After the table was cleared and a desultory round of toasts launched with the usual fond wishes for the king's health were made, Nath cleared his throat and announced, "As some of you have no doubt conjectured, Admiral Weymouth has done the *Alarum* the honor of entrusting her—and us—with a private mission of some importance. I fear I cannot give you the full details, but I can say—"

"Sir!" Master Harde half stood and slapped his open hand on the table with enough force to rattle the wineglasses upon it. " 'Ware what ye say in this company! Recall the warnin' I gave ye!"

"No, Mr. Harde!" Nath roared as he surged to his feet. "You recall your place! I have borne more impertinence from you than I can bear!"

Enid was astounded at the magnitude of Nath's sudden anger and the volume at which it was expressed. It seemed almost supernatural—much too fierce a wrath to be reasonably supportable by his slight form. "Now hear *my* warning: I will not have one of my officers slandered and the confidence of the crew shattered to support your obvious ambitions and self-serving grudges!"

Harde's eyes bulged, and his mouth worked silently for a moment before he hissed, "Why, you jumped-up whelp! Captain Ambrose would have—"

"Damn you and your beloved Ambrose," Nath shouted, the veins in his neck and forehead clearly visible. "I command you to silence!"

Harde quailed noticeably but regained enough of his bluster to scowl around the table and point an accusing finger at Enid.

"What sort o'spell has this ghost-talker laid on you that you'd hazard the king's ship t'defend her?"

The dreadful word "ghost-talker" brought everyone in the cabin up short with a gasp of shock. Enid found herself under the suspicious gaze of Oxley and Harcourt.

"That's right, sirs," Harde continued in a tone of unctuous malignity.

Merryweather's eyes hardened and her features went flat and expressionless. "Sir?"

"Stuff and nonsense!" Nath snapped. "Master Harde came to me with no more evidence than the word of one of his hand-picked rascals! I assured him the matter would be looked into discreetly, but he has ignored my wishes in the matter, a preference that will cost him his warrant if I have any say in the matter!"

"Rascal!" Harde puffed up in resentment at the choice of word. "This 'rascal' is our master's mate, Kendal! You know him of old, Lieutenant Merryweather, and if he says he heard this Rat parlaying with ghosts, you can set your accounts on it he did!"

"Yes, I know him of old," Merryweather drawled. "I know he was one of your particular creatures aboard the old *Brazen* and that he brags in his cups. He was made a mate because of the esteem you hold for him. Neither of these things suffices to merit blind trust regarding accusations against his betters, especially as the details of that accusation are still unknown to me."

"Then allow me t'acquaint ye with 'em more closely, sir. Kendal was on an errand belowdecks when he passed by Spell's workspace down in t'orlop when what did he hear but this Rat summoning up and conversing with the dead! She is a ghost-talker and y'know what the foremast jacks will think o'that!"

"Enough!" Nath roared, instantly silencing the sudden eruption of babble following Master Harde's accusation. In a lower, more menacing timbre, he continued, "Mr. Harde, you may consider yourself under arrest."

Nath silenced his protest with a curt slash of his hand. "I will not countenance an officer who treats his fellows with such contemptibly public disrespect. You are relieved until further notice. Lieutenant Harcourt, be so kind as to escort Mr. Harde to his quarters and place him under guard. When that is done, send word along for Mr. Gaines and rejoin us here."

Harcourt and the sergeant acting as a table servant took the enraged master in hand, their faces grim and set. As he was guided out of the cabin, Harde bitterly excoriated the gathered officers for allowing a rantipoling coxcomb's lewd favoritism to take precedence over the safety and good discipline of his command.

A long, uncomfortable silence followed Harde's removal. Enid sat stoically, pointedly ignoring the inquisitive glances of the remaining officers. Nath displayed an even colder reticence as he stared out the stern gallery windows, his hands clasped behind his back. His expression was a study in barely suppressed rage. He turned as Harcourt entered the cabin in the company of a white-faced and rather stricken-looking Mr. Gaines. Nath acknowledged the youngish-looking man's salute and briskly informed him that he was now the *Alarum*'s acting master.

"What of Kendal, sir? He is master's mate and . . ."

"And he preferred to report a potential hazard to the ship's discipline to Mr. Harde rather than to me or my lieutenants. I trust you would not have made the same sad error in judgment in his place?"

Mr. Gaines stiffened to rigid attention. "Absolutely not, sir!"

Nath's only acknowledgment of Gaines's assurance of undivided loyalty was an abrupt gesture for him and Lieutenant Harcourt to be seated.

"Since Mr. Harde's willful disobedience has made a discreet inquiry into Kendal's accusations against Magister d'Tancreville impossible, I'm obliged to look into the matter immediately. I call upon you gentles to bear witness and offer your opinions regarding the necessity of a court-martial."

A subdued chorus of assent circled the table and Enid found herself the focus of several gravely objective stares, each of which she entertained with an expression equally devoid of obvious emotion. With a peculiar synchronicity, both she and Nath steepled their fingers on the table. When the captain spoke, his voice was grim and flat. It was quite unlike his normal conversational voice, which was warm and gentlemanly, or his command voice, which was strident enough to pierce the roar of storm or combat. It was the voice of judgment, and it sent a chill up her spine.

"Magister d'Tancreville, attaching no question to your honor, I must ask you to swear that you will answer the questions put to you by myself and these, your fellow officers, honestly."

Enid answered with a cool smile. "Of course. I understand completely and do so swear."

"Mr. Harde and Master's Mate Kendal have accused you of summoning a ghost to commune with it. How do you answer this accusation?"

There was no trace of cordiality in Nath's voice.

"I have never summoned a ghost, nor any other spirit save those used in legitimate sorcery—sylphs, salamanders, undines, and the like," Enid answered with smooth, unhurried dignity.

"They have also accused you of being a ghost-talker. How do you answer that?"

Enid sniffed disdainfully. "If you thought I was a hedge wizard or charlatan, I doubt you would have asked me to serve as your ship's magister, Captain Nath. The accusation is preposterous."

"And yet it must be pursued. Now, answer directly: How do you answer the accusation that you are a ghost-talker?"

"I deny it. I am no ghost-talker, nor do I sell wards against the evil eye or beads to snare a lover's heart."

The captain studied her face for a long moment and then nodded peremptorily, apparently pleased with what he saw. "Good. Reminding those present that Lady d'Tancreville is a gentlewoman and the product of one of the world's most prestigious sorcerous academies, have you any questions for her?"

Nath cast a slow glance around the table, but no one offered any further questions.

"Stuff and nonsense," Harcourt commented, breaking the silence. "Harde is a fool and Kendal a known rascal."

Merryweather nodded grimly and snarled, "An attempt to divide the crew against one another and their officers. You'd best have his cur, Kendal, arrested as well, sir."

Nath shook his head. "He will be disrated, that is enough—and it is not the question at hand: Do you believe the magister should be held over for court-martial based on Harde's and Kendal's accusations?"

All of them answered firmly in the negative, the new master a bit too loudly.

Nath nodded and rose to fetch his logbook from its place on his small writing desk. He brought it to the table with a pen and pot of ink and wrote on one page with a swift, precise hand. Finished, he passed the log to Merryweather.

"Read it, Lieutenant Merryweather, and if you agree with the assessment, affix your signature below it. Let each of you do so and then we will be about our proper business."

When the log finally shuffled to Enid, she found it contained a bald and absolutely accurate account of the accusations against her and her answers to them followed by a brief paragraph indicating that the undersigned had agreed that the charges were unfounded and required no further action.

"You need not sign it, Magister," Nath informed her. "But you may add to it if you feel I have omitted anything to the detriment of your honor and reputation."

Enid pushed the log across the table to Nath. "I have nothing further to add. Will Harde be held under arrest until we return to Gisbon?"

"Yes. Why?"

"I understand he is the by-blow of an aristocratic lady?"

Nath instantly saw where the question led. "Yes, he is known to be the bastard son of Lady Therusa of Owick. But he was not truly the author of the accusations against you. Giving him the lie would only revert to Kendal, who is purely of common birth."

"I am not referring to Kendal's accusations. They mean nothing to me. Harde has called me a Theocrat, and that is a lie that cannot be left unpunished." Enid raised a hand calmly as several voices were raised at once.

"I will do nothing to jeopardize the discipline of this ship, but he must answer for this lie. I understand it is frowned upon for challenges to be issued at sea, so I will wait until we have returned to Gisbon."

"Do as you will ashore, Magister," Nath answered with steel in his voice. "But do not give him the lie until the cruise is finished. I forbid you from seeking his company until you are both ashore at Gisbon."

Enid bowed her head in acknowledgment of the command and smiled. "Never have I been given a ban more to my liking, sir. It will be as you say."

"To our business, then. As I said, Admiral Weymouth has honored us with secret orders of great import. We are to take a ship for him, a particular ship whose capture will be a great moral victory for Albion."

Enid watched the eyes of the officers around her widen and then narrow in sudden speculation. They exchanged quick glances, all obviously thinking the same thing, although what that thing was, she had no idea herself. After a pause, whose purpose was apparently to allow just such a shared revelation, Nath continued, "We will stand off and on from Monte Ybarre for the next two weeks. We'll no doubt have plenty of opportunity to take prizes, but we will be as abstentious as Portella's older sister. We will save our favors for a very specific suitor. I realize this may cause some dissatisfaction among the ship's people, but I conjure you all to reassure them that the kisses will be sweeter for the wait."

Enid doubted if many of the men recognized the allusion to Bazin's *Three Sisters of Gyronne*, but their self-satisfied smiles as they nodded made it clear they took their captain's meaning nonetheless.

"It is imperative that we ensure the new men are as thoroughly drilled as possible," Nath continued. "But I fear we may not indulge ourselves in live fire. The Rats are even tighter with their powder than the Admiralty and I very much desire to be taken for a Rat. Work the men at running the great guns in and out until the new men are worked in as smoothly as possible with the old. When the prize shows herself, we must be ready to take her."

Lieutenant Oxley cleared his throat and asked creakily, "How shall we know her when we see her, sir? The prize, I mean?"

The question elicited some low chuckles and knowing looks exchanged between the other officers, but Nath raised a hand to silence them and answered earnestly, "Thank you for asking, Lieutenant Oxley: You will fetch me, no matter the time of day or night, whenever any ship is sited. I will identify the prize myself. I am intimately familiar with her."

Lieutenant Oxley sat straighter in his chair, obviously affected by the respectful tone of the answer.

Nath turned to the marine lieutenant. "I assume, Lieutenant Harcourt, that your men will not object to eschewing their lobsters in favor of more nondescript coats while above deck?"

Harcourt's face melted into what Enid could not help but think of as an amiable smile as he answered. "Oh, I'm sure they'll miss 'em, sir. The stocks especially. But they're a doughty lot and will prosper despite their disappointment."

Nath chuckled and stood. "Very well. I have my orders and now you have yours. A last drink with you, and then to your stations."

chapter 14

Word of Harde's arrest was common knowledge among the crew before Captain Nath had finished briefing his officers on the *Alarum*'s private orders. The mood of the ship when Enid emerged on deck was subdued and wary, reminding her of the breathless, still hours before a fierce summer storm. She practically fled to her little berth off the side of the gunroom, but no sooner was the thin door closed behind her than it was rattled by an insistent knock. She half expected to find a mob of common sailors, intent on casting her overboard when she opened the door. Instead, she found Rondelle, his unpleasant face screwed up into its usual disapproving frown.

"I beg your pardon, Magister," he said in a tone bereft of the slightest note of apology. "I realize the hour is growing late, but there is a matter I must speak to you about at once. In private."

Enid groaned inwardly but stepped aside to allow the surgeon to enter her cabin. Without asking, he took the chair, leaving her to make do with one of her sea chests. Before she could offer him wine or tobacco, Rondelle exclaimed, "I have heard about Harde's incarceration and find no cause to regret it. He is as impertinent and disagreeable a man as ever graced a jail cell, and inevitably, he has found his way into one."

Enid made no answer but thought that if impertinence and unpleasantness were grounds for imprisonment, Harde would soon find a cellmate in Rondelle, who continued in a more accusatory tone, "But whatever my feelings toward the rascal, I am given to believe that he was arrested for accusing you of speaking with ghosts. Is this true?"

"No." Enid was gratified to see the man startle slightly at the vehemence with which she pronounced the word. "He was arrested for showing an insolent disregard for Captain Nath's person and command."

"But he accused you of speaking to ghosts? And you *denied* it?"

Enid nodded wordlessly. The direction this conversation would take was obvious, and she would need to handle Rondelle carefully. She had caused Nath enough trouble with Kendal and Harde—nothing good could come of it if more of his officers and men joined in the accusations against her.

"Then I am in an uncomfortable position." Rondelle's posture and voice smacked more of gloating than discomfort as he continued, "You see, I am quite familiar with the late Magister Dunaughy's voice and vocal mannerisms. The man was odious company and that loathsome singsong tone of his is ingrained so deeply in my consciousness that I fear I will never be rid of it. So there is no doubt in my mind that I would recognize that voice, should I ever hear it again, and hear it again I did, emanating from this very room and coupled in conversation with your own! Before taking this observation to the captain, I thought I would extend you the opportunity to explain yourself. After all, we are both educated people and recognize the truth can sometimes ring as falsely as a lie."

Enid's hand clenched into a fist at her side, but she resisted the urge to strike the man. After all, the reasonable portion of her mind argued, this awkward and unpleasant man probably felt his speech to be conciliatory and gently put.

"Harde accused me of summoning the dead to commune with them and of being what your countrymen call a ghost-talker. Both accusations are false."

Rondelle nodded slowly, a smugly discerning expression on his sour face that rankled her inexpressibly. "Like me, you are required by your calling to possess an exacting mind and I'm sure you share my disdain for imprecise language, so I have no doubt that you answered truthfully. You did not summon Dunaughy's shade, so it must have sought you out. You are not a ghost-talker, per se, but you have spoken with Dunaughy's ghost. Am I mistaken?"

"You are not, other than in your insistence on referring to Dunaughy as a ghost."

"Well, he is dead, is he not? And he speaks to you from beyond the grave? What else could he be but a ghost? I value precise language but have no love for sophistry."

Enid bit back a sharp retort and answered coolly, "It is no sophistry, I assure you. Let me put it in terms you are more familiar with: Both the heart and liver are internal organs required for life, yes? By your example, however, we could call either of them 'spleen,' as it also meets both criteria. Dunaughy is no more a ghost than your heart is a spleen, Dr. Rondelle."

"Oh, well said!" Rondelle brayed. "I take your point and accede to it! It is only to be expected that your profession would have its own jargon. So, if Dunaughy is not a ghost, what is he?"

"In my profession, I would categorize him as a relict," Enid answered carefully. "He has left a part of himself behind, the greater part, to be sure—his intellect and his love of service."

Rondelle rubbed his long nose thoughtfully for a moment. "He is a spirit that refuses to cross over, then, regardless of the nomenclature applied to his situation. How is this different from any other specter?"

"Ghosts, as your common sailor uses the term, are what educated folk such as ourselves would call a revenant," Enid said, schooling her tone to that of one professorial master to another. "They are jealous of the living and are intent on spiting or harming them. The revenant cannot tolerate the company of the quick, no longer being counted among them. These are your rustic haints that frighten the travelers in lonely places, or the phantoms that rattle chains or moan woefully to drive newcomers from their ancestral manse. Worse, they can be the terrible specters whose bony claws rend flesh and glowing eyes banish reason."

Rondelle nodded as if she were covering familiar ground for a deep philosopher such as he. Enid couldn't fail to notice the faint rolling of his eyes toward the darker corners of the dimly lit berth, as if he expected to see the looming form of Dunaughy's vengeful spirit.

"Dunaughy, or at least what is left of him, does not meet these criteria," Enid continued. "He has no malicious intent toward the living, I assure you, only an undying desire to serve his king."

Rondelle rubbed his sharp chin skeptically. "If he has no malicious intent toward the living, death has improved his nature considerably. How is it that this 'relict' can serve his king?"

"By familiarizing me with naval sorcery. There are considerations to practicing the High Arts at sea that would cause me no end of problems without his guidance. I'm sure it is the same with your practice, but you have had years to adjust to the differences between the ailments peculiar to sailors and those suffered by landsmen, and I have been thrown instantly into performing duties I have never even contemplated. As a fellow savant, I'm sure you understand my situation."

Enid shrugged and adopted an expression she hoped Rondelle would interpret as cordially deferential.

"Of course, it is perfectly clear to me now," Rondelle said slowly, his pinched brows compressing further. "Your competency is not with maritime magic, so it is only natural that you would accept discreet counsel from this relict of yours—and you were right in being circumspect about it. But tell me, how can you be certain Dunaughy's . . . relict . . . has no argument with the living? His complaisance with you may not extend toward the living as a whole."

Enid leaned forward and, with a conspiratorial smile, placed a comrade's hand on the doctor's shoulder. "Your wit is as sharp as your scalpel blades! You have cut directly to the pertinent question! I suppose it is your medical training that allows you to pierce distractions and see to the quick of a problem. I'm sure you've arrived at the same conclusion as I have regarding this sticky question!"

"Well," Rondelle said in his deepest voice after clearing his throat. "I have drawn my conclusion, but I believe it would be best to hear yours first, to ensure it corroborates my own."

"Of course. Of course," Enid said, nodding gravely. "It's best to treat this as the serious philosophic conundrum it is."

"I agree, and confess I'm with child to hear your theorem, Lady d'Tancreville."

"Then you shall have it, Dr. Rondelle. I admit the same question troubled me, although I didn't realize its import with the same rapidity. How could I be sure that Dunaughy wasn't felicitous toward me because of our shared vocation, yet might flay the skin from those who'd offended him? And, Dr. Rondelle, I own that in the brief time I've been in noncorporal communication with him, it is clear to me that his Murchadhan temper is always near the surface of his thin skin. The smallest criticism is bruising to his esteem. One sour glance is never forgotten once glimpsed. He is a vindictive creature in death, as I suppose he must have been in life."

"My experience supports your supposition," Rondelle said, and squinted surreptitiously toward the room's shadowed corners again.

"He seems also to be a man of precipitous passion, which he took little care in constraining." Here she glanced at Rondelle, who nodded grimly. "As I thought. And I also posited that you and he were at odds frequently, due to your rational, dare I say *scientific*, approach to problems as opposed to his more instinctual, undereducated reactions to challenges. I found that supported in his journal. It seemed he viewed you as his singular rival to intellectual supremacy aboard the *Alarum*."

"I suppose he would see it thus, the benighted wretch."

"Indeed, and I mourn to think of what the two of your minds working in concert could have accomplished, although I hope to see the results of a similar congress between ours. But back to the question at hand: How do I know that Dunaughy is as harmless to others as he is to me? Although I'm sure you've already seen through to the answer as I blather on, my thoughts running wild without the regimentation of a physician's finely disciplined logic."

"No, no," Rondelle protested. "It is a pleasure to observe the insightful workings of another professional mind. I do not think our scrutiny is as separated by our callings so much as you might infer. Pray, continue!"

"Well, it occurred to me that Dunaughy was a creature of impulse and malignity in life, quick to act on petty hurts and slow to forget them. So why would he be different in death if his cantankerous nature followed him there? And if he were capable of exacting all the small revenges that crowded the back of his pugnacious brain, whom would he have visited them on first? What person did he feel had oppressed and challenged him the most in life?"

Rondelle swallowed visibly. "Me?"

"Indeed! And have you suffered any spectral importunities? Rattling of chains, wailing, unwonted visions of death's dire visage?"

"No." Rondelle's voice was hushed at first, but grew stronger as he considered her words. "No. Not at all. Not so much as a cold draft or a whisper in my ear."

"There you have it. I'm sure we're of a mind on the matter now!"

"Yes," Rondelle said, some of his bluster returning with the pronouncement. "If Dunaughy were a ghost, he would have heaped abuse on me from beyond his watery grave. I would be so haunted that young Captain Nath would set me adrift in the *Alarum*'s smallest boat. So it follows, inarguably, that Dunaughy is not a ghost, but merely a relict of his best parts, left behind while the worst of him has been plunged into some pagan hell."

Enid clapped her hands together. "Exactly my reasoning, sir! I suppose I should leave it to you to explain all this when you report it to Captain Nath."

Rondelle produced an ostentatious pipe from his coat pocket and chewed its stem without loading or lighting it. After a moment, he looked up at Enid with what she felt must be his best estimation of the semblance of paternal concern. "No, I think not. In fact, I think reporting this would be unwise at best, and needlessly compromising at worst. Most of the officers aboard are good men, but woefully ignorant of matters such as these. And the common sailors? Savagely superstitious. They would have grave difficulty reconciling the differences between 'revenant' and 'relict.' They are so fearful of ghosts, I don't credit them with the wisdom to listen to our arguments, prima facie as they are, but would rather react with fear and unrelieved ignorance. No, no, Enid, I think it best we keep this matter between ourselves, as both dutiful professionals and inquiring savants."

"Then you are satisfied? You will not speak to the captain of it?"

"Of course not. You have been honest in every way and have made a decision based on your professional wisdom, which you have detailed for me most persuasively, and I would no more question a decision of yours than you would offer an opinion on the reduction of a femur!"

"I am happy to have your support, Dr. Rondelle," Enid said, not without a degree of genuine relief. "Now, as pleasant as it is to speak to a fellow scholar, the day has left me quite drained . . ."

"Say no more! It is time I checked on the recovery of a couple of malingerers in the sick bay. I will leave you to your rest. Seek me out should you require any guidance of a non-sorcerous nature. Do not let the gulf that separated Dunaughy and myself attach itself to us."

The surgeon took his leave with a condescending smile and a coy wink.

Sickened by the necessary simpering, Enid took immediately to her suspended cot upon Rondelle's departure, pointedly ignoring the increasing chill of the new silver ring on her right hand. By morning, she thought, Harde's accusations against her would spread through the ship like a plague. Experience taught her that there were no maladies more contagious than fear and suspicion.

Dunaughy's low chuckle rolled from the very shadowy corners that Rondelle had searched with nervous eyes. "I see you are indeed a courtly creature, Lady d'Tancreville. You played poor Rondelle like a fiddle."

Enid stared at the planks overhead and said, "He is a much simpler instrument than that—perhaps tin whistle might be more accurate. I apologize for impugning your character, though."

"No need for that. The Sea Service comes before personal concerns. Besides, you said nothing to him he did not already believe."

Dunaughy chuckled again. "Death, or at least dying, has given me a different perspective on the good doctor. He is a prickly man and full of himself to overflowing, but he is also a good man. As I lay dying on that Rat frigate's deck, he did all in his power to save me and I felt his tear on my cheek when he could not. There is a heart under that bundle of thorny vines, and do not doubt it."

Enid waved a noncommittal hand in the air and Dunaughy fell silent again.

She slept fitfully that night, her slumber filled with dreams of fog, fire, and death. Dreams imbued with the crystalline precision of prophecy.

The next day found the *Alarum* standing just off Monte Ybarre, holding a position that allowed the watch high on her mainmast to survey traffic both shoreward and farther out to sea.

The weather was glorious, the sun bright in a clear sky and a warm, brisk wind whipping a fine white spray from the peaks of the evenly rolling emerald-green waves. Enid stood at the rail in the aft quarter of the waist, dividing her attention between the wild Naveroñian shore and her observation of the crew working diligently around her.

To her infinite relief, her fears of a sullen and resentful crew were unfounded. The sailors went about their tasks with obvious enthusiasm, grinning broadly and knuckling their brows with gusto at the orders shouted by their officers. Even the officers, normally rather staid and reserved, seemed more animated and cheerful as they stood their watches. The atmosphere aboard the *Alarum* seemed charged with high spirits and purpose.

Finding herself momentarily alone on the quarterdeck with Lieutenant Oxley, whose watch it was, she inquired after the source of all this excitement.

"You heard the captain last night, Magister," Oxley answered with a gruff suspicion, as if he feared her question was some manner of trick designed to either incriminate or humiliate.

"I did, indeed," she answered patiently, swallowing her annoyance with some effort. "But I'm not as familiar with naval ways as an experienced officer like yourself. I do not doubt that you and I heard the same pronouncement. I simply failed to apprehend its full meaning. Something about a private mission to capture some ship or another?"

Oxley regarded her for a long moment, weighing the sincerity of her words against the risk of being made to look a fool. At last, he shrugged and smiled shyly, an expression that seemed to drain years from his careworn visage.

"I forget that having a mage's education don't make you less the landsman—no offense meant by it."

"And none taken," Enid assured him. "While my family's home estate lies near the Merentian, I spent much of my life in the mountains and none of it in boats."

"Mountains? Truly?" Oxley seemed as impressed as if she'd said her nursery had been on the moon. "I have no stomach for high places. I'm always afraid the side of the mountain will slide off and carry me away. I've a mortal fear of falling."

Enid arched a brow and glanced up at the mastheads tracing spiral patterns against the clear blue heavens. The lieutenant followed her glance and gave a good-humored chuckle.

"It's not the same. I *know* the state of the rigging. I can look at a rope or spar and judge its soundness as easily as you can read a spell. But your mountains, see, there's no way to judge them by their looks. God alone knows how much the weather has eaten at their bones or what bushel will break their back. I've heard tell of whole villages fallen into the sea and no one who could say the cause of it. Who's to say it weren't because one poor wight too many put his weight on the wrong side of some crack too far down in the rock for anyone to see?"

"I cannot counter your logic. I have myself seen vast rockslides triggered by the movement of one small pebble. But to the matter at hand, what escaped my landsman's ears from the captain's words last night yet had such an energizing effect upon the crew? Especially in the face of the evening's unpleasantness?"

"Oh, as to that, Captain Nath has vouched for you and that is enough for all but Harde's meanest creatures." Oxley shot a meaningful glance toward the waist, where a sour-faced Kendal was employed in re-blacking one of the great guns, a task far below his former post as master's mate. "Most will see his slander as another attack on the captain's authority. He tried to paint Captain Nath as a foolhardy pup from the start, but prize money soon shouted that down."

The aging lieutenant lowered his voice. "And prize money has this lot in such a high fettle. To your common sailor, a private mission means only one thing: rich prize money—especially when the mission is given to a young captain who has proven he can accomplish a great deal with very little."

Enid nodded, somewhat disgusted at heart.

Later, standing on the quarterdeck after a private dinner with Captain Nath followed by a presentation of the pivotal scene from Act III of Reverte's *Council of Crows* by the mids, Enid commented to Nath on the character of his crew.

"They are a mercenary breed, are they not?"

"Undeniably," Nath agreed, smiling. "But can you blame them? Their pay is always in arrears and does not compare favorably with that of the meanest soldier ashore." He pointed at one of the topmen hurrying aloft on an errand to fine tune a key element of the ship's complex rigging. "That fellow is paid less than some lubber in one of the king's regiments who has been beaten till he can walk a straight line despite a belly full of stolen grog. Can you fault him for seeking a windfall whenever and wherever he may?"

"Intellectually, I concede the point. Viscerally, such cupidity offends my sense of what is honorable."

Nath chuckled complaisantly, leaning on the rail, and removing his hat to allow the evening breeze to run its cooling fingers through his auburn hair. "You may assure your bowels that avarice has little to do with our mission and honor everything. There is certainly more glory than gold at stake in this affair."

"Then we do not seek a Naveroñian treasure ship?"

"God, no!" Nath answered quietly, grinning. "How did you arrive at such a fantastical theory?"

Enid shrugged. "It is not my theory. It is the most popular conjecture among the crew. I have overheard it voiced several times. They seem to find the prospect most gratifying."

"I daresay," Nath said. "Such a capture would make the grossest landsman aboard as rich as a lord!" He shook his head slowly. "No, it is not a treasure ship we seek, more's the pity. If anyone deserves one, these poor lads certainly do." Sighing, he straightened and replaced his hat upon his head, once more assuming the appearance of a rigid, "taut" officer.

"Have your studies of nautical spellcraft been to your satisfaction? We may have need of magical support."

"Yes," Enid said, closing her right hand around the icy silver ring on her middle finger. "I flatter myself to believe you shall find me ready to serve satisfactorily upon demand."

Nath smiled, pleased with the answer. "Good. I expect to be demanding your assistance soon. Very soon!"

chapter 15

Sadly, Captain Nath's fond hope remained unfulfilled. Two weeks of fruitless cruising in and out sapped the avaricious good cheer out of even the most sanguine crewmen. The watch called Nath to the masthead at least a dozen times to scrutinize some ship-rigged vessel. Each time the crew's hopes rose with him as he scrambled up the mainmast, only to be dashed as he slid down the stays, shaking his head. Wags opined at mess that the *Alarum* must take two treasure ships to make up for all the rich prizes they'd allowed to pass without so much as a challenge.

Nath made every effort to appear unmoved by the profitless effort, but his growing impatience was evident in the increasing rigidity of his posture and the cessation of nightly theatrical readings in his cabin.

The captain did not sequester himself entirely from his officers, however. He continued to host regular dinners and accepted two invitations to dine in the gunroom and, on all occasions, proved congenial.

Nor did he neglect his crew. He staged regular inspections and greeted the men, even the newcomers from Gisbon, by name. While he continually drilled the men at the great guns, he also allowed for a dancing contest, pitting the starboard watches against those of the larboard. The winning watch (the jubilant larbowlines) received an extra rum ration while the losers were treated to a dancing lesson from the captain himself, a spectacle that left them in breathless hilarity and dispelled any illusions that the stress of command had reduced him to a grim parody of his former self.

On the morning of the fifteenth day off Monte Ybarre, the by now familiar call for Captain Nath was again passed down from the masthead. He rushed up the mainmast with his best glass slung over his shoulder as all the *Alarum*s on deck watched raptly and held their collective breath. That breath was released in a more or less universal sigh of disappointment as Nath shook his head, snapped his glass shut, and swarmed deftly down the rigging.

Back on deck, Nath turned briskly to Lieutenant Oxley and snapped curtly, "Prepare a boat, Lieutenant, to pull me across to that vessel, which is the *Murtherer* frigate, unless I am entirely mistaken. Have a side party ready in case her captain decides he'd prefer to come across himself."

The Honorable Captain Jerome Odenton chose not to come across himself, finding it far more agreeable for the junior officer to make the crossing. He'd heard a bit about this Nath fellow from the admiral, who seemed quite taken with him, and from his first, who had shared a commission with him aboard the *Redoubtable*, 74, under the then captain, now Admiral Emuel Barrington.

"He is small in stature, but possessed of a remarkable amount of presence," First Lieutenant Manlann had recollected as they watched the signal flags run up the mast that would summon the object of their discussion aboard the *Murtherer*. "His family's prestige in the Service was widely known, but I must admit he never sought to parlay it to his advantage. Most of the ship's officers and people held him in the highest esteem, including Admiral Barrington, who perfectly doted upon him."

"He is a toady, then?"

"No, no, nothing like that, sir." He frowned, obviously finding it hard to speak of his fellow officer with approbation. Odenton was well aware there was no love lost between the two men, but he was also certain that his lieutenant's sense of duty would abrogate his distaste for the subject at hand. Manlann would give him the most honest and accurate assessment of Nath and save his obloquy, justified or not, for the gunroom. "It was more his dash that Barrington loved, that and his obvious affection for the common sailors."

Odenton nodded absently as he observed the *Alarum* lowering a boat away the instant the last flag of the summons unfurled. Nath's dash had obviously not diminished in the year since his departure from Barrington's command.

"He is one of those popular captains, then?" He pronounced the word *popular* with the same affection he would have imparted to *pederast* or *rapist*.

Manlann shook his head firmly. "No, sir. He is a taut officer and, in most ways, an admirable disciplinarian. There is nothing of the martinet about him, nor yet the panderer after popular opinion."

"And yet you have a pronounced dislike for the man? No, sir, do not disavow it. Your feelings are obvious, writ large in both your tone and expression."

Manlann stifled his protestations and stared across the startling-blue Merentian waters, recognizing Nath's compact form as he descended surely into the boat bobbing at the *Alarum*'s quarter.

"He has a presence about him, sir. Damnably confident, if I may be blunt. Overconfident, I would say. He behaves as if the mark of eagles were inscribed upon his brow and the doors of destiny were already flung wide to accept him into history. A typical Westlands scrub. And you know of the nonsense his father is up to in the Sugar Islands. Can you credit it? An admiral grubbing in the dirt like a common farmer."

Odenton arched a brow but refrained from comment. His family was of ancient lineage and today supported an earl, two viscounts, and a handful of barons, but his own father was a gentleman farmer in Hemethshire. Instead, he cleared his throat and asked, "I understand there was a scandal at the end of the cruise?"

"No scandal per se, sir," Manlann blundered on, oblivious to his indiscretion. "An affair of honor that arose, in my opinion, more from a minikin's prickly pride than from any real insult offered." Recognizing the tension in his captain's jaw, he continued more carefully. "Lieutenant Hefflin made a jest of Nath's love for theater—a tiresome fascination made worse by his maddening habit of quoting some play or another seemingly at every instant—Nath took injury from it and called Hefflin out. Barrington threatened to court-martial them both if they pursued the affair, but Nath could not be persuaded to accept Hefflin's apology."

"What? An apology was offered, and Nath refused it? On what grounds?"

"He claimed he had been struck a blow, sir, and that words could be withdrawn but a blow could not."

"And there is the right of it." Odenton was not a man who believed in the disdain for dueling that seemed to take root among some of the more "modern" young officers. "But was he struck?"

"Well," Manlann answered reluctantly, "Hefflin threw a book of plays at Nath. No harm was meant by it, and it could hardly be called a blow. She was making a jest."

The captain sniffed distastefully. "Her intent would mean nothing to a gentleman, sir. A blow is a blow regardless of the motive behind it and any *jest* that culminates in indignity to a gentleman's person is hardly a gentleman's jest!"

"Yes, sir, as you say, sir!"

"And how was the affair resolved?"

"They met at the end of the cruise, at Warrington Field, a park on the south side of Middlesea often used for the purpose." Manlann's tone became audibly bitter as he recalled the event.

"I was Hefflin's second. There was quite a bit of drinking the night before, as there often is before such occasions. No one had any doubt about the outcome. Hefflin is a good foot taller than Nath and possessed both of a greater reach and a more powerful touch."

The lieutenant shook his head in disgust before painting the rest of the picture. "So, there was Hefflin, bleary-eyed and grinning as if the appointment were already resolved in her favor—and Nath, clear-eyed and grave as a chaplain. In Hefflin's defense, though, I doubt her condition made much of a difference in the outcome."

"Our little captain has a fine wrist, has he?"

Odenton narrowed his eyes and carefully studied the small lieutenant taking charge of one of the *Alarum*'s boats. From this distance there was certainly nothing impressive about him, although his boat crew snapped to with admirable alacrity. He allowed his eyes to stray back to Nath's little sixth rate and once again found her rigging and deck in perfect order—more than perfect order, in fact. The taut lines and neatly organized gun deck spoke of a crew that was as proud of their little barky as they were able in its handling.

Manlann nodded soberly. "As fine as I've seen outside demonstration matches, sir. He made short work of Hefflin without giving any serious hurt and accepted his rather discreditable apology with perfect grace. If the man were not a king's officer, he could easily make a living as a dueling instructor."

"Hmm. From the sound of it, he has done a bit of dueling instruction despite being a king's officer." Odenton turned his back on the rail and straightened his coat. He found he now regretted the news he must deliver to Nath.

"Prepare a side party for Commander Nath. I will receive him in my cabin."

Two hours later found the *Murtherer* setting her sails and bearing off to continue her cruise while the *Alarum*'s boat crew strained at their oars to bear their captain swiftly home. Lieutenants Merryweather and Oxley stood at the rail studying the departing frigate and surreptitiously dropping their glasses slightly to learn what they could of their captain's mood. The *Murtherer*'s performance left nothing to criticize, but Nath's appearance, rigid in the stern sheets of the boat, was a definite cause for comment.

"Oh, he don't look happy," Oxley muttered from the side of his mouth, his words intended for Merryweather's ears alone. "Must've been bad news."

Merryweather grunted in agreement, closed her glass with a snap, and replied in the same low tone. "End of the cruise, I'll warrant. Off to escort some lumbering merchantman or run messages along the blockade line. I'd best see that the side party is sharp. It looks as if a squall may be upon us."

Oxley closed his own glass contemplatively. Squall? He doubted it. He'd seen Nath respond sharply to direct impudence, such as Harde's outburst against the new magister, and overt incompetence, as in the regrettable incident in which the Number Three gun crew contrived to drop a ball on the deck and the rammer over the side in the same evolution, but he'd never seen Nath lash out against his men in frustration.

There'd been plenty of opportunity for that sort of behavior to raise its head in the early days of the cruise. Oxley could plainly recall the crew's glum reception of their new commander, who Master Harde painted as a jumped-up mid whose familial interest had raised him rapidly through the ranks and unfairly leveraged him into a command that rightly belonged to a true sailor's captain. He was ever ready to remind them of Nath's youth and inexperience at command each time he made changes that impinged upon the *Alarum*'s settled routine.

Most of those changes were met with obdurate, foot-dragging resistance that made even the simplest, most reasonable policy a horror to implement. Inwardly, Oxley hung his head at the memory. He'd done precious little to make Captain Nath's life easier and had actually encouraged some of the resistance to his efforts to convert the *Alarum* from what amounted to a yacht into a true warship.

He would have liked to have blamed his complicity on the fact that by the time of Nath's arrival, he had already been thoroughly beaten down and cowed by his last cruise with Harde and Captain Ambrose. He was old for a lieutenant, consistently passed over for command not from any lack of ability, but more for a lack of any spark, a fact that mortally injured his own esteem to the extent that he often found it preferable to follow the path of least resistance rather than take a stand against complacency. As shameful as that admission was, and he had come to terms with it years ago, he was more deeply embarrassed by the sure knowledge that it was not the root of his poor behavior toward Nath. He was too honest a man to fail to recognize his own motives, however malignant he might find them. No, it was not his damnable sheepishness that was to blame; rather it was resentment—a quiet, virulent resentment toward a man who had achieved so much at such an early age, a man whose very existence underscored Oxley's own pathetic failure to prosper.

Despite the forces arrayed against him, however, Nath made his will reality without resorting to the sort of savage reprisals that were perfectly within his rights as a captain. This stoic strength of character had done as much as the sudden flow of prize money to win the crew's heart. This turn of events seemed to bring out the meanest, most vicious aspects of Harde's personality, which did little for the master's influence.

Like the crew, Oxley's resentment gradually faded in the face of the young captain's calm self-confidence and fair treatment. He was embarrassed to admit to himself that it had taken Harde's arrest to break the final manacles that prevented him from giving Captain Nath his full support, an embarrassment he was resolved to assuage by turning over a new leaf. He told himself it was never too late to change one's character, a declaration that filled him with a subdued elation and a resigned sense of looming failure all at once.

⟨———— ≫ ————⟩

Enid was invited to dine with Nath that night and found him in an unsettled mood. In stark contrast to the unflappable, professional image he presented on deck mere moments before, in the privacy of his cabin he was full of nervous energy that set his fingers tapping on the table and further evidenced itself in the regular crossing and recrossing of his legs.

Conversation during dinner was subdued and Nath did not seem to open up until the plates were cleared away and they settled down with a decent fortified wine purchased with the advance against his prizes. As usual, Enid dipped into her private—and dwindling—stock of fine cigarillos to give the final touch to the post-meal ritual.

A less than comfortable silence reigned until Nath broke it, picking up their earlier conversation as if moments rather than weeks had intervened.

"No, it is not a treasure ship we seek, Enid. But it is something that might prove more valuable to our cause than a dozen galleons loaded with bullion. Morale is dearer than gold in times like this."

Enid nodded agreeably, but could not resist jibing, "As you say, sir, but one might also say that gold is worth its weight in morale if I understood your past explanation of the import of prizes to the common sailor."

Nath nodded in absent agreement. "Yes, yes, of course. But gold isn't the only coin with which it can be bought. There is also pride and a sense of righteous vengeance, both of which can be wondrously efficacious motivators to do whatever must needs to attain victory."

"Yes, you have the right of it there, sir," Enid agreed earnestly. "I can personally vouch for the truth of it. So, this ship we seek would bolster Albion's pride and serve as vengeance for some past wrong?"

"Indeed." Nath took a long, thoughtful draw on his cigarillo before continuing in a less agitated tone. "And I would be disingenuous to deny it would do wonders for my own pride and, more significantly, my career. If we succeed in this, I cannot see how I would not receive post. Merryweather would certainly receive a command of her own. Perhaps even poor old Oxley."

"Then we must dedicate ourselves to the task! I know nothing of nautical maneuver, but it seems plain to me that if our prey must pass Monte Ybarre, the course we maintain will make it impossible for her to pass without our notice."

"If we are here when she passes."

Enid raised a brow. "You are considering abandoning our vigil here?"

"It is not a matter of consideration," Nath said with a sigh, frowning. "It is a matter of being recalled before we can spring our trap. Captain Odenton bore grave news affecting the Sea Service in general and our endeavor in particular. Sea Lord Dunbow, Providence bless him, has passed, carried away by a paroxysm. He has been replaced, at least for the nonce, by Theon Morrin, the Duke of Morrin. Admiral Weymouth has received orders from the Admiralty that Lord Ambrose of Aixely, Morrin's godson, is on route to Gisbon to assume command of the *Alarum*. I am to be relieved."

Enid leaned forward in alarm. She had no firsthand knowledge of Ambrose, of course, but she had a vivid impression of his character thanks to her new "relationship" with Dunaughy. It was not an impression that left her with any eagerness to find herself subservient to him rather than the eminently more agreeable Nath.

"Surely Admiral Weymouth places more importance on your mission here than on the convenience of this disagreeable wretch?"

"Oh, he does," Nath assured her. "That we are here at all is evidence of that." Nath tapped a slim leather letter case on the desktop.

"His orders indicate I may return immediately in order to be on hand for Captain Ambrose's arrival, or, at *my* discretion, I may remain on station here until word reaches us that Lord Aixely has arrived in Gisbon. In fact, according to Captain Odenton, it is Admiral Weymouth's plan to leave us on station here and send Captain Ambrose out with the *Murtherer* to relieve me, rather than require us to run in to receive him. Unfortunately, that buys us a week's time at most."

"At least the mission itself will not be lost, although it is regrettable of course that you will not receive full credit for the action. Surely you would still benefit from it, though, just as Merryweather or Oxley would?"

"No, I fear Captain Ambrose will have vastly different orders from ours," Nath said, sighing ruefully. "Admiral Weymouth has no interest in seeing Ambrose take our prey."

"Perhaps Fortune would favor him even if the admiral does not, and offer him an opportunity to bring her to action independent of orders?"

"Hmm." Nath struggled for a moment with his natural reticence to speak ill of another officer, but found it outweighed by his need to confide his doubts to someone he felt he could trust. Despite her annoying tendency toward a reflexive personal secrecy, he felt an overwhelming confidence that Enid would prove as discreet a companion as an officer could ever wish. "Well, even if the opportunity presented itself, I doubt Captain Ambrose would avail himself of it."

"You believe Ambrose would attempt to avoid action? Or that he lacks the skill to close with an enemy to engage them in action?"

Nath looked up from his drink and met her eyes through the swirls of blue-gray smoke, much the same hue as his eyes. He peered into her eyes for a long moment, his teeth thoughtfully working the inside of his lip. At first, she thought he was considering his answer with great care and then, in a flash of insight, she realized it was not the content of the answer that required such consideration, but its very pronouncement. Finally, he reached a decision and spoke.

"Yes."

She knew the pronouncement of that single word represented a more portentous confidence than any other Nath had yet shared with her. It was not an admission he would make to another officer, no matter how much he might trust and respect them. It would violate his code of "officerly" behavior. It seemed Dunaughy's ambition for her was fulfilled: she had become Nath's confidant.

"Well, I would not call another officer shy or cast aspersions on his abilities." Nath mouthed the caveat out of rote, it seemed to Enid. "But Ambrose's record includes no prizes—nor even any chases. He is either the most ill-starred captain in the fleet's history or . . ."

"Or he is a coward."

"Still, it is neither here nor there for us, Enid." Rue's voice was flat with resignation. "We will be returning to Gisbon aboard the *Murtherer*. Aixely has learned of your provenance and mistrusts you. He will bring his own magister to assume your post."

Enid sniffed and waved a hand. "He and I are of a mind, then. I have no desire to serve under Harde. Perhaps I can find a place aboard your next command?"

"With all my heart," Nath said. "Should I ever see command again."

"You have powerful friends, both near and far. Your navy is not so different from Achard's court. You will receive some sort of command, or I'm no judge of politics."

Rather than comment one way or the other, Nath unrolled a chart of the coastline and changed the subject. He tapped a spot on it with his finger. "This is Puerto Galeno. I believe our prey is there, waiting us out."

Enid leaned over the map and recognized Monte Ybarre and the nearby Puerto Galeno. "How? They are aware of our intent?"

"I doubt they are aware of our intent, but I think it is likely they are aware of our presence. We have taken pains to avoid revealing our nature and nationality, but I would not be surprised if Galeno has been warned that an Albion warship is patrolling nearby. The captain of the vessel we seek would be particularly cautious of such reports, having much to lose from running afoul of any Albion man-of-war."

Enid exhaled a slow stream of smoke and leaned back in her chair. "And what is this mysterious vessel we seek? I do not ask from personal curiosity, although I own to a large amount of it, but that I might use my arts more effectively in assisting your cause. There is some slim hope that the name of the vessel may prove helpful in scrying for her."

Nath considered for a moment and then shrugged.

"Of course. I must ask you not to reveal it to any of the other officers, however. It is best to keep it to ourselves until the time seems right to me. Have you heard of the *Redemption*?"

Enid smiled, pleased to finally answer one of Nath's questions affirmatively. "Of course! She is the ill-fated vessel that came under such a tyrannical despot of a captain that the poor wretches in the crew were forced to take up arms and destroy him. I saw Rouland's version performed onstage in Berre, *The Damned Ship*."

"Hmm. Well." Nath frowned over his wine. "I trust you realize that the fabrications of Rouland are overtly political. The true events of the *Redemption*'s mutiny probably bear little resemblance to his fiction. Still, conditions aboard her were apparently harsher than normal and she was indeed seized by the crew. Once in power, they slew every officer aboard, even the youngest of the mids. The mutineers turned her over to Naveroña in exchange for sanctuary from the king's justice. It is our aim to reclaim her."

Enid had a clear recollection of the crowing in her father's court when news of the mutiny became well known. Considering the malicious pleasure taken by the Ardain nobility at the news, she could easily imagine the shame and consternation the event must have produced among the proud officers of the Albion navy.

"Yes. Yes, I can see how retaking her would be a boon to morale." She considered a moment, and then asked, "But did you not say you were intimately familiar with our prey? You served aboard her?"

"No, no, nothing of the sort. But I saw her once in Middlesea Roads . . . before she was taken under Ourey's command. Rumor was she was an unhappy ship even then. That observation coupled with information Admiral Weymouth had from sources in Naveroña should allow me to identify her easily enough."

"Has she always been an 'unhappy ship'?"

"I cannot say she always has been," Nath said, shrugging. "But happy or no, we must pray Providence puts her in our hands." Nath paused for a moment, smiling. "And nothing unusual in praying for redemption, is there? Or in finding damnation in its stead?"

Enid chuckled perfunctorily. "Well, I will attempt to scry for her, but I cannot guarantee much."

"If you can tell me if she is even near, you will ease my mind greatly."

"Then I will do my utmost to do so."

Nath tapped out his cigarillo in a pewter salver on the table and rose. "Very well, then. I will free you to be about it. I have new orders to present to the watch at any rate. As usual, your company has been a pleasure, Enid."

"A pleasure reciprocated in full, sir."

In her cabin, Enid withdrew a sheet of cheap paper from her desk and dipped her quill in ink. On the paper she wrote "scry?" The silver ring chilled instantly and as her hand wandered aimlessly across the page an internal dialogue began within her head. It was still disturbing to find her mind crowded with Dunaughy's thoughts. She was infinitely grateful that she had insisted on placing limitations on his ability to freely impinge upon her consciousness. The on-again off-again chilling of the ring was distracting enough and the times, such as this, when she opened a "conversation" with him were far more unsettling than any discourse with his free-ranging spirit had ever been.

Still, Harde's and Kendal's accusations against her proved that Dunaughy's rebinding was a wise, if self-interested, move. It allowed her to communicate with him without speaking aloud and gave her the limited ability to seek his counsel outside the cabin he had previously haunted.

"Have you any suggestions to make my efforts to scry for the *Redemption* more effective?"

"There is no need to scry for her, Enid." Dunaughy's voice within her still held the same brogue but seemed somehow younger, more vital. This, she suspected, was how his thoughts sounded to him when he was alive: ageless and robust. "She is near."

"How can you be so sure?"

"If you had my senses, you would not ask. The dead call to the dead and too many fell aboard that poor barky to escape my notice now."

"Can you tell me where she is?"

"No, I'm afraid I cannot, lass. I can only tell you she is very near. I can still recognize proximity, but the longer I am without my body the more difficult it is for me to recognize direction or placement. It is a fascinating phenomenon I'm sure I would find more interesting were I not dead."

Enid's mind filled with his mirth, a profoundly unpleasant experience that simultaneously caused the hair on the back of her neck to rise and forced the corners of her lip up in an involuntary empathic spasm.

"Well, let us be back about our lessons. You were about to explain how weather manipulation at sea differs from on land."

"Yes," Dunaughy answered, his "voice" sounding cheerful. "Well, the first difference is obvious—the dominant element is clearly quite different at sea than ashore. You must learn to tailor your castings to take this into account . . ."

Enid's hand traced formulae on the sheet of paper, formulae she would understand later but now, with her eyes rolling in her head, she could not see, let alone read.

chapter 16

Over the next few days, Enid watched the *Alarum* transform from a creature of exuberant energy to one of nervous urgency. Whether news of Ambrose's imminent return had somehow leaked to the officers and crew, or they were simply able to discern from their captain's rigid posture and redoubled intensity, every soul aboard her understood that time was no longer their ally.

Enid's assurances that their quarry was near seemed to add to Nath's discomfiture rather than relieve it. Still, he seemed to find her presence on watch comforting, perhaps deluding himself that she would suddenly point toward the horizon and declare the hunt at an end. So it was that Enid found herself standing next to Nath when the main watch shouted, "Strange sail!"

"Where away?"

Enid winced at the boom of Nath's command voice at such proximity. She stepped aside with alacrity to avoid a collision as he bound away from his place at the rail to peer up at the masthead where the sailor on watch pointed away to the sou'-sou'east. A nearly incomprehensible exchange of shouted jargon followed, the gist of which Enid took to be congenial, judging by the fierce grin on Nath's face and the barely repressed jollity with which he addressed her.

"An answer to my most earnest prayers, Magister d'Tancreville! A schooner with Ardain privateer written all over her. Mr. Gaines! Set a course to bring us alongside that schooner!"

Time passed, demonstrating the odd dilation that Enid associated with events of great anticipation whether the end contemplated were for good or ill. Hours dragged like years as the two ships converged across the gemlike sea and then, suddenly, they were near enough that she could plainly see the activity of the schooner's sailors and all the intervening hours seemed reduced to mere instants in the face of the moment's culmination.

"Mr. Yeardly!" Nath's shout broke Enid's philosophical reverie. "I desire you to run up the black pennant. Sharply, lad, sharply!"

Enid frowned as she watched the black Confessor's flag rise briskly into the air. "Why do you raise that filthy rag? The Ardainne colors would be just as effective and far less offensive to the eye."

"If that schooner is Ardain, as I suspect, she'll immediately haul her wind for a Confessor, where she might hesitate if she thought we were merely a naval vessel. If she is not Ardain, she'll do the same for fear of the consequences."

"I must admit that I find the use of false colors objectionable in principle," Enid remarked sourly. "And to use such a fearsome instrument only adds to the odiousness of the practice."

"Your objection is noted." There was no trace of rancor in Nath's tone and more than a little amusement, which Enid found more rankling by half. She was about to expand her remarks to include a diatribe against patronization when Nath called out, "She does not seem to see us. Give her a gun, Mr. Hall!"

One of the *Alarum*'s great guns boomed and a moment later the schooner seemed to be seized by a frenzy of confused activity. Nath snorted in disapproval. "I thought they were simply playing coy with us, but apparently we truly have caught them all unawares. I'd have their watch's hide at the grate—Mr. Yeardly! Down with that rag and up with our own colors! Mr. Hall! Be ready by the guns if these rascals prove to be fools!"

The schooner's captain showed no signs of being a fool, however. His only bellicose action was the firing of a single gun, which Nath identified to Enid as a "long-nine," well ahead of the *Alarum*'s bow. Enid expected to see the impertinent shot answered by a wrathful blast from the *Alarum*'s larger cannons, but Nath cheerfully explained that the single shot had more to do with the schooner captain's dignity than his desire to fight.

"Who wants it said that they hauled their colors without firing a shot?" Nath asked rhetorically before bellowing for Hall to "stir up that schooner's wake with a ball." He turned back to Enid with a smile.

"Now both of our logs can read that he surrendered only after he exchanged shots with us, a much larger vessel. In that way, the honor of all involved remains untarnished and their honesty strained but a little."

"I trust this is another of your naval traditions and not an innovation of the moment?" Enid said with a sniff.

Nath nodded absently, his full attention dominated by the cheerful sight of the schooner striking her colors and heaving to. "What? Oh, yes, it is a custom immemorial. Why do you ask?"

"It occurs to me that many of the 'glorious victories at sea' that I have seen heralded with such joy and admiration in the papers were likely pro forma exchanges of customary courtesies of just the sort I am witnessing now!"

"Well," Nath answered with a wry smile, "I cannot answer for your foreign papers, but Albion's require a far more profligate expenditure of powder, shot, and blood than we have spent today to gain their attention. The blood must flow freely before the ink ever will, they

say—Lieutenant Merryweather! Assemble a boarding party and secure the prize! Send her captain straight across! I desire to see her in
a state to sail before nightfall!"

"As you will, sir!" Merryweather began shouting up her party,
finding no dearth of hands eager for first crack at whatever they could
lay hands on aboard the privateer.

In less time than it took to say "ship," Merryweather and her party
secured the schooner and loaded her captain into a boat bound for the
Alarum.

"What an ill-looking lot of ruffians," Nath said as they watched
Merryweather's party herd the schooner's crew into her bow at gun-
point. "And at least forty of the devils! They must have been stacked
belowdecks like cordwood. We are lucky we caught them so off their
guard or we would have had a far harder bargain of it."

Enid, intrigued by the habits of the Albion press, returned to the
matter as they watched the ship's boat carry the schooner's captain
across the waves. "So even your action against the *Artagny* is unlikely
to see print? I recollect your losses were light, your poor magister
aside, of course."

"Our casualties were indeed very light in that instance," Nath
agreed, somewhat distracted as he watched the actions of his people
aboard the schooner with all the intensity of a mother raptor. "But I
flatter myself enough to believe that our little barky's victory over a
bloody great frigate will merit a line or two in the *Naval Times*."

He gave her a wolfish grin and touched the wood of the rail for
luck. "And Fortune willing, we will soon see an action that will demand
the expenditure of barrels of ink even if we do not spend so much as a
drop of blood ourselves!"

Enid found herself somewhat unnerved by his enthusiasm, but felt
compelled to ask, "So you value mention in the journals so much?"

"Of course! Many is the captain who made post thanks to a lucky
splash of ink. But look, the boats approach and I desire to put the

schooner's captain on the carpet in my cabin—he looks quite saucy despite losing his sword. Will you be so kind as to attend should your mastery of the Ardain tongue be required?"

"It would be my honor and pleasure, sir."

Citizen Captain Herme, Enid determined, was indeed "saucy." Tall and lanky, the young captain had the long, mobile face so common among the nobility of the Ardain duchy of Artagny. He was dark-skinned, and his deep brown eyes were alert and intelligent. Since girlhood she'd found Artagnac features handsome in a relatively plain, manly way. Unfortunately, as pleasing as Artagnacs were to her eyes, so was their accent odious to her ears.

"Captain Nath, I am Antoin Herme, citizen captain of the *Tape a'Bord*." Herme made a courteous leg and doffed his battered bicorn hat as he was escorted by Lieutenant Merryweather into the captain's cabin. Enid found it astounding that the man contrived to imbue the Albion language with the same thick, rustic accent that doubtlessly reduced his Ardain to nearly unintelligible gumble-gabble.

"It is an honor, sir, I assure you!" Herme straightened, a disarming smile on his face and a bright twinkle in his eye that had nothing of defeat in it.

"Hrmm. Allow me to introduce my ship's magister, Enid d'Tancreville."

Nath left the reason for her presence unspoken. She hoped the cocksure privateer would assume the worst. After all, the Theocrats weren't alone in their truth-seeing and insight magics. She studied Herme closely for a long moment, hoping to see some trace of unease, but, alas, the devil seemed perfectly sanguine.

"Your papers, sir?" Nath held out a hand.

"Your charming and gallant lieutenant has them in hand, sir." The Artagnac bowed slightly toward Merryweather, who placed a thick folio of papers in her captain's hands and, at his nod, took her leave. Nath's lips moved as he puzzled out the complexities of written Ardain. As a brief silence fell, Herme cast an appraising glance in Enid's direction. She returned his curious and openly admiring gaze with cool hauteur, a faint sniff her only answer to his eloquently arched brow. She was not here to answer questions, after all. He was.

"A letter of marque, then?" Nath asked, holding an official-looking document by its corner between his thumb and forefinger in the same way he might have dangled a drowned rat by its tail. If Citizen Herme noticed the contemptuousness of the gesture, he chose not to acknowledge it.

"Indeed, sir, and I am lucky to have it. You may perceive my antecedents were not of a nature to encourage the confidence of the Theocratic council in charge of naval appointments. I could not retain my commission, so . . ."

The Ardain privateer shrugged philosophically.

"You were an aristocrat and a naval officer prior to the Theocracy?" Nath made a note in his log. "And your commission, sir?"

"The same as your own, sir, unless I misjudge your attire." Herme made a laconic, loose-wristed gesture that took in Nath's uniform from boot to hat. "I had the honor to serve Ardainne as a lieutenant commander, an honor I ardently hope will be revisited soon."

"Then yours is a forlorn hope," Enid observed coldly in formal Ardain, garnering a puzzled frown from Nath. "Once the traitors are overthrown, your service to them will invalidate you for service in the Crown's navy, and, if they are not, you may bear your old rank again, but you will not have the honor of serving Ardainne. Ardainne will be dead."

"Come, m'lady," Herme answered with easy equanimity. "The Ardainne we knew is as dead as the god-king of Kemet and there is no power on earth that can restore it. As for the Theocrats, their time in the sun is running down. They will find their needs outstripping their

prejudices before their inevitable collapse. As will the regime that follows. In circumstances such as these, the ambitious need only be flexible to prosper."

"Flexible or facile?" Enid rejoined acerbically.

Herme opened his mouth to answer, but Nath raised a silencing
hand and snapped, "Please! Restrict your comments to the language
of Albion, both of you!"

In the silence that followed, Nath, Herme, and Enid put their eyes
to earnest, if decidedly diverse use: the captain, oblivious to all else,
scrutinized the infamous letter while Enid, through the conveyance of
a remarkably inimical glare, poured a palpable flood of contempt upon
Herme, whose twinkling brown eyes regarded her with a combination
of merriment and physical appreciation, the warmth of which seemed
to increase paradoxically as the glacial chill of Enid's gaze deepened.

"Well," Nath said at last. "All seems to be in order here. Captain
Herme, you and your people will be my guests for a short time to
come. It is my intention to release the lot of you ashore, without parole,
as soon as it is convenient to our operations. Since your stay with us
will be short and will culminate in your freedom, there is no reason
for your people to get up to any foolishness that will only result in the
injury or death of their fellows."

"I will convey your sentiment to my crew along with my sincer-
est endorsement, sir," Herme assured him with a smile. "I see no
reason that our brief stay should not be as pleasant as possible and
hope time will permit us the opportunity to profit from a few social
moments together." He punctuated his wish with a brilliant smile for
the still-scowling Enid.

"That is wondrously congenial of you considering the circumstances." Nath could not help smiling at the fellow's sanguine, even
cheerful acceptance of his capture and loss of his ship.

"Congenial? And why not?" Herme's smile broadened. "Didn't
Bleobris counsel Chlodric, 'These troubled times may have the better

of us but that is nothing to deter us from making the best of them'? Besides, Fortune, especially in times of war, is a wheel. Rather than resent you for playing host on this occasion, I prefer to look forward to returning your hospitality on the next."

Nath clapped his hands once and flashed his own broad grin. "Oh! Well said, sir! Well said!" He noticed Enid's baleful stare turn on him and exclaimed, "Come now, Magister! Surely a quote from Orillon merits some charity?"

Enid responded with an icily delivered Orillon quote of her own. " 'While I have pledged my body to my captain's command, I remain lord of my own conscience.' "

A cautionary rejoinder reminding Enid of the courtesy expected of one of His Majesty's sea officers was forming on Nath's lips when Herme, a laugh in his voice, asked to be excused to see to the housing of his people and the delivery of their host's message to them. Nath called for the marine stationed at his door, who escorted the Ardain privateer from the cabin.

"Really, Enid," Nath muttered reproachfully. "There's no cause for such overt animosity. I have no love for privateers, either, but this man has given up his sword with good grace."

"As you say, sir." There was nothing of accord in Enid's curt reply.

Nath pushed back from his desk with a sigh. "Enid, I understand your feelings, but—"

"Your pardon, sir," Enid interrupted with quiet vehemence. "But you do not. You have not lost your entire family, your entire way of life, to a pack of scripture-quoting devils. Dogs like this Herme are worse than the fools duped by the Theocrats. They at least believe their treason is for a broader cause. He is only interested in his own ambition. It does not matter a whit to him if Ardainne is reduced to rubble as long as he profits from it!"

"Do not deceive yourself that you are alone in your familiarity with loss of either family or lifestyle, Magister," Nath answered sharply, his

eyes flashing dangerously, but he continued with more of the humanity she had grown accustomed to in their moments of private conversation. "Don't deceive yourself that Citizen Herme's bonhomie deludes
me, either. He is not a good man or likely to be an honorable one. However, one of the first lessons one learns in the mids' berth is that it
doesn't take a good man to be good company. A bit of good company
is probably the best treasure we can hope for off any prize, especially
one as mean as Herme's little *Toucher du Bois*."

Captain Nath had to admit he was wrong, however, and the proof of
his error lay in the unbelievably fine bottle of Artagnac brandy holding down one corner of a chart taken off the *Toucher du Bois*. The
bottle came from one of two cases removed from the Ardain schooner
and now safely nestled in his personal stores. Both the brandy and the
chart, which showed this section of the inner coast of Naveroña in exquisite detail, were taken from Herme's cabin. Nath was hard-pressed
to decide which was the more valuable prize.

The chart illustrated Puerto Galeno's approaches and Herme,
whatever the quality of his character, was obviously diligent in maintaining his maps. The new boundaries of a shifting shallow were
clearly defined by fresh pencil lines and dated three days past. He
saw no serious navigational hazards in the harbor, certainly none that
would affect vessels of the size he intended to take in. Satisfied, he
rolled and stowed the chart.

He turned his chair to face out the stern gallery windows and
sipped brandy as he watched the *Alarum*'s phosphorescent wake fade
into the near distance. By this time tomorrow, he thought, the outcome
will be determined for good or ill. Staring out into the deepening darkness, he felt he should experience anticipation, dread, or a mixture
of the two. Instead, he felt nothing more than a comfortable fatalism
hearkening back to his days aboard his aunt Dolorous's command, the

Alianor. It was her habit to employ a schoolmaster for the edification of her young gentles. His fellow mids always suffered greatly the night before Master Curtwaithe's exams, particularly those who tested their knowledge of classical Velascin. So had he his first year.

Sometime during his second year, however, he had a revelation: Curtwaithe's devilishly difficult exams were an elemental force of nature. It was impossible to predict every peril they might present a hapless student or prepare for every eventuality. The best one could do was prepare diligently for the worst and hope either inspiration or, more likely, Fortune would make up for any lack. The books were now set aside, the studies complete: all that remained was the exam—and a rather late dinner.

chapter 17

The atmosphere around the captain's table was less companionable than he might have wished, but Nath was pleased to see Enid seemed to have recovered her courtly graces and Mids Cullen and Yeardly had gone to some effort to present themselves before the guest of honor with clean faces, hands, and uniforms even if he was a mere privateer. Merryweather, of course, was as officer-like as ever. Her pleasant professionalism was never in doubt. Nath was slightly chagrined that Herme's "uniform" coat, an amazingly well-tailored garment constructed of a cloth that shifted from the brightest crimson to the deepest burgundy with the slightest movement, so thoroughly outshone the couture of the *Alarum*'s officers.

There was nothing to be ashamed of in the dinner set before them, at least, although it was true that the fine wines and most of the fresh meat and vegetables had come from Herme's own pantry aboard the *Toucher du Bois*. Nath was not embarrassed in the slightest to be serving the viands to their former owner, however. The stuff had been transformed by the magic of conquest into *his* provisions and he felt rather grand to be sharing such a fine repast with the commander of a mere letter of marque—and only a *schooner* at that.

With everyone warned to be on their best behavior and Enid's pride still stinging from Nath's earlier rebuke concerning the proper treatment of guests aboard a man-of-war, the meal passed uneventfully but, to Nath's mind, rather successfully.

Herme regaled them all with astounding tales of the latest goings-on in Ardainne while tactfully skirting the subject of the ongoing purges save for one indelicate remark concerning the use of the cloud of carrion birds that circled Arleonne's central square and the city's Roget Device as a navigational aid. Enid blanched to hear it and set her fork down upon the table with a clank.

"How can you chuckle in the same breath with which you speak of such savagery? What humor is there in murder at such a scale?"

"There is no humor in murder regardless of scale, m'lady," Herme answered mildly. "That said, it is somewhat ironic that the simple fishermen of Arleonne, rather than being frozen in place by such horror, choose instead to turn it to their advantage as they struggle to wrest a meager living from the unforgiving sea. Those of noble blood, our blood, have always sought to guide the commons, and continue to do so even in the face of their own extinction."

"Our blood, is it?" Enid snapped. "And yet you choose to serve the very authors of its extinction. I'm sure a sardonic fellow like yourself finds the humor in that as well."

"Come, come," Merryweather interceded before Nath could let fly. She laid a hand over Enid's, who was seated next to her. "Citizen Herme here will be free soon enough and, Providence willing, you'll have the opportunity to make your argument more forcefully the next time our courses cross. For now, lay it aside and edify our youngsters here with the seemly complaisance of a true Ardain gentlewoman."

Enid glanced at the mids and felt a sudden and infuriating rush of shame. Cullen's handsome face was taut and colorless with forced geniality. Yeardly, next to him, fixed Herme with such a contumelious gaze that Enid wondered for a moment if steel would be drawn. Nath regarded her from the head of the table with a cool expression of silent remonstration that struck her more deeply than it should have. She looked down at her plate and cleared her throat before the uncomfortable silence could stretch further.

"I apologize for disturbing the amicability of the meal. My deliverance from the machine our guest speaks of is too recent for me to comfortably accept it as a topic of casual dinner conversation. Perhaps it might be best if I excused myself . . ."

"Nonsense," Herme interrupted with a laugh. "It is we who should apologize for our boorish disregard for your feelings. It would be *best* if we recognized your obvious and well-justified discomfort and demonstrate our good character by changing the subject."

"I could not have said it better," Nath agreed, leveling a warning glance at Yeardly, who seemed about to speak. "What should we discuss? Art, theater, music? Perhaps Lieutenant Merryweather will lead us in a song?"

Merryweather smiled and raised a demurring hand. "All of you have suffered through what passes for my singing too many times already. If our purpose is to entertain rather than to torture, why should we subject our poor guest to such pain? I think the mids would profit more from comments on your Western Ocean cruise aboard the *Alianor*. I understand you gained firsthand experience of the Darghaur there."

Nath was about to decline when he caught the expression on the mids' faces, all wide-eyed and open-mouthed at the prospect of a tale of blood, thunder, and otherworldly evil.

"Well," he began reluctantly, "I was a true younker then. Nine years old and fifth mid aboard the *Alianor*, 74, under the command of my aunt, Captain Dolorous Nath."

"What a forbidding name," Herme said.

"Fit for her forbidding person," Nath said with a tight smile. "You might think sailing under my paternal aunt would have been an easy berth for a young mid, but I assure you it was anything but the case. She only took me aboard at the behest of my father, her brother, Captain Grief Nath, retired. They are both flag rank now, of course."

"Rue, Dolorous, and Grief," the privateer exclaimed. "What a grim taste in given names runs in your family!"

"I have a cousin named Grim," Nath said, chuckling. "She was testing for lieutenant just afore I took leave of Middlesea. It is a tradition, based on an old story that has been passed down in our family for unknown generations. In the region of the Westlands my folk are from, it used to be common to give children names that might foreshadow their future fortunes. Glory, Comfort, Hale, and so forth."

"Amiable, too," Lieutenant Harcourt interjected with a wry smile.

Nath grinned and raised his glass to the marine officer. "Aye, and Amiable, too! Now, the family story goes that one of our ancestors ran afoul of a hag who placed a curse upon him and all his kin, declaring that all the generations that followed would suffer the opposite of the fate portended by their name. Since then, all Nath children have received names that others might consider an evil presentiment, but, due to the letter of the curse, are actually blessings."

Herme laughed and snapped his fingers. "And there's that to your curse, hag! The awful creature wasn't very clever in her hexes, was she?"

"Nearly any curse can be turned to the victim's favor," Enid said with a sniff. "But I must agree this ogress was not the brightest of her ilk."

When the jolity died down, Nath continued.

"Captain Nath, Dolorous Nath, that is, had been given a spanking-new seventy-four and an independent cruise in the region of the Sugar Isles. It was a show of force to discourage Ardainne from sending more frigates to the area. Typical naval one-upmanship. We loitered around the approaches and snatched up several prizes, but eventually my aunt set her mind on a patrol between the Lower Approaches and the Darghaur Verge. The Vermustan pirates were restive there at that time and she desired to instill the fear of His Majesty in their bones."

"Good on her," Merryweather said sternly. "The Vermustans are the basest lot of pirates. We should plant a governor there and be done with it."

Herme gave a good-natured snort. "Phah. The same might have been said of Albion not so long ago. You may recall that anyone who lived within a day's ride of any navigable waters lived in fear of your reavers and their longships."

A retort formed on Merryweather's lips, but it died there as Nath continued his tale.

"Pirates or reavers or what have you, the Vermustans curse the *Alianor*'s memory to this day, I'll warrant. My aunt had no mercy on them. We took no prizes, but we sent a dozen or more commerce raiders to the bottom.

"It was an exciting time," Nath said. "But the adventure took a dark turn. Vermustan vessels became fewer and further between, which we credited to word of our presence spreading until we fell into the company of an Ardain merchantman that signaled for a parley. We were at peace then, Magister."

Enid nodded patiently.

"The merchant's captain advised us to make for safe harbor with haste and asked to sail under our protection. A Darghaur war barge had been spotted on a course for the Three Sisters."

The mids gasped and their seniors exclaimed troubled glances. War barges were the stuff of nightmares. Few were those who'd seen one and lived to tell the tale.

Nath let the pause get with child for effect before continuing.

"Fleeing a fight isn't in Aunt Dolorous's nature, if you'll forgive the informality. She sent the merchanter off and the *Alianor* set a course contrived to intercept the barge, which we did as night fell."

"What did it look like?" Yeardly asked in a hushed tone.

"It looked perfectly hellish," Nath said, his eyes growing distant at the recollection. "Easily half again as long and broad as our *Alianor*. Not a sail on it, but four banks of rowing tiers. Its deck was even with the first step of our mainmast, if you can credit that.

"In the dark, it was a mass of shadow, lit within by red flames and eerie greenish light. There wasn't a figure to be seen on its deck, neither Taken nor Darghaur, but there were innumerable black tubes—the so-called organ guns that the creatures prefer to honest cannon."

"Gods," Harcourt said. "Did your aunt think better of her folly?"

Nath laughed. "Not for a moment. We steered a course to bring her stern under our guns at the very limit of their range. The Darghs wanted none of that and opened up with their cursed guns and turned to deny us her stern. At the range we engaged, though, their awful shot fell short, sending up great geysers of steam where they struck the waves. And outmaneuvering a taut, fresh-bottomed ship like the *Alianor* with that great slab of oars and guns? A laughable stratagem at best."

"When we were positioned just so, Aunt Dolorous ordered that the guns should fire carefully as they bore. The *Alianor*s were crack gunners and I'm proud to say that the gunners in my division were among the best. There were very few splashes in that first volley. Nearly every round struck true."

Herme and the other naval officers leaned forward in shared professional interest, and the Ardain privateer asked, "And to what effect?"

"Negligible, at first," Nath admitted. "At least in respect to damage to the barge itself. The stern of a barge is as stout as its scantlings. There is no stern gallery to be blown and no rudder to damage. Still, some of our shot penetrated and cut a bloody swath through the human slaves manning the oars. We could hear their wails of pain and fear faintly but clearly over the distance between us. Soon we saw their bodies, both living and sorely wounded, dropped through gratings at the bottom of the rowing galleries for just that purpose."

Enid winced at the words. "Were you able to rescue any of the poor souls?"

Nath shook his head grimly. "No. They were still bound in chains that drug them to the bottom as quickly as they struck the water. I can only imagine that fresh slaves were forced onto the blood-soaked benches of their predecessors, the pitiful wretches."

Even the irrepressible Herme looked grave. "The monsters have no inkling of good or evil, pity or remorse. May the Redeemer save us if they ever leave their Fastness in force again."

"Redeemer save us, indeed," Nath agreed somberly before continuing his tale.

"The damage we wrought on that monstrous barge was slight but incremental. Soon it was literally trailing a red wake as blood poured from the rowing banks. A horrible, choking stench arose from the thing that was perceptible even at a distance. I suspect it indicated some of our shot had found a Dargh or two.

"When it became clear that we would not close with them, the Dargh assailed us with magic. It still haunts my dreams. Some of our people threw themselves into the sea or tore open their veins with their teeth in a frenzy of terror."

He tugged his stock down to reveal a ragged scar on his throat, just below his jawline. "I hurt myself thus with my bare fingers and surely would have opened my throat completely if one of our doughtier hands had not physically restrained me."

Enid visibly paled. "The art required to do such a thing—it boggles the mind. The monsters' magic is manifestly strange and powerful. Pray, how did you survive to tell the gruesome tale?"

"Larger ships-of-war, such as the *Alianor*, carry a master magister and several assistant magisters. Through their combined efforts, the miasma of terror that afflicted us was reduced, if not outright dispersed. We continued our tactic of raking the barge's stern until, at last, it turned and set a course back to the Fastness."

"A resounding victory!" The other officers at the table supported Merryweather's judgment with an enthusiastic round of "Hear, hear!"

"It didn't seem so resounding at the time," Nath said gravely. "Although we were never so much as grazed by Darghaur shot, we lost twenty-nine *Alianor*s in the engagement. All to self-inflicted wounds."

"I suppose that the common folk bore the brunt of the Darghaur magic's predations. They are weak-willed by nature and poorly suited to resist such sendings."

Nath fixed Enid with a sharp look. "They did suffer the worst in sheer numbers, of course. That is to be expected. They form the majority of the ship's inhabitants, after all. But more to your point, our gentle officers fared worse by proportion. Of the twenty-nine lost, nine were officers or warrants of gentle blood, including two lieutenants and the captain of marines—and I would have been among them if it hadn't been for a common sailor who restrained me until the fit had passed. We were forced to return to Trebon in the Isles to find suitable replacements."

Enid sat back in her chair, her brow clouded in thought.

"Did you ever clap eyes on one of them, sir?" Cullen asked. "A Dargh, I mean?"

Nath seemed to snap back to himself and gave the mid a sad smile. "Not a living one, but we did fish the corpse of one from the water. It was an awesome and disturbing sight."

"The thing was well above seven feet in height and was heavy as the devil it was. Even in death, its posture was somewhat hunched. I suspect standing fully upright, the demon would have topped nine feet. Its back, chest, and part of its abdomen was covered by a carapace so black that it absorbed light completely without so much as a glimmer reflected."

"Curious," Dr. Rondelle commented, taking notes in a pocket journal with the stub of a pencil.

"Only the beginning of a long list of curiosities," Nath said. "Its hands had four fingers, as ours, but seemed to have thumbs on either side of 'em. Its feet were cloven hooves, as befitting a devil. But the head, the head was its oddest feature. It was covered with the same darker-than-night chitin that covered its back and chest and was roughly shaped like a rounded triangle, with a point where our chin would be. It possessed no visible eyes, nose, mouth, or ears."

"Did it have hair?" Yeardley asked, eyes wide with wonder and a touch of fear.

"Unlikely," Rondelle snorted. "Did you not note the captain said it was covered with *chitin*?"

Yeardley bristled a bit under the rebuke. "I have seen hairy spiders, and they are chitinous as well!"

Rondelle was about to respond, but Nath cut him short by saying, "No, there wasn't a trace of hair on the thing. It did possess antlers, however. A large prodigious one on the right side, with four tines. The one on the left side was sawn off some six inches from its skull and capped with plain, unadorned iron. The bone between the cap and skull was painted red with horizontal black stripes."

"There are historians and philosophers that opine Darghaur antlers indicate their rank and clan," Enid said. "But obviously, none can say for certain."

"Did it stink?" Like Yeardley, Cullen was on the edge of his chair. "Like you suspected?"

"And what was the cause of death?" Dr. Rondelle asked. "Was any study made of its innards?"

"It stank to high heavens," Nath said, taking the questions in order. "Although 'stink' is not altogether accurate. Better to say its odor was overpowering, unpleasant in an inexplicable way, and difficult to define. It had a strong smell of something akin to cinnamon.

"As to how it died, there was nothing mysterious about that: it was run through the chest by a wooden splinter thicker than my thigh. Our doctor and mage wished to make a study of its inner works, but the sight and smell of the thing was more than most of us could stand at that point, so my aunt ordered it returned to the sea."

Dr. Rondelle clucked his disapproval. "Such a waste."

"You were not there, sir," Nath responded with uncharacteristic sharpness. "Or you might think differently."

Rondelle raised an apologetic hand and said, "I speak only from the perspective of a man of medicine, sir. I do not question your aunt's judgment in the matter."

Nath received the apology, such as it was, with a curt nod.

"Well," he said, after a short silence, "that is the story of my encounter with the Darghaur. I'm happy to say that Aunt Dolorous's stratagem for turning the barge is now taught to all captains assigned to the Verge and their environs."

"It is a drama worthy of the stage," Herme said, without a trace of sarcasm.

"You know, I have always had an inkling's desire to try my hand at a play," Nath admitted reluctantly. "I suppose we all desire a vocation at some point that we cannot have. I wouldn't doubt that Marbury secretly desired to be a sailor, as often as he wrote of 'em."

"Or perhaps a king," Herme said, winking slyly. "He wrote of them often enough, too. I must say given the choice between the two, I'd take the crown of a king on my head rather than the king's crown in my pocket."

Nath laughed out loud at the jest and was about to expound upon it when, up on deck, the ship's bell rang the hour. He sighed and pushed away from the table.

"Well, four of Ostoporto's finest soldiers are dead on the table before us and the hour has become late," Nath said, taking in the empty oporto bottles with a broad wave of his hand. "I fear I must wish you all a pleasant evening. Merryweather, a moment if you please."

Enid and the mids made their obedience and slipped out of the cabin, where a marine was waiting to return Herme to confinement.

After a mawkish bow, the Artagnac privateer followed the marine below, humming one of his mountainous homeland's shepherd's tunes.

"I dislike that fellow," Yeardly hissed. "He is too pleasant by half. A smiling snake's whitest teeth are its fangs, my old granddad used to say."

Enid was barely aware of Cullen's reproachful words as he hustled Yeardly off to the mids' berth. Her mind was too occupied with the evening's conundrum: Was the valor ascribed to the commoners in Nath's tale anomalous, or did they represent a profound indictment of her imperfect understanding of the character of the base-born?

It was easy enough to accept that commoners were capable of harmonious and efficient labor without that much intervention from their betters. The easy, cohesive manner in which the *Alarum*'s crew carried out their duties was eloquent proof of that.

Nor did such an observation prove too startling a revelation: She was well aware that the lowborn were responsible for much of Ardainne's industry and agriculture—a fact that Theocratic agitators harped on endlessly in the days leading up to the revolution. To accept them as her moral equals on the battlefield, however, was too incredible. Still, Nath did not strike her as prone to romanticism, at least so far as the performance of those under his command was concerned, and Merryweather, who obviously shared his opinions, struck her as absolutely pragmatic.

Her reverie was interrupted by the shuffle and stamp of the marine guard at Nath's door coming to attention as Merryweather closed it behind her. Enid turned in time to catch a sly and rather pleased smile on the lieutenant's face before it was reabsorbed into her usual expression of stern amusement.

"Well, Magister, I give you joy for a remarkable performance under trying circumstances." Merryweather took Enid by the elbow and led her toward the companionway. "That privateer is a cocky fellow, and I can only imagine how much his smiles and japes must offend you, representing the antithesis of your nation's welfare as he does. I found you to be quite moderate in both word and glance, all things considered. My admiration for your restraint knows no, well, restraint."

They shared a smile as they stepped out into the relative cool of the deck. Enid lit a cigarillo for Merryweather as they lingered a moment by the rail. Night had deepened since she went below, trading its cloak of rich blue for one of elegant black. She was always struck by the brilliant abundance of stars when she went on deck at night. Millions or more of them, scattered across the sky like diamonds strewn over a sable cloth. No emperor ever wore such a fine raiment, she thought, no earthly grandeur could signify in comparison.

"You know your stars, Enid?" Merryweather asked, following her gaze as she leaned on the rail and savored her cigarillo.

"Moderately well." Enid shrugged, lighting a smoke for herself. "Some of the more complex rituals involved in advanced formulations require familiarity with the celestial sphere. They interest you, beyond their obvious beauty?"

"They do. I have recently read a monograph, kindly loaned me by Captain Nath, describing how the stars can be used with a timepiece to accurately plot the position of a ship upon a chart."

Enid snorted smoke. "What is the benefit of such an exercise? It seems an unwarranted amount of effort to achieve what must be a grossly inaccurate result."

"Oh, yes," Merryweather agreed with a chuckle. "Quite impracticable in comparison to navigation by ley lines, of course. Still, it is an interesting philosophical puzzle. Such things have fascinated me since I was a girl. Had I not gone to sea, I believe I might have pursued a career in academics—perhaps in the physical sciences."

"Your talents are put to better use in your current profession than in the pursuit of trivial knowledge, I think. Tell me, though, why did you go to sea if your interests lay elsewhere?"

Merryweather took a long draw on her cigarillo and exhaled her answer with a long stream of smoke. "Tradition."

Enid nodded. "Ah, I see. You are from a naval line, then?"

"Oh, veritable merfolk, we Merryweathers," she answered with a wistful smile. "My father is a rear admiral on Saint Mahaute Station, and all my older brothers and sisters are post captains. Most of my aunts and uncles are in the Sea Service as well."

Enid chewed her lip thoughtfully before finally relenting to her curiosity. "In Ardainne, a gentleperson only seeks service in the navy if they lack the funds to purchase a position in one of the cavalry regiments. We look upon the Sea Service as a viable option for nobility who are too poor or too ill connected for a more glorious appointment. I do not mean to offend, Augusta, but is it thus in Albion as well?"

Merryweather hid her amusement behind a cough and shook her head. "Far from it, Magister, far from it. You see, we are an island kingdom with a long history of naval glory, dating back to the fearsome reavers who preyed upon every coast within reach of their longships, even your own. In modern times, protecting our homeland has fallen to our navy more often than our armies. Albion's cities require no stone walls around them as long as the kingdom's wooden walls still stand, as the saw goes."

"I believe I've heard a song to that effect," Enid said with a wry smile.

"Oh, it is a hackneyed expression, I'll grant you that. Still, clichés are not always groundless. Truths are repeated as often as fancies, after all."

Merryweather turned her back to the rail and leaned against it with her elbows. Crewmen nearby paid the women little attention, other than to give them a wide enough berth to avoid the appearance of eavesdropping. The *Alarum*'s ability to create the illusion of privacy where there was none was a source of constant wonder to Enid.

Merryweather tossed the butt of her cigarillo over the rail and Enid asked, "Would you care for another?"

Merryweather waved the offered smoke away with a polite smile. "I don't have the same appetite for them as our captain does. You won't have a chance to replenish your stores till we return to Gisbon, so you'd best save them to share with him."

Enid smiled slyly. "He smokes like a furnace, doesn't he? I think when I first came aboard you thought I might contribute to another of his vices as well."

Merryweather coughed again and lowered her voice to a whisper. "That was before I came to know you. Captain Nath has a reputation for his good fortune in turning up lovely ladies in the most unlikely places."

"And yet you said you wished to dance with me the moment you saw me."

"I offer no excuse for it, either," Merryweather said. "And having danced with you once, I am tortured by each moment that delays me from doing so again."

"It is a mutual torture, I assure you."

"One that shall be relieved the instant we are ashore and at liberty," Merryweather said. The husky near-growl of her voice tasked Enid's self-control as thoughts of their lips crushed together filled her mind.

"I suppose there are still a few aboard who think I am little more than a useful adornment for their illustrious captain?"

"Nonsense. We've seen the hand you've taken with the young gentles' education, particularly with Mr. Yeardly and Ms. Harlech. You've been most conscientious in your efforts to learn the ship's routine and your role in it. Do not think the long hours you spend at your studies go unnoticed, Enid."

Enid let the compliments pass without comment.

"Does our captain have any other reputation I should be aware of? I don't mean to indulge in idle gossip, of course, but it might be helpful to understand the man more completely if I am to serve him effectively."

Merryweather grinned. "I would never stoop to gossip, dear, especially as I know so little of our captain beyond what I've witnessed myself under his command. Still, while we were in Middlesea awaiting his arrival, I heard nothing worse than his liberal affections."

"And his family?"

"As maritime as my own," Merryweather said. "As you've probably gathered. Most of his clan is in the Sea Service or employed in its support. His father is a flag officer famous for his frigate actions during the Naveroñian Troubles. Naval service was a foregone conclusion for young Rue, so his father and aunt conspired to see him listed on the naval rolls when he was very young."

"Ah," Enid said, "I assume his mother had already vanished?"

"Vanished," Merryweather said with a confused expression.

"Oh, that is an Ardain expression. I believe you say 'passed away' in Albion."

Merryweather chuckled. "Yes. In the king's navy we say the deceased has 'given up their number.' The dead have no more need for the numbered brass chits used to draw their mess. It will be reissued, you see, hence we also say 'their number is up,' meaning it's available for a new—"

"The poor boy," Enid said.

Merryweather nodded and paused to direct a nearby crewman to bear her regards to Mr. Dinwitty, whom she had just espied slumped in the shadow of one of the ship's boats, sleeping. "Tell that lazy rascal that since he has demonstrated such devotion for a good caulk, he can lead a party in inspecting the seams on the morrow."

"Was it worrisome to come under the command of such a young officer?"

"Not at all," Merryweather said in a lower voice. "In fact, I was quite relieved. The Red Witch of Hathesby would have been more welcome to most of the officers and crew than Lord Aixely. I normally would rather be flogged than speak ill of an officer, but that man's indolence and lack of regard for the Service is infamous."

"You served under him in the past?"

"Yes, on his last cruise in the old *Brazen*, 32. He'd just made post and come over from the sloop *Vigilant*. His interest was powerful enough to secure him an immediate command while more senior captains marked time ashore on half pay. He brought his favorite officers and warrants over to the *Brazen*, not that he had many. That's how we came by Master Harde, for instance. I suppose I qualified as a 'favorite,' too, else I wouldn't have been selected for his first cruise as post captain, nor sent aboard the *Alarum* with his toadies. I should be grateful not to be on half pay ashore, but I can tell you the best news I've had in some time was that Devil Aryl had given the *Alarum* to another captain, even if he was a callow youngster that barely topped my shoulder."

"What made Lord Aixely such a dreadful commander?"

"His innate character," Merryweather answered with a smirk. She studied Enid for a moment and then said, "I find I could use a little more smoke, but not enough to light another cigarillo. Share a puff or two with me as we talk?"

"With pleasure," Enid said, passing her smoke to Merryweather, who took a long puff from it before handing it back.

"Delicious," she breathed, and then carried on with her indictment of Aixely. "As I said, his very character makes him a poor commander. He is arbitrary and cruel—and none but the most hardened sycophants can stay in his good graces. Captain Nath proved to be far more even-handed. He distributes his pleasure and ire where reason and the custom of service dictate, without regard to favorites."

"He does seem well loved by the officers and common sailors alike. Such esteem is the natural consequence of just rule, I suppose."

Enid passed her cigarillo to Merryweather, who leaned close to accept it and did not pull away afterward.

"You may rely on it. A taut, fair captain may not guarantee a happy ship, but it comes as close as can be. Of course, it cannot be denied that a captain's star rises apace with his people's prize account. I can name at least one utter scoundrel who fills his ship with volunteers who can hand and reef a sail at the start of any cruise because he is known to be a prolific prize-taker. Many are willing to hazard a few extra stripes on their back if they're certain of ending a cruise with a prize or two to their account. Our captain Nath excels in that regard as well. He is like a starving man at the table when prizes are within sight. He'll snatch up whatever morsels are near at hand without regard for their provenance. The crumbs will serve as well as the bread."

"He is driven by avarice, then?" Enid was reminded of her early impression of Nath as a grasping shopkeeper aboard the *Marie*. "I thought his family was of some consequence. Has he fallen on bad times? I know that I value a sou more than I once did now that my familial lands are lost to the Republic."

"Well, do not fail to budget for the Lithain water. It is intoxicating." Merryweather relinquished the stub of the cigarillo to Enid and resumed the course of their conversation. "I thought the same thing at first, but I've come to believe that where Captain Nath is concerned, the value of the prize don't signify against the glory of its taking. Between you, me, and the rail here, I believe our captain has set his sights high and looks for glory in battle to elevate him to the point that his shot might land where he desires. It is providential that his skills appear to match his ambitions, otherwise any who sailed with him would be doomed."

"Hmm." Enid studied the burned-down butt of her cigarillo thoughtfully for a moment before flicking it over the side. "Well, as delightful and educational as this has been, the hour grows late, and I suppose I should retire."

"It might be best for us both if you did," Merryweather agreed, with a gleam in her eye. "I have not been in less command of my passions since the first time I was smitten."

"You'll have to share that story with me at some point," Enid said, stepping away from the rail. In a louder voice she said, "Thank you for sharing your nautical wisdom, Lieutenant. You are an accomplished instructor."

Merryweather touched the brim of her bicorn in a casual salute and said, "Rest well, Spells. Tomorrow may prove eventful."

Enid smiled, took her leave of the lieutenant, and retired to her cabin. Had they been ashore, and out of ship's discipline, she would not be slipping under the covers alone nor in modest sleep clothes. She put that thought from her mind and settled into her cot. After muttering a calming cantrip, she settled into immediate slumber.

chapter 18

Enid arose excruciatingly early, awakened as usual by the muffled scrape and roar of the holystones on the deck directly above her head. As impressive as the clean, white sweep of the *Alarum*'s deck was, even to her landsman's eyes, she did not believe it was worth the clamor required to maintain it. Unfortunately, the scant time she'd spent on the *Alarum* convinced her nothing short of imminent capsize would deter the work teams from the routine of their sand, water, and holystones.

"Magister d'Tancreville!" Nath greeted her as she approached the quarterdeck. "I was about to send Mr. Yeardly here to fetch you! I trust the morning finds you well?"

"Passing well, thank you." She made an expansive gesture at the hectic activity on deck. "If you would not think it too forward, what is the cause for all this bustle? Has an enemy been spotted?"

She shielded her eyes against the rising sun and scanned the horizon to seaward, half expecting to see a man-of-war bearing down upon them.

"No, nothing of the sort," Nath answered with an airy grin. "But with any luck at all we shall spot him before lunch."

"You can be so certain the enemy will pass by us here?"

"Certainly not, but I can be fairly certain we will pass by the enemy there." He pointed over her shoulder toward Monte Ybarre's morning-mist-blurred outline in the distance. "Well, at least some of us shall. It is my intent to take Citizen Herme's *Tape a'Bord* into Puerto Galeno and put an end to this search once and for all. I think it can safely be said that if we do not find our prey there, our part in the hunt will be over. I thought you might be interested in accompanying me, especially since such a personal reconnoiter might be to our mutual benefit later."

"I would be honored to take part, sir." Enid felt her spirit stir at the opportunity to prove useful for more than charging spell-locks. "Are there any particular preparations I should make?"

"Dress in plain costume. Bring a brace of pistols if you have them. If not, draw them from the armorer. And your sword, of course. Wear nothing to identify you as an Albion officer." Nath thought a moment, pinching his lower lip between his thumb and forefinger, and then shrugged. "And whatever magical accoutrements you feel may be of use to you on a scouting mission. We will avoid combat at all costs—ours is but to see and report for now."

"As you will, sir."

Enid hurried belowdecks to prepare her weapons and certain sorcerous preparations she felt might be of use. As she charged a pair of matched Kreitzer spell-lock pistols, she felt the silver ring grow chill upon her finger. She closed her eyes and engaged Dunaughy in a short, internal conversation in which he advised her to take particular care in preparing a link to several sylphs should the schooner require extra speed to escape. In less than an hour, she finished all her preparations, both martial and arcane, and presented herself to Nath clad in the plainest clothes in her possession.

Nath raised a brow at the sight of her and bit his lip to avoid laughing.

"I fear we shall not be riding this morning, Magister d'Tancreville."

Enid glanced down at her riding clothes and frowned. "This costume has served me hunting and I cannot see why it would not serve in this." She plucked at the buff sleeve of her jacket, a sleeve that was only partially covered by elaborate floral stitchwork designs. "This is buckskin, as you can see, and stout enough to turn a blade—a characteristic that might prove useful in this endeavor."

"That may well be, Magister," Nath answered with a barely subdued grin, "but you must believe me when I tell you that whatever sort of attire the people in that port might expect to see on the crew of an Ardain privateer, they most certainly do not expect to see tooled buckskin riding togs. A slop coat should cover your finery at the distance at which we are likely to be observed, however, Yeardly! My compliments to the purser and a large slop coat for the magister! Make haste!"

Nath smiled at Enid, who seemed caught in a state between indignant fuming and nonplussed bemusement. "You will not find slops to your liking, I'm sure, but you may take comfort that your captain will be dressed no better."

"As you will, sir."

"Our guests are all safely settled in, Lieutenant Merryweather?" Nath asked.

"Yes, sir. As surly a lot of hard bargains as I have ever clapped eyes on, too. Lieutenant Harcourt's marines have them well in hand, though."

Nath nodded. "Set a pair of swivel guns to cover the hatch. That should discourage any foolishness."

"As you wish, sir, but I assure you, the marines have the matter well in hand . . ."

"I do not doubt it, Merryweather." Nath punctuated his remark with a respectful nod to Lieutenant Harcourt, who stood at Merryweather's left hand. "I have every confidence that the marines could instantly repulse any attempt to break out of the hold. However, it is quite possible that most of his lobsters will be unavailable for the task tonight. The swivel guns should make up for the lack."

He gestured toward the captured schooner and explained, "If we find our quarry in port, as I believe we shall, darkness will find us cutting her out. We won't have the luxury of leaving many marines behind to play nursemaid for our unwilling guests."

Merryweather began to speak but swallowed her words with some effort. As eager as she was to finally discover the nature of their prey, a crowded deck was no place to ask. If there was to be any impertinence, it would not be hers, nor after her example. Nath noticed his lieutenant's restraint and admired it. He was in no wise certain he would demonstrate the same control under similar circumstances. Soon, all would be revealed. He cast a quick eye over the schooner and found her manned and ready.

"You have command of the *Alarum*, Lieutenant Merryweather. I will repair to the *Toucher du Bois*. Have Mr. Yeardly join me there with the magister's coat. I will rejoin you here by nightfall. If I fail to appear by morning, make all sail for Gisbon immediately."

Bosun's pipes skirled as Nath's hat vanished below the level of the *Alarum*'s deck, closely followed by a sour-faced Enid d'Tancreville.

Enid watched as Monte Ybarre slid by on the *Alarum*'s larboard side and a smaller prominence, unnamed as far as she knew, matched its pace to starboard. She had the unsettling impression of drifting slowly into the maw of some predatory beast, a sentiment her pinched expression conveyed clearly to Nath, with whom she was standing near the schooner's helm.

"I see the sailor's soul growing within you, Lady Magister. Land on three sides is unsettling, is it not?"

"Indeed. It conjures images from d'Troyen's *The Golden Ship*, although I doubt there are any angels loitering nearby to save any of us from 'a fatal ride upon a foal of foam.' What if the wind shifts? Will we not be trapped?"

"'A foal of foam!' Phah. A ride upon a foal can only be fatal to the poor beast itself. The body of d'Troyen's work is admirable, but the lengths he would go to in the name of alliteration were often deplorable." Nath shook his head and indicated the wind's direction with a gesture of his hand. "We have a soldier's wind. We can sail out as easily as we are sailing in. We can reach handily in either direction."

"I'm glad to hear it. I am much reassured." Her gaze lingered apprehensively on the spray-blackened, craggy face of Monte Ybarre despite her words and the game sentiment behind them. She pointed at the rocky peak and asked if there were cannon emplaced upon it.

"No, thank the Redeemer. Nor on that other damned rock, Arethusa. There is a fine fortress situated nearer the mouth of the actual harbor, though, covering its approaches. And of course, there are gunboats stationed there as well, like hounds waiting to throw themselves against any wolves that might threaten the sheep in their care. All of this should be perfectly visible as soon as we round the point there."

And so it was, along with another sight that produced a delighted exclamation from Nath.

"She is there!" he exulted, pointing toward the base of an impressive fortification. "And look, her spars are crossed! No doubt they intended to sneak her out soon, and farther down the coast to Cadice. Well, we'll do them a favor and take her south a bit sooner than they'd expected!"

Enid muttered a short cantrip to increase the acuity of her vision to study the vessel in question more closely. It was simplicity itself to recognize *Redemption*, as she was the only vessel of any size in the anchorage, safely tucked beneath the forbidding mass of a formidable fortification that literally bristled with cannon. To her untrained eye, *Redemption* seemed very much like the *Alarum* in appearance. The similarity between the two vessels ended there, however. *Alarum* seemed a trim, gallant vessel, despite the ominous false colors under which she sailed at the time. The first sight of *Redemption*, however, knotted her stomach with dread. The vessel emanated an aura of patient, implacable enmity, as if she were waiting for an opportunity to do her worst, like an asp coiled in one's shoe. While Enid felt no sign of a magister aboard the frigate, unfamiliar magic lurked in the dark spaces behind her freshly painted timbers. As Enid studied *Redemption*, she had the distinct impression of looking upon a slumbering beast that would surely awaken and rend the flesh from her bones if she stared too long.

"She is poorly named," she observed somberly. The faint quaver in her voice caught Nath's attention and he turned to regard her with troubled blue eyes.

"What is the matter, magister? You look as if you've just seen a ghost."

"I very nearly believe I have."

They rejoined the *Alarum* just as the sun was sinking below the horizon in the sort of blazing glory so adored by poets and artists. Nath was immune to the display as he climbed aboard to the accompaniment of skirling bosun's pipes. He returned Merryweather's salute briskly and turned to offer Enid a hand up. She accepted his assistance in silence, still disturbed by the impression the *Redemption* made upon her.

"All officers to my cabin immediately," Nath barked at Merryweather, who promptly began passing the word. A small smile broke through Enid's dour mien as the shouts began traversing the vessel from end to end, setting mids scurrying to carry their captain's compliments to the ship's various officers. The controlled chaos of such moments was one of the facets of shipboard life that made it so fascinating to her. Despite the racket raised by the "passing word," it seemed to Enid that a tense hush gripped the vessel, an anticipatory silence that no amount of noise could drown out. She followed Nath into his cabin, and at his gesture, joined him at his table. They sat together in profound silence as the portentousness of the discovery weighed upon each of them in its own way, setting Nath's mind afire with barely sub-limated dreams of shipping his captain's epaulette from the beneficent hand of the Hero of Filsterhead himself, while Enid's thoughts took a darker course, rooted in her belief that such an obviously ill-fated vessel was where it lay.

In less than a quarter of an hour, they were joined by the remain-der of the *Alarum*'s officers, who gathered around their captain's table, their faces schooled to a blank professionalism that clashed almost comically with the avidity of their posture. They reminded her of noth-ing more than a pack of hounds straining against the leash after catch-ing the scent of blood. Even the cadaverous old surgeon, Dr. Rondelle, who normally held forth at length in strident, brassy tones concerning the inevitable results of battles won or lost ("Mind me, gentlemen, it is all songs and glory till someone has an eye out!"), seemed on edge with anticipation.

"My *Alarum*s," Nath began crisply, "His Majesty's Ship the *Re-demption*, taken by mutineers and delivered for specie to the Nav-eroñian crown in '81, lies under the guns of Castle Ybarre. Her spars are crossed, and her decks are in good order. She appears to be fully manned by a Naveroñian crew. I intend to take our boats in and cut her out."

Lieutenants Merryweather and Harcourt exchanged pleased glances and Oxley seemed about to stutter out something encourag-ing, but his mouth snapped shut audibly as Nath pressed on, describ-ing his plan.

"I will take the pinnace and lead a pair of boats around the *Re-demption*'s starboard side. Magister d'Tancreville will accompany us and attempt to mask our approach with her arts. We must come on stealthily, as there are gunboats to be dealt with and the castle's guns to be considered. Lieutenant Merryweather will take the gig and a pair of cutters to the larboard. When we board, I desire enough men to be left in the boats to take the *Redemption* under tow if necessary. Once we have taken the deck and fire has abated, topmen will ascend and release her topsails. Once the topsails are down, the carpenter and his mate will cut her hawsers. I'll want the men in the boats to pull her head round so we can gain steerage way on the instant."

An agreeable murmur circled the table. Enid did not add her voice to the supportive babble. Her ignorance of naval tactics made any pronouncement effectively valueless. Nath allowed the cheerful nattering to go on for a moment before raising a silencing hand.

"This will be no fiddler's green! The *Redemption* lies at anchor well within range of Castillo Ybarre's guns, great murthering guns fed with good iron shot and hot shot as well, if my eyes did not deceive me. You saw the furnace smoke, did you not, Magister?"

"I saw smoke, thin wisps of the stuff," Enid answered primly. "But I cannot say whether it came from furnaces or no. I lack your expertise in such matters, sir."

Nath made a noncommittal noise in the back of his throat. "Be that as it may, there are over two hundred guns in that castle, any one of which could smash our boats to flinders as we approach or hull the *Redemption* as we take her out. There are also gunboats to be dealt with, or better yet, avoided. This is no lark, I assure you."

He met the gaze of each of his officers in turn, and the uncharacteristic severity of his pale blue eyes reinforced his words with sobering effect. He nodded his approval of their sudden gravity and continued.

"That is not to say that I fear the outcome of the undertaking. To the contrary, I have no doubt but that we shall succeed in this fortunate task. But if we wish to succeed with a butcher's bill that does not sicken our hearts and bleed the *Alarum* white, we must proceed with cool sobriety and careful planning. Now, if you will join me, I believe I will speak to the men before turning them over to you to prepare for the evening's action."

Every eye on deck had followed Nath's back as it retreated purposefully toward his quarters after reconnoitering Puerto Galeno. Now the same eyes, reinforced by the presence of the idlers and the off-duty watch, greeted him as he reemerged on deck. His officers trailed behind, their faces masks of professionalism tinged with only the faintest hint of enthusiasm. Enid stood among them, wincing minutely as Nath said a word and the bosun's pipes began to shriek "all hands on deck."

Enid watched Nath as the crew rushed to form up in their divisions. He stood at the quarterdeck's rail, his feet shoulder-width apart and his hands clasped firmly behind his back. She envied the easy way his body swayed to the Merentian Sea's gentle swell and noticed that his left hand clenched and unclenched in rhythm to the rise and fall of the deck. The action brought to mind the great Velascan thespian, Agnolino Lorri.

Theater lore had it that Lorri, perhaps the greatest actor of the last century, finished each line by clenching his fist with such force that his palm was stained with blood at the end of each act. She wondered if this reflexive tensing of Nath's left hand indicated nervousness at addressing his men en masse, or an uneasiness regarding the subject of the address. Neither seemed likely based on what she'd seen of the man so far, but there was no other likely explanation for his fidget than fiercely sublimated anxiety. When Nath spoke, however, there was no sign of nervousness in the booming clarity of his voice.

"*Alarum*s!"

Nath's "command voice" carried from one end of the light frigate to the other. Enid did not doubt that he was clearly heard by the few men left as a prize crew on the *Toucher du Bois*, which bobbed calmly off the *Alarum*'s stern. She wondered what the privateer's crew, locked in the hold below, and their sanguine "Citizen Captain" would think of Nath's address. She frowned at the ease with which his smugly insouciant features crystallized before her mind's eye. Pursing her lips petulantly, she returned her full attention to Nath's speech.

"Fortune has favored us with the opportunity of a lifetime! An opportunity to serve our king! To avenge the honor of our Service! Each one of us will, before dawn, have gained a share in such glory that our children's children will bask in the fame of our posterity!"

Nath paused for a moment, his glance taking in the solemn faces of his crew, some grave and, yes, a little fearful, others more speculative. He smiled as he leaned over the rail and went on in a bantering tone. His left hand continued to spasm.

"Some of you are old hands. You have sailed with me since departing Middlesea, since the taking of the *Artagny* frigate, the *Marie*, and the others. You've made your king and captain proud . . . and put aside a bit of tin in the process!"

Enid noticed all the ship's people, whether truly old hands or those who had been recruited by Nath less than three months ago, stood a little straighter and tossed each other self-assured glances from the corners of their eyes. There were precious few of them left, Enid realized. Probably less than a third of the original crew remained, the rest parceled off to serve in prize crews.

"The rest of you, you newcomers added to the books at Gisbon— do not think that your hard efforts at sail and gun drill have gone unnoticed! If the *Alarum* is a lucky ship, then she is twice as fortunate to have drawn such as you to serve aboard her!"

More than a few sheepish smiles appeared among the "new people" at Nath's words. More significant, though, Enid thought, were the nods of agreement from several of the original *Alarum*s. These gestures of solidarity bode well for the acceptance of Nath's next words.

"Lieutenant Merryweather informs me that the last three gun drills have carved two seconds off the speediest drill on record before Gisbon. No crew divided between old and new hands could work so smoothly at the great guns. Only a crew that acts as one, with trust and confidence in the skills of their division mates, can fire volleys so swift and sharply! You are no longer the old or the new *Alarum*s, but simply *ALARUM*S!"

The answering cheer was ragged at first but reached a gratifying level of cohesion and volume by the third "hurrah!" Nath raised a hand and held it above his head until the appreciative tumult subsided.

"Yes, you deserve a cheer," he continued, the hint of a somber smile in his voice. "You are a solid, gallant crew and just the sort of fire-eaters for the task at hand. It has fallen to us to set right a wrong that another crew perpetrated, a terrible crime against their king and and shipmates."

"Five years ago, the HMS *Redemption* was seized by mutineers off the coast of Osberia. Not well enough pleased with mutiny, the villains sailed the *Redemption* to Cadice, sold her to the Naveroñian Crown, and added the black mark of treason against their names as well. The continental kingdoms crowed in delight at this outrage, which made our king—*our king*—and the Sea Service—*our Service*—look ridiculous!"

Most of the *Alarum*s were familiar with the *Redemption* affair and grumbled at the shameful memory. The few to whom the story was new scowled right along with their brethren in-the-know. No one in their right mind wished to be seen as complacent toward mutiny and treason. Nath recognized the perfunctory response, but was pleased by their reaction nonetheless, and continued in a stronger, more eager tone.

"Oh, yes, they rubbed dirt on the honor of our Service and our king, but now we have been given a chance to wipe the grin off the traitors' damnable faces and choke those arrogant continentals on their own damned japes!

"There," he shouted, pointing landward. "There is Puerto Galeno, and anchored there, wrapped up like a Winter's End present, is the *Redemption*! They've snugged her down right under the guns of their old castle, covered her with two hundred guns, and set a wolf pack of gunboats to block the approaches—and why? Because the perfume-sniffing dons know it took two score Albion traitors to deliver them the *Redemption*, but it would only take a half dozen solid Albion tars to take her BACK!"

Nath may have said more, but if he did, his words were lost in the savage roar that suddenly erupted from his crew. Although Enid knew that none of their bloodthirsty energy was directed at her, she was nonetheless grateful that she stood on the quarterdeck behind Nath rather than down in the waist. Her first reaction to the sudden display of ardently vocal enthusiasm was to balk and take a step back, the inarticulate shouts bringing the vicious mobs that now ruled the streets of her beloved Arden instantly to mind: hateful masses consumed by resentment and disenfranchisement, united into a single, voracious monster with an unquenchable thirst for blood. A glance at their upturned faces dispelled that initial impression, however. Theirs were not the mad, rolling eyes of the Theocratic mob. No, their eyes were locked with fierce adoration on the slim form of their captain, the man who had instilled this sudden, shared purpose in them.

Far from a brutish, uncontrolled beast bent on senseless mayhem, this creature summoned by Nath's words quivered with discipline and a desire to be unleashed upon whatever task he desired. When Nath turned to glance over his shoulder at her, he wore his impassive "officerly" expression, but his face was still radiant with the joy of what he'd done, of what he'd created.

The crew's belligerent shouts coalesced into organized cheers. As the third "huzzah" was echoing across the waves and before a fourth could take flight, Nath shouted, "We will cut her out, *Alarum*s! We will cut her out as fast as you can say 'knife!' Now, Officers, to your divisions! Organize the cutting-out parties! The crew to eat once they're assigned their boats and duties!"

Nath turned briskly on his heel as his officers took his noisy, energetic crew in hand. As he passed, Enid's hand snapped to salute all of its own accord. He smiled as he touched the brim of his hat and paused long enough to say, "I'd be honored were you to dine with me tonight, Magister, were you so disposed."

chapter 19

Enid found dinner to be plain but plentiful, the atmosphere redolent with a mixture of subdued enthusiasm and ferocity that made itself felt in the form of exaggerated formality tempered by the occasional outburst of coarse, raucous humor that apparently passed for wit in naval circles. Nath restricted the flow of alcohol after the first volley of toasts, ordering Alston to strike the wine and port in favor of small ale.

Conversation was vague for the most part, and Enid suspected the gathered officers conspired to avoid subjects of any real substance. All references to the impending action were circumspect and quickly dispensed with. The strongest allusion came from Nath himself when he observed Merryweather might soon "ship a swab of her own" if all went well during the night. Although Merryweather was obviously abashed by her captain's comment, she was just as obviously pleased. Later, after the other officers excused themselves to prepare for the cutting out, Enid asked what the arcane phrase meant.

"This bit of tassel and gilt is referred to familiarly as a swab," Nath informed her, tapping the epaulette on his left shoulder. "It is my intention to put Merryweather in command of the *Redemption*. If I were post myself, bringing such a prize into port would be enough to make her post as well. Even as things are, though, the least she can expect for the honor is a command of her own—and a commander's swab to go with it."

"And there will be some sort of reward for you as well?"

"Oh, there will be reward enough to go around. Post for myself, I'd imagine—no, honestly, I pray!" Nath chuckled amiably and tapped his knuckle on the wooden table.

"What is this famous *post* you speak of?"

"To be made post is the dearest desire of every lieutenant or commander in the king's navy. It's an apotheosis of a sort, a sanctification that once granted cannot be rescinded." Nath flashed a boyish grin and explained, "As a commander, I am only considered a captain while in command of a king's warship. Without a vessel to command, I'm only a lieutenant—and worse, once made a commander, a lieutenant is too tainted by pride to serve humbly under another officer's command. So, if there are no ships available at the end of this cruise, I will languish ashore at half pay—which by the peculiarities of Admiralty mathematics equates to something like a third."

Enid gave a little snort. Between the odd weights and measures used by the purser and the confusing use of ranks, she was not surprised that a maritime "half" would not be the same as she was used to ashore.

"Now, once made post, all such fears are banished. A post captain is a true captain and will be treated as such regardless of his fortune in finding an actual command. What is more, his name is added to the *Navy List*."

"And this is some sort of signal honor?"

"Well, to those on it or aspiring to it, yes. But beyond the honor is the fact that those on the list will someday rise to the rank of admiral should they live long enough. Think of it! To be an admiral! Whole fleets at one's command and an eighth of all their prizes!"

"Fortunes are to be made in the service of one's king, then?"

"Never doubt it. Earl Weymouth will have an eighth of all I and any of the captains beneath him take without ever stirring his flagship from anchor. Your admirals down in the Sugar Isles? Why, a year on station leaves them richer than three bankers and all their lawyers!"

"So, all this gallantry is aimed at attaining a position where you can profit from similarly ambitious officers some day?" Enid inquired in a carefully flat tone.

"Not at all," Nath answered seriously. "The truth of the matter is that while I can barely imagine myself an admiral, a heartbeat rarely passes that I do not think fondly upon the day that I may be made post."

He turned to stare at his reflection in the glass of the stern gallery windows. "And it has nothing to do with pay or rising up the list—or very little to do with it, at any rate—and everything to do with command, the assured continuity of command.

"I must own that there is nothing on earth I love so much as command. All the terror of it, all the joy—I cannot imagine how empty my life would be without the prospect of it, nor envision suffering such a meaningless existence." Nath's shrug was vaguely apologetic.

"My father once said much the same about the rule of his lands," Enid said. "It is a common sentiment among rulers. I suppose there is something intoxicating in the enforced obeisance and obedience of others."

"Only the vilest of hypocrites would deny it," Nath agreed wryly. "And yet it is only the smallest part of my feelings toward command. You know of schoolmasters?"

"I'm sensible of them," Enid admitted with a touch of humor. "And I have recently developed a more sympathetic understanding of the hardships of their calling."

"Well, think of them then: They have the purest mastery over their wards. A single word is enough to bring painful justice down upon the disobedient or insolent. As I am fortunate in the matter of education,

I'm quite qualified for such a position, but would rather be flogged. Do you take my meaning?"

"I believe so, but a further elucidation could do no harm."

"Then you shall have it: Mastery over men is not so gratifying to make a vocation agreeable to me purely by virtue of receiving it. It is the command of the *Alarum* herself, people, timber, and guns, that captivates my genius."

"More so when that command is set against a difficult challenge, I'll wager." Enid lit a pair of cigarillos and handed one to Nath, who accepted it with a grateful smile. "You have troubled yourself that your distaste for Captain Ambrose has led you into disobedience to spite him, but I believe you would make the same try for the *Redemption* regardless. It seems clear to me it is not in your nature to be satisfied with any attempt save the strongest. You remind me, if you will forgive the comparison, of this new breed of Albion terrier that once set upon a confrontation will not withdraw, no matter the size or ferocity of their opponent."

"Parson Riordans," Nath said with an amiable chuckle.

"I beg your pardon?"

"The new breed of terrier that everyone is so on about, they're called after the sporting parson that first bred them." Nath leaned back in his chair and took a long, lung-filling draw on his cigarillo. "Beautiful little brutes with prodigious spirits. I must admit I'm with child to lay hands on a pair of them!"

"Fox hunter, then?"

"Loathe the sport, actually. What a dreary waste of time and energy, all spent in pursuit of an inedible scrap of meat! But those Parson Riordan terriers are such handsome and intelligent-looking creatures, and it is not unheard of for a captain to take his dogs aboard—or even his cats, if you can credit that!"

Nath, obviously no longer in the mood for more personal conversation, rattled on about the abomination of cats and the advantages of

certain breeds of dogs over others until their cigarillos were nearly
burned up. The ship's bell tolling the hour brought him up short amid
describing a peculiar race of small dog bred specifically to prey on
shipboard rodents.

"Well, it is nearly time," he said lightly and stubbed out his cigarillo. "Have you ever been in battle, Enid?"

"I have gone out to meet someone on two occasions thus
far." She paused at the sudden memory of flaming figures fleeing into the night as her uncle's body cooled at her feet—and the
terror-frozen face of his murderer as the darkness consumed him.
"And there have been—scuffles in the street as well, but nothing
one might call a true *battle*."

"Are you disturbed by the prospect? I'm not insinuating you might
be shy, of course. My only interest is in comparing your feelings with
my own on the occasion of my first battle."

"Well, for the sake of comparison, then," Enid said, strangely relieved
by the opportunity to share her feelings with a man she had not known
long enough to qualify as an acquaintance under ordinary conditions.
Enforced proximity, it seemed, had a remarkable quickening effect on
personal relationships. "I will freely admit to a degree of anxiety, although no more than seems natural for the situation."

"Oh, a certain level of anxiety is natural," Nath assured her. "It
would only be remarkable if you felt none. Do you also feel a peculiar
anticipation, an eagerness to get to it at once and resolve the matter
for good and all?"

"I do, indeed, and it is not an entirely unpleasant anticipation. Was
it the same with you?"

"In the main." Nath absently ran the tips of his fingers over the hilt
of his hanger, which hung from the back of his chair. "I found myself
wildly happy at the prospect and I remember the first luff scolding me
for laughing as we prepared to board."

"And did battle meet your expectations?"

"It exceeded them in both joy and horror."

"I have heard that both are to be found in abundance under such circumstances, but I have always suspected that most of the joy is discovered at the battle's end—by its survivors."

"You may find experience turns your suspicions on their ear."

"Well, in any case, I hope you'll accept my fondest wish that the outcome of this affair brings you naught but joy."

"Oh, happily accepted! I will even drink to the sentiment with you. No, no—put away that weak child's brew! I do not think a single strong drink now will bring us to sorrow. Alston! Brandy for the magister and myself—and take care not to spill any of it. I will smell it on your breath!"

⸻

The powerful smell of licorice in Enid's cabin mixed sickeningly with the brandy fumes lingering in her nostrils. Dunaughy, she thought distastefully, must have had a devilish addiction to absinthe for his phantom to smell so strongly of it.

"A ghost that reeks of spirits!" Dunaughy crowed merrily within her mind. "That's an amusing turn of a phrase that would be worthy of your playwrights were they not so dead set on the fragrance of funeral earth and corruption!"

"I'll mention it to the next one I meet, which is a promise predicated upon my survival of this evening's drama. Tell me, are there any particular nautical considerations I should bear in mind during my preparations?"

"Tell me what you have in mind, and I will make suggestions and criticisms if I think you might profit from them."

Enid mentally ran down the list of formulations she intended to perform to prime the area for the required summoning. These castings would require a deft touch to be powerful enough to be productive but subtle enough to avoid the attention of any Naveroñian or Ardain sorcerers ashore or at sea in the local area. Beyond that, the matter was fairly straightforward and involved no unfamiliar forms or techniques.

A long, empty silence settled over her mind as she finished the accounting of her plans. For a moment she wondered if it were possible for the spirits of old men to drift into ghostly slumber, but the notion was utterly exploded by the sharp, silent crack of Dunaughy's voice in her brain.

"Where did you learn to normalize humors after the Blassingale Method? I did not believe that refinement was known outside the Royal Navy. The gods know we've made every effort to keep it so."

She was momentarily taken aback. Where *had* she learned that technique? It had seemed so natural to her as she used it, but now loomed darkly in her consciousness, as unsettling as finding a strange cloak tossed over a chair in one's supposedly empty apartments. How did it come to be there, insolently disrupting the comfort of familiarity? What did it portend?

Out loud, she wondered quietly, "How did that come to be there?"

"By affinity of connection." Dunaughy's voice was dolefully flat in her mind's ear. "I've read of it. It is one of the potential perils of the arrangement between us. As a lady of Ardainne, you are no doubt familiar with the tales of Cardinal Arundel and the fate that befell him after donning the medallion of his predecessor, Cardinal Gisboneaux?"

A sudden chill seized Enid, colder by far than the band of silver ice around her finger. "It is said that the medallion contained the spirit of Gisboneaux, confined there at his own request that he might continue to act as his young successor's mentor even after death. The story holds that Arundel's will was too weak to survive in such close contact with the greatest mind of its age—that he began to speak in the same manner and cadence of his departed mentor, to carry himself with the same regal hauteur where before his carriage had been that of a slump-shouldered clerk. More than one historian has said that the brilliance of the second half of his life was not his own—that Gisboneaux lived again through him, and that Arundel was little more than a powerless observer to the great deeds credited to his name."

"That is the kernel of it, indeed. The Red Mage himself prepared the talisman and placed it on Gisboneaux's narrow breast as he breathed his last. The amulet contained some item, lost to us now, that Gisboneaux wore from the time he was a student in the Academe Militaire and did not part with after taking orders and donning the crimson cloak. It must have been as familiar and dear to him in his last days as the *Alarum* was in mine."

Enid lurched to her feet and grasped the silver ring in her other hand, poised to wrench it from her finger. "And you believe this is happening to me? That I know your damned formula because my will is so weak that I absorbed it unconsciously as your persona slowly supersedes my own?"

"Not a bit of it," the ghost reassured her in a voiceless voice, redolent with fatalistic resignation. "Quite the opposite, in fact. I believe it is my genius that has proved insufficient to withstand the force of yours. I have felt less and less tangible of late, like a thick smoke dispersed by a soft breeze, gently but inexorably. I fear that the ring has brought us into such proximity that one of us must eventually be sublimated by the other despite the careful compartmentalization of person we have both diligently maintained. It seems clear to me which of us will become the footnote to the other."

"I have no desire to see your . . . self . . . diminished or lost for my personal gain. I must break the enchantment on the ring. You must move on and leave me to my own ends. You hazard too much with too little surety. I must warn you that while I find life at sea interesting, even satisfying, I am far from certain that I will not accept Captain Nath's offer to release me upon our return to Gisbon."

"You must follow your own conscience and leave me to follow mine. There are steps we can take to forestall the process after the conclusion of the matter at hand. Now, you've made a minor overcompensation in your formulations regarding the sylphs. Let us go over it together..."

chapter 20

Dinner, although comparatively light by Albion standards, weighed heavy on Enid's stomach as she sat stiffly in the stern sheets of the pinnace. The night was relatively still, and the air was turgid with humidity that clammily adhered the silk chemise beneath her leather hunting tunic to her skin. There had been some comment over her choice of clothing by Dr. Rondelle, who pointed out that it was more prudent to wear a clean silk blouse and hose than hunting leathers.

"Let you catch the ball from a spell-lock, Magister, that leather will not offer you protection. Indeed, the great wad of the stuff that will be driven into your flesh by the impact will almost certainly cause your wound to fester and putrefy! I implore you to consider a clean coat, and stockings and shirt of clean silk instead!"

She did as he said—that is to say, she considered his recommendation and then, after reflection, rejected it. She had little fear of any small-caliber spell-lock balls penetrating the wards she had cast upon herself—wards so efficacious they may have even saved Dunaughy's life, had he known them. Anything larger that struck her would surely cause such trauma that infection would be the least of her worries. Stray sword blows, however, were another matter entirely and her finely made—and cunningly charmed—hunting leathers would do far more against them than any amount of silk.

In the distance, rising and sinking with the swells, were the glittering lights of Puerto Galeno. The brilliant, flickering points of light, slowly growing in size and intensity as the little flotilla neared the mouth of the harbor, seemed to deepen the darkness around the boat. She could barely discern the boats on either side of her own, but the sounds of their muffled oars creaking in the oarlocks and digging into the waves seemed deafening. She clearly heard Mid Yeardly cursing sibilantly from one of the other boats, apparently encouraging one of his men to smoother strokes by reminding them that the oar would be more comfortable seated in his hands than inserted in his nether regions. She shot an alarmed glance at Nath, seated next to her, but he seemed unconcerned by the noise. He did notice her glance, however, and obviously took it for nervousness. The assumption chagrined despite its validity. She found herself possessed of none of the ebullient anticipation of Nath's youth but a dull and powerful longing to see the whole adventure behind her.

"All is well, Magister," Nath said softly as he lay a calming hand on her shoulder. "Sound carries well over the water, but the nearer sounds of surf and rigging will mask our approach. You can be sure, too, that the nearer we come to our destination, the more attentive everyone will be to working as silently as possible. Close proximity to peril concentrates the senses wonderfully, I've found."

Enid nodded. There was no arguing the effect. Even now her entire vision seemed filled by the small promontory upon whose approach they'd settled as the point at which she should cloak the little armada with mist and fog. It was barely visible in the darkness, conspicuous in large part only because of the white flicker of waves breaking at its rocky foot. It seemed to have snuck far closer during the brief period she'd allowed her eyes to glance from it to Nath.

After a long, narrow-eyed contemplation of the distance between their boats and the dread point of land, she determined the time had come to work her prepared formulations. Once the decision was made, she seemed to relax wondrously. Incidental sounds of their passage no longer reached her ears and the image of the little promontory and the expanse of water between it and her boat took on a crystalline quality. She felt the silver ring chill significantly on her finger and found its cool touch as reassuring as it was unnecessary. She did not require Dunaughy's help for a task such as this—it was well within her abilities—but his attention and support were comforting nonetheless.

She pulled a deep breath of warm, humid air into her lungs and reached out beyond herself to summon a bank of fog. Her task was eased by the thin veil of murk that already hung heavily just above the break of the waves, a wispy veil of heat mist that responded quickly to her call, gathering upon itself to thicken with gratifying ease and rapidity around the *Alarum*'s boats. Indeed, the formulation was accomplished with such ease that her primary worry was not summoning the cloak of fog, but rather in amassing such an abundance of the stuff that the boats could not find their way through it. Once she had the fog settled, she sought and found several sylphs amenable to driving the smoky stuff along at a rate matching that of the boats.

When she was certain the fog would persist and the sylphs were of a sort that would continue about a given task without constant supervision, she allowed more of her consciousness to return to its accustomed seat within her physical body. She shifted uncomfortably on the seat, which had grown exponentially harder during her brief absence from her corporeal form. A soft breeze, cool and slightly damp, brushed her skin and fleetingly recalled the susurrating voices of the sylphs to her ears. A quick glance around revealed the fruits of her brief labor: a bank of heavy mist, thinner than an actual fog and thus more natural for the season, stretched across the mouth of the bay, its swirling tendrils creeping forward in concert with the progress of the boats.

"Does this suit our needs, sir?" Her voice felt as hoarse as if she had not used it for days rather than minutes, but Nath seemed to hear her clearly enough and nodded briskly.

"Perfectly done, Magister," he murmured with a smile. "A capital effort. I doubt they will see us till we are on them, so we need only guard against some careless noise giving us away."

"Well, as to that, I have also instructed a sylph to thin the air twixt the edge of the mist and the shore." She gestured absently in the direction of land, surprised at the lethargy that made such a simple action require an unwarranted amount of effort. Were there counter-formulations at work here? It seemed unlikely as she could detect no sign of another mage of any consequence within range of her senses. "That should dampen the passage of sound to some degree and further muffle our approach."

"Very well done," Nath said, beaming. "Very well done, indeed! I doubt even old Dunaughy would have been so thorough in his preparations!"

Enid bowed her head in recognition of his praise and silently hoped that the *Alarum*'s old magister would not take offense at it. While it was true that the old man's shade had not suggested the extra step to render the boats' approach more silent, there were half a dozen other things she would never have considered without his counsel. She held no illusions regarding her reliance on the ghostly intellect that now made its home in the cold silver band encircling her finger. She flattered herself that her understanding of the specialized nuances of nautical magery was expanding rapidly but accepted that she was by no means prepared to rely upon her own knowledge alone as of yet. This understanding, coupled with the evening's earlier revelation of the peril Dunaughy placed himself in by aiding her, did little to raise her spirits.

"It is nothing, really. I took the precaution of working as subtly as I may, but unless one has cloaked themselves most effectively against my attentions, it is apparent that the *Redemption* has no mage aboard. My work, therefore, went unopposed."

"No mage aboard?" Nath ruminated softly. "That portends well for our little enterprise. Perhaps none of their officers are aboard—these Naveroñian officers would rather forsake the Patriarch than spend an unnecessary night aboard. They're fierce enough, but their discipline to service is somewhat lacking."

She excused herself from further conversation by informing Nath that she must mind her castings lest they slip. He left her in silence then, free to quietly observe the progress of their undertaking and wonder at the rising unease that tightened her belly. She thought the ordeal of escaping Arden and the near capture of the *Marie* by a Confessor's frigate had left her nerves incapable of experiencing further shocks, but found that the long, slow approach toward an inevitable, bloody conflict left her feeling as taut as a fiddle string. There was an odd fluttering in her chest that she shamefully recognized as a symptom of extreme anxiety, perhaps even fear.

Did Nath feel the same dread, she wondered, or was he inured to such physical concerns from years spent at sea in constant peril of death by squall, disease, or the predations of foes? He certainly seemed unfazed as he sat quietly next to her, his posture upright and erect as an officer's should be without evidencing the unwonted rigidity of tension or apprehension. His faded blue eyes were alertly mobile but did not jerk to and fro or fixate randomly as those of a fearful man might. No, she thought, this young Albion officer obviously possessed a physical courage superior to her own.

From experience, she knew she had no qualms concerning purely personal hazard. She'd had the honor of participating in duels of both the mundane and magical sort while a student and later, during those last few years before the Theocratic Revolution—a period that, in retrospect, represented the nobility's frantic attempt to dispel the rising peril to established order by embracing traditional pastimes such as dueling and fashionably excessive fetes with a fervor unknown since the days of Achard XIII. None of those affairs had affected her as deeply as this long voyage toward the *Redemption*.

She supposed the difference lay in expectations. In a duel, one could take comfort in the ritual of the affair. The expected forms would be followed slavishly, and when the moment of violence did come, it was neither unexpected nor particularly unwelcome. The clash of rapiers or sorcerous energies was merely the dénouement of a well-known and oft-told tale. The matter at hand, though, this "cutting out," was as strange to her as some Khorivian faerie tale with its walking huts and murderous siblings. She had no comfortable process from which to hang her expectations. There was only a headlong dash toward some indefinite climax that would certainly involve riotous mayhem and chaotic death. As she carefully unclenched her fists and stole another glance at Nath, another thought struck her: Perhaps he was no more courageous than she, but simply more familiar with the forms of this particular ritual. She found the idea comforting.

"Damme!" She heard Nath's coxswain, Bell, curse from his position, standing in the pinnace's stern. "Look'ee, sir! The gunboats!"

She followed Nath's gaze, amazed at how far the men's tireless sweep of the oars had borne them during her long moment of introspection. They were now well into the bay and over halfway to their quarry. The boats were spread out in a rough line, vaguely separated into two small "squadrons." Nath's group, bound for the larboard side of the *Redemption*, formed the left half of the line, while the right was comprised of the boats under Lieutenant Merryweather's command. It was toward Merryweather's section of the line that Nath peered fixedly.

Through the ragged mist, Enid could make out three bright beacons of light which seemed to be closing rapidly on Merryweather's boats. It was difficult for her to judge their distance, but it was clear the lights would soon be among the boats on the right hand. She assumed the bright, steady lights were illumination orbs suspended above the gunboats' prows.

"Can you thicken the mist there?" Nath hissed. "Perhaps they'll swerve to avoid chancing a real pea soup?"

Enid nodded once and immediately extended herself toward Merryweather's imperiled squadron. She quickly coerced an undine to expel a thick breath of warm moisture into the air, which exhalation the sylphs already under her control promptly cooled to produce a thick fog between the gunboats and Merryweather's gig and cutters.

She returned quickly to herself to observe the effectiveness of her handiwork. The gunboat lights were now reduced to three faint nimbuses, little more than slightly glowing patches of fog beyond the starboard squadron. She smiled as one of the faint lights swerved to steer clear of the fog and onto a course that would take it aft of Merryweather's boats. A moment later, a second boat followed suit and she heard Nath release a long-held breath. She was about to make an allusion to Marbury's famed "paths lost in the fog of life" verse when the third nimbus seemed to lurch forward and visibly brighten. A heartbeat later and the proud, slim prow of the gunboat cut through the thickest of the fog and the orb hovering before it bathed Merryweather's starboard-most cutter in bright, sickly yellow light. A startled Naveroñian oath split the silence, followed a breath later by the strident blasts of a horn.

"Well, stap me," Nath sighed fatalistically. "So much for surprise, eh? The canny bastard in command of that galley must have thought the sudden thickening of the soup a bit suspicious and pushed on through. Would to God he could have been as lazy and witless as his fellows! Ah!

Look, Merryweather is turning to take him bows on. They're too close for the gunboat to bring her main gun into play and that will stop her ramming her, too."

Nath was obviously pleased at his officer's initiative, but his voice became somber as he continued. "But his fellows, look, they're coming around now, too. They'll play merry hell with us once they have a clear view of us. Merryweather and her cutters may be too close to fire upon, but *we're* perfectly positioned to be served up properly."

The first of the trailing gunboats broke through the fog as Nath spoke, its orb goaded to full brightness by whatever officer commanded her. Enid squinted against the glare and noticed that it picked out bright auburn highlights in Nath's hair, giving him the fleeting appearance of wearing a halo borrowed from some Eastern saint's ikon.

"Lay onto your oars with a will, lads!" Nath shouted. "It's neck or nothing now!"

No sooner had the command left his lips than its echoes were drowned out by a thunderous boom. A cascade of water drenched Enid and for an instant she thought she was actually overboard. Dunaughy's vision of her demise filled her mind, and she was momentarily paralyzed with terror. Then she recalled that her last moments in that premonition had been spent watching the sun fade from sight as clear green waters closed over her. If it was an accurate prophecy of her death, she could take comfort that it was still several hours till dawn and therefore several hours of life were left to her. A mad urge to laugh seized her but was stilled as she heard Nath snarl, "A thirty-two-pounder, if it's an ounce. Pull for it, men! Those Naveroñian dogs have enough trouble hitting the water with their shot, a moving target will be right out for 'em!" A volley of spell-lock fire rippled across the water, sounding faint and tinny after the roar of the gunboat's bow gun.

"Lieutenant Merryweather is settin' her lads against t'other galleys, sir!" Bell barked. "Shall we steer to her aid or bear on?"

"Bear on!" Nath cried. "Bear on with a will. Merryweather will make quick work of 'em and we've more than enough men left for the *Redemption*!"

The men let out a hoarse cheer and the pinnace surged forward as they bent to their oars with enthusiasm. Enid spared a glance back toward Merryweather's boats and was rewarded with the sight of one of the gunboats vanishing in a sudden gout of fire and noise as a grenado hurled by a marine found her powder stores. Staccato gunfire punctuated by howls of pain and fury drifted toward her from the general melee unfolding as Merryweather's other boats closed on the two remaining gunboats, which soon found themselves locked in a knot of struggling men and shattering oars as the Albions sought to overwhelm them. Even from a distance, she could discern the gunboats carried far more men than the *Alarum*'s gig and cutters, but what Merryweather lacked in men she made up for in energy. Her encouraging shouts were plain to hear over the roar of gunfire and screams of men dying and doing others to death. Enid saw the cutter nearest Nath's squadron turn toward Merryweather's aid, but the lieutenant shouted him off with a strident cry of, "To Captain Nath! We have it in hand here! To Nath!"

Enid turned her face forward, expecting to see another wave of gunboats rushing toward them and finding instead a rather serene panorama. The lights of Puerto Galeno still glistened calmly in the distance, apparently unconcerned by the sudden fury of combat that erupted not so far off her shore. Nearer, surprisingly nearer, loomed the *Redemption* herself, her tall masts cutting black lines against the starlit mass of Mount Ybarre.

She glanced up worriedly at the fortifications on the mountain's shoulder, half expecting them to vanish in a cloud of flame and smoke as their two hundred guns belched iron and fire. Instead, she was treated to the oddly peaceful and undeniably beautiful sight of a pair of illumination flares soaring skyward, trailing soft lines of vermillion smoke behind them before bursting high in the air to release a cloud of brightly glowing orbs that hung suspended on charms designed to slow their fall to a feather's pace. Shouts drew her attention back to the *Redemption*, whose deck was seized by a sudden paroxysm of frantic activity. A series of sharp retorts rang out and Enid ducked her head reflexively.

Nath elbowed her lightly in the side and muttered sternly, "Do not flinch from fire, Magister. It is terrible for the people's morale." He flashed a quick smile and leaned closer to observe, "And that was not fire, but merely the clatter of firing ports being opened briskly. Ah. Look. They're running the guns out now."

She turned to look, marveling at the way he could say "they're running the guns out now" with the same equanimity he might say "my cigarillo has gone out." Her cheeks burned slightly at being chided for flinching, and she vowed she would never allow her reflexes to compromise her dignity again.

The blunt, black muzzles of the cannons emerging from their firing ports were clearly visible in the light of the illumination flares and Enid found no comfort in the sight of them. The guns' black maws seemed to grow with each sweep of the boat's oars. When they were large enough to accommodate the entire pinnace with room to spare, she heard a single Naveroñian word shouted from somewhere aboard the *Redemption*. A sailor seated near her apparently spoke Naveroñian and muttered sardonically, "For what we are about to receive . . ." She was about to ask Nath what the fellow meant when the world was suddenly filled with a ragged roar of tangible sound. The night was instantly banished by an actinic flash that, combined with the fearsome thunder that preceded it, left her momentarily blind and deaf.

When her vision returned a heartbeat or two later, she stared dumbly into Nath's laughing face. He was pointing toward the *Redemption*'s smoking guns with a broad grin and shouting. She shook her head and whispered a restorative cantrip that succeeded to the extent that she could hear his words as from a great distance and overlaid with the buzzing of swarms of angry bees.

". . . held off too long and let us get too close! They'll never get another broadside off before we're over her side, not as sloppy as their gunnery is! Not that we'd have aught to worry about judging by past performance! A whole bloody broadside and not a ball struck a thing save water!" He half rose and shouted, "Pull 'round to the loo'ard, lads! Even if they have their battery ready, we'll be too close for 'em to bear! To the loo'ard and up and at 'em!"

They skirted under the *Redemption*'s bows, the air singing with spell-lock balls from above. The marines aboard Nath's pinnace raised their own carabines to return fire, but their sergeant shouted for them to hold their fire. "Wait till we're aboard her, lads, then we'll stand and deliver, line and volley!"

Enid was nearly thrown to the bottom of the boat as the pinnace lurched to an unexpected stop. Coxswain Bell's fluent profanity filled the air until Nath shouted him to silence. He stood and shouted at the other boats of his squadron, "We're tangled in the bow lines! Shift your positions aft and we'll take the fo'c'sle! Lieutenant Harcourt, pray pass by and take the quarterdeck! Yeardly, get you to the waist!"

Once the other boats were safely past, Nath took stock of the situation. Enid saw his expression grow grim as he took in the boarding nets hanging in limp tendrils above the bulwarks. The loose netting served to entangle anyone who sought to scramble over them, slowing boarders long enough for a defender's pike to find their vitals. The netting had not been hung earlier and such preparations proved that the *Redemption* expected an attack. Nath doubted the Naveroñians had either the foresight or energy to hang them at dusk each day, but he could see no other explanation.

As spell-locks began to poke through the netting and grenados came sizzling over the side, Nath shrugged and shouted, "Mr. Bell! Grapples away! Boarders away! First men over to cut down these bloody nets!" The words were barely out of his mouth before the air was filled with grapples and the flying forms of men leaping for hand-holds on the frigate's beakhead. "Wait for us here, Magister, until we've won the fo'c'sle. No use risking your person in brute work."

Enid had never seen such a uniform, focused ferocity in her life. Even the bloodthirsty mobs of Arden lacked the singularity of purpose possessed by these Albion sailors. Howls of determined fury on their lips, they threw themselves at the *Redemption*'s bulwarks with abandon, each carrying an assortment of knives, clubs, hatchets, and spell-locks thrust through their belts or hanging from lanyards around their wrists and necks. She could not imagine that anyone could stand before such a savage onslaught and, indeed, it seemed at first that the ferocious Albion tars would swarm over the nets in a trice. She was searching for a place among the sailors to insinuate herself when the assault failed.

The Naveroñians, momentarily taken back as much by the volume of the Albions' battle cries as by the savagery of their assault, recovered under an officer's harangue and the *Alarum*s found themselves facing a veritable forest of thrusting pikes. Combatants voiced battle-cries and cursed as the iron points found soft flesh. Although the shouts of pain were as much Naveroñian as Albion, the tide was finally turned and Enid had to scramble back to avoid being trampled by a wave of retreating *Alarum*s, many of them bleeding from minor wounds and at least one crumpled up around a mortal wound to his abdomen. Nath was among the last off the nets, a mad look in his eye and blood streaming from a deep gash in his left cheek.

When Alston attempted to dab the blood away from his wounded face with a surprisingly gentle hand, Nath brushed it aside with a snarl.

"There's no time for that!" He turned his bloody face on the men in the pinnace as spell-lock balls whistled through the air around him and struck splinters off the boat's inner gunwales and deck with dull smacks.

"Once more, *Alarum*s! Once more, and they are ours! Damn their nets and damn them if they think they'll keep us from what is ours! Now, at them! Every other man to fend off the pikes and the rest to climb the netting or else cut a hole through it!"

The second assault, though carried out with the same vigor as the first, was also thrown back, this time leaving a woman dead in the netting, three more men wounded, and Nath slowly pulsing blood from a deep stab wound through his right biceps. Unintelligible jeers rained down on the retreating *Alarum*s, along with a spell-lock ball that struck Alston in the foot, carrying away his smallest toe, which set him cursing like a cutter and dancing in tight, agonized circles. The spectacle brought more laughter, insults, and missiles cascading down on the pinnace and its bloodied, grim-faced occupants.

Nath winced as one of his topmen tied a bandage around his wounded arm to the accompaniment of a steady stream of profanity from his steward. He was about to speak when there was a sudden cry and scramble to clear the center of the deck. The dead woman, shoved free from the netting by laughing Naveroñian pikemen, landed with a dull thud in the cleared space. She lay there, staring up at the *Redemption* with a pained expression frozen on her features.

Nath stepped forward and pointed at the dead woman.

"See her? Hear their laughter? Do we require any further reason to take this ship?"

Rather than shouts of enthusiasm, this time his words were met with a low, animal growl. They marshaled themselves again, silently readied their weapons, and waited for their captain to give the word. Enid took a place next to Nath. He frowned at her and began to speak, but she cut him short, announcing loudly, "I have prepared a formulation, but I must see the Naveroñians to target it. When I shout, everyone must close their eyes tight for a heartbeat! Remember! Shut your eyes fast when I shout!" Nath and the nearest *Alarum*s, already taut as bowstrings in anticipation of mayhem, nodded jerkily in acknowledgment.

Silence settled suddenly over the pinnace, as if her exclamation had killed all sound as the firing of cannon was purported to slay the wind. Every *Alarum*'s eye was on Nath, she realized, waiting for him to give the signal. She was mortally aware that spell-lock balls still sizzled through the air around her, that Naveroñian sailors still shouted challenges and taunts from the fo'c'sle above, facts her senses resolutely denied. She wondered if the same insulating veil surrounded the rest of the *Alarum*s or whether the unnatural reticence of her ears to hear was a singular symptom of her barely sublimated trepidation acting in synthesis with her fierce effort to maintain concentration on her hastily prepared formulation. Would they hear her shout of warning? Perhaps she should have proposed a hand signal, such as the one Nath used now, his arm spearing straight into the air and then falling in a swift, forward arc.

And then she was in motion, her body moving of its own accord, a mote caught up in a gale of bloodlust and determination. She saw Nath leap and grasp one of the grapnel lines left uncut by the overconfident Naveroñians and followed his example. Her soft-soled boots scrabbled on the timbers of the *Redemption*'s tumble home as she pulled herself up the rope. She stared dumbly for a moment when confronted by the boarding net at the end of the knotted grapnel line. Through the loose, dangling loops of the net, she saw a file of fierce-looking Naveroñian sailors and soldiers armed with pikes, cutlasses, and spell-locks. Their pikes thrust through the net slowly, as if forcing through some thick, transparent substance just beyond the bulwarks. Poisonous yellow smoke blossomed languorously as a dozen or more spell-locks spat .75-caliber balls toward the *Alarum*s struggling to hack through or climb over the netting.

Splinters thrown up by one of the balls stung her left hand, and the glance down at her smarting fingers nearly caused her to miss the Naveroñian sailors' charge. They ducked beneath their mates' pikes, cutlasses, and belaying pins, poised to strike as soon as they were within reach. She filled her lungs and shouted for the Albions to look away but doubted if she would be heard—she could not hear her words herself, after all. A pike head shoved into her shoulder but the charms on her hunting tunic turned a forceful lunge into a gentle nudge. Ignoring the distraction of the impact, she closed her eyes, opened her mind, and released the formulation.

The world flashed red through her eyelids, the brightness apparently shocking her ears back to life as they were suddenly filled with murderous howls, shrieks of pain and fear, and the vicious bark of spell-locks. She opened her eyes upon a scene of bedlam and carnage.

The Naveroñian line across the fo'c'sle was reduced to a milling mass of staggering sailors, some of them clawing blindly at their smoking eye sockets, the more fortunate among them blinking rapidly in confusion and uselessly rubbing their intact, but temporarily blind eyes. A heartbeat later, her view of the Naveroñians was blocked by the backs of a half dozen *Alarum*s who had bested the net. Nath was among them, a pistol in his left hand and a graceful hanger in his right. More men followed, some rushing to join in the short, one-sided melee against the *Redemption*'s foreguard, others turning to quickly hack the boarding net down with their hatchets.

Enid ducked beneath the now-loosened lower edge of the boarding net and scrambled on deck. She was shoved unceremoniously forward by *Alarum* sailors and marines as they surged onto the fo'c'sle themselves. To her amazement, Alston was one of the men who shoved past her, his face fierce and eager despite the blood seeping through the hastily applied bandages around his injured foot, which stained the deck with blood as he advanced with a limp.

The marines, seeing that the sailors had the blinded Naveroñians well in hand, began to form up around their sergeant, incidentally shielding Nath from any fire from abaft.

"Put a volley into those rascals," Nath shouted in a voice that carried clearly over the din of battle. "Let us clear a way for Mr. Yeardley to come aboard!"

Sergeant Garrick snapped a series of commands at his men that culminated in a blast of spell-lock fire delivered in such precise unison that it seemed more the roar of a single weapon than that of a little over half a dozen. The effect of the smallish volley was remarkable.

A group of Naveroñians, sensible of the turn of events in the fo'c'sle and determined to reverse matters, found their determination shaken as two of their number dropped dead on the spot and a third let out an ear-splitting shriek as a ball shattered his arm just above the elbow. Their resolve for bloody deeds dampened by the sight of their own blood, the Naveroñians were left off balance, moving about indecisively and glancing this way and that for someone to spur them on or give them the command to withdraw. Nath saw no reason to allow them time to regain their composure and let out a blood-curdling shout that his people immediately recognized as an invitation to charge the hapless Naveroñian soldiery crowded into the *Redemption*'s waist.

And crowded they were, too. There seemed to be hundreds packed in among the cannons below and nearly as many jamming the catwalks that connected the fo'c'sle to the quarterdeck. Perhaps the Naveroñian numbers would work against them in such close quarters now that the *Alarum*s had a foothold aboard the *Redemption*, Enid thought as she found herself instinctively following Nath into the fray, her viscera apparently dominating whatever reason the shock and clamor of combat had spared her.

She rushed after Nath as he hurled himself at the Naveroñians holding the larboard rail against Mr. Yeardly's boarders, dimly aware that the Albion lobsters were charging down into the mass of sailors, soldiers, and marines that filled the main deck from stem to stern.

She saw Nath parry a cutlass slash at his face with an indolently precise movement of his own blade and reply to the affront by shoving the muzzle of the pistol in his left hand into his attacker's face and discharging one of its two barrels. She had the leisure to observe the little Albion captain dispatch two more Naveroñians, one with an elegantly lethal lunge that confirmed her earlier impression of his familiarity with the salle and the second with an almost absent-minded flick of the tip of his hanger across a hatchet-wielding sailor's throat before her own situation demanded her full attention.

A burly Naveroñian sailor loomed suddenly before her, his fiercely mustachioed face screwed up into an equally savage scowl. His ham-sized fist waved a thick-bladed cutlass as if it were a willow wand. Enid's own weapon, a fine small sword from the famed forges of Mittelsohn, came on guard as if of its own accord.

Her weapon surged forward an instant later as her opponent cocked back his arm for a powerful overhand slash. The hulking sailor collapsed to his knees on the deck, one nerveless hand clasped over the crimson fountain that sprung from his chest and the other pinned to the deck by the hilt of a sword he no longer possessed the strength to lift. Another Naveroñian leveled a spell-lock pistol at her body, but he was near enough that it took less than an instant's focus to fix the ball in place so that when the powder ignited the pistol exploded and left her attacker staring in white-faced shock at the bloody ruin of his hand.

She saw a woman she assumed was a Naveroñian marine based on her uniform, far more elegant and overtly martial than the slops worn by the raggedly dressed sailors, strike down one of the *Alarum*s with her sword and bound over his body to rush toward Nath's unprotected

side. A peculiar sound that combined a laugh and a snarl escaped
Enid's lips as she leapt forward herself, covered the intervening space
with two long strides, and drove her Mittelsohn through the base of
the Naveroñian woman's neck.

Nath seemed utterly unaware of his close brush with mortality, or
at least utterly unconcerned by it. He pressed ahead, beating a pike
aside here and slashing at the eyes of an axman there. She was at his
side, her own sword dancing red in the night, flashing to interrupt
the metronomic cutlass drill of a scar-faced man whose eyes glinted
with confidence until his routine was interrupted by several inches of
cold steel through his wrist. They pressed forward together, *Alarum*s
crowding in behind them and fighting at their sides where the narrow
breadth of the catwalk would allow.

Something like joy swelled in her breast and something like lust
as well. The stamp and slash of their progress toward the quarterdeck took on the grace and synchronicity of a dance and, like a dance,
warmed her blood to a salacious temperature that only impassioned
kisses or deftly delivered blows might cool. And yet, as blow followed
blow and foe after foe fell, she found that her ardor only grew and, in a
brief pause as she planted her foot on a fallen man's knee to wrest her
blade free from his thigh, she wondered whether she was depraved,
and, if so, could she find it within herself to be concerned by it after the
joy of the prolonged moment was passed.

Enid was momentarily confused when she suddenly found no
enemies before her, save those fleeing toward the quarterdeck. She
turned to Nath for direction and saw blood fly from the wound on his
cheek as he shouted the names of several *Alarum*s and directed them
to cut down the boarding net. She spared a glance at the gun deck
below and was astonished at the chaos there. The marines, augmented
by the *Alarum*s who had not followed Nath's charge down the catwalk,
were creating a terrible confusion in the waist as they slowly pressed
forward. Despite the combat in their midst, though, many of the

Naveroñians continued to work the *Redemption*'s great guns, producing ragged broadsides she assumed must be directed against Merryweather's orphaned half of the expedition, which led her to believe the Naveroñian gunboats had been dispatched or the *Redemption*'s crew had a wondrously cool attitude regarding their countrymen's welfare.

As one of the cannons erupted directly beneath her feet on the deck below, she marveled at how distant it sounded, nearly muted by the peculiarly selective nature of her senses. She turned to look over the rail, all but oblivious to the spell-lock balls that were pattering around her with increasing intensity from the quarterdeck, and was gratified to see the narrow, pockmarked face of Mr. Yeardly appear from below, his pale visage ruddy with excitement and split by a wolfish grin that seemed to contain far too many teeth—an effect that did nothing to improve his already doubtful looks. The mid was followed by more *Alarum*s, howling in their eagerness to get some of their own back after repeated, frustrated attempts to force their way aboard.

Nath grabbed Yeardly by the arm and shouted directly into his ear. "Mr. Yeardly! I would admire it if you and your people would silence the guns below while the magister and I secure the quarterdeck!"

Yeardly grinned and nodded eagerly before turning so energetically to his task that he nearly left a piece of his sleeve in his captain's grip.

Nath waited just long enough to see Yeardly and his command scramble down into the gun deck and then shouted, "Mine to me and take the quarterdeck!"

The men remaining to him took up a shout of "The quarterdeck! The quarterdeck!" and Enid found herself adding her own voice to the cry as they stormed forward along the catwalk. The quarterdeck end of the catwalk was blocked by a double file of carabiniers dressed in smart but garish uniforms of pink and green. The front rank was suddenly obscured by a great cloud of foul yellow smoke and the air was instantly alive with whirring balls of lead. She heard a meaty smack behind her followed by a stunned groan and saw the second rank step forward and kneel to fire as the first rank began to reload with mechanical precision. She had no doubt that the dweomers woven into her hunting garb would protect her from the second volley but doubted if the men behind her would fare so well—or Nath, for that matter. If too many of the *Alarum*s fell, or worse yet, their *captain* fell, the entire endeavor would fall with them. With that in mind, she howled an inarticulate battle cry and sprinted past Nath.

She quickly outpaced him, as he was far shorter than she in stature and stride and was soon far ahead of him. She positioned herself in the center of the catwalk so that the charms enveloping her would do the most good for the *Alarum*s behind her. The smoke from the Naveroñian soldiers' second volley billowed out to meet her and she heard the high-pitched scream of charm-deflected balls veering violently away from her. She was in among them as the retired rank was attempting to finish loading, her small sword darting over the head of a crouching carabinier to run their startled officer through the throat. Freeing her blade with a deft twist, she slashed madly to either side to clear a space and was gratified to see the stunned and now leaderless soldiers accommodate her desire.

It didn't take the cowed Naveroñians long to realize Enid was alone, however, and a pair of the bolder among them were thrusting at her with their bayonets. They were quickly reinforced by comrades inspired by their bravado and Enid found herself hemmed in by a small grove of sharp steel at the end of stout carabines. When one of the Naveroñians thumbed back the hammer of her weapon, Enid slashed at the weapon's muzzle, forcing it away to discharge into the deck. A bayonet danced before her eyes, and she took a quick, reflexive step backward. Her feet tangled in the sling of a fallen man's spell-lock and, without quite knowing how she came there, she found herself flat on her back.

The mizzenmast loomed above her, pointing like a dark, cable-festooned finger at the circling stars above, and she experienced a moment of absolute clarity. Time stopped an instant, leaving her at the center of some strange tableau whose every detail stood out as if backlit by the light of Providence. After an indefinite period of stasis, time lurched back into motion, its progress so unnaturally rapid that it seemed bent on making up for lost momentum. Her vision was filled by a circle of pink-and-green uniforms and the dull, wicked glint of bayonet points, all moving in jerky, high-speed syncopation.

She struggled to raise her sword, but found it pinned to the pale wood of the deck by one of the soldier's boots. A bayonet slammed into her belly and only the charmed leather prevented her from being pinned to the deck as well. As it was, the breath was knocked from her, leaving her nerveless and gasping for air. One of the soldiers stood astraddle of her and aimed his bayonet at her throat with an expression of murderous glee. To her horror, she saw his lips mouth a simple but effective cantrip which, though not sufficiently efficacious to defeat her protective dweomers, might weaken it enough to allow him to lay open her throat.

The bayonet rose, cocking for the blow, but before it could fall a plume of smoke darted across her field of vision and the soldier staggered backward, his carabine dropping harmlessly to the deck as he fell across her body. She saw Nath leap over her, negligently dropping his double-barreled pistol and slashing to either side with his hanger to drive back the Naveroñian carabiniers. He was followed a moment later by several sailors whose hard-swung cutlasses and boarding axes sent the Naveroñians scrambling back. Alston, his missing toe apparently forgotten in the heat of the engagement, leaned down, rolled the dead soldier off her, and helped her to her feet with a calloused, bloody hand.

"Yer has t'be more careful o'where ye caulk, Magister," Alston said with a grin and a wink. She nodded with a weary smile of her own and a grateful pat on his shoulder before staggering over to Nath's side.

"Well done, Magister!" Nath's appreciative smile was made a bit horrible by the blood flowing down his face from the wound on his cheek. He thrust his hanger toward a tight knot of armed men farther aft along the quarterdeck and shouted in her ear, "There is the captain! One last set-to and we can bring this scene, this act, to an end!"

Enid nodded, her shortness of breath all but forgotten in the thrill of the moment. Here were the *Redemption*'s officers, her captain, and a lieutenant or two at the very least, each of them gentleborn and worthy of her efforts. True, they were ringed about by powder-blue-coated men she assumed were marines, but she had no doubt the *Alarum*'s people would prove sufficient to brush them aside long enough to allow her an opportunity to cross blades with worthies of her own stature. Filled once more with a passion for mayhem, she answered Nath with a meaningful glance toward the waist and her own shout, "Let's be about it, then! The audience below has grown restive!"

And so they had. The Naveroñians packed into the waist continued to make a creditable showing. While the great guns had been silenced under the ferocious attack led by Yeardly from the larboard rail, the great number of Naveroñians had stopped them from sweeping the waist entirely clear or uniting with the marines pushing toward the stern from the fo'c'sle. A stabilized "front" developed that held the *Alarum*s in place in the forward quarter of the gun deck and no farther in than amidships larboard. Some of the Naveroñian soldiery aft had obviously observed the Albions push onto the quarterdeck and appeared to be milling about in an effort to get organized enough to do something about it. Nath took it all in with a glance and whirled to call out to the *Alarum*s with him, "There is their captain! I'll have her sword in my hand, or she'll have mine in her belly! At 'em, *Alarum*s!"

Spell-locks barked as the Albions tore across the quarterdeck, but this time Enid took no mind of it. The bloodlust was upon them, and she doubted if the *Redemption* sinking beneath them would halt their charge, let alone the fall of a comrade or officer, no matter how beloved. She knew nothing short of the drowning prophesied by Dunaughy would keep *her* from her quarry, a tall Naveroñian lieutenant whose confident poise and determined expression lit a fierce, bright fire of desire in her. The *Alarum*s crashed into the Naveroñian captain's guard, and the relatively ordered line of soldiers and sailors immediately dissolved into a mass of individual melees. Some fought in breathless silence, others to the accompaniment of howls of rage-tinged terror. Enid was sensible of her own shouting but was so caught up in the joy of the moment that she could not for the life of her discern the sense of it.

Through the chaos and jumble of hard-fought personal contests, she found the lieutenant she desired before her, his fine small-sword held at a perfect guard and his eyes gleaming with an intense anticipation that matched her own. They danced passionately, exchanging ardent glances over glittering blades, and Enid came to love the proud fellow in the moment before she drew his sword out of line and plunged her own through his heart. Turning, she found herself momentarily isolated on the embattled quarterdeck. Casting about for a new love, she found herself treated to the final movements of Nath's duet with his Naveroñian counterpart.

The two captains stomped and lunged across the deck, stepping lightly over fallen men of either side, their faces different as night and day, but set in identical expressions of grave concentration.

It was instantly apparent to Enid that the Naveroñian captain was a skilled practitioner of her country's lethally scientific fighting style. Her sword moved with geometric precision in response to Nath's every thrust and slash—but her moves were definitely *responses*. Nath led the dance and the Naveroñian was hard put to keep up with the sure, rapid tempo he set. Arabesque followed arabesque and for a moment Enid thought the contest would last forever. The much larger Naveroñian's back obscured Nath for heartbeat and Enid saw the bright blade of Nath's hanger appear as if by magic between her shoulder blades.

Nath wrested his blade free from the downed Naveroñian and bawled out to Alston, "Cut down those colors! The rest of you prepare to hold the quarterdeck against all comers!"

There was a brief flurry of action as some Naveroñian sailors and marines swarmed across the catwalk in an effort to save their colors and avenge their fallen captain, but it was to no avail.

A moment later, and a sorrowful cry went up from the Naveroñians as they saw Alston cut down their colors and allow them to stream away into the darkness on the night breeze. The sight of their banner forcefully struck and their proud captain gasping her life away at Nath's feet was sufficient to persuade the now-outnumbered Naveroñians on the quarterdeck to drop their weapons and call for quarter in poorly accented Albion and Ardain. Nath ordered Bell to take charge of the prisoners with the aid of a pair of lightly wounded but brutal-looking *Alarum*s.

He then turned his attention to the fight in the waist.

Enid followed Nath to the quarterdeck railing in time to see young Mr. Yeardly brain the Naveroñian lieutenant in command of the waist with a deftly thrown belaying pin. The Naveroñians gathering to charge the quarterdeck faltered as a dismayed cry arose from the men who'd witnessed their leader's death and at that critical moment, Merryweather's and Harcourt's divisions, finally free of their melee with the gunboats, swarmed over the starboard rail. Harcourt's lobsters rushed to deliver a volley into the packed Naveroñians below but were hardly formed into a line before Naveroñian pikes, cutlasses, and the odd spell-lock began thudding onto the deck and hands were lifted skyward in surrender.

Redemption was theirs.

A cheer went up and another would have followed, but Nath broke in with a command that carried clearly from stem to stern of the captured vessel.

"Marines! See the prisoners below and secure the hatches! I want the t'gallants shaken loose and the hawsers cut as soon as we begin to gather steerage way! The boats to tow! I want us out from under that castle's guns as soon as dammit!"

Then, with a mischievous grin he said, "Alston! Fetch Lieutenant Merryweather! Her quarterdeck awaits!"

When Alston didn't answer, Nath cast his eye around the quarterdeck. Enid felt dread clutch her heart as the quarterdeck fell silent, save for the pained sounds of the wounded and the disgruntled murmuring of the beaten Naveroñians. She winced as an expression of profound grief flashed across Nath's face, utterly erasing the expression of joyful fatigue that had reigned there a moment ago. She felt her own face stiffen with his into a mask of stoicism and the same dire presentiment that seized them both was proven when one of the hands called out quietly, "Here, sir."

Alston lay dead near the ratlines he had ascended to cut down the Naveroñian colors, a boarding ax buried in his chest. There was a faint smile on his immobile features and a spell-lock smoking in his right hand. Next to him lay the body of Mid Cullen, with a blood-clotted cutlass clutched in his hand. Several dead Naveroñians lay nearby.

Yeardly, who'd scrambled up from below to join his captain on the quarterdeck, stared at his dead friend a long moment, as if he refused to recognize the cold clay as the remains of his boon companion. Then he fell to his knees beside Cullen and used the kerchief from around his neck to dab the blood and powder smudges from his friend's handsome face.

It was clear from the position of the bodies and the nature of their wounds that Alston and Cullen had fought like lions against a group of Naveroñian sailors intent on avenging their fallen colors and, perhaps, rallying their fellows to further action in *Redemption*'s defense. The skirmish near the ratlines had gone unnoticed in the general combat on the quarterdeck, but the number of dead Naveroñians was a sure indication of its savagery.

Nath stared down at the bloody, still forms arranged side by side on the deck and Enid saw his jaw muscles bunching and relaxing in a manner that reminded her of the clenching of his fists during his speech to the crew before the attack on the *Redemption*. She more than half expected a quote from Marbury when he turned to address the crew, but instead he called out in a fine, clear voice, apparently untroubled by loss or doubt.

"Lieutenant Merryweather! Get more way on her! Lieutenant Harcourt! Get these prisoners belowdecks! Yeardly! Get any hands that may be spared from manning the rigging to the guns! We shall not allow further impertinence from any remaining gunboats to go unanswered! Sharply now, *Alarums*! Sharply!"

Sunset the following day found the *Alarum*, *Toucher du Bois*, and *Redemption* in company and out of sight of land, a merry little armada the sight of which filled the venal hearts of the *Alarum*'s officers and hands with glee despite the cost of its formation. Pride of accomplishment formed a large part of their satisfaction, but avarice was not to be ignored, either. More than a few of the *Alarum*s were happily doing their sums to determine what their share of the prize would be, their computations based on an estimate of the captured frigate's value that, while a trifle optimistic, would have done any of the Prize Board's surveyors proud.

The head money for the *Redemption* alone, if it were allowed under the peculiar circumstances, would come to a tidy amount, crammed from stem to stern as she had been with soldiers, sailors, and marines. Beyond such notional valuations, the vessel herself was possessed of fine lines—an obvious thoroughbred—and was laden down with spare spars, cordage, sails, shot, and powder. Many a knowing glance was exchanged as *Alarum* after *Alarum* reached their own estimate of the *Redemption*'s princely value.

Enid was a bit put off by the atmosphere of cupidity, which reminded her of her first uncomplimentary impression of Nath as a greedy shopkeeper aboard the *Marie*. She was left with no doubt of the abundant gallantry and valor possessed by *Alarum*'s officers and crew, despite their inglorious avidity. When confronted with glowing estimates of the fortune awaiting her from one of the hands, most of whom now referred to her familiarly as "Spells" beyond her hearing owing to the good impression *she* made upon them during the cutting out, she would simply smile and nod in much the same manner that a mother would smile and nod at a child's whimsical ambition to conquer the Faerie King and lay his fey treasure at her feet.

She stared over the rail at the *Redemption* as sailors swarmed about her rigging to set to right the mischief done by the Castle Ybarre's guns as she fled before them toward the open sea. In her mind's eye, she could still clearly see the eerily diffuse flowers of light that bloomed through the fog she summoned to obscure their retreat and confound the enemy gunners. Each of those pale pink roses represented the discharge of a monstrous gun, none smaller than a thirty-two-pounder she later learned, and heralded the arrival of a massive ball of heated iron that would crush men, splinter wood, and set their prize to burning if it were fortunate enough to strike home.

Whether from the efficacy of her fog or the unseen hand of Providence, the worst the *Redemption* suffered in her passage to freedom was a few damaged spars and a bit of cut rigging. The gunboats that disrupted their approach to the *Redemption* were nowhere to be seen as they sailed her out. One had been destroyed when its small store of alchemical powder ignited, another holed during boat-to-boat fighting, and the rest so thoroughly mauled by Harcourt's marines and

Merryweather's *Alarum*s that they wanted nothing more to do with the night's play.

The high spirits with which the *Redemption* and the returning cutting-out party were greeted had held through a hard night of frenzied labor to prepare their prize for further flight, and, although their cheer labored under the weight of lost friends and shipmates, it was never fully crushed. They would miss the lost, as their solemn expressions and downcast eyes testified whenever the names of the dead were mentioned, but they had expected to lose far more of their fellows to the action.

Despite the difficulties in gaining the *Redemption*'s deck and the fierce fighting against overwhelming odds that followed, only nine *Alarum*s were slain and less than a dozen wounded sorely enough to require the expertise of Dr. Rondelle and his loblolly boys. Lieutenant Oxley assured her it was a light toll to pay for such an undertaking, especially considering the enemy's losses. Less than an hour of pitched combat had cost the lives of one hundred and twelve of the three hundred and sixty Naveroñians crammed aboard the *Redemption*.

One of the *Alarum*'s wounded was Lieutenant Merryweather, who received a deep cut across her left cheek. She'd only allowed Dr. Rondelle time to perform the most rudimentary of treatments before hurrying to the *Redemption*'s quarterdeck to join the frenzy of action required to get the captured frigate out from under Castle Ybarre's furnace-heated shot. The last Enid saw her, she was calling to someone high up in the rigging a cack-handed lubber and threatening to reassign him from topman to ballast stone. There was a glitter in her eye that was plain to see, even from a distance, and her face was flushed with a mixture of pride and pleasure. It was a combination that rendered her beautiful to Enid's eyes and left her staring until Lieutenant Oxley begged her pardon and pleaded with her to board the gig before Captain Nath sent marines to drag her aboard.

The *Redemption*'s captain, Guillien de Suarez de Acacena, survived

Nath's sword passing through her lungs and showed none of Merry-weather's satisfaction but every sign of a full recovery under Rondelle's acerbic ministrations. She shed some light on the overwhelming num-bers found aboard the frigate. Simply put, the Naveroñian crown was fully aware of Albion's desire to retrieve the *Redemption* and kept her overmanned at all times as a hedge against just the sort of action as last night's cutting out. Captain de Suarez also made it quite clear her king would view the night's action as an act of unprovoked hostility that would likely lead to war between Albion and Naveroña.

Nath had amazed her with his sanguine reaction to such a dire pronouncement. He simply shrugged and instructed the Naveroñian-speaking sailor translating for de Suarez to reiterate his compliments on her gallantry in the *Redemption*'s defense and to see she was ren-dered whatever aid she required. Once back on deck, he'd simply shrugged at Enid's concerned expression.

"War with Naveroña is inevitable. The sanctimonious swine are sure to take Ardainne's side if only to spite Albion. Still, I doubt the *Redemption* will be the excuse they'll choose for a war against us. It would mean openly admitting that a few dozen men snatched her out from under the watchful eyes of nearly four hundred of their picked sailors and marines—never you mind a couple hundred cannons in Castle Ineffectual as well. I should imagine there will be a strongly worded letter to our ambassador in Cadice, at worst."

He'd frowned then and stared toward Gisbon for a long moment before saying quietly, "I'm far more concerned with how Admiral Weymouth will react to my impertinence in cutting her out against his orders. I can only hope his joy at having regained the *Redemption* will outweigh his ire at the means by which she was restored." He shrugged again, then, more dismissively than fatalistically said, "The die is cast, and it is too late to call it back into the cup."

As if summoned by her thoughts of him, Nath appeared at her elbow. He had been speaking with Lieutenants Oxley and Harcourt regarding the shifting of prisoners from the *Alarum* and the *Redemption* to the *Toucher du Bois*. At present, the *Alarum*'s oversized marine contingent was split between the two larger vessels to keep the Naveroñian and Ardain prisoners from attempting to turn the tables on their captors. As long as the prisoners were cowed by their recent defeats, there was sufficient force to restrain them. Should they take heart, though, perhaps under the encouragement of one of their officers? Well, Nath was less sanguine regarding that potentiality than some purely notional war with Naveroña. He stood quietly for a long moment, watching as the Ardain privateer was brought under the *Alarum*'s lee in preparation for receiving her captives.

"Most of the Naveroñians have been taken off the *Redemption*," Nath observed. "Packed like cordwood in *Toucher du Bois*'s hold. She's a bit low in the water, but not perilously so. It will not be a comfortable voyage for them, but it should be safe enough."

"You're still resolved to release them, then?" Despite understanding the necessity of ridding themselves of a dangerous surplus of prisoners, Enid found grudging support was the best she could summon for their release. As voluntary supporters of the Theocrats, and worse, volunteers whose support was based more on the opportunity for profit than any revolutionary zeal, they were beneath her contempt. Unlike Nath, she also found it difficult to adopt a "sporting" attitude toward the Naveroñians. Mid Cullen's and Alston's deaths loomed too large in her consciousness to allow for such niceties. She found the thought of them all locked away in some Albion dungeon or rotting prison hulk far more pleasing than the idea of them taking up arms again to slay more gallant men and women. "How can you think that they'll respect their parole?"

Nath shrugged.

"Each to their own conscience, I suppose. For the Naveroñians, it doesn't signify in any case. We're not at war with them, so we can hardly take them as prisoners of war. As for Citizen Herme and his—"

Nath frowned as Enid interrupted with the word *pirates*, but refrained from correcting her at the sight of a grim-faced Yeardly approaching with Citizen Herme in tow.

"Captain Nath. Magister d'Tancreville." Citizen Herme made an elegant leg and stole a glance past them at the *Redemption*. The sight evinced a good-humored smile. "I must congratulate you both on your victory, the fruits of which I see fresh plucked. I wish you joy in her and the best of luck in keeping her. I imagine the news of this will encourage a bit more activity out of your Naveroñian counterparts."

"Which will encourage a fair lot of activity among Albion's prize agents." Nath chuckled. "Let them come!"

Herme shared Nath's mirth with good nature. "I'm sure you and your agents will end life as wealthy as lords, sir, and old as saints." He gestured toward the members of the crew that were being herded on deck, blinking against the soft light of sunset after the pitchy darkness of the *Alarum*'s hold. "I gather that my men and I are to be released?"

Nath nodded. "Even so. I hope you will not feel too put upon, considering the situation, if I trouble you to ferry the prisoners from the *Redemption* to shore?"

"I assure you that I'm honored to be of any service to such a kind host, Captain Nath." Herme laid his hand over his heart and bowed from the waist in the modern fashion. His eyes sparkled with amiable sarcasm as he spoke and Enid was disturbed to realize that she found them attractive. "My only sorrow is that I will not have the opportunity to share your table again, or the company of your lovely magister, the Lady d'Tancreville."

He extended his hand palm up to accept hers in order to press a courtly kiss to it, but Enid contrived not to notice and clasped her hands at the small of her back in unconscious imitation of Nath and the other Albion officers. Herme's smile widened slightly, and he continued as if he hadn't noticed the slight. "I suppose you'll desire my parole and that of my officers?"

"No," Nath said. "I see no reason to so discommode you, Captain Herme."

"Or to waste time on futile gestures?" Herme chuckled sardonically.

Enid snorted disdainfully. "You see? He makes no pretext of honorable behavior!"

"And why should I?" For the first time, there was a trace of heat in Herme's voice. "To satisfy some outmoded tradition that in no way serves Ardainne? If I am to swear I will not raise arms against my country's enemies, then why should I desire they release me? For my own comfort? Phah. Let them take me prisoner, then, and waste their treasure in feeding me and their strength in guarding me!"

"And I thought you eschewed zealotry in favor of self-interest!" Enid sneered. "Yet just now you sound the perfect Theocrat."

"I am no zealot," Herme shot back coolly. "I am a patriot. I may decry the Theocracy's excesses, but I applaud the fact that they have put an end to many of the 'honorable' traditions that have starved our countrymen and seen our nation reduced from the preeminent power on earth to a veritable hostage of an island of fisher-folk and trades-people!"

"Politics aside," Nath interrupted, frowning at the characterization of his homeland, "let me be clear: I am releasing you and your men for the sole purpose of ferrying unwanted prisoners to shore. You will find that your guns, such as they were, have gone over the side. Your armory has been disposed of likewise, leaving you only a brace of pistols in your cabin. I doubt a privateer captain can rest easily unarmed, even for so short a time as it will take you to reach Puerto Galeno."

The privateer nodded slowly, and his customary half-smile reappeared as he cast a meaningful glance toward the *Redemption*. "The same might be said of the captains of men-of-war, apparently."

"Well, any captain might find himself unfortunate in his crew, I suppose," Nath replied evenly.

"Of course," Herme agreed, grinning profligately. "And a villainous crew is inevitably the cause for all mutinies, yes? What good ship's folk would rise up against their wise and benevolent captain?"

"Oh, come now!" Nath snapped. "Of course the blame is not always entirely with the ship's crew, but the greatest portion of it invariably is! The sailors of a king's vessel swear their obedience and loyalty to their captain and if that captain proves undeserving of that oath, it is for Admiralty to rectify and nobody else!"

Herme began to reply, but Nath cut him off with a raised hand. "No, sir. As edifying as further exploration of this topic might prove for us both, I fear we have no time for it."

"I'm sure you're correct, sir," Herme answered with a deferential but uncowed nod. "Still, I hope you'll forgive me for looking forward to continuing the conversation with you as my guest. It would be my honor to return the hospitality you have so freely extended to me."

"I'm afraid my social calendar is in the hands of Providence," Nath answered with a smile. "And yours, I fear, is in mine.

"Once the *Toucher du Bois* has taken on all the prisoners, you are to take them directly to Puerto Galeno and disembark them. If you deviate from this course and fall into my company farther south of our current position, I will have no choice but to interpret the meeting as a forlorn attempt on your part to retake the *Redemption* or warn other Ardain or Naveroñian men-of-war of our approach. While it would trouble me to send an unarmed vessel crowded with equally unarmed prisoners to the bottom, it would not trouble me so much as failing in this undertaking out of some misplaced sense of compassion. I trust you take my meaning?"

As Captain Herme's smile flickered, another was born on Enid's face. She dearly loved to see the man's jovial composure shaken, however slightly.

"Perfectly, sir," Herme replied amiably. "It will be just as you say.

Of course, once I have seen my guests safely home and refit my dear little schooner, my calendar will be free again. I look forward to some future assignation with you and your lovely magister."

"You forget yourself," Enid snapped, jerking her hand away as Herme bowed and reached for it. "I am an Albion officer, not some salon flower eager for your attentions! You will respect the dignity of my rank or answer for it with your body!"

Although his good humor didn't waver, she was gratified to see Herme take a cautious step backward and touch the brim of his hat in a formal salute. "Your pardon, Magister. I meant no offense, although I must own that my body is ever eager to answer to you."

A heated reply formed on Enid's lips, but Nath interrupted with an observation that the last of the *Toucher du Bois*'s hands were about to go across to her and perhaps their captain should join them. Herme nodded briskly, exchanged salutes with Nath, and went off with Yeardly to rejoin his emasculated command. Enid watched him go, her body rigid with wintery rage at the impertinence of the arrogant dog with his flashing eyes, bright smile, and quick wit. Her eyes followed his boat across, and she muttered a curse as she saw him pick her out along the rail and purse his lips in a blown kiss.

"Why the sour look?" Nath inquired, standing next to her to watch the privateer get underway.

"The ill-bred dog presumed to blow a kiss in my direction," Enid fumed. "Despite the firm clarity with which I have rebuked his every attempt at my attentions!"

Nath raised a brow. "You are certain of this?"

"Indeed, I am! I saw it with my own eyes as clear as I see you next to me!"

"Then your eyes must rival those of our best watch in the tops," Nath replied dryly. "From this distance I can make out who Herme is by his build and bearing, but I couldn't tell if his lips were forming a kiss or singing a dirge. I'd need a spell or glass to see his face so clearly from such a distance and I fear *I* do not find it nearly interesting enough to be worthy of the trouble."

Enid's posture stiffened further, becoming as rigid as scripture. "If you will excuse me, sir, I have matters to attend to before we are underway ourselves."

"Of course," Nath answered. "My compliments to you upon your admirable attention to detail."

Enid touched her brow in salute and stalked off to her workroom below.

At dawn, as the rising sun painted the *Alarum*'s sails red and gold, she gave up her dead to the sea. Nath read from the naval edition of the Reformed Rite of Albion and Enid was touched by the sincere emotion he put into the archaic phrasings of the funereal selection. She suspected he harbored more piety than he probably cared to admit behind his carefully constructed modern exterior. Harlech began to sob as her captain read, "Their flames never to be extinguished, but rekindled when the sea surrenders her dominion to the Redeemer to claim their reward" and closed the holy book with a soft thud. Enid lay a hand on her shoulder and the girl looked up, tears streaming down her face. As the drums began to roll, the mid turned and buried her face in Enid's coat.

It was a terrible breach of discipline, but Enid truly doubted that any mention would ever be made of it. Cullen had been like a brother to Harlech, and Alston was loved by the entire crew for not putting on airs as the captain's steward and occasionally acting as a conduit for their concerns. She felt the girl's shoulders convulse as each shroud-wrapped body slid sibilantly down a plank to vanish beneath the waves with a dull but audible splash. Damning the discipline that kept Nath coolly erect as the drums beat their somber tattoo, Enid fell to her knees and clutched the girl tightly to her shoulder, unconsciously murmuring comforting words in Ardain into her sob-reddened ear. Enid held the girl long after the last body went over the side and the drums rattled to a stop. When she finally stood, it was only to take Harlech below and tuck her comfortably into the cot in the magister's tiny berth off the wardroom. She stood by the rocking cot and sang soft shepherd's songs until the girl was asleep. She passed the night herself sitting at her cramped writing desk in the company of ghosts, some awkwardly near, others more distant and infinitely more dolorous.

chapter 21

The return voyage to Gisbon was relatively uneventful, much to Nath's obvious relief. He had no desire to see his hard-won prize lost due to a chance encounter with a more powerful Ardain or Naveroñian force. Sails were twice spotted that may have been men-of-war and twice the *Alarum* and *Redemption* altered course, crowded on sail, and sank them below the horizon.

The *Redemption* was immediately recognized as she worked into the anchorage at Gisbon behind the *Alarum* and a great cheer had greeted the two vessels from each ship they slid slowly past before dropping anchor. The smoke from the *Alarum*'s salute to Admiral Weymouth had barely cleared before the signal flags atop the Admiralty building were flashing up her number and the signal "Captain Repair Aboard at Once." Nath snapped his glass closed and handed it wordlessly to Mid Harlech to stow. She caught Enid's eye and beamed up at her for a moment before scurrying off to replace the telescope in Nath's cabin.

"Well, there it is," Nath said with a sniff, shooting the cuffs of his best coat, and smoothing its front with his hands. "I think it best that you accompany me, Enid, as Admiral Weymouth may have some questions regarding your part in the affair."

"As you will," Enid answered.

As quick as could be, they were both seated in the stern sheets of the captain's gig, both clad in their most elegant uniforms. The long strokes of the immaculately turned-out boat crew pulled them swiftly toward the steps. Enid stole a sidewise glance at Nath, who presented the perfect model of a dignified, aloof officer, his hat seated just so upon his carefully clubbed hair and his white-gloved hand resting on the hilt of his hanger. There was nothing in either his bearing or expression to reveal any feelings he might have concerning his imminent appearance before Admiral Weymouth. She knew from their conversation the night before, however, that he was not nearly the bastion of calm certitude he presented to the world and was all the more impressed by his stoicism.

"When I decided to disobey Admiral Weymouth's orders and cut the *Redemption* out, my heart was easy," Nath had assured her over a glass of a very fine plum wine taken from Captain de Suarez's personal stock. He had invited all his officers together for one last dinner before their arrival in Gisbon. She'd stayed at his request after the other officers had withdrawn, and he'd confided in her, "Now I find myself considerably less sanguine."

"You seemed utterly unconcerned about the diplomatic consequences before. What has changed?"

"Nothing. I remain unconcerned. Naveroña will not declare war on Albion over the recovery of a stolen frigate. Indeed, King Juan-Charles has expressed extreme embarrassment in the past over the shameful conduct of his Admiralty for awarding bloody-handed mutineers with anything other than a rope collar and a dance at the end of a yardarm."

Nath took a long sip of his wine and followed it with an equally prolonged drag on one of the last of Enid's depleted stock of cigarillos. "No, that's not what concerns me."

"Then what?" Enid asked around her own smoke.

"I dread telling Weymouth I disobeyed him. The proof is in the pudding, of course, and he'll find the *Redemption* a pleasant pudding indeed, but the fact remains . . ." Nath trailed off miserably with a wave of his cigarillo.

"That you have sworn an oath of loyalty and obedience?" Enid pursed her lips thoughtfully as Nath nodded disconsolately and re-filled their glasses.

"Exactly. I dread facing the man and admitting I have broken that vow."

"I suspect," Enid said cautiously, "that he will see it less as dis-obedience than as initiative. You confirmed that the *Redemption* was anchored in Puerto Galeno and prepared to sail at a moment's notice. If you had not taken her when you did, what might have become of her? She may have slipped out during the dark of the moon or through some other contrivance. And didn't I hear some of the men talking about some startling aspect of her provisioning?"

"Yes, she had enough fresh stores crammed aboard to make Ul-tremare without stopping to resupply. That is odd and does argue that a plan was afoot to break her out soon. It may even excuse my initia-tive, but the fact is that I would have gone in for her even if she had not been in such a state. If her masts had been down on deck, I dare say I would have raised 'em to sail her out."

He sighed and swirled the wine in his glass. "I do not deceive my-self that it was from an avidity to serve the Crown, either. No, I was spurred on by ambition and spite, and as motivations go, neither of those are particularly comforting to a troubled heart."

Enid arched a brow. "Spite? Toward the Naveroñians?"

Nath laughed. "Never for a moment! I don't fancy your Naveroñians, and I do not deny it. They're too haughty by half and I like nothing better than taking them down a peg or two when opportunity allows."

"Well, you certainly took Captain de Suarez down. Nearly mortally so. I saw a bit of your swordplay with her, enough to see that she was a skilled practitioner of what the Naveroñians call 'La Ecuación Sublime.' My old dueling master warned me that the Naveroñians have distilled all the motions of offense and defense into a series of mathematical formulae. Duelists who have mastered those formulae are nigh impossible to best."

"Apparently I am simply faster at my sums than our good Captain de Suarez. It is probably an unforeseen benefit of so much time spent dwelling upon prize shares and purser's claims."

"Well, if not spite toward the Naveroñians—Lord Ambrose of Aixely?"

"Yes." Nath frowned darkly and shook his head. "But we'll speak no more of it tonight, if for no other reason than the well-known fact that some devils are summoned by the pronouncement of their names."

The boat crew shipped their oars, and the gig glided to a halt at the base of the steps. Bell and one of the hands leapt out smartly and steadied it for Nath and Enid. Nath acknowledged his coxswain's salute and left him with instructions to return to the *Alarum*.

"The magister and I will hire a boat. Inform Lieutenant Oxley that it is unlikely that we will return until well past dark."

At the top of the stair Nath hired a coach despite the expense. Enid was unable to see much of Gisbon as he insisted the windows remain shuttered against the fine dust that added its weight to the oppressively hot, still air. They found a crowd of officers awaiting them when the coach clattered to a stop outside Admiralty House, most of whom stopped their gossiping to unabashedly gawk.

"They look like a gallows crowd," Nath observed quietly from the side of his mouth, "here to see us kick up our heels a last time."

The crowd parted before them as they approached, and Enid saw a furtive smile here and an amiable wink there that revealed their curiosity was apparently not malevolent. In point of fact, they reminded her more of the awestruck faithful she had seen lining the streets of Velasca to steal a glance at the Patriarch as he passed in his gilt-laden carriage than the morbid mobs that frequented public hangings. Her impression was supported as one elderly lieutenant, obviously past any concerns regarding promotion, leaned close to Nath as he passed, clapped him on the shoulder, and muttered, "Good on you, sir!" in a hoarse, conspiratorial tone. Nath gave the fellow a bemused smile and thanked him for his kindness.

Inside Admiralty House's relatively cool antechamber Nath shared a significant glance with Enid. Word of the prize frigate entering in consort with the *Alarum* had apparently spread quickly and it was likely her identity had as well. Still, to judge by the pinched and sour expression of Weymouth's clerk, once they were ushered into his office by the antechamber's younger clerk, not everyone took the same delight in it as the officers without. The shriveled wight continued to scribble on a long sheet of ledger paper for several moments after they entered his domain and did not see fit to grace them with his rheumy gaze until after he had sanded and blotted the sheet.

"My compliments to the admiral," Nath began to announce himself. "I am—"

"I know good and well who you are, *Lieutenant* Nath," the clerk interrupted sharply, pronouncing the word *lieutenant* as if the shaping of it might ulcerate his tongue. "And Admiral Weymouth is expecting you. Past expecting, I imagine, as long as it took for you to comply with his signal. And who is this severe-looking lady at your side?"

Nath swallowed a sharp retort with some effort and replied, "Marquise Enid d'Tancreville, acting magister of His Majesty's Ship the *Alarum*."

The clerk frowned and chewed his lip for a long moment before shrugging contemptuously.

"If you wish to present yourself to Admiral Weymouth in the

company of your vessel's entire wardroom it is not for me to comment. Wait here, and I will announce you."

"You cannot let fellows like that provoke you," Nath hissed from the side of his mouth. "They are the gatekeepers to the celestial powers and rarely fail to have whatever humanity they may once have possessed burned away by the glare of reflected glory."

One corner of Enid's mouth quirked into a wry, subdued smile. "I know the sort," she assured him quietly, thinking back on her father's odious valet with a strange fondness. What had become of him? she wondered. Although of common birth, the man had emanated the social superiority of a duke. She doubted that his ponderously correct grammar, lethal acerbity, and carefully cultivated lisp would have been of any great aid in the face of a Theocratic mob.

The clerk reappeared and gestured impatiently for them to follow him into the admiral's office. He had barely announced them—Enid noticed he pronounced her name with a flawless Cite d'Arden accent—before the admiral was out of his chair and around the massive desk to grab Nath's hand and pump it vigorously. A second man stood as well, rising more slowly and evincing none of the admiral's enthusiasm as he sized Nath up from beneath grim, half-lidded eyes. He stood quietly aloof as the admiral continued to rattle Nath's knuckles and exult, "Good on you, sir! Oh, by God, good on you! Words fail me, sir!"

Obviously unnerved by such a demonstrative display from a "celestial power," Nath's smile was bright but constrained. "You are too kind by half, sir. I was fortunate and I am only pleased that my good fortune serves you."

"Oh, it has served me right well! Right well, indeed! Reyfort! A bottle of that fine claret and four glasses!"

As his sour-faced assistant rushed off for the wine, Admiral Weymouth took Enid by the elbow and turned her gently toward the stranger. "Magister d'Tancreville, allow me to introduce Lord Aixely, Captain Carlysle Ambrose. Lord Aixely, Marquise Enid d'Tancreville."

Ambrose's amber eyes were cold and reptilian as they swept over her, laden with contemptuous dismissal. Tall, aristocratic, and arrogantly handsome as the man was, Enid had no doubt he was used to that basilisk's gaze reducing his social inferiors to abashed deference and those inferior in naval rank to cowed obsequiousness. If this was the effect he hoped to achieve with her, however, he was doomed to disappointment. Mortally certain that her pedigree was at least as rarified as his and cavalier in her attitude toward military rank, Enid's only reaction to his baleful glare was a haughty sniff and a chilly, half-lidded stare of her own. Her lips pursed with amusement as his eyes slid angrily away from hers.

"Well," Ambrose greeted her in a strangely affected, nasal drawl, "I'm sure the honor is mine, Marquise."

"I will not argue your judgment in such matters, Captain." Enid was gratified to see the man's eyes narrow at the sting but carefully concealed any signs of gloating behind a courteously demure smile.

Weymouth released Nath's hand and retook his seat behind the massive, paper-covered desk. Still beaming, he took in the office's several straight-backed chairs with a broad gesture and invited them to be seated. As soon as each of them had a glass of wine in their hand and the aide had departed, leaving the cantrip-chilled bottle on a silver tray on the desk, the admiral eagerly leaned over the desk and jubilantly pressed Nath for details of the *Redemption*'s capture.

"Did you catch her in the offing to Cadice, then?" Weymouth demanded. "How heavy were your losses? Come, lad, speak! Captain Ambrose and I are with child to hear every smallest part of your tale!"

"Indeed," Ambrose agreed coolly in his indolent, nasal drawl. "There is nothing I would rather hear than an accounting of your recent actions."

Nath carefully rested his glass on one knee and cleared his throat casually before plunging directly into an informal report of the action.

He complimented Admiral Weymouth on the accuracy of his intelligence regarding the *Redemption*'s location and described finding her in Puerto Galeno through the capture of the *Toucher du Bois*. Admiral Weymouth listened intently as Nath described the *Redemption*'s crossed spars and the other indications that she was prepared to sail at a moment's notice.

Enid noticed a faint tightening of his expression as Nath recounted his decision to cut the frigate out and related the plan he had laid down toward that end. She saw the lines at the corners of his mouth and the indentation between his brows deepen as the gunboat's untimely arrival and its unsettling effect on the flotilla of the *Alarum*'s boats was described and thought, *Oh, there is trouble ahead. This admiral is not so pleased with the result that he will ignore the methods by which they were attained!* A quick glance at Ambrose, whose somewhat sullen expression at the start of the tale had transformed into a look of smug righteousness, did nothing to allay her uneasiness.

If Nath noticed the change in his audience's demeanor, he paid it no heed and pressed on to describe the short, sharp action aboard the *Redemption*. He told of the boarding nets, of Enid's blinding formulation and its effects on the defenders, the overwhelming odds against the *Alarum*s once past the net, the fight for the fo'c'sle—all of it described in the same spare terms and matter-of-fact tone with which he might have described the particulars of yesterday's breakfast. The only real emotion that entered his voice during the telling was as he praised the actions of Enid, Merryweather, and Yeardly— and as he gave an accounting of the butcher's bill.

"My God," Admiral Weymouth breathed as Nath finished. "Nine dead and a dozen wounded . . . your steward and senior mid among them."

"A dreadful loss of life," Ambrose snapped disapprovingly. "Especially in the pursuit of what can only be described as self-aggrandizing adventure! I hope you were not as careless with my ship as you were with her crew, *Lieutenant* Nath!"

Nath opened his mouth, but Admiral Weymouth spoke first.

"A dreadful loss of life? I dare say it was for the Naveroñians with their hundred and twelve dead, but it seems to me *Captain* Nath's care for the *Alarum*'s people is amply demonstrated by how few of them were lost in what was obviously a difficult and daring action."

"Oh, certainly it was daring," Ambrose agreed, a trace of sneer in his overcultured voice. "It's quite daring to invade a friendly nation's waters at the risk of war just to take what could have been had freely if he had been patient enough to wait in the offing. Or would 'reckless' be a better word?"

"I waited patiently for a few weeks, sir," Nath replied evenly. "But as I said, Captain Herme of the *Tape a'Bord* warned of a large Ardain frigate prowling the same cruising grounds. If she had come upon the *Redemption* first and fallen into company with her, the *Alarum* would have had no chance against the pair of them. Worse yet, if she fell upon us with the crew split between the *Alarum* and the *Redemption*, we would have stood a good chance of losing both vessels to Ardainne."

Ambrose snorted disdainfully. "I see you are cognizant of the importance of proper manning when it serves you, Lieutenant. If only you'd given the same careful thought to the crew you put aboard the *Artagny*."

Nath's jaw dropped in puzzlement. "The *Artagny*? What of her?"

"She was retaken by her people, who found the prize crew you left in charge of them too few in number," Ambrose said coldly. "Criminally few, in fact. You may as well have presented them to the Confessor as a gift for all the concern you showed for Lieutenant Bascombe and her crew."

Nath went stiff in his chair and Enid was taken aback by the cold, expressionless set of his features as he addressed Ambrose. "Has this been confirmed, sir?"

"Confirmed that you sent a promising officer to her doom, or that you are the dangerous scion of a family that has always put glory before the interest of the Crown or the Sea Service?" Ambrose shrugged airily. "The questions are as one, as is their answer: yes, it has been confirmed."

Nath half rose, before Admiral Weymouth interjected in a menacing baritone, "Here, now! We will limit our remarks to the matter at hand, which is the *Redemption* and not the *Artagny!*"

"As you will, sir," Ambrose answered flatly. "And on that subject, when do you intend to call for a court-martial?"

"A court-martial? Whatever for?"

"Why, for making war on a peaceful nation. I mean it is all fine and good to have the *Redemption* back, but to do so at the risk of war with Naveroña? Or barring that, willful disobedience to orders. Captain Odenton of the *Murtherer* delivered sealed orders to Lieutenant Nath in my own hand directing him to return to Gisbon at once and to take all steps possible to avoid exposing the *Alarum* to further peril. I have also seen a copy of your orders to Nath, as is my right as the *Alarum*'s new captain, and I could not help but notice that you were quite specific in forbidding him from undertaking the very sort of operation he has just described in shameless detail."

"My orders trump yours," Weymouth said tightly, his expression visibly darkening. "And they granted him the flexibility to remain on station until advised you were physically present to assume the *Alarum*'s command. And they directed him to take any reasonable risk to capture the *Redemption*, which order he obeyed to my great satisfaction!"

"And I wish you joy for it, sir," Ambrose said, sniffing primly. "But the fact remains that he disobeyed a direct order prohibiting him from cutting the *Redemption* out."

"You may interpret it that way," Weymouth growled. "But you'll note that I also gave Captain Nath leave to take 'extraordinary measures' to ensure the *Redemption* did not reach Cadice."

"I do not for an instant believe you would wish any of your subordinates to interpret 'extraordinary measures' to mean 'disobey the lawful orders of your superior officers.' As admiral of the Merentian, it is your duty to—"

"You presume instruct *me* regarding *my* duties, you vomit-gobbling young cur?" Both of Admiral Weymouth's fists crashed down on his desk in unison, upsetting the bottle of claret and, Enid would later swear, bouncing the ponderous mass of oak and brass a full inch off the floor. The admiral half stood and seemed to loom over them all like a sudden storm cloud. His broad shoulders blocked out the light and his flashing eyes threatened to strike down anyone they settled upon with a thunderbolt of wrath.

"You would instruct me? You who left your command rotting at anchor with no provisions and too few men to work her pumps as the hull rotted beneath 'em? You *pretend* to lecture *me* regarding *duty*? Be careful with your bleating about courts-martial or you will find yourself standing in front of one yourself!"

Ambrose flinched under the admiral's thunderous rebuke but was not cowed. He stood to attention and answered in a voice that barely quavered. "There is nothing censurable about my behavior regarding my command. If there were any irregularities in the manning and outfitting of the *Alarum* the blame lays squarely at the feet of my replacement, assigned as a favor to the Young Briar Party to discomfit their rivals without a care for his ignorance and brazen foolhardiness!"

Enid was certain the claret glass made some sound as it shattered in Nath's grasp, but the tinkling of its destruction was utterly lost in Weymouth's indignant gale.

"You are a damnable scrub to blame the man who surely kept you

from a court-martial yourself!" Weymouth roared. "You think your interest is sufficient to have saved you if the *Alarum* had not sailed when
ordered? You deceive yourself, sir! The Service would have eaten you
whole, friends in the House of Lords or no! None of your toadying
would have saved you! What Nath did in the time your procrastination
allowed does him nothing but credit!"

"The Admiralty lords disagree, sir," Ambrose replied haughtily,
producing an oilskin cartel from inside his coat. "Here are their orders directing and requiring me to relieve Lieutenant Nath from duty
aboard the *Alarum* and directing him to return directly to Middlesea,
there to answer for his dereliction of duty in inadequately preparing
the *Alarum* for action and for the resultant loss of the prize frigate
Artagny and the capture or death of all the Albion officers and crew
aboard her. I am to assume immediate command of the *Alarum*. You'll
find copies of his orders there as well."

He placed the cartel on the desk, fastidiously avoiding the spreading pool of claret and tapped it with an elegantly long forefinger. "You'll
also find, sir, that it directs me to remove any officers, warrants, or
crew I deem to have contributed to Nath's dereliction and dispatch
them with him to face the same charges. I will have that list for you
before sunset. I fear it will almost certainly include the names of my
surviving lieutenants, so I pray you will indulge me in approving the
appointment of Master Harde as an acting lieutenant."

"That will prove difficult," Nath interjected dryly as Admiral Weymouth's indescribable wrath left him dangerously silent for a moment,
"as Master Harde is under arrest for insubordination." He touched a
slight bulge beneath his own coat. "I have the formal charges here,
along with a letter to the Naval Board requesting the revocation of his
warrant."

It was Ambrose's turn to be choked to silence with rage and surprise, a silence that Admiral Weymouth filled with a low, dangerous
laugh. "Hah! If the dog isn't hung, or isn't crippled by the lash, or

doesn't catch the fever in a prison hulk and die, perhaps you can rate him 'able seaman' and not be completely bereft of the services of a talented lickspittle! I can't imagine he would be so high in your favor were he aught else!"

Ambrose stiffened and tapped the cartel again. "I will have the names of the other officers to you before sundown, sir. If you wish, I will prepare the *Alarum* to transport them back to Albion. It will be necessary for me to testify, in any case, so—"

"That will not be necessary, Captain," Admiral Weymouth said as he slapped his hand down over the oilskin envelope and dragged it across the desk. "I have alternate transportation in mind for Lieutenant Nath and his 'confederates.' And I have better uses for you and the *Alarum* than playing transport. I fear you'll have to put your testimony in the form of a deposition due to pressing needs of the Service. Have the officers and men you wish to accompany Nath to Albion ready to shift their gear before dark. I will send Nath to take charge of them and shift his own dunnage."

"And Master Harde?"

"Send him to my flagship under arrest and in the custody of marines. I'm sure I can find appropriate accommodations for him until the matter of his warrant can be reviewed. You are dismissed."

"As you will, sir." Captain Ambrose saluted languidly and slipped from the room without a backward glance.

"Arrogant bastard," Weymouth snarled at his back and then shouted for his aide. He opened the cartel and skimmed over the documents inside as his wizened old assistant mopped up spilt claret and muttered under his breath. After the old fellow was gone and Nath's hand was bandaged—"Never mind the glass, Lieutenant, but I cannot have you bleeding all over the upholstery or Lady Weymouth will have *me* bleeding as well!"—he laid the papers down with a sigh.

"Did you roger this fellow's mistress before you left Middlesea,

Nath?" Weymouth shot an apologetic glance at Enid, who only shrugged. "The devil seems to have it in for you. Normally I'd say you could shrug off such nonsense as this, but Lord Ambrose is very well connected."

"So I'm to be court-martialed?"

"So it seems. On charges of dereliction of duty." The admiral snorted contemptuously. "He claims you are fully to blame for the *Alarum*'s poor state and failed to request additional time to ready her because you were in a hurry to get about taking prizes. Blames the loss of the *Artagny* on your failure to raise a large enough crew to support your greedy pursuit of prizes, which left you too short-handed to put a creditable prize crew aboard her. Dereliction that resulted in the loss of one of His Majesty's ships—and somehow the devil has convinced the sea lord to consider the *Artagny,* a prize that never came within eyeshot of a prize court, a 'king's ship'—"

"The charges are ridiculous, sir," Nath observed wanly. "Surely they cannot stand."

Weymouth grunted noncommittally. "Well, whether they stand or not, you certainly must answer for them. I suggest you waste no effort in preparing your defense."

"I shall commit myself directly," Nath agreed perfunctorily.

Weymouth frowned and gave Ambrose's papers a distasteful shove across the table.

"The joy has certainly been taken out of the day. Leave your logs with Reyfort for my review and fetch your dunnage and whoever Ambrose is determined to banish from the *Alarum*. I will have orders for the lot of you delivered to the Briar and Thistle. You know it?"

"Yes, sir." The Briar and Thistle stood at the top of the stair and was well-loved for its Albion atmosphere by the officers who could afford it.

"Very well. Do not provoke Ambrose or allow yourself to be provoked by him," Weymouth cautioned. "Gather your things, gather your people, and be gone. Do not add fuel to the fire. You're too likely to be burned by it already. Now off with you both! I've a damnable lot of work to do. Reyfort! Get your scowling phyz in here and prepare to take a letter or three!"

Whether by the expression on Nath's face or Ambrose's stormy departure earlier, the officers outside Admiralty House parted to allow them to pass without comment. Nath approached a loitering trap driver, and they were soon clattering back down Mt. Gisbon. They rode in silence for a quarter of an hour before Enid broke it at last.

"It will come to that?" Enid asked in disbelief as Nath stared grimly down into the bloodied wrappings swathing the palm of his left hand. "Death or exile from the navy?"

"It could," Nath answered gravely. "Apparently our Lord Aixely believes he throws enough weight in interest to support these specious charges."

He looked up from his hand and frowned. "And that is troubling, as he must be aware that Admiral Barrington holds me in some esteem. After all, it was Sir Barrington who put my name forward to command the *Alarum*. Then, of course, there is my father."

"Your father is powerful in the navy?"

"He is an admiral of the Yellow and has a fine history of service," Nath said. "But he's in a bad odor with Admiralty."

"I confess that these colorful admirals of yours leave me perplexed. What fleet does the Admiral of the Yellow command?"

"None. Admirals of the Yellow are officers of the Admiral's rank who have no command assigned to them. They are, in essence, retired officers." Nath scrutinized his wounded hand closely in a manner that Enid suspected was intended to forestall questions about his father.

"Admiral Weymouth seems to have your interests at heart, too," Enid ventured, ending the uncomfortable conversational lull. "He is held in high esteem, is he not? A national hero, by your account?"

"Certainly." Nath sighed and gingerly clenched his bandaged hand into a fist. "I have a fair amount of interest, but you can wager your last cent that Lord Aixely's father and uncle will spare no expense or blandishment of interest in seating their creatures as judges of the court."

"Well, surely your partisans will rally behind you, too?"

"They will, and though they aren't as numerous or near to the throne as Lord Aixely's, they are all good, copper-bottomed naval officers. I believe I have fewer guns, but more throw-weight, if you follow."

Enid stared at him.

"I mean to say when it comes to interest, it is six of one and a half dozen of the other in this case. My fate is not sealed, but it will be a close thing."

The hack clattered to a halt and she and Nath stepped down onto the sun-bleached steps.

"Well," he muttered, squinting against the glare. "Now I'd better find us a bumboat or we'll both have to thrash our arms and swim like fish out to the *Alarum*."

———— ⚬ ————

Their boatman proved to be a ferociously scarred man, a native of Albion by his accent, whose wooden leg and three-fingered right hand hardly seemed to hinder him in propelling his passengers rapidly across the bay's choppy waters to the *Alarum*'s anchorage. As they came within earshot, Nath hailed the ship. He was answered by the traditional "Who goes?" from the watch and nearly shouted "*Alarum!*" in reply. He was no longer in command of the ship looming larger over the shoulder of the grisly-featured boatman, though, so that answer would not do. Instead, he shouted out, "Nath!"

Nath pressed a coin into the boatman's hand and told him his services would not be needed for the return trip. A few moments later found them on the deck. They came up the starboard side at Nath's direction to alleviate any embarrassment over a side party or lack thereof. The ship, which Enid suddenly realized had taken on the warm familiarity of home during the last few months, now seemed a strange and potentially perilous place. Whether from empathy or hostility, the sailors on deck avoided their eyes and made no move to acknowledge their presence at all.

A strange lieutenant strode toward them, touching the brim of his hat as he came. Nath returned the courtesy and the man introduced himself in a carefully neutral tone.

"Lieutenant Nath, I presume? And Magister d'Tancreville?" At their nods, he smiled slightly, revealing a set of even, white teeth. "I'm Lieutenant Darwood. I was sent across to replace Lieutenant Bascombe. Captain Ambrose has directed me to assist you in shifting your dunnage ashore. The longboat is at your disposal."

"Most kind of him," Nath drawled flatly. He glanced up at a net laden with chests suspended above the deck. "I see my things have already been swayed up. Is there any point in looking in my cabin for anything else?"

"No, sir," Darwood answered, a touch of color at his cheeks despite his crisp, military tone. "Captain Ambrose saw to it that your coxswain made a clean sweep of things before . . . going ashore."

"Kind of him, indeed," Nath said stiffly. "I'll stay clear till Magister d'Tancreville's dunnage is brought topside. I trust you'll put a few men at her disposal to aid in the task?"

The *Alarum*s chosen to help her pack her cabin and workroom and rouse her chests from the hold were touchingly diffident once they were belowdecks and out of sight of the quarterdeck. They helped her pack with near-wordless efficiency and many a searching glance. In less than an hour the chests she stored in the hold after crossing over from the *Marie* were swayed up on deck and her personal dunnage was being manhandled from below.

Before they emerged on the deck, one of the *Alarum*s touched her lightly on the elbow and muttered hoarsely in what amounted to a whisper for a man more used to howling gales and roaring guns than the hushed tones of conspiracy, "Give the cap'n our best wishes, won't ye, m'lady? 'Tis a powerful wrong done to him an' while we hain't no voice in't, we dearly desire 'im t'know the esteem b'which we hold 'im!"

"Your words will be a great comfort to Captain Nath," Enid assured him earnestly, keeping her face turned away from the quarterdeck where Ambrose and his first lieutenant, Langlin, looked on like grinning vultures.

She joined Nath and stood next to him as their gear was lowered into the boat. She followed his example and stood with hands clasped behind her back and set her face in as near an approximation of some marble-sculpted saint as was within her means. Enid found she was not nearly as successful at it as Nath, especially as Langlin and Ambrose made a great show of amusement at their discomfiture.

After what seemed an eternity, the last of their baggage was in the boat and Lieutenant Darwood dismissed the detail. He turned to Nath and Enid and announced that all was prepared for their departure. At the entry port he exchanged a salute with Nath and, turning so that his back was to the quarterdeck, said quietly, "Best of luck, Commander Nath. I reviewed your master logs when I came aboard and only a fool would believe you were in any way derelict."

"Thank you for your kind words, Lieutenant Darwood," Nath answered quietly. "But be careful with your opinions. Your new master has the sea lord's ear and many friends nearer to hand."

The younger lieutenant's face screwed up in a moue of distaste. "A handful among the crew you sailed with and a whole retinue of 'em brought over from Albion just to fill the berths of those he purged. The *Alarum* is an unhappy ship. I've heard some of the old salts venture that the accursed spirit of the *Redemption* has passed into her."

Before Nath could answer, First Lieutenant Langlin's strident voice called out from the quarterdeck, "See those people over the side, Mr. Darwood! We have work to do and no time to prattle with super-numeraries!"

As their boat pulled around the *Alarum*'s stern and made for shore, Enid heard Nath utter a quiet curse. She followed his gaze and saw Ambrose standing at the taffrail watching them. His face was virulently smug, and she felt her blood rise hotly at the sight of him.

"Enjoy your frolic while you can, you arrogant, whoreson prig," Nath hissed, turning away. "Enjoy it while you may."

Enid continued to stare at Ambrose as Nath fixed his eyes on the shore. After a moment, she cupped her right hand around her mouth and whispered something.

"What was that?" Nath asked. "I couldn't make out what you said."

"It was nothing," Enid assured him, smiling as she saw Ambrose start and visibly blanch before turning and walking shakily away from the rail. "I merely made a promise to myself and shared it with the wind. It is a custom among the girls of my homeland. Silly, I suppose, but I find that the rituals of childhood often ease the rigors of adulthood."

The longboat, now commanded by Captain Ambrose's coxswain, slid up to the steps and the hands manning it shipped their oars with machine-like precision. Nath paused before stepping out of the boat to give them a warm look and a grateful nod. They were all *his Alarum*s and their gesture spoke volumes to him.

He turned to Enid and said, "Well, we've arrived. Let's see who is to join us in exile, shall we?"

They ascended the broad, low flags of the Admiralty Steps under the heat of Gisbon's dusk. The day seemed to hold its breath in anticipation of the cooling caress of a night breeze, a fond desire held in vain at this time of year when the blanket of night seemed intent

on smothering everything that fell beneath it. The weight of the stifling heat seemed to bear down particularly cruelly upon the file of
sailors who stood before the Briar and Thistle. Although a squad
of marines stood guard over them, most of the banished *Alarum*s
looked too dispirited to desert. Chins rested on chests and the shoulders of many were so rounded with despondency that the straps of
their rucksacks could barely find purchase. Enid was amazed to see
so many of them.

"It's a full third of the hands," Nath marveled. "Bell, Merryweather, Oxley, plus Yeardly and all the younkers! He's even put off
old Rondelle!" He gave his head a bemused shake and strode up to the
expatriate *Alarum*s. As he neared, Yeardly approached.

"Captain Reordan sends his compliments, sir, and wishes to speak
with you inside immediately regarding the particulars of our orders."

Nath nodded grimly. "Very well, Yeardly. Make sure the people
are ready to move. I'm sure this won't take long and once it is finished, we'll be off to whatever quarters the Service has seen fit to
provide for us."

"A fine berth aboard the *Black Agnes*, I shouldn't wonder, sir."
Yeardly named a notorious prison hulk moored in Middlesea.

"I shouldn't either," Nath answered, sharing a sardonic grin with
the young mid before trudging up the flagged path to the Briar and
Thistle. Enid followed, determined to know their fate at the same moment as Nath. Her stomach felt much the same as it did as the *Artagny*
bore down on the *Marie*. She had no desire to wait an instant longer
than necessary for whatever news might set it to rest.

The interior of the inn was hot, but not as stiflingly still as outside
thanks to a dweomer that sent unseen sylphs chasing each other about
the room in slow circles. It was considerably darker inside, however,
and the light orbs still hovered quiescently in their cressets, awaiting
their owner's word to shed their radiance over the room. Nath squinted
through the gloom and finally set his eyes upon a naval captain sitting

alone at a small table. Noticing Rue's glance, the officer stood and called out, "Lieutenant Rue Nath?"

"Aye, sir," Nath affirmed, touching the brim of his hat as he approached the man. "And the Marquise Enid d'Tancreville, former volunteer aboard the *Alarum*."

"Captain Avram Reordan," the stoutly built officer introduced himself, motioning them to sit with him. "Flag captain, the *Conqueror*." He raised a hand as Nath seemed about to surge to his feet again. "No, no, Lieutenant Nath. No need to jump from your skin like a schoolgirl seeing the king's carriage for the first time. You've shared wine with the Hero of Filsterhead, you have nothing to dread from me. I am not one of the gods. I am merely one of their messengers."

"As you will, sir," Nath answered skeptically. "But the dreadfulness of the messenger depends greatly upon the message he bears, I think."

Reordan's laugh was deep and pleasing, inexplicably bringing well-aged brandy casks to Enid's mind. He pushed a fat envelope across the table to Nath, who looked down at it in much the same way a man might survey a deadly asp so near to hand. The captain laughed again, shaking his head. "You're a wary one, aren't you, Nath? Though I must admit I can't blame you, considering your situation. Still, sometimes a strange sail is a friendly one, no?"

Nath nodded slowly, turning the envelope over in his hand to study the seal on it.

"Well, those are your orders," Reordan said breezily. "And since the Earl of Filsterhead bade me to ensure you obey them with all possible dispatch, let me give you the key points now. You can read the details later at your leisure."

Nath nodded again, more briskly, and visibly braced himself for the worst. Enid, true to her earlier observation regarding the "rituals of childhood," crossed her fingers beneath the table.

"You and that lot outside are to report immediately to the *Redemption*."

"For transport to Albion?" Nath said grimly. "Will the magister and I be confined to our cabins until she is ready to sail?"

"Whatever suits you," the flag captain said, chuckling. "But I would think you'd prefer to take a more direct hand readying your command for sea, especially considering the charges Ambrose has levied against you."

Enid saw an expression flash across Nath's face that she had never seen there before: bewildered surprise.

"My command?" he breathed lowly, as if speaking the words too loud might startle him awake, ending the precious dream.

"Yes, your command, Captain Nath." Reordan waved a powerful, thick-fingered hand at the epaulette on Nath's shoulder. "You'll need to shift that 'cross deck, Captain Nath. Admiral Weymouth has made you post. Your commission is in the envelope, along with your orders to make the *Redemption* ready for sea and take her to Middlesea, there to stand court-martial."

He stood and tossed a handful of coins on the table. "I fear my duties require me elsewhere but allow me to contribute to the evening. I trust you will not neglect tradition in wetting the swab?"

"No, sir!" Nath gasped, standing himself and reaching out for Captain Reordan's hand, which he pumped energetically. "I— Give my regards to Earl Filsterhead, my compliments— I-I have no words to express . . ." He trailed off, releasing Reordan's hand as an afterthought.

"Nor did I, when the time came." The older captain smiled, laying a tanned hand on Nath's shoulder. "And I wish you the joy of your promotion and the best of luck in this matter with Ambrose. Do not waste what you have been given!"

Nath sat down heavily next to Enid and stared bemusedly at

Reordan's back as it disappeared through the gloom of the inn. Enid frowned at the money that had been tossed on the table and sought to make sense of the exchange she'd just witnessed.

"You are given command of the *Redemption* despite the pending court-martial? You have attained the famous rank of *post*?"

"So it seems, but let us see for certain." Nath broke the envelope's red seal, which appeared black in the poor light, and pulled out a thick fold of papers. He unfolded the papers and squinted at them, angling them toward the dim glow of the inn's open door. Enid rolled her eyes and a small orb of light appeared over Nath's right shoulder at a wave of her hand.

"Ah! Thank you! That is much better . . . Now, let us see, yes, it is no cruel jest. 'You are directed and required to take command of His Majesty's ship now designated the REDEMPTION'—it appears they plan to rename her—and here"—he held up a sheet of vellum with obvious reverence—"here is my commission, making me post. I am made post, Enid! Can you credit it?"

"Credit it? Of course I can. But is this appointment of any consequence in light of your current difficulties?"

"All the consequence in the world," Nath said, grinning. "All the consequence in the world! I'm no longer a lowly lieutenant facing charges from a post captain. I can now meet Aixely on level ground, with no step of rank between us. This is more than a grand gesture from Admiral Weymouth, it is a lifeline for my career!"

"And well deserved, I would say. Your actions have added luster to the admiral's name as well as yours. Should we begin this ritual of 'wetting your swab' immediately?"

Nath returned Enid's rare smile but shook his head. "Not yet. I must read myself in aboard the *Redemption* and see to getting her underway as soon as possible. The wetting may need to wait until we are in Middlesea."

The *Redemption* and *Alarum* were anchored within two cables of each other in Gisbon's crowded harbor. Nath had already witnessed the punishment of two men he'd been forced to leave behind when Ambrose assumed command of the *Alarum*. He recognized them through his come-hither glass as a man and woman brought aboard at Gisbon. Both good sailors, but a little rough around the edges. Neither had approached a level of indolence or impudence under his command that merited a turn at the ship's grate, but he'd seen them both seized up to receive an even dozen lashes each. He wondered what their crime might have been, to drive Captain Ambrose to admit a failure in command under the very eyes of Admiral Weymouth. For what else could one consider the rigging of the grate for a flogging if not a captain's failure to maintain the good discipline of their crew?

He was brooding at the rail when Enid approached. She took in his general mood and the direction of his gaze and said, "I suppose it is natural to miss a vessel that has been both your home and instrument of warfare for so many months. I find I miss her myself, despite my negligible experience with her compared to yours."

"Aye, the *Alarum* is a good ship, and despite my circumstances, she was a happy ship." He turned to face Enid full on and said, "Do you know I never found cause to flog one of her people while she was under my command? Not even with that serpent Harde fomenting whatever trouble he could in the gullible hearts of the common tars."

"That is obvious proof of your talent at command," Enid said. "I expect to see the same results aboard the *Redemption*. You are a fine example and guardian of your people."

Nath frowned at that. "Not so fine that I kept Lieutenant Bascombe and her people from falling into the Rats's hands. I've received word that Bascombe and the prize crew have attracted the particular attention of the Theocratic press, who are painting them as fire-breathing assassins, utterly bereft of humanity."

Enid saw a morose curtain descending behind Nath's eyes, so she sought to distract him with a more immediate concern. "How go the preparations?"

"We are still a little shorthanded, but not so much more than any of His Majesty's ships these days. Most of the people we've recruited are experienced salts who know their ropes and pulleys. Not a landsman among 'em.

"Moreover, her hold is stuffed to bursting with stores, courtesy of the King of Naveroña. We shall want for nothing on our voyage to Middlesea." He sighed and cast a gloomy glance at *Alarum*. "Still, it rankles me to see *Alarum* sitting so low in the water from all the stores I purchased for her on account. The price of them will be deducted from my prize money to the profit of that jackal, Ambrose.

"It is not all easy sailing, though," Nath said. "We are short on powder and shot. All the Naveroñian munitions were condemned, so she must be fully resupplied. Gisbon has yet to recover from the inroads made on its stores by the blockade fleet, so there is precious little food for the cannons available."

"We must go to sea unarmed, then?"

"No. I've secured enough munitions to defend ourselves if we have no other choice, but not much more. I fear there will be no prizes taken on our homeward voyage."

Enid shrugged. "I am in no way dismayed. A peaceful cruise will give me time to pursue my studies in maritime magic."

"Well, I'll leave you to your studies then, Magister," Nath said with a half bow. "I must prepare to read myself in. I'll send Yeardly to summon you when the time comes."

A soft knock at her door broke Enid's internal conversation with Dunaughy, who silently informed her that Merryweather awaited her outside, so she was not surprised to find the lieutenant standing without.

"Is it time for Captain Nath's famous reading?"

"Not quite yet." The bandage on Merryweather's cheek bunched up as she smiled gingerly. "Dr. Rondelle suggested I speak to you about my wound. Easing its scarring is beyond his magic, but he thought you might be able to help."

"Of course, come in and sit," Enid said, gesturing to her writing desk's small chair. "I'll see what I can do."

Merryweather took her place and Enid knelt before her and carefully removed her bandages. The wound beneath was long and had been left untreated long enough that it had closed poorly.

"Oh, Augusta." Enid gently stroked Merryweather's cheek with the back of her fingers.

Merryweather's eyes dropped. "I understand if there is nothing you can do, Enid."

"No, no, I can help. The scarring can be reduced, but it cannot be erased."

"I shouldn't care. Scars such as this are a sign of honor and accomplishment. I fear I'm vain, though, and loathe the idea of looking hideous."

Enid took Merryweather's face in her hands and lifted it until she met her eyes. "You are not hideous, Augusta, and never will be. You are luminous and no scar can dim your glow."

As Merryweather turned her head to wipe unofficerly tears from her eyes, Enid stood and said, "We will begin work on this when next you are off watch. I'll have you ready to be adored as a hero before we reach Middlesea."

All hands were called on deck when the sun was an hour short of sinking below the western horizon. Everyone aboard was crammed onto the weather deck as Captain Nath read himself in as the *Redemption*'s new captain. Enid stood in the front row, with the other commission and warrant officers, but Nath's pride would have been obvious were she in the very back, cloistered with the most lubberly of the *Redemption*'s people. When he'd finished reading his orders, he returned them carefully to his vest pocket and looked out over his small but attentive crew. They returned his gaze expectantly.

"We are all of us *Alarums* and always will be, forged to it as we have been, and bound to our mates lost while cutting out this very ship—" Here Nath was forced to pause until three cheers had wafted across the harbor, disturbing squabbling gulls and drawing a frown from Captain Ambrose as he paced the quarter deck of the *Alarum*, anchored nearby.

"We are short-handed, but there are enough of us to sail *Redemption* and man one of her broadsides at a time. That should still leave us with the advantage against any Ardain frigate foolish enough to try her hand against us on our triumphant return to Middlesea!"

When the crew's renewed cheers subsided, Nath grinned and, in a voice loud enough to be heard by the crew, said, "Master Gaines! An extra tot for all hands during the dogwatch and all divisions to their duties! We sail for Middlesea on the morning tide!"

It was shockingly early when Enid joined Nath at the taffrail. She'd stayed below and out from under the crew's feet as the *Redemption* worked her way out of Gisbon Harbor and only emerged on deck after Yeardly alerted her that they were in the offing. The Fist of Gisbon was half-sunk below the horizon before Nath's acting steward arrived with a pewter tray bearing cups and a steaming pot of coffee, the odor of which was an immediate balm to Enid's mood.

She took in Nath's calmer expression and the smoothness of his brow and said, "You seem more at ease at sea. I've come to suspect that you are some saltwater amphibian that can function on land but prefers the water."

Nath chuckled. "Having the great barky underway is gratifying, while scrabbling for butter and balls ashore is pure frustration."

"Once this farce of a court-martial is dispensed with, I assume you will be given new orders?"

Nath frowned and accepted a cigarillo from Enid, who had replenished her stock in Gisbon-town.

"Assuming all goes my way, perhaps. Even if the charges against me are repudiated as calumny and stuff, Lord Ambrose has powerful friends in the Admiralty and the king's court. Depending on the prevailing political winds in Albion, I may be added to the long list of captains who have been consigned to shore duty for the duration of their career."

Seeing her friend's previous jollity evaporate before her eyes, Enid said, "Well, when you assume your next command—and I'm mortal certain that you shall—I will be happy to serve as your magister again."

"That's as kind as can be, Enid," Nath said. "I would heartily regret sailing without you. If I find a safe passage through these troubled waters and receive a new command, I'll have the choice of the old *Alarum*s to crew her. Can you imagine what we could accomplish with a ship of more substance than the little *Alarum* and the officers and crew that cut out the *Redemption* despite the enemy's numbers and ferocity? History would be ours to write."

Enid smiled and tapped the lip of her coffee cup to his. Nath's renewed enthusiasm was irresistible, but her mind kept going back to the court-martial as they sped toward Albion. She fervently hoped he would emerge unscathed from the traps and snares arising from the jealousy of Captain Ambrose, Lord Aixely. If not, dark storms lay on the horizon, which might shatter his hopes and hers upon the rocks of a political lee shore.

END

Regarding the Albion Royal Navy

INDICES

A NOTE ON THE PRESENTATION OF SHIPS' NAMES

It is customary in Albion dispatches and reports to show the name of Albion vessels in all capitals, i.e., ALARUM, and enemy vessels in italics, i.e., *Artagny*. We have dispensed with that practice in this volume as it may be jarring to the eye of readers unversed in naval custom. Instead, all ship names are shown in italics, and it is the hope of the author that their respective allegiances will be made clear by their actions as described in this chronicle.

NAVAL RANKS

The Albion Royal Navy during the Theocratic War was the largest organization in the kingdom outside the Crown government itself. It was far more rigorously structured than Albion's army and infinitely more coherent in both hierarchy and purpose. What follows is a brief description of the rank structure encountered within this chronicle. An actual accounting of every facet of the Royal Navy's organization would be both unnecessary and tedious to all but the most devoted historian of the period.

Our circumscribed examination of Royal Navy ranks begins at the pinnacle of power and responsibility encountered in our tale and concludes with the least empowered but nevertheless vital members of a ship's people.

The Sea Lord

The sea lord is responsible for administrating all aspects of the Royal Navy, albeit through the devices of their appointees with regard to concerns beneath their lofty rank. The position is filled by the sovereign's appointee who maintains their seat at the Crown's pleasure. Since the Albion Royal Navy is the kingdom's largest and most lauded department of the royal government and brings with it access to near-celestial power and wealth, the office of the sea lord is much sought after, particularly by admirals of a political bent.

FLAG RANKS

Admirals

Hoisting an admiral's pennant is the ambition of all but the dullest Royal Navy officer. Every post captain will eventually gain the rank, should they live long enough to be at the top of the Captains List when an existing admiral passes on, but truly energetic, capable, and clever (or cunning) captains can be elevated to an admiral's post at the sea lord's command.

An admiral can be appointed to command one of the navy's great fleets, in which case they are identified with the flag associated with it. The admiral of the Merentian Sea, for instance, is referred to as the Admiral of the Red. Admirals can also be assigned to lead specific task forces or to the command of naval bases. Admirals in name only, with no commands beneath them, are referred to as Admirals of the Yellow or Yellow Admirals. This, in essence, is the retirement provided for post captains who remain in the Sea Service their entire lives.

An admiral in command of a fleet or a naval region is in an enviable position to multiply their wealth, as they receive a share of all prizes taken by officers under their command or in their region of responsibility.

Commodores

A commodore is a post captain who has been assigned command of a squadron of ships or a naval base that doesn't merit the attention of an admiral. This rank may be temporary and endure only so long as the task to which a commodore's command has been assigned, or it may become unofficially permanent, which is often the case with land-based commodores.

Like admirals, commodores receive a share of all prizes taken by officers under their command or in the region for which they are responsible.

COMMISSION RANKS

Post Captain

All commissioned offers dream of being "made post." Once promoted to post captain, an officer's name is added to the Captains List, guaranteeing their rise to the rank of admiral, mortality permitting. Post captains in command of a vessel receive a large share of any prize she takes. They also receive full pay when not employed at sea, rather than the half pay with which other beached commission officers must make do.

Primarily, though, a post captain is given command of a post ship, a real fighting ship of twenty-eight guns or more, and will never again be consigned to unrated vessels with which a commander must be satisfied. Aboard their own ship, a post captain is the embodiment of the navy and speaks with its authority. They are expected to represent the Crown's authority and act in its best interest on their own initiative.

Commander

A commander is a lieutenant who has been given command of a vessel that does not meet the requirements of a post ship, such as schooners, sloops, or brigs of war. Aboard their own ship, they have all the authority of a captain (and are, indeed, referred to as such) and have authority over other lieutenants assigned to the vessel. Being made commander is, in effect, a trial period in which a lieutenant can prove they are fit to assume the duties of a post captain. Until then, their authority lies between that of a lieutenant and a post captain.

Once a lieutenant has been made a commander, they are never employed as lieutenant again. If their ship is lost or paid out, they're stuck ashore on half pay until a new command becomes available or they resign their commission.

Lieutenant (Wardroom Officer)

When a mid's captain believes they are ready, they will recommend them to stand before the Lieutenant Board. This is a mixed blessing for the mid in that it indicates their captain is pleased with their performance and believes they are suitable for a commission, but the Lieutenant Board is one of the most harrowing experiences the navy has to offer.

The Lieutenant Board consists of three or four post captains who scrutinize the hapless mid's bona fides in search of the slightest deficiency before peppering them with a series of rapid-fire questions in which the wretch must describe how they would respond to situations that beggar the imagination. If the mid's papers, references, and, most importantly, responses to the questioning meet the board's approval, a new lieutenant is born. If not, the crestfallen applicant must return to the mids' berth to study and await the next board. A newly made lieutenant is usually assigned to a new ship, as their current captain likely has a full complement of lieutenants.

Lieutenants assigned to the same vessel are ranked by the time they've held the commission, with the first lieutenant having the longest time in rank, the second the next longest, etc. Each lieutenant commands one of the ship's watches and assists in training the ship's mids. The first lieutenant acts as the captain's executive officer.

WARRANT RANKS

Acting Lieutenant (Wardroom Officer)

Particularly active and knowledgeable masters and master's mates are sometimes temporarily promoted to the rank of acting lieutenant, usually to fill the slot of a slain officer. They act with the authority of a lieutenant but are subordinate in rank to them. Acting lieutenants can petition their captain to stand before the Lieutenant Board and, should they pass, become full-fledged commission officers.

Master (Wardroom Officer)

The master is responsible for a ship's navigation and sailing. They maintain charts of all the waters in which they've sailed. They are appointed by the Navy Board. A ship's master has the authority of a lieutenant but is subordinate to lieutenants as they are not commission officers.

Purser (Wardroom Officer)

The purser is responsible for provisioning a ship and keeping its accounts. This position offers many opportunities for profiteering, often at the expense of the common sailors. For this reason, pursers are not well loved before the mast.

Magister (Wardroom Officer)

A ship's magister is a practiced magician who specializes in maritime and war magic. They put their arts to use in the ship's upkeep, charging spell-locks, slowing spoilage, dispersing ill humors, etc. There is also a martial aspect to the magister's role, as they are employed to cast and counter sendings aimed at damaging or compromising the sailing and fighting properties of a warship. Some also practice healing magic that they use in conjunction with the ship's surgeon—although many surgeons don't appreciate this intrusion into their domain. The talent and capabilities of magisters varies wildly, but those found on ships of the line tend to be the most talented.

Surgeon (Wardroom Officer)

Like magisters, the skill of surgeons is highly variable. Some are skilled at their art and others are little more than charlatans. Good surgeons (or sawbones) are loved by their crew, while they avoid bad ones, sometimes at the expense of their health. Surgeons are assisted by "loblollies," who are usually stout, strong-stomached lubbers who aren't good for much more than holding a screaming amputation patient down while the surgeon plies their saw.

Chaplain (Wardroom Officer)

Some pious captains employ chaplains to see to the spiritual health of the officers and crew. They are rarely welcome additions to a ship's wardroom and some sailors believe they are bad luck to have aboard.

Coxswain

A coxswain (cox'n) is a sailor assigned to helm one of a ship's boats and supervise its crew. The captain's coxswain is responsible for his boat and is often tasked with specific duties by the captain.

Volunteers

Children of common laborers could join the navy as volunteers. Initially, they would serve as "powder and shot carriers," referred to by sailors and popular fiction at the time as "powder monkeys." Volunteers were usually under the care of the master and gunner. Those that survived and had an aptitude for working the ship or gunnery could expect to progress rapidly to the rank of master or gunner.

SHIP RATINGS OF THE ALBION ROYAL NAVY

Unrated

Unrated naval vessels are commanded by a lieutenant who has been awarded the title of "commander." They include the Royal Navy's innumerable sloops of war, gun brigs, and cutters. Such vessels are used for a wide variety of purposes, ranging from delivering communications between larger vessels to active patrols against smugglers, small trading and fishing vessels, and armed vessels of the same diminutive proportions. A number of the Royal Navy's great captains achieved early fame in command of such humble vessels.

Sixth Rates

Classed as "frigates" and considered "post ships," sixth rates are ships-of-war that carry between twenty-four and twenty-eight great guns on a single gun-deck. These are usually nine- to twelve-pounders. Lighter guns are mounted on their upper deck, including swivel guns and chase guns.

Fifth Rates

Fifth rates are long, swift ships-of-war that mount all their great guns on a single gun-deck. Often used for trade interdiction. Like sixth rates, they are classified as frigates. They mount between twenty-eight and forty cannon. These are usually eighteen-pounders on the gun deck and nine-pounders on upper decks.

Fourth Rates

Classed as "ships of the line," meaning that they are considered to be strong enough to take their place in a line of battle, fourth rates are mounted with between forty-six and sixty cannon, on two dedicated gun decks. Fourth rates are used extensively wherever a shallow draft is required. They are increasingly seen as too weak to stand in the line, particularly those with less than sixty cannon, and are thus being pressed into other service.

Third Rates (Line-of-Battle Ship)

Third rates carry between sixty and ninety guns on two gun decks, but most now in service are ships of the line carrying seventy-four cannons on two dedicated gun decks. These usually consist of twenty-eight-pounders on the lower gun deck and thirty twenty-four-pounders on the upper gun deck. The balance of the cannon are nine-pounders carried on the quarterdeck and forecastle. Seventy-fours are fast, agile, and heavily armed—arguably they are the height of speed, handling, and gunpower. They are often deployed as large commerce raiders and used to snatch up smaller enemy vessels.

Second Rates (Line-of-Battle Ship)

Second rates are line-of-battle ships carrying ninety to ninety-eight guns on three dedicated gun decks. They normally carry thirty-two-pounders on their lower gun deck, eighteen-pounders on their middle gun deck, and twelve-pounders on their upper deck. Their relatively short length and greater height gives them poor sailing qualities with regard to both speed and handling.

First Rates (Line-of-Battle Ship)

First-rate ships are the most powerful of the ships of the "line of battle." They carry one hundred or more guns mounted on three gun decks and carry eight hundred or nine hundred crew and officers. Like a second rate, they carry their cannon on three decks, normally long thirty-eight-pounders on the gun deck, twenty-four-pounders on the middle gun deck, and twelve-pounders on the upper gun deck. Although first rates are longer hulled and handle better than second rates, they suffer from low gun ports on the gun deck, meaning the thirty-eight-pounders can only be brought into play on fine days.

NUMBER OF ALBION NAVAL SHIPS
COMMISSIONED, BY RATING

Rating	Number of Ships Commissioned
1	9
2	20
3	133
4	25
5	135
6	44
Unrated	310

Glossary

Aback: Movement of a ship toward its stern, either purposefully by the set of the sails or inadvertently by a shift in the wind.

Abaft: Closer to the stern.

Abeam: Objects to the starboard or larboard of a ship.

Accommodation Ladder: A set of steps by which officers and visitors can board or leave a ship.

Admiralty: The royal office that oversees the navy under the direction of the sea lord.

Aft: Toward the rear.

After-Cabin: The cabin reserved for the captain's use, located in the ship's aft.

After-Guard: The ordinary sailors and landsmen responsible for working the aft sails. They are posted to the quarterdeck and poop deck.

A-Lee: The lee or sheltered side of a ship.

Amidships: The middle section of a ship.

Athwart: Across the ship, from one side to the other.

Barky: Sailor's slang for a happy and/or well-loved ship.

Beam Ends: A ship "on its beam ends" is laying over so steeply that it is in immediate danger of capsizing.

Before the Mast: Someone berthed forward of the foremast, in other words, a common sailor.

Belay: To make something fast, such as securing a rope to a cleat, or to cease or disregard something, as in "belay that gabble" or "belay my last command."

Belaying Pin: Iron or wooden pins stored in holes in the pin rail around a mast. They are used to store coils of rope and can be pressed into use as a weapon if necessary.

Berth: A sleeping area.

Bilge: Both the lowest-lying area in a ship and the foul liquid that accumulates there.

Binnacle: A small cabinet near the wheel in the ship's ley-line in which navigation instruments are stored. At night, the binnacle is often illuminated by a low orb of light.

Blacking: A paste used to protect an object from rust or rot. The polish blackens the item.

Blackstrap: A fortified wine of inferior quality.

Block: A strongly made pulley used to set the rigging or lifting the anchors or other heavy items.

Boarding Net: Nets strung along a ship's rails to discourage and entangle boarders.

Bogaraets: Nonhuman natives of several islands in the Shards. While they have a nasty reputation as man-eaters and pirates, the majority of Bogaraet communities are peaceful fishers, and it is against their religion to consume the flesh of sentient creatures. Unlike humans, they refuse to eat dolphins, whales, or octopi. They will, however, consume Darghaur.

Bosun (Boatswain or bos'n): A petty officer responsible for inspecting the ship's sails and rigging and reporting on their condition to the officers of the watch. They are also responsible for overseeing the raising/weighing of anchors, sail-handling, and other routine actions required to work a ship. Their orders are broadcast to the crew using coded calls from the bosun's silver whistle.

Bosun's Chair: A swing-like chair used by sailors working aloft or to safely hoist lubbers aboard ship.

Bow (Bows): The forward end of a ship or boat.

Brig: A square-rigged, two-masted ship.

Broadside: The total number of guns on one side of a ship or the firing of all such guns in a single volley.

Buffskin or Buff: Leather made from buffalo or ox hide. It is a dull light yellow in color.

Bulkhead: The partitions that form a ship's cabins. A wall.

Bulwark: The wooden "wall" enclosing a ship's upper deck.

Bumper: A glass filled to the rim with wine or spirits.

Capstan: A horizontal wheel on the deck that turns an axle below-decks. It is used to raise the ship's anchors. As the capstan wheel is turned, a cable is wound up that lifts the anchor. A series of pawls are engaged as the wheel turns to prevent the cable from unwinding if the capstan is released. The capstan is pierced around its circumference by a series of sockets into which capstan bars can be inserted to give the hands more leverage to turn the wheel.

Captain: The commanding officer aboard a warship. Captains can only be placed in command of post ships. They are commissioned officers and all other officers and ratings aboard a ship are their subordinates.

Carabines: Carabines are muskets with short barrels. This makes them less accurate at long range, but very handy for boarding or antiboarding actions.

Cat (Cat-o'-nine Tails): A whip used to deliver floggings for violations of the Articles of War. It consisted of nine cords attached to a thick rope handle. The cords, each about a foot and a half long, are each knotted three times along their length. Sailors are usually tied bareback to one of the ship's grates, where their punishment is witnessed by the assembled crew.

Cathead: Sturdy wooden beams projecting from the side of a ship's bow. They are used for hoisting and storing the ship's anchors.

Colors: A ship's flag that indicates its nationality.

Commander: A rank above lieutenant and below captain. A lieutenant who has been approved for the command of small, non-post vessels. It is increasingly common for master and commanders to be referred to simply as "commanders." A commander's rank is higher than a lieutenant's but subordinate to a post captain. Officers of this rank are referred to as "commanders" only when they are not assigned a command. While in command of a vessel, they are referred to as "captain."

A commander's uniform distinguishes them from lieutenants, most notably by the single epaulette worn on the left shoulder.

Commission: The orders requiring a captain to take command of a ship or the document confirming the rank of a commission officer.

Commodore: A captain placed in command of a squadron of ships on a particular mission. Also, a rank granted to the commander of a given naval station, such as the Commodore of Far Harbor.

Complement: The official number of sailors and officers required to crew a ship. It is a fortunate officer who finds himself with a full complement at the beginning of a cruise, let alone at its end.

Corsair: A pirate or privateer or a ship employed in either pursuit.

Courses: The sails depending from the lowest spars. There are normally two courses, the forecourse and the main course: or the compass point toward which a ship currently sails.

Coxswain (Cox'n): The sailor assigned to helm one of a ship's boats and supervise its crew. The captain's cox'n is responsible for his boat and attends to him.

Crack On: To carry as much sail as a ship will bear to coax as much speed from her as possible.

Cutting Out: Capturing an enemy ship at anchor with a surprise attack by boats.

Darghaur: Nonhuman creatures that inhabit the continent known as the Darghaur Fastness. The Darghaur are inimical to humanity. They are obviously intelligent and possessed of highly advanced magic, but they have never communicated directly with humanity. They wage an off-again, on-again genocidal war against humanity, but have currently withdrawn into the Fastness and have not launched any major attacks in a century or more. They are sometimes referred to as "Dhargs."

Deckhead: The "ceiling" of a space belowdecks.

Dophir: A colloquialism for a wealthy merchant who made their riches in the Shards. Derived from the Bogaraet word for "chief."

Dunnage: A sailor's or passenger's baggage.

Ensign: A flag that announces a ship's nationality.

"First" or First Lieutenant: A ship's second-in-command and executive officer.

Flag Officer: An admiral, vice admiral, rear admiral, or commodore.

Fo'c'sle (forecastle): The deck forward of the foremast is referred to as the forecastle, or fo'c'sle by nautical types.

Fore: Toward the front.

Frigate: A three-masted fifth- or sixth-rate ship built for speed and firepower. Too light to take a place in a line of battle, they are used to patrol against or perform commerce raids, scout for a fleet, or carry out independent cruises.

Gig: One of a ship's boats. A gig is a light, graceful boat that can be propelled by either oars or sails as required. It is usually reserved for the use of the captain.

Grating: The cover for a hatchway. It is composed of a grid of wooden slats. Its secondary use is to secure a sailor for punishment.

Grog: A strong mixture of water and rum that is served to Albion crews twice a day. Other spirits may be substituted if necessary.

Hanger: A short, often curved sword worn on one's belt.

Head Money: A reward paid for the prisoners taken from a captured ship.

H.M.S.: "His/Her Majesty's Ship." A ship of the Albion Royal Navy.

Holystone: A soft sandstone roughly the size of a thick holy book. Used to scour a ship's decks.

Jolly Boat: One of a ship's boats. Its bluff bow and wide stern make it an ideal workhorse. It is usually carried suspended from a ship's stern for quick and easy access.

Landsman: A sailor with no naval training, fit only for hauling and pulling on ropes.

Larboard: The left side of the ship, looking forward from the stern.

Launch: The largest of a ship's boats. It can be rigged with a fore-and-aft sail.

Lee: The lee side is the side away from or protected from the wind.

Lieutenant: The lowest commissioned rank in the navy. They are referred to numerically according to their seniority, with the most senior lieutenant being the first, the next senior the second, and so forth. The number of lieutenants aboard a ship depends on its rating.

Loblolly Boy: An assistant to the ship's surgeon.

Lower Deck: The deck upon which a ship's sailors are berthed, situated above the orlop.

Lubber (Landlubber): A person who is grossly ignorant of life at sea. The term can be extremely derogatory when aimed at a fellow sailor or affectionate when directed at, say, a ship's rather exotic and attractive magister.

Make a Leg: To bow with one leg drawn back and the other bent, normally to the accompaniment of doffing one's hat.

Master: A ship's master is responsible for its navigation and sailing. They are appointed by the Navy Board. They have the authority of a lieutenant but are subordinate to them as they are not commissioned officers. Also, the commander of a merchant ship.

Master's Mate: Petty officers subordinate to a ship's master. They are the only rating allowed to take command of a prize vessel.

Mid: Also referred to as a ship's "young gentles." The Albion Royal Navy requires any person seeking a career as a commissioned officer to serve as a mid until such time as they pass their lieutenant's examination. Mids are accepted from age ten on. Despite the youth of most mids, they are expected to take responsibility for the supervision of the sailors assigned to their division.

Not all mids are children or teens, however. Unfortunate, would-be officers can be stuck as mids for their entire career if they continuously fail their lieutenant's exam, although most find a new line of work rather than suffer the shame of being called a "long-toothed mid."

Navy List: An official quarterly publication printed in Middlesea. It lists the officers of the navy and their seniority within their rank.

Orlop: The lowest deck on a ship. The space is below the waterline and has areas reserved for use by the ship's surgeon and magister, in addition to providing storage for spare cables.

Petty Officer: A naval rank similar to that of a noncommissioned officer in the Albion army.

Pinnace: A ship's boat, generally used as a light tender.

Post Captain: An Albion naval rank indicating an officer who has received orders to command a post ship. Once an officer has received this honor, referred to as "making post," they will never be assigned to a non-post ship. If they live long enough, they will eventually rise to the rank of admiral.

Post Ship: A rated ship with no less than twenty-four guns.

Purser (Pusser): The officer responsible for provisioning a ship and keeping its accounts.

Quarterdeck: The area of deck described by the space between the mainmast and a ship's poop, or should it lack a poop, its stern.

Rake: The angle of a ship's masts, which can be raked forward or aft. Also, a particularly devastating attack in which a broadside is fired into an enemy's bow or stern, the two weakest sections of its hull. The balls from such an attack tend to run the length of the ship's decks, causing terrible destruction and death.

Scantlings: The breadth of a vessel's planks. The larger the vessel, the stronger the scantlings are and the more resistant they are to iron shot.

Sea Service: The navy.

Spanker: On a square-rigged ship, a fore-and-aft sail rigged in place of the mizzen course during fair weather. The spanker is sometimes called the "driver." It can be used to increase the speed or even steer a vessel.

Spell-Lock: Spell-locks are enchanted "locks" used to ignite the alchemical powder used in guns of all types, from pistols to massive siege cannons. An unenchanted lock will not ignite alchemical powder. They are kept "charged" by the ship's gunner, armorer, mids with the required training and ability, and, if absolutely required, the ship's magister.

Starboard: The right side of the ship, looking forward from the stern.

Stern Gallery: An ornately carved and painted balcony built on the stern of the ship. Its glass windows face aft.

Taken: The colloquial name for humans who have been enslaved by the Darghaur.

T'gallants (Top Gallants): Pronounced "t'garns'ls." The square sails immediately above topsails.

Topsail: The sail mounted on the topmast immediately above one of the courses. There are three topsails, listed from stern to bow: *mizzen topsail*, *main topsail*, and *fore-topsail*. Also referred to as "mizzen top," "main top," or "foretop."

Wardroom: A mess (dining) area reserved for the use of commissioned and warrant officers of wardroom rank. The gunroom serves as the wardroom on smaller vessels, like the *Alarum*.

Warrant: A certificate of appointment issued to officers below commission rank.

Wheel: A ship's wheel is located on the quarterdeck. It is attached to a mechanism that allows it to control the rudder and thus steer the ship.

Younker: A youngster.

SKETCH OF *HMS ALARUM* EXECUTED BY MID MR. YEARDLY FOR THE EDIFICATION OF MARQUISE ENID D'TANCREVILLE

1. Mizzenmast
2. Mainmast
3. Foremast
4. Mizzen Topgallant
5. Mizzen Topsail
6. Spanker
7. Stern Gallery
8. Main Topgallant
9. Main Topsail
10. Mainsail or Maincourse
11. Mizzen Staysail
12. Capstan
13. Main Topgallant Staysail
14. Middle Staysail
15. Main Topmast Staysail
16. Mainstaysail
17. Fore Topgallant
18. Fore Topsail
19. Foresail or Forecourse
20. Fore Staysail
21. Galley Stovepipe
22. Fore Topmast Staysail
23. Jib
24. Flying Jib
25. Flying Jib Boom
26. Jib Boom
27. Dolphin Striker
28. Bowsprit
29. Beak and Figurehead

Acknowledgments

I owe a debt of gratitude to my agent, **Caitlin Blasdale**, who took a chance on a manuscript from a new writer recommended by a dubious source. Caitlin has been a patient mentor and ally in this process. If not for her, you wouldn't be reading this, unless you are one of my grievously put-upon friends.

The manuscript for this novel wouldn't exist at all if not for the open-hearted encouragement and skilled guidance of **Joel Dane**, an honest-to-gosh pro-fessional writer who is the best friend I've never laid eyes on.

Speaking of people without whose contributions I never would have written this book (or anything else), I'm obviously indebted to **Gary and Roberta Carpenter**, the most supportive parents a nerdy loner of a boy could ask for. They filled me with confidence and self-assurance, which my younger brother **Robby Carpenter** took special care to cut down a notch or two when it reached unsupportable levels.

I'd be actionably remiss if I didn't praise the invaluable contributions of **Emma P. Dog, Ellie Bellicus, Kona the Barbarian, Aoife BEP, and Nadja, Queen of the Night**. They all earned their kibble during the process of bringing the adventures of Enid and Nath to life. Good girls, every one of them!

Shawn Drake was extremely helpful in developing names for some of the eastern nations in addition to being a supportive Discord buddy and generally a good guy. He's also a fine game designer. If you like tabletop role-playing games, please check out acoupleofdrakes.com. Shawn and his equally talented wife, Navi, write great games.

I'd be disingenuous if I failed to credit the naval authors who inspired me and this work: **Patrick O'Brian, C. S. Forrester, Dudley Pope, Alexander Kent, Dewey Lambdin, and Frederick Marryat.**

Stephen Brust and his masterful play with archaic language forms in the PHOENIX GUARD books emboldened me to have fun with the voice in this novel.

Finally, and most importantly, I'm obliged to recognize the support of my wife, **Peggy Carpenter**, my tireless best friend, confidant, advisor, one person pep-club, and a far more talented writer than I am. Without Peggy, I would be lost, rudderless on a lee shore.